HORROR
MOVIE
FREAK
BY DON SUMNER

Published by

700 East State Street • Iola, WI 54990-0001
715-445-2214 • 888-457-2873
www.krausebooks.com

To order books or other products call toll-free 1-800-258-0929
or visit us online at www.krausebooks.com or www.Shop.Collect.com

Library of Congress Control Number: 2009937511

ISBN-13: 978-1-4402-0824-9
ISBN-10: 1-4402-0824-7

Cover Design by Shawn Williams
Designed by Heidi Bittner-Zastrow
Edited by Kristine Manty

Printed in China

Front cover movie stills: main photo: *Underworld*-Subterranean/Screen Gems/The Kobal Collection/Egon Endrenyi; bottom photos, from left: *Dracula*-Universal/The Kobal Collection; *Dawn of the Dead*-United Film/The Kobal Collection; *Saw II*-Twisted Pictures/The Kobal Collection; *Jeepers Creepers*-Zoetrope/United Artists/The Kobal Collection/Gene Page; Freddy Krueger-New Line/The Kobal Collection; *The Descent*-Celador/Pathe/The Kobal Collection. **Back cover:** *Psycho*-Paramount/The Kobal Collection/William Creamer. **Contents page, from top**: *30 Days of Night*-Ghost House/Columbia/Dark Horse; *The Mummy*-Universal Pictures; *Alien*-20th Century Fox Productions/Brandywine Productions; *Splinter*-Indion Entertainment Group/Magnet Releasing.

Dedication

To Mom and Dad, Polly and Barry
for giving me roots and wings.

Acknowledgments

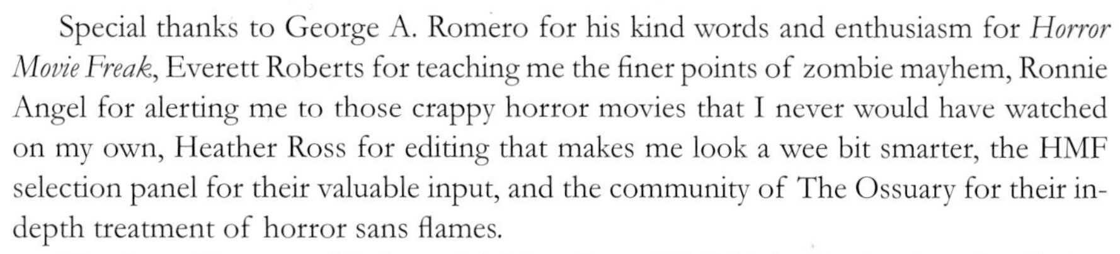

Special thanks to George A. Romero for his kind words and enthusiasm for *Horror Movie Freak*, Everett Roberts for teaching me the finer points of zombie mayhem, Ronnie Angel for alerting me to those crappy horror movies that I never would have watched on my own, Heather Ross for editing that makes me look a wee bit smarter, the HMF selection panel for their valuable input, and the community of The Ossuary for their in-depth treatment of horror sans flames.

Thanks to Rosemary Marks and Adrian Carr of Tall Order Productions for filming my introduction to the enclosed *Night of the Living Dead* DVD. I appreciate their talent, and patience with an on-camera amateur.

Also a big thank you to Ricky Byrd at The Picture Desk (www.picture-desk.com), the online home of The Kobal Collection, a film photo archive with over a million images from the early days of cinema to the present.

Thanks as well to The Cult Movie Network, Alberta, Canada.

About the Author

Don Sumner is a Horror Movie Freak from an early age, ever since sneaking up in the middle of the night to watch *Terror Train* on cable at the age of 10, and suffering weeks of nightmares as a result. As the founder and editor in chief of Best-Horror-Movies.com, Don has been engulfed in horror movies nonstop since 2006 and is an oft-quoted enthusiast of independent horror and bloody zombie gore. As the expert on Horror Movie Locales for *USA Today*, Don seeks out the locations of famous horror movies and visits them one by one, hoping that an overlooked slasher may somehow appear. Don spends his time on his farm in Athens, Tennessee, battling beaver dams and avoiding wearing only panties when investigating strange noises outside.

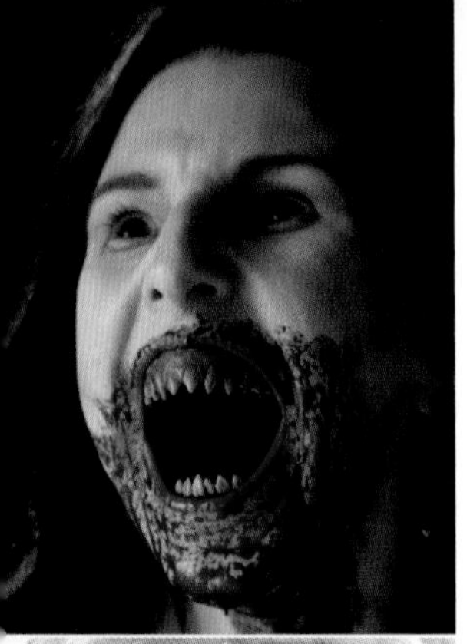

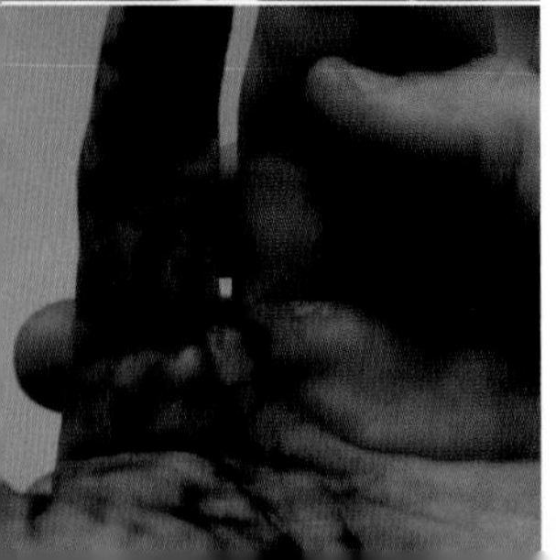

Contents

With its levels of violence and Technicolor gore unheard of at the time, Hammer Studio's 1957 *The Curse of Frankenstein* brought the movie monster back to the spotlight. Peter Cushing is Victor Frankenstein and Christopher Lee is the creature he creates. Cushing and Lee, along with Terence Fisher, who directed several of their movies, are the trio of terror of Hammer's horror legacy.

Hammer Film Productions

Count Dracula (Bela Lugosi) and Lucy Weston (Frances Dade) strike a classic vampire-and-victim pose in a publicity still from the 1931 film, *Dracula*. *Universal*

Why We Love Horror Movies

Why do we love horror movies? This question has been posed many times over the decades by people from all walks of life.

Sometimes the query takes on an accusing tone, such as one coming from a date who wants a nice dinner and night at the symphony rather than catching the midnight showing of the new *Zombie Carnage* indie flick. Other times the tone is one of concern, as from parents confused about their child's disdain for *Sesame Street* in favor of the Sunday morning horror fest showing of *The Brain That Wouldn't Die*. Still others take a tone of disbelief—what is WRONG with you, anyway?

Although some of our friends and family don't understand our passion for terror, the craving just does not subside. Why is that?

Every Horror Movie Freak is unique, but there are certainly some common threads that run among horror lovers the world over. Where else can a worst-case scenario of carnage and terror be played out before our eyes, all within the safety and comfort of our living rooms or local theater multiplex? All entertainment has an element of escape, but Horror Freaks crave more—the RUSH! In fact, many horror aficionados are searching for a particular rush, one reminiscent of the utter fear felt when they watched their first horror movie.

Think of the first time, as a child, you rode that frightening-looking roller coaster at an amusement park. Mom didn't think you were ready yet, but you knew you were…or at least thought so. Never showing your inner apprehension, you climbed into the car and pulled down the harness. The car lurched forward and you gasped and wondered what you had gotten yourself into. Slowly the coaster moved up the initial grade and you realized how high in the air you were and wondered if it was too late to get off. As the car plunged over the crest and down the first big drop it hit you: No! You weren't ready!

What followed was the longest three minutes of your life, so terrifying that hardly a scream could escape your lips and your knuckles turned white from your death grip on the restraining bar as you were certain you were heading toward doom. Finally, after an eternity, the car screeched to a halt and the safety bar released. You made it! You just had the most terrifying experience ever, lived to tell about it, and felt a rush of excitement…and you wanted to ride it again!

The same thing applies to horror movies. The first time we disobeyed our protective parents and crept into the living room in the wee hours of the morning to watch a scary movie on cable, we paid the price. Nightmares followed. Weeks were spent peering around corners in search of the certain monster waiting to grab us. We slept with the light on and made sure the closet door was closed all the way so that creepy ghosts couldn't see us through the crack. But we lived! We got the heart-pounding terror without the consequence of death and dismemberment. We prevailed over the most frightening of scenarios, and now want that feeling again. And again…

The search for fright is the driving force for many Horror Freaks, but horror movies also have certain elements that make the experience unique to any other movie genre. The stars, the scares, and the concept of good vs. evil play an enormous role in a Horror Freak's satisfaction—and overcoming adversity is such an integral part of the experience that certain rules for surviving a horror movie have also emerged.

The Stars

There are many ingredients to an effective and enjoyable horror stew: storyline, special effects, script, and scenery, but one of the most important is the star. Not the actors and actresses in the film, but the *real* stars—the heroes, villains, ghosts, and monsters.

The best horror-movie monsters are those that capture the imagination, and nightmares, of Horror Freaks everywhere, and are the true stars of the show. How many serial killers do you know who have high schoolers sporting T-shirts with their likeness or tots scampering off to school with their images emblazoned across their lunch pails? What about serial killer action figures and scenes, so that kids can reenact the more grisly of their murderous rampages? I can name a few noted horror movie villains off the top of my head: Jason Voorhees, Freddy Krueger, Leatherface, and Michael Myers. Maybe because these stars act out vengeance and retribution with bloody gusto, horror villains are simultaneously feared and revered.

So, if the monster is the star, the hero is the co-star. Heroes are the characters who represent us. They are just a little smarter than their sliced-up compadres, a little more level-headed, a bit tougher, and a lot luckier. Horror Freaks love to imagine that they, too, could be the individual to rise above the terror and emerge from the carnage alive and victorious. The house says "get out," and we get out. A crazy guy says that anyone who stays the night in an abandoned summer camp is doomed, and so we get a hotel. If we are alone in a cabin in the woods and hear a noise outside, we lock the door and call for help…or at least get dressed beyond our panties before venturing outside crying, "Is anyone out there?" The more resourceful the hero, the more satisfying it is to join them on their surge for survival.

Of course, even a hero can do something stupid, and when they do, all bets are off. The Horror Freak can sit back smugly as the hero-turned-victim takes a machete to the skull and quip, "Yep, she deserved that one."

The Scream Queens, of course, trump all as the stars of the show. Should any film feature one of these irresistible divas of dismemberment, that is reason enough to watch it. The most royal of the Queens of Scream have their own section on P. 220-229.

The Scares

What is so scary about a horror movie? Ask that question a hundred times and you're likely to get a hundred different answers, which is why there are so many different sub-genres of horror.

Some Horror Freaks are fans of the "jolt scares," those tense moments when an unsuspecting victim is creeping toward an ajar door investigating a strange noise, only to be given a heart attack by Fluffy the cat leaping unnaturally from the shelf that has the Malt-o-Meal. The "Fluffy factor" is a bit cheap, but accomplishes the goal of causing a "yell out loud" moment. Other, less cheesy jolt scares, like when a monster bursts forth from behind a tree or a hand emerges from an underground gravesite to grab an ankle, can be very satisfying and keep the energy rolling during the horror experience. Some Horror Freaks even gauge the success of a horror movie by the number of times a spontaneous shriek escapes their lips.

Suspense scares are more gut wrenching, and for a longer period of time. Alfred Hitchcock once said that his goal was to "always make the audience suffer as much as possible," and suspense scares do just that. You just know that something terrible is about to happen…it is just a matter of time.

The longer the anticipation of a horrifying event is drawn out, the more we are compelled to hide our eyes or get up for a drink of water, but can't. Glued to the screen and unable to breathe, we await the inevitable horror unfolding before our eyes. Sometimes, when horror filmmakers are feeling particularly sadistic, they will combine the suspense scare with the jolt scare—suspense builds to an intolerable level only to immediately dissipate when the feared monster is not in the hall closet after all…he jumps out of the laundry hamper instead.

Unexpected scares can certainly cause a loud yell, but are different from jolt scares. These are the brief visions of something horrifying, presented without pomp or circumstance. Maybe a menacing face appears in the window for an instant, an alien passes across the alleyway in the background of a newscast, or a brief vision of ghostly feet standing on the bed while Mom is making it would all certainly qualify as an unexpected scare. These scares can be clever and extremely effective when used correctly.

Phobia scares are a cornerstone of horror movie concepts and play to the individual fears of Horror Freaks. Uncomfortable with the thought of toy clowns coming to life while you sleep and smothering you with a pillow? There are horror movies about that. How about childhood panic over a monster hiding under the bed? That's covered, too. The effectiveness of phobia scares depends on the deep-seated fears of the viewer. Because one Freak's phobia is another Freak's Shangri-La, horror movies

English filmmaker, producer, and "master of suspense" Alfred Hitchcock once said his goal was to "always make the audience suffer as much as possible." He accomplished just that in his masterpieces including *Psycho* and *Rear Window*. He also made us look at our feathered friends in a whole different way after watching *The Birds*. *Universal*

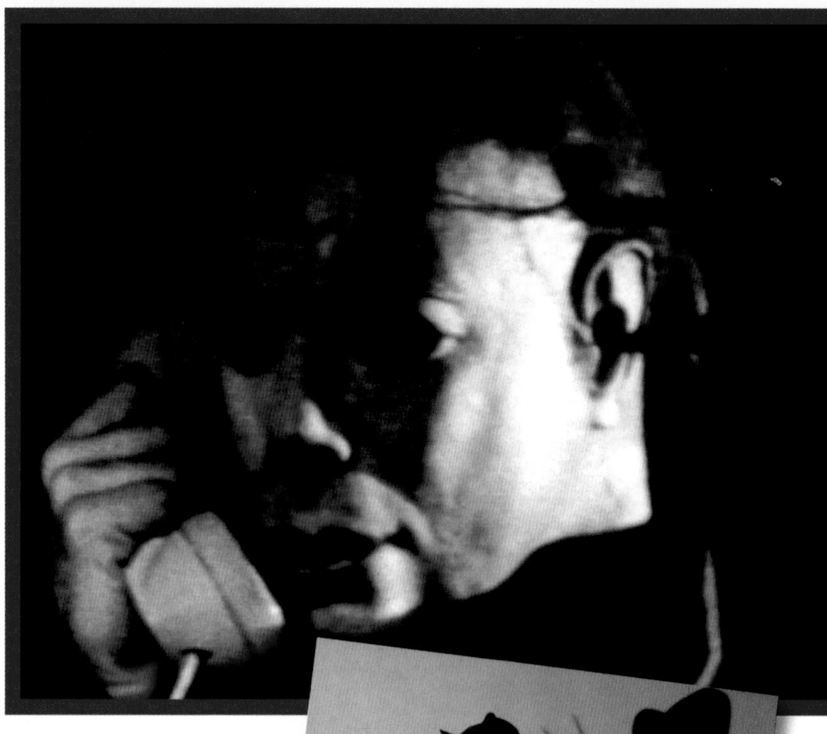

Three of the biggest, baddest, slashiest, and best-known superstars in horror movies: Jason Voorhees, Michael Myers, and Freddy Krueger. They have been slicing and dicing their way through randy camp counselors, babysitters, and dreaming teens for years in their respective movie franchises of *Friday the 13th*, *Halloween,* and *A Nightmare on Elm Street*. Freddy and Jason even battle each other in the 2003 movie, *Freddy vs. Jason*.

As a testament to his pop-culture status, Jason was awarded the MTV Lifetime Achievement Award in 1992, the first of three fictional characters to get it (Godzilla got it 1996, and Chewbacca in 1997). The hockey mask-wearing maniac, who bloodies up Camp Crystal Lake with the help of his machete, has ripped through more hapless victims than Freddy and Michael combined and seems to be an unstoppable killing machine. But the other two villains are no slouches. Dr. Sam Loomis, the child psychiatrist who spent years trying to help Michael, doesn't say he has the "devil's eyes" for nothing: this mad slasher is pure evil. Freddy, with his horribly melted face, grimy red-and-green sweater, and razor-sharp glove, is a child murderer who slashes teens in their dreams.

Each of these iconic villains continues to terrorize a new generation, as each franchise has had new installments: encapsulations of *Halloween* in 2007, *Friday the 13th* in 2009, and *Nightmare* in 2010. It's probably a safe bet that we'll see plenty more bloodletting from these villains in the future.

Photo credits, from top left: Jason Voorhees-Paramount/The Kobal Collection; Michael Myers-Falcoln International/The Kobal Collection; and Freddy Krueger-New Line Cinema.

A Nightmare ON ELM STREET

Long before Jason, Michael, and Freddy came on the scene, monsters were the shining start of horror movies. Monsters capture our fears in one grotesque physical form. These beasts have what it takes to bring societal angst to life so that they can hide under the bed and get us in our sleep. Some monsters have a personal tragedy to correspond with their murderous appetites. Werewolves, when in their human form, often live in torment from the atrocities they commit while under the influence of the full moon; others, however, don't: when lead character Ginger is transformed into a werewolf in *Ginger Snaps* (depicted on the publicity poster at top left), she relishes tearing things to pieces with no remorse. Other monsters are merely trying to survive and don't understand why their prey is so darned violent. Still others are just looking for love, as is the case with the creature in *The Creature from the Black Lagoon* (center photo), after he spots a lovely lady. At right, Christopher Lee is a monster created by human hands in *The Curse of Frankenstein*; his impassioned performance as the creature made him a star. Monsters continue to be a mainstay in Horror Freaks' movie collections, and with good reason: they scare the bejesus out of us.

Photo credits, from top: Lions Gate/TMN/Telefilm Canada; Universal/The Kobal Collection; Hammer Film Productions.

with phobia themes must utilize other fear-inducing tactics in addition if they want to fill the theater.

Some scares do not involve any specific fright-inducing techniques, but instead are completely wrapped up in atmosphere. Atmospheric scares are less of an immediate reaction and more of an overwhelming feeling of fear and dread that infiltrates the senses of the Horror Freak and sets the tone for fright and unease. A natural for atmospheric scares are ghost stories and evil from hell, but good scary atmosphere will heighten the fright factor of any horror movie, and should not be overlooked.

Good vs. Evil

The concept of good vs. evil is a required theme in any horror movie, and it shows itself in a variety of ways.

The most obvious conflict between light and dark is between the hero and the villain, with the hero representing good and the villain evil, but horror can be much more complex than that. Aside from the obvious evil of ripping someone into a million pieces with a hay hook, is the villain really the evil one? What if the "victim" is actually a shiftless scumbag who caused the mental breakdown of the villain by playing a vicious prank on them years ago in the frat house? The line between retribution and evil, in these cases, is blurred.

There are varying degrees of evil among an entire cast of potential victims: the smiling "best friend" may be secretly scheming on someone else's boyfriend, for example, and that football star just may have some backward and derogatory attitude toward women. Is the villain who sends these miscreants to their untimely demise an evildoer, then, or just a purveyor of justice?

Then there is the ultimate horror theme that guarantees that having sex or doing drugs equals certain death. Sinners will be punished, and horror movie villains are just the ticket to hand it out. Villains who deal the consequences for such behavior are little more than a puritanical force of penance, albeit an evil force themselves. Horror Freaks are drawn to cheer the villain on in their murderous quest, then, not out of a deranged desire to be harbingers of doom but rather a righteous longing to have no bad deed go unpunished.

When you look at it that way, Horror Freaks are downright civilized.

The obvious exception to all of this is found in films portraying pure biblical manifestations of good and evil, the power of God rising to crush Satanic apparitions. Unfortunately for Horror Freaks, years of Sunday school provided the ultimate horror movie spoiler...we all know how it's going to turn out.

Regardless of which character is the ultimate good and which the ultimate evil, there is an underlying hope that good shall prevail, and it usually does in horror movies. Sometimes it doesn't, but that's what sequels are for.

Rules of Survival in a Horror Movie

Countless lists, and even books, have been written on the rules for survival in a horror movie. Wes Craven's *Scream* is a horror movie about horror movie clichés, and outlines three basic rules:

1. Don't have sex. Sex = Death

2. Don't drink or do drugs. Drugs and alcohol = Death

3. Never say "I'll be right back," because you won't be.

These rules are, indeed, the basic no-brainers for horror movie survival. Countless other lists of survival rules exist and tend to detail specific dos and don'ts, often inspired by decisions made by victims in particular movies that led to their painful ends. However, without going into movie-specifics, there are a few additional rules that tend to always apply:

4. Don't wander around in your panties, and DEFINITELY do not go outside with them as your primary garment. When a Horror Freak sees a young coed venture into the woods investigating a strange noise in

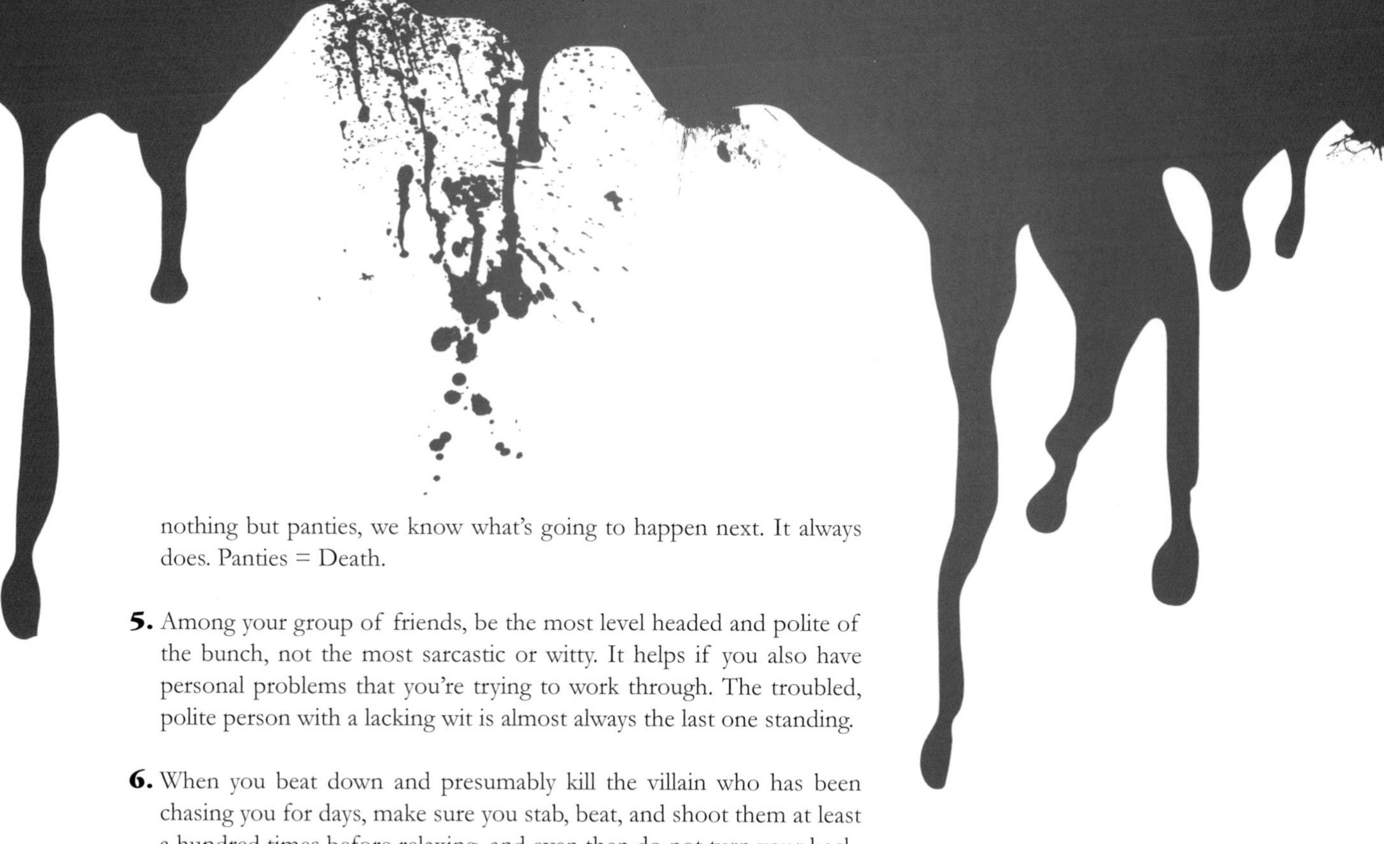

nothing but panties, we know what's going to happen next. It always does. Panties = Death.

5. Among your group of friends, be the most level headed and polite of the bunch, not the most sarcastic or witty. It helps if you also have personal problems that you're trying to work through. The troubled, polite person with a lacking wit is almost always the last one standing.

6. When you beat down and presumably kill the villain who has been chasing you for days, make sure you stab, beat, and shoot them at least a hundred times before relaxing, and even then do not turn your back. They ARE going to get up.

7. If you are in a horror movie with a young starlet known for crude behavior in her public life, steer clear. She's gonna get a fence post through her skull.

The rules for surviving a horror movie are not, unfortunately, hard and fast. Every once in a while a film will break the rules by killing off the good girl or letting the presumed hero be snatched through an open window by a hungry monster. Rules were made to be broken, it seems, and the best movies will break, or at least bend, these and other rules to keep Horror Freaks on their toes. That's how we like it.

Finally, there is one single bottom-line rule for surviving a horror movie that has not yet been mentioned: Do not be an idiot. Once the idiocy begins, so does the carnage. Guaranteed.

What Makes a Horror Movie Great: The Rating Methodology

What factors elevate one horror movie to your "classic shelf," while hurling another to the bargain bin in a gas station mini-mart? The answer from some may be as simple as whether they like the film or not, but that's not easy to measure or duplicate.

Over the course of creating the 100 Best Horror Movies list for Best-Horror-Movies.com, a verifiable and semi-scientific rating methodology was created, partly to ensure that there were actual criteria other than personal preference behind inclusions in this list, and partly to have some way of defending those choices since getting any two Horror Freaks to agree on the top 100 films is an exercise in futility.

Horror Movie Freak is not a listing of "best" horror movies, but rather a collection of ones that fall into a variety of horror subgenres with the simple inclusion criteria that they don't suck.

To construct such a group of horror movies, and their appropriate categories, the Horror Freak Selection Panel of Experts was organized. The members of that panel were responsible for assisting in the generation of the Master Horror List, categorization of each film and to provide a stopgap against any individuals' favorite horror being included in spite of the fact that to most folks, other than the nominator, it sucks. They are:

Don Sumner (yours truly), Certified Horror Freak with an uncanny ability to watch a horror film for the 30th time and blank the mind of all coming scares to watch it anew each time like a child.

The favorites and "must-haves" of the selection panel were considered, along with four years of top 100 horror from Best-Horror-Movies.com, and the "irrefutable best horror list" from members of the BHM online community, The Ossuary.

The list was narrowed down via my emotional reaction, and then further thinned by a reality-check session with the panel. The resulting collection of horror favorites is included in *Horror Movie Freak*!

Everett Roberts, resident Zombie Master for BHM, first discovered his passion for the undead while studying at Miskatonic University, where he eventually majored in zombology and reanimation theory and minored in camp counselor. While preparing for the upcoming zombie apocalypse, he somehow found time for a wife and family. He currently resides in Memphis, Tenn., where he is studying the political effects of the dead voting.

Bill Burda, child of the sixties, was raised on "Famous Monsters of Filmland" and EC comics. He was fortunate enough to see *Night of the Living Dead* at a drive-in, and also actually got to take a date to see John Carpenter's *Halloween* during its initial run. Long-time home haunter, he currently blogs for BHM on the merits of forgotten horror classics. Bill is a resident of Richmond, Va., home of Edgar Allen Poe, and knows where all the "Yankees" are buried. Bill likes doll mutilation and burying things that still have a little twitch left in them, and dislikes horror directors who don't know the difference between "disgusting" and "scary."

James Lasome is a mad scientist by trade residing in the wilds of New Jersey. In his spare time, you can find him wandering the BHM forums, writing reviews from all corners of the genre and the world, and attending and blogging about horror conventions and related events around the Mid-Atlantic and New York City.

Heather Ross is editor and feature film reviewer at Horror Freaks Media LLC. She grew up on the backdrop of a Stephen King novel — Tucson, Ariz. — so she was introduced to horror at a young age, as well as snakes, scorpions, and creepy desert stuff. Her first horror movie was the classic *The Nanny* with Bette Davis, which Heather watched on TV at the ripe old age of eight. It scared the bejesus out of her and after that, she was hooked on the adrenaline. To this day, Heather remains a horror junkie, hooked on it as only a horror queen could be.

A scientist conducts an experiment that has horrific results in the 1958 chiller-thriller, *The Fly*. See more on P. 78. *20th Century Fox*

Essential Horror Movies: The Categories

The movie genre "horror" is broad, and means different things to people. For some, nothing less than flesh-feasting zombies will do, while for others, ghostly apparitions are what it takes to get the heart pumping and shrieks erupting.

Luckily for the Horror Movie Freak, there are many sub-genres under our beloved horror umbrella. Each sub pertains to a particular kind of horror movie theme and, therefore, a particular type of fright. Is the villain human, animal, alien, or apparition? There's a subgenre for each. Is the human meanie always a murderous freak, or do they appear normal in day-to-day life? There's a subgenre for that. Is that inhuman freak actually from hell or merely otherworldly? We've got that covered, too.

No matter what freaks out the Horror Movie Freak, subgenres likely have a slew of films just right for an evening of horrifying delight. Then again, there are some freaks who love every kind of horror film, and for those, the subgenres are nothing more than a basis for a horror collection filing system. After all, nobody wants to accidentally play a dark Asian ghost story on vampire night. That's just wrong.

Within each category, movies are listed in chronological order.

One other note on the categories: they are in no way absolute. Most, if not all, of the horror films listed here can be accurately classified in several categories. Therefore, if a film has been selected in one category, it will be absent from any others, no matter how appropriate those others may also be. Keep that in mind before you craft an angry letter calling for the author's untimely demise at the collective hands of a hungry zombie horde.

Photos credits from top: 28 Weeks Later-Fox Atomic, a subsidiary of 20th Century Fox Film Corp.; Boris Karloff as the Frankenstein monster-Universal Pictures; and The Exorcist-Warner Bros. Pictures.

A super-giant bear munches and crunches its way through *Grizzly*. This was the most financially successful independent movie of 1976, earning an impressive world-wide box office total of $39 million. It held this record until *Halloween* broke it in 1978.

Film Ventures International

Aberrations of Natu

Ah, nature. Long drives in the country-side, peaceful lakeside picnics, and hikes on mountain trails next to babbling brooks…and sprinting for your life, as a huge bear with razor-sharp claws bounds after you, bits of bloody flesh from your camping partner dangling from its ferocious fangs. Nature is all well and good, until it turns upside down into a pristine backdrop for murderous mayhem.

Nature run amok is a regular villain in horror through the decades, from killer bees and giant ants to carnivorous plants and genetically altered cockroaches. What is this fascination with "nature gone wild?"

The answer lies in the very core of horror movies and why Horror Movie Freaks love them—to be scared. Many people are scared by psychotic dudes with bloodlust or monsters hiding under the bed, but the concept of normal everyday things changing their tune and becoming harbingers of doom are, for some, particularly terrifying. The familiar, even the peaceful, is suddenly transformed into the realization of a horrific nightmare. Safety in any circumstance is an illusion, and that cute little rabbit scampering across a meadow could stop, eye you hungrily, and lunge for your jugular at any moment.

Nature horror also plays to the worst-case scenarios that people push from their consciousness and try not to acknowledge. Do you REALLY know what is under the water swimming around your toes while you wait for the speedboat to take off and pull you topside on your water-skis? Are

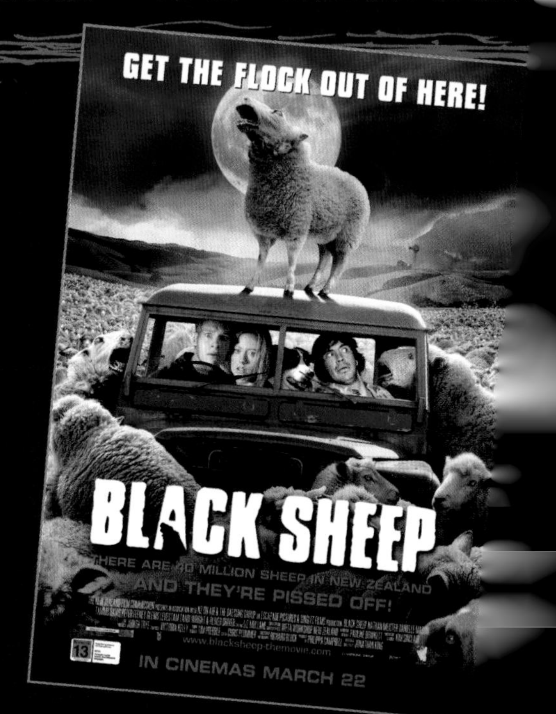

the inhabitants of that anthill truly satisfied wit are they dreaming of a large, warm human m seems sweet enough, but how will we handle t when survival instincts of centuries of hunting b modus operandi?

Ghosts and goblins are scary enough, but i maintain a position that these are not real, an they wreak couldn't actually happen. Aberrat provide this luxury. No matter how outlandish flock of birds suddenly swooping down and p most certainly could happen. By entering the ture horror infiltrates the deepest repressed fe Freak and plays them out for all to see.

Even when the movie is over, they are st time you embark on a lovely stroll through th you are also on a survival mission…and the

Melanie Daniels (Tippi Hedren) fights off a feathered friend gone mad in *The Birds*. *Universal/The Kobal Collection*

The Birds

RELEASE March 28, 1963 (U.S.)
DIRECTED BY Alfred Hitchcock
WRITTEN BY Daphne Du Maurier (story) and Evan Hunter (screenplay)
STARRING Rod Taylor, Jessica Tandy, Suzanne Pleshette, "Tippi" Hedren, Veronica Cartwright
RATING PG, for birds pecking people violently

The Birds is an Alfred Hitchcock original and depicts an aberration of nature with the horror and suspense that only he could achieve.

Melanie Daniels (Tippi Hedren) is a wealthy young socialite who follows Mitch Brenner (Rod Taylor) to his home in the coastal town of Bodega Bay. After some playful pranks and romantic posturing, Melanie is in a small motorboat in the bay when a seagull attacks her and pecks up her face.

As time goes by, the passive-aggressive and blossoming romance between Melanie and Mitch continues, and the strange behavior by the local birds intensifies. Gulls smash into glass windows to their deaths, crows hurl their bodies against the front door, and the strange avian behavior results in a dead friend of Melanie's found in a bedroom. The bird threat becomes a true deadly menace, as thousands of birds converge on the area leaving death and peck marks in their wake.

The Birds is a wonderful example of the genius of Hitchcock and truly illustrates how deserving this director is of the title "master of suspense." The threat grows slowly, and the anticipation of the ghastly events proves more uncomfortable than when those events actually occur. The chemistry and interaction between Mitch and Melanie plays well in this film also and proves that human banter can be as unexplainable as crazy acts of nature.

The screaming woman on this famous poster art is not Tippi Hedren as commonly believed, but Jessica Tandy. *Universal*

All Horror Movie Freaks must have a working knowledge of Hitchcock films, and the most well known are minimum requirements in the quest for this knowledge. In terms of an aberration of nature, *The Birds* is certainly a shining example of danger lurking in the seemingly harmless faces of creatures we see every day.

> DO YOU HAPPEN TO HAVE A PAIR OF BIRDS THAT ARE... JUST FRIENDLY?
> –MITCH BRENNER

Jaws

RELEASE June 20, 1975 (U.S.)
DIRECTED BY Steven Spielberg
WRITTEN BY Peter Benchley (screenplay, based upon his novel) and Carl Gottlieb (screenplay)
STARRING Roy Scheider, Robert Shaw, Richard Dreyfuss, Lorraine Gary, Murray Hamilton
RATING PG, for violent attacks by a giant psychotic shark

Jaws became a worldwide phenomenon that terrified audiences at the time and inspires phobia and fear surrounding swimming in deep water to this day.

The film opens with one of the most famous scenes in horror movie history: a woman swimming toward a buoy in the ocean is suddenly ripped at and pulled under the water by an unseen attacker.

Sheriff Brody (Roy Scheider), the lawman of the tourist town where the attack happens, immediately begins a crusade to have the beach closed down so that a proper search for the attacker, determined to be a great white shark, can be conducted.

Unfortunately, tourist season is approaching and the town relies on the revenue, so the mayor denies any request to turn the money spenders away. Bad idea.

After a few more deadly shark attacks, Brody sets off with shark hunter Quint (Robert Shaw) and boat captain Hooper to find and kill the deadly shark.

The shark, however, has other ideas, and with the determination of the most brutal horror movie slasher, conducts some hunting of his own.

Jaws is, indeed, a horror movie in the aberration of nature category, but the film is a classic for other reasons. The villain shark is not portrayed as merely a mindless, deadly creature, but rather as a calculating killer single-mindedly hunting his prey.

The psychotic killer qualities of this particular shark, along with its size and the fact that it could conceivably exist in any coastal body of

The animatronic shark was nicknamed "Bruce" and director Steven Spielberg also reportedly called it "the great white turd" when he got frustrated with it. *Universal*

The famous opening scene [illegible]hristine “Chrissie” Watkins (Susan Blacklinie) being attacked by something menacing under the water has left an indelible mark on horro[illegible]. *Universal/The Kobal Collection*

water, allows *Jaws* to transcend nature horror of the past to become a full-fledged classic with a lasting impact.

There are those horror fans who argue that *Jaws* is based on too much natural possibility to actually be a horror movie, and is instead a thriller with a naturally occurring creature as the antagonist.

The perspective of a Horror Movie Freak, however, is that a homicidal slasher is what it is, regardless of the species.

THIS SHARK, SWALLOW YOU WHOLE.

-QUINT

Grizzly

RELEASE May 21, 1976 (U.S.)
DIRECTED BY William Girdler
WRITTEN BY Harvey Flaxman and David Sheldon
STARRING Christopher George, Andrew Prine, Richard Jaeckel, Joan McCall, Joe Dorsey
RATING PG, for bloody bear carnage

Considered by some to be "*Jaws* on land," *Grizzly* (aka *Killer Grizzly* and *Claws*) shows that a pleasant camping trip can go terribly wrong when an 18-foot bear is on the loose.

Grizzly opens with two women breaking camp in a pristine national forest. Suddenly, one of them is attacked and violently killed by a giant grizzly bear. The second woman escapes to a nearby cabin, but only for a minute, as the bear tears down the cabin wall and rips her to shreds.

The park's chief ranger, Michael Kelly (Christopher George), immediately begins a crusade to shut down the park so that a hunt for the killer bear can be conducted. Alas, tourist season is approaching and the park supervisor denies the request. After several more killings and an unsuccessful open hunt by enthusiasts looking for a bounty, Kelly strikes off on his own to face the beast and bring it down.

Does all this sound familiar? It should, as most story components seem to be taken directly from the blockbuster *Jaws*, which released to huge audiences just one year prior. *Grizzly* is not the only film to be accused of following the new-found success formula of the vicious slasher shark, but is possibly the highest quality. The story is strong, the use of a real bear instead of some guy in a suit works well, and the film is a frightening account of an aberration of nature with the cunning of a driven serial killer.

Horror Freaks, then, will enjoy the theme of natural beast as serial killer from two standpoints, by land and by sea. Add *Grizzly* to your library and think about it the next time you zip up the tent and settle into your sleeping bag made for two for the night.

Actress Mary Ann Hearn is the first victim of the 18 feet of man-eating terror. *Film Ventures Int/ The Kobal Collection*

"IF YA FEEL A WET SNOUT IN YA FACE, WHATEVER YOU DO, DON'T MOVE. AND DON'T KISS IT 'CAUSE IT AIN'T ME."
- DON STOBER

Black Sheep

RELEASE June 22, 2007 (U.S., limited)
WRITTEN AND DIRECTED BY Jonathan King
STARRING Nathan Meister, Peter Feeney, Matt Chamberlain, Nick Fenton, Sam Clarke
NOT RATED Expect gore galore as killer sheep go on a rampage

Black Sheep, a horror/comedy from New Zealand, explores the side effects of genetic tampering and the horrific aftermath of the dreaded "weresheep."

Henry (Nathan Meister) lives with his family, who tend a large herd of sheep in the New Zealand countryside. Jealous of Henry's knack for sheep farming, brother Angus (Peter Feeney) plays a cruel joke on him that leaves his pet lamb dead and skinless, and Henry with a severe sheep phobia that drives him to move off to the city away from the ovine threat.

Years later after the father's death, Henry returns to the farm to sell his share to Angus. Unbeknownst to Henry, however, Angus has been conducting genetic experiments on the sheep in an effort to create a better lamb chop. The resulting mutated sheep fetuses are thrown into a pit, presumably to be buried later, but when a couple of eco-terrorists get their hands on one of the fetuses, they inadvertently unleash a mutated creature that proceeds to turn the entire flock into a vicious wooly pack of zombie sheep.

HENRY: ARE YOU *OK?*
EXPERIENCE: I WON'T BE *OK* EVER AGAIN.

Black Sheep has something for the lover of nature gone wild, fans of zombie attacks, and monster enthusiasts who are open to the possibility of weresheep, which result from a human bitten by mutton run amok. The gore is first rate, the monsters are actually scary in their incredible ridiculousness, and the serene New Zealand countryside is beautiful as the deadly heard of carnivorous ewes crest the horizon.

Farm animals, comedy, and zombie (well, actually 'not-a-zombie' zombie) mayhem await the Horror Freak with *Black Sheep.* Just don't forget the mint jelly.

An investor in the experiment to breed new sheep (Jono Manks) gets a return on his money he wasn't quite expecting.

Livestock Films/ New Zealand Film Commission/The Kobal Collection/Ken George

Cabin Fever

RELEASE September 12, 2003 (U.S.)
DIRECTED BY Eli Roth
WRITTEN BY Eli Roth, Randy Pearlstein
STARRING Rider Strong, Jordan Ladd, James DeBello, Cerina Vincent, Joey Kern
RATING R, for strong violence and gore, sexuality, language

The directorial debut of Eli Roth, *Cabin Fever* captures the grit and violence of 1980s horror and launched the career of a director now known as one of the new generation of horror movie creators, the Splat Pack.

The film begins with a hermit living a solitary life in the wilderness with only his faithful dog for companionship. When the dog does not respond to calls, the hermit investigates and finds that most of the canine's flesh has rotted away.

> "THAT GUY ASKED FOR OUR HELP AND WE LIT HIM ON FIRE. YOU'LL UNDERSTAND IF I'M NOT IN A PARTICULARLY SOCIAL MOOD."
> - KAREN

Later we meet some young people on their way to a glorious vacation in an isolated cabin in the woods. Trouble materializes early when one accidentally shoots the hermit, thinking he is a deer. Instead of coming to his aid, the shooter leaves him in a ditch to die and slinks back to the cabin and his friends. Shocker, then, when the hermit shows up at the cabin the next day both wounded and infected with some strange sickness that causes him to vomit blood all over everybody. What do the youngsters do in response to the crazed blood-puking hermitized whack-job? Set him on fire, of course. Who wouldn't?

What follows is the speedy progress of flesh-eating bacteria as it consumes the bodies of the campers one by one. Add a cameo by Roth as a tent-camping pothead, a vicious killer German shepherd, inbred country folk with murder on their minds, and a crazy kid who spontaneously launches into fits of acrobatic karate moves, and you have *Cabin Fever*.

Marcy (Cerina Vincent) takes a defiant stance. *Down Home Entertainment/The Kobal Collection/Scott Kevan*

Cabin Fever spawned the movie-making career of Roth for good reason—it brings graphic gore and disastrously bad decisions back to the forefront of good horror. Often the most terrifying of all is the way seemingly normal human beings behave in times of peril and certain doom, and this one puts the inner darkness of humanity in the spotlight in every graphic detail…to the delight of Horror Movie Freaks and gorehounds alike. Getting "the flu" has never been more frightening.

The flesh-eating bacteria mercilessly eats away the once-pretty face of Karen (Jordan Ladd) in *Cabin Fever*. *Down Home Entertainment/The Kobal Collection/Scott Kevan*

The Ruins

RELEASE DATE April 2, 2008 (U.S. premier)
DIRECTED BY Carter Smith
WRITTEN BY Scott B. Smith (screenplay and novel)
STARRING Jonathan Tucker, Jena Malone, Laura Ramsey, Shawn Ashmore, Joe Anderson
RATING R, for strong violence and gruesome images, language, some sexuality, nudity

The Ruins takes the murderous potential of nature to new heights, this time pointing to plants as the harbingers of doom rather than furry or feathered friends.

The film begins with two couples on vacation in Mexico. They meet a German tourist and agree to accompany him on a search for his missing brother, who joined an archeological dig of a Mayan temple in the jungle. Soon after discovering the temple, the group is confronted by a band of armed and enraged Mayans. These Mayans turn their weapons on the others and force them to climb to the top of the temple, preventing their escape with regular armed patrols.

"THE POLICE, OUR PARENTS, THE GREEKS, SOMEBODY. SOMEBODY IS GOING TO FIND US. WE JUST HAVE TO BE ALIVE WHEN THEY DO."
- JEFF

The now captives quickly realize that there is something sinister about the vines, as they witness them move of their own accord, mimic sounds, and eventually take root inside their bodies.

Killer plants are typically not as exciting as ferocious creatures in the aberration of nature category of horror. *The Ruins*, however, breaks the fright barrier by focusing both on plants with seemingly conscious actions and the torturous hell experienced by the humans of the film. Infighting, bodily dismemberment, and cutting themselves open in search of the growing vines adds to the dramatic fright of the situation and provides for some extremely explicit and disturbing gore.

Horror Movie Freaks with an interest in horrific nature should have a variety of both animal and plant terror tales at their disposal. *The Ruins* covers the plant, and will certainly cause second thoughts of venturing across that vine-laden expanse.

Stacy (Laura Ramsey) wakes up to an unwanted visitor creeping up her leg. *DreamWorks SKG*

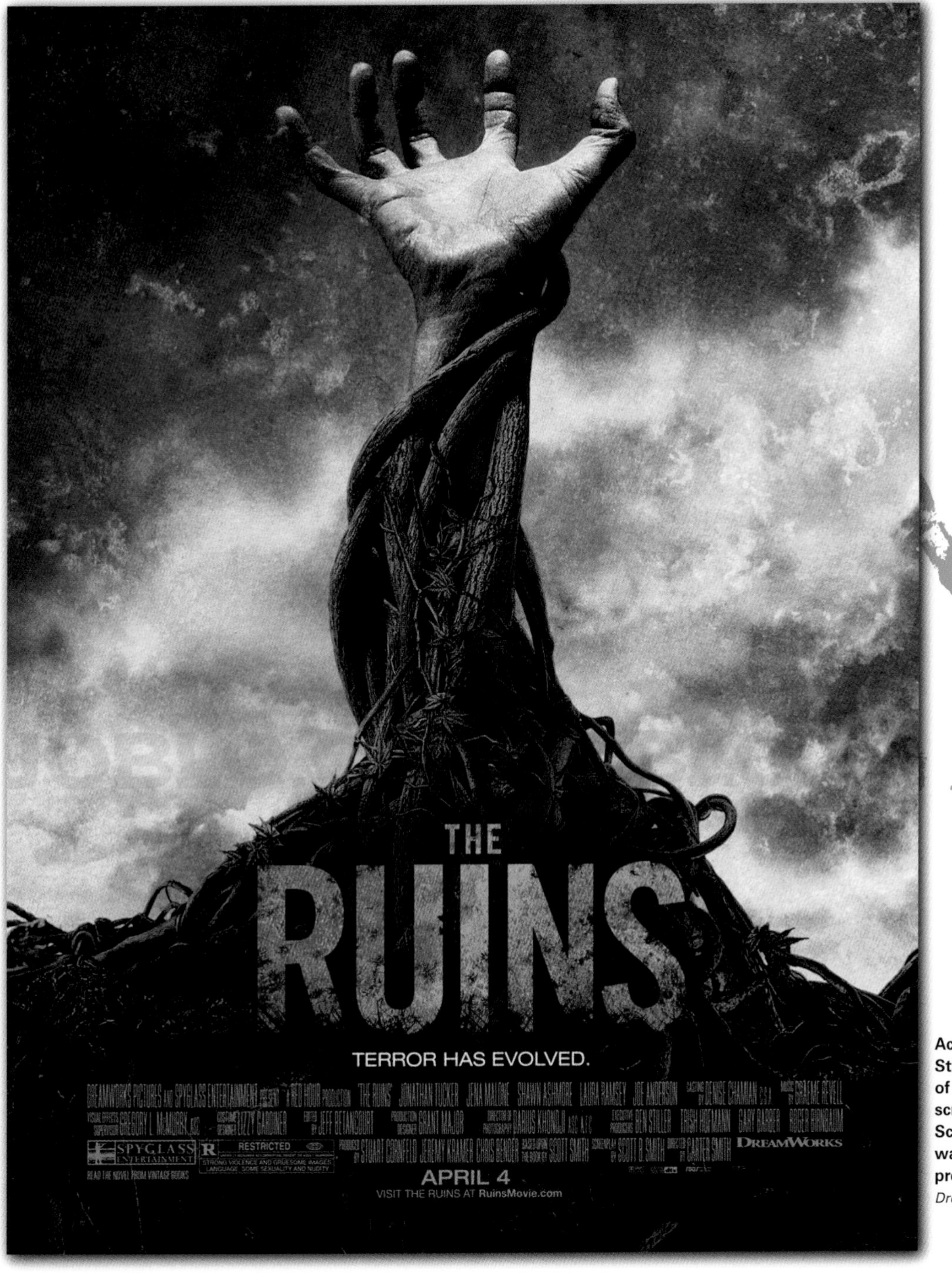

Actor Ben Stiller, a friend of novelist/screenwriter Scott B. Smith, was an executive producer of this.
DreamWorks SKG

The title character in *Alien* gets ready to strike. *20th Century Fox Productions*

Aliens and Outer Space

There is a long-standing debate surrounding the classification of movies with outer space or alien themes as horror movies, rather than science fiction. Let's put that debate to rest once and for all, shall we?

Bottom line: does the film have a slasher? How about a monster determined to make a meal of unsuspecting humans? Maybe there is a ghost haunting the halls of that great space station in the sky. If these things occur, it's a horror movie. The elements that make up a horror movie, namely inspiring fear and dread by conjuring up known and subconscious fears and bringing them to life, exist whether the setting is an old house on a hill or a space freighter headed for the next galaxy. A monster is a monster, even if it is hovering over your stasis chamber instead of hiding under your bed.

Incorporating aliens into the equation opens an entire universe of new and unique monsters and other villains. No longer limited to the confines of earth-borne possibilities, the extraterrestrial monster can take any form necessary to maim and mutilate, confined only by the imagination. Acid for blood, the ability to assume the form of friends and pets, and even causing children to develop glowing eyes as they plan their parents' painful demise can all be done, and have been. The alien factor is great for horror and horror movie monsters.

The added dimension to horror that happens in outer space is the isolation and inability to flee. If you're confined to a spaceship, for example, it's difficult to run out the front door and ask your neighbor to call the police. With nowhere to run and nowhere to hide, horror can transpire unencumbered by the possibility of rescue or escape. Space is ground zero for the final showdown between villain and hero, and only one will escape alive. Plus, in space they have Tang and food in a tube, so what's not to love?

With so many similarities and points of intersection between science fiction and horror, it may seem curious that the fan base between the two is not identical. Sure, there are a large number of Horror Movie Freaks who also enjoy science fiction, as well as science-fiction junkies who appreciate horror…but they are still different. The Horror Freak craves the fright, with the galactic backdrop playing second fiddle to the murderous mayhem and terrible apparitions.

When it comes to horror movie monsters, villains and specters originating from other planets, galaxies, and spatial grids, the Horror Movie Freak says, "Bring it on!" How bad could it be, right?

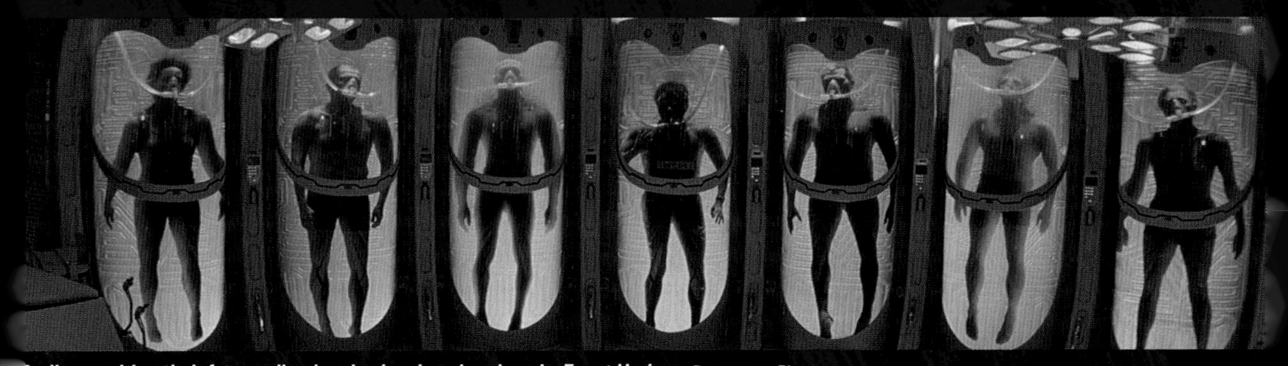

Bodies awaiting their fate are lined up in sleeping chambers in *Event Horizon*. Paramount Pictures

Invasion of the Body Snatchers

RELEASE February 5, 1956 (U.S.)
DIRECTED BY Don Siegel
WRITTEN BY Daniel Mainwaring (screenplay) and Jack Finney (*Collier's* magazine serial)
STARRING Kevin McCarthy, Dana Wynter, Larry Gates, King Donovan, Carolyn Jones
NOT RATED Has some mildly frightening scenes

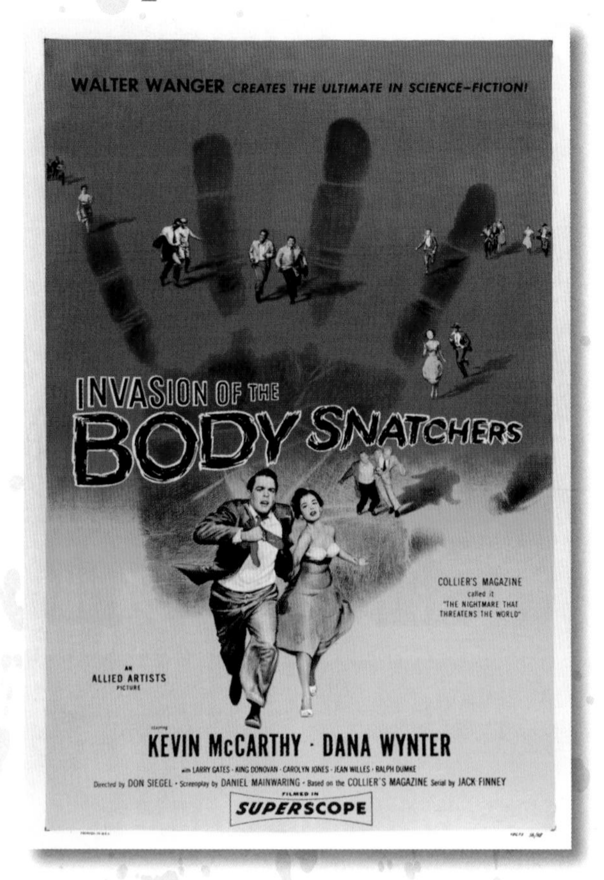

In June 2008, the American Film Institute ranked this No. 9 on its list of the 10 greatest films in the science-fiction genre.
Allied Artists Pictures/Walter Wanger Productions

The tale told in *Invasion of the Body Snatchers* has been restated time and time again through multiple remakes over the years. This is the original.

The tale begins with Dr. Bennell (Kevin McCarthy) dealing with a rash of townspeople claiming that their families and loved ones have been replaced by imposters.

At first this is disregarded as mass hysteria, but it soon becomes clear that the fears are indeed real. Large alien pods are disposing of human beings and growing exact duplicates in their place, distinguishable only by their utter lack of emotion.

"THEY'RE HERE ALREADY! YOU'RE NEXT! YOU'RE NEXT, YOU'RE NEXT...!"
— *DR. MILES J. BENNELL*

In this original film adaptation, the menace involves the overtaking of the human race by aliens and is, for the most part, considered science fiction. The film is scary, however, as the loved ones of the un-replaced are indeed monsters in their own right.

As this film continued to be remade, the replacement of humans by the pods became more and more the platform for political and social commentary. The question becomes one of which is better, the fighting of humans amongst themselves or the seeming harmony of the replaced individuals motivated by a common mind?

Horror Movie Freaks should watch all in the series as a study of the progression of horror as technology and filming techniques change, as well as a view into the societal angst of the day and the effect it has on the interpretation of the same story. Horror depicts worst-case scenarios, but what if that worst case is better than the status quo?

nes, Kevin McCarthy, and King Donovan fend off alien attackers in *Invasion of the Body Snatchers*. *Allied Artists/*

Alien

RELEASE May 25, 1979 (U.S.)
DIRECTED BY Ridley Scott
WRITTEN BY Dan O'Bannon and Ronald Shusett
STARRING Tom Skerritt, Sigourney Weaver, Veronica Cartwright, Harry Dean Stanton, John Hurt, Ian Holm, Yaphet Kotto
RATING R, for violence and some gore

The central themes of *Alien*, specifically the facts that there is an alien and the action happens in outer space, may to some imply a science-fiction film. Horror Freaks disagree.

The film begins on a mining space ship with the crew in hypersleep for a long journey. Suddenly the ship's computer, "Mother," awakens the crew and sounds an alarm. There is a distress signal coming from a nearby planet that must be investigated.

Several members of the crew go to the surface to investigate and discover thousands of objects that look like large eggs. One of the eggs opens up and when a crewman peers inside, some sort of creature leaps out and attaches to his face. Later, after the creature has fallen off the crewman and apparently dies, an alien bursts out of his chest and scurries away. The simple mining ship becomes the scene of a stand off between the deadly alien and the crew, and in space…no one can hear you scream.

"YOU STILL DON'T UNDERSTAND WHAT YOU'RE DEALING WITH, DO YOU? PERFECT ORGANISM. ITS STRUCTURAL PERFECTION IS MATCHED ONLY BY ITS HOSTILITY." *- ASH*

Lt. Ellen Ripley (Sigourney Weaver), the heroine
20th Century Fox Productions/Brandywine Productions

Alien logically falls under the Aliens a
the existence of, well, aliens, but that is wh
fiction film ends. *Alien* is a horror movie t
categorized as an aberration of nature
The fact that this is an alien becomes irre
destruction of the crew one by one in a m

The production of *Alien* is amazing,
film was made in the 1970s and therefore
All of the effects were created the "old f
models, and animatronics and yet are so co
that you might wish all movies were done

Alien is a true classic of the horror ge
vered spot in the Horror Freak's collectio
come along that are complete no brainers
fits the bill.

Event Horizon

RELEASE August 15, 1997 (U.S.)
DIRECTED BY Paul Anderson
WRITTEN BY Philip Eisner
STARRING Laurence Fishburne, Sam Neill, Kathleen Quinlan, Joely Richardson, Richard T. Jones
RATING R, for strong violence and gore, language, some nudity

Event Horizon is the name of a space ship, and also an astrological event described in the general relativity theory about the edge of a black hole and its affect on the perceptions of events from different points of view.

The ship Event Horizon is testing a new drive technology, which seeks to create a black hole to bend space and reduce travel time, when it suddenly vanishes.

Seven years later, the ship reappears with the crew dead and something strange existing at its core. Members of the rescue crew begin having visions of their innermost fears, and it seems that whatever happened to the ship has opened a gateway to another dimension—one of pure chaos and evil.

Bringing together space travel, the general relativity theory, and the concept of an entire ship possessed by what is effectively the devil makes for some dramatic and confusing horror.

The basis for the film is deep and could easily drag the entire thing into the black hole of pure science fiction, if it weren't for the fright.

The vision of each character's worst fears being brought to life before their eyes is beyond unsettling. Horror is all about the worst nightmares of people being acted out on the screen to horrify and exhilarate, and in this regard, *Event Horizon* achieves this goal directly rather than anecdotally.

Event Horizon is an excellent film often forgotten by popular lists of the best horror movies, but Horror Movie Freaks know better. This film may take just a little bit of thinking, but the horror is pure emotion.

Dr. William Weir (Sam Neill) investigates something in the green-tinged venting system.
Paramount Pictures

MILLER: OH. MY. GOD. WHAT HAPPENED TO YOUR EYES?
DR. WEIR: WHERE WE'RE GOING, WE WON'T NEED EYES TO SEE.

A bathing beauty is about to discover that's no rubber ducky in the bathtub with her in *Slither.* *Universal/The Kobal Collection/Chris Helcermanas-Benge*

Slither

RELEASE March 31, 2006 (U.S.)
DIRECTED AND WRITTEN BY James Gunn
STARRING Don Thompson, Nathan Fillion, Xantha Radley, Elizabeth Banks, Michael Rooker
RATING R, for strong violence and gore, language

Slither is a monster movie, or rather "monsters" movie, but the source of these monsters moves the film to the Aliens and Outer Space category.

Starla Grant (Elizabeth Banks) is a lovely young woman married to the older, and richer, Grant Grant (Michael Rooker) in her small country town, but things aren't going very well. After a fight, her husband ventures off to the local bar and hooks up with a floozy, and suddenly sees what appears to be a meteorite crossing the sky and landing in the woods. He investigates the object and comes across something moving along the forest floor, which promptly shoots him in the neck with some sort of dart and then dies.

"GRANT LOOKS LIKE A SQUID, DON'T KNOW WHERE HE'S GONNA HIDE... SEAWORLD MAYBE." - *BILL PARDY*

Grant begins to change as a result of his alien spearing, and impregnates a woman with some sort of slugs that incubate inside her and emerge ready to overtake the town and turn the inhabitants into alien-controlled zombies.

Slither is a good film, although it didn't do very well at the box office and ended up losing millions of dollars. The reasons for this vary, but some possible explanations are that the concept of alien slugs had previously been done in *Night of the Creeps*, and horror fans at the time didn't appreciate the duplication.

Musician and horror movie director Rob Zombie makes a voice cameo as Dr. Grant. *Universal Pictures/Gold Circle Films*

This movie is promoted as a horror/comedy and yet the comedy isn't very funny. *Slither* does, however, have a great monster, some really gross visuals, and giant slugs that crawl down the throats of unsuspecting townspeople and put them under the control of Grant, who becomes quite a disgusting monster himself. Slowly this film is gaining recognition and popularity and will one day be considered a cult classic of the genre. Horror Movie Freaks had better get a head start.

Spiral shapes figure prominently in *Uzumaki,* and things sometimes end in death for those spellbound by them. *Omega Micott Inc/The Kobal Collection*

Asian Horror

Although Asian horror falls squarely into the category of foreign horror from the point of view of an all-American Horror Movie Freak, this is a bit of a special situation. Although there are many horror fans and aficionados who have a leaning toward horror from one country or another, Asian horror, and most notably Japanese or J-horror, is both particularly popular and particularly dark in its presentation.

Movie "formulas," so prevalent in U.S. horror, are either non-existent in Asian horror or so different from the recognized norms that they throw a wrench in the whole works and seldom fail to shock, disgust, and terrify. Cultural norms, differences in rating systems of "suitability," and centuries of spiritual history undoubtedly contribute to the uniquely unsettling quality of Asian horror films.

There are Asian horror "purists" amongst us who consider J-horror, or Asian horror generally, to be far superior to any domestic offerings. These fanatics will not tolerate even a mention that any Asian horror film has a single flaw, and certainly will not accept an Asian horror film remade for U.S. audiences under any circumstances. Many of these Freaks are similar to the ravenous devotees of Macs who would rather engage in a bare knuckle brawl than admit that there is a remote possibility of a software flaw in their laptop operating system. Others are members of the dreaded "horror intelligentsia" who have latched onto the horror sub-genre as a way to belittle the common horror releases and discuss films that nobody has ever heard of in an effort to feel superior, while wearing all black, of course. There are also others, however, who simply recognize the powerful allure of Asian horror and prefer to be engulfed in the dark experiential mayhem of it all.

The truth is, there are a great number of J-horror and other Asian horror films that are, indeed, uniquely compelling and shocking. Asian horror can be highly atmospheric and dark, a bit confusing, and very scary with original themes and existentialist outcomes. To find out what is really running through the minds of Horror Freaks on the other side of the world, find out what scares them. Chances are good it will scare you, too.

A normal-starting day in the South Korean film, *The Host*, quickly turns to terror and makes people run for their lives. *Chungeorahm Film/The Kobal Collection*

Audition

RELEASE May 7, 2002 (U.S. DVD premier)
DIRECTED BY Takashi Miike
WRITTEN BY Ryû Murakami (novel) and Daisuke Tengan (screenplay)
STARRING Ryo Ishibashi, Eihi Shiina, Tetsu Sawaki, Jun Kunimura, Renji Ishibashi
RATING R, for torture and violence, sexuality

Audition by director Takashi Miike has definite leanings into the psychotic category, and the dark themes are characteristic of the best of J-horror.

Shigeharu Aoyama (Ryo Ishibaski) is an aging widower of seven years. Others in the family want to move on with their own lives, yet do not want to leave Aoyama alone, so they devise a plan to find him a mate. They schedule an audition, presumably for a part in a new film that will allow Aoyama to meet and eventually marry the appropriate companion.

Of the beautiful women who try out for the position, Asami (Eihi Shiina) catches Aoyama's eye. After some awkward beginnings, it seems as if Asami returns the interest, but we see the first shades of something wrong as she sits on the floor in her apartment manically waiting for Aoyama's promised telephone call. Slowly the story and tension build, leading up to the final 15 minutes of horrific mayhem that has been described as "controlled chaos."

Miike is a masterful storyteller who has been sometimes criticized for his exceedingly dark and violent themes and attention to detail when it comes to gore and carnage. There are even those who claim that the level of shocking gore and realism are too graphic to allow for an enjoyment of the film itself. This film has also been admonished by feminist groups for the portrayal of women as stereotypes and the definition of the "ideal woman" by male-dominated Japanese culture. The controversy, however, only serves to make this film more appealing to Freaks seeking variety and a taste of varying points of view when it comes to their horror.

Asami Yamazaki (Eihi Shiina) knows her way around needles. *Omega/The Kobal Collection*

The realistic interpretation of the macabre and the violent results of subscribing to societal constructs are powerful and clearly illustrate the difference in scope and execution of horror from cultures outside the United States. Miike regularly claims, as he has with *Audition*, that social commentary is in no way a factor in his films, but a cursory viewing of the movie proves this to be untrue. The commentary is indeed there, whether it is "on purpose" or not.

"THIS WIRE CAN CUT THROUGH MEAT AND BONE EASILY."
- Asami Yamazaki

Uzumaki

RELEASE May 3, 2002 (New York)
DIRECTED BY Higuchinsky
WRITTEN BY Junji Ito, Kengo Kaji, Takao Nitta and Chika Yasuo
STARRING Eriko Hatsune, Fhi Fan, Hinako Saeki, Eun-Kyung Shin, Keiko Takahashi
NOT RATED There is some violence/gore and disturbing images

Uzumaki is a highly c[illegible] on a Japanese "manga," kno[illegible]vel in the U.S.

Kirie (Eriko Hatsune)[illegible] sign of trouble when she wit[illegible]er of her boyfriend seemly obse[illegible] spirals on a snail's shell. He tak[illegible]cination with the spiral shape further and [illegible]ther. He films anything having such a shape for a video scrapbook, makes whirlpools in his soup, and eventually climbs inside a clothes dryer to film the world from a spiral point of view.

Before long, the entire town is swept away in the spiral. Hair curls on its own, corpses wrap over themselves in gruesome ways, and eventually everyone begins to sprout snail shells. Kirie is committed to a mental institution due to her new-found fear of the spiral, which culminates in her trying to cut the spirals from her fingerprints. She becomes entwined in a race to both figure out what is happening and to get out of town before she is caught up in the spiral.

Uzumaki is a strange movie that is confusing and full of creative and gory references to the emergence of the evil spiral and the havoc it wreaks on the town's inhabitants. For Horror Movie Freaks who believe they have seen it all, this one will certainly swirl that thought out of their brain. It is not advisable that you attempt to fully understand this film, but rather that you watch it and revel in the different themes and points of view Asian horror offers.

A whole town in *Uzumaki* is swept away by mysterious spirals, even hair.
Omega Micott Inc./The Kobal Collection

Ringu

RELEASE March 4, 2003 (U.S. video premier)
DIRECTED BY Hideo Nakata
WRITTEN BY Hiroshi Takahashi (screenplay) and Kôji Suzuki (novel)
STARRING Nanako Matsushima, Miki Nakatani, Hiroyuki Sanada, Yuko Takeuchi, Hitomi Satô
NOT RATED Has some violence/gore and disturbing images

When *Ringu* released in Japan in 1998, it was the highest-grossing film ever in that country, and inspired the beginning of a huge rush of Asian horror remakes for U.S. audiences. Based on a novel of the same name, the movie uses as its basis a popular myth in Japan called "Bancho Sarayashiki," where a woman is thrown down a well and becomes a "vengeful spirit."

Ringu begins with two teens discussing an urban legend about a cursed videotape that brings death in seven days to all who watch it. It is later revealed that one of the teens watched a found videotape with some friends exactly one week earlier, and she is then killed by an unseen force while her friend watches in horror.

Later, an investigative reporter doing a piece on urban legends discovers that her niece and three friends were mysteriously killed on the same night, their faces distorted in terror. Her quest to find the cause of the deaths results in her finding the cursed tape and watching it herself. Now she has seven days to unravel the mystery and avoid becoming a twisted-face victim of the curse.

"THIS KIND OF THING...IT DOESN'T START BY ONE PERSON TELLING A STORY. IT'S MORE LIKE EVERYONE'S FEAR JUST TAKES ON A LIFE OF ITS OWN. - *RYUJI TAKAYAMA*

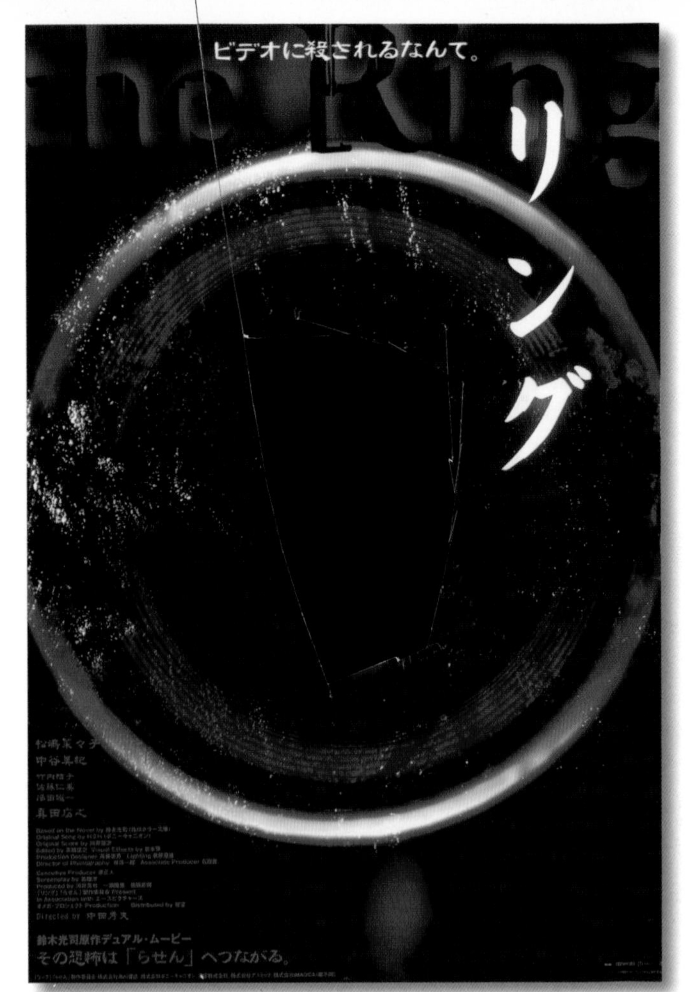

One of this movie's taglines is, "One curse, one cure, one week to find it."
Omega Project

Ringu is, for many horror fans, one of the scariest movies ever made, and it resulted in a remake that began many Freaks down the path of searching for another film that would elicit similar levels of fear.

Ringu is the perfect example of dark and gritty themes, production methods, and frightening cultural myth. That, and the fact this film has inspired so much domestic fright and retellings of Asian horror in the United States, elevate it to unquestionable must-see status. Regardless of your preference for the original or the remake, watching the inspiration for so much horror-related activity and progress is a necessary distinction between the casual horror fan and bonafide Horror Movie Freak.

Shown above is the vengeful spirit that wreaks havoc in *Ringu*. Koji Suzuki, who wrote the novel this movie is based on, says he g[illegible] inspiration from American horror classic, *Poltergeist* (reviewed on P. 104). *Omega/Kadokawa/The Kobal Collection*

Ju-On

RELEASE November 9, 2004 (U.S. DVD premier)
DIRECTED AND WRITTEN BY Takashi Shimizu
STARRING Megumi Okina, Misaki Itô, Misa Uehara, Yui Ichikawa, Kanji Tsuda
RATING R, for some disturbing images

A low-budget production that went straight to video, *Ju-On* later became a surprise hit that inspired a string of sequels, as well as English-language remakes.

Ju-On is a ghost story that expands on the popular Japanese horror myth of the vengeful ghost, or "onryo." The legend of the *Ju-On* describes this as a curse that can take a mind of its own, causing the ghosts of those killed by the curse to kill others and further spread itself via new cursed ghosts. The curse begins when someone dies while harboring a "deep and burning grudge."

"THANKS FOR THE EFFORT."
- *HIROHASHI*

Ju-On chronicles the affects of such a vengeful ghost, taking refuge in the house where the ghost's body died. All who enter the house or come in contact with a cursed person are themselves affected by the curse, and when they die, they spread the evil wherever it is they frequented during life.

This movie was not expected to take the horror-loving community by storm, illustrated by the micro budget and straight-to-video status. It may be this very fact that made the film so successful. Without money for gore or effects, it was up to writer and director Shimizu to instead build feelings of dread and foreboding, making the anticipation of events scarier than actually seeing them for yourself. Shimizu is also noted for his willingness to actually show his ghosts onscreen, something that typically has been implied in other ghost stories.

Ju-On has had an incredible impact on the horror genre, resulting in several Japanese sequels as the curse spreads from area to area, and inspiring some highly profitable Asian-horror-for-U.S.-audiences remakes. In this regard, *Ju-On* can be credited with helping to fuel the modern love-affair production studios have with J-horror remakes as it proved the profitability and acceptance of such films.

Due to the dark qualities of *Ju-On*, as well as the references to Japanese myths and its inspiration of prominent English language remakes, Horror Movie Freaks are best served to be familiar with this film and add it to their general horror knowledge base. J-horror has many appealing attributes, and *Ju-On* is one of the films that led the way in exposing Horror Freaks worldwide to disturbing Asian myths and film-making methods.

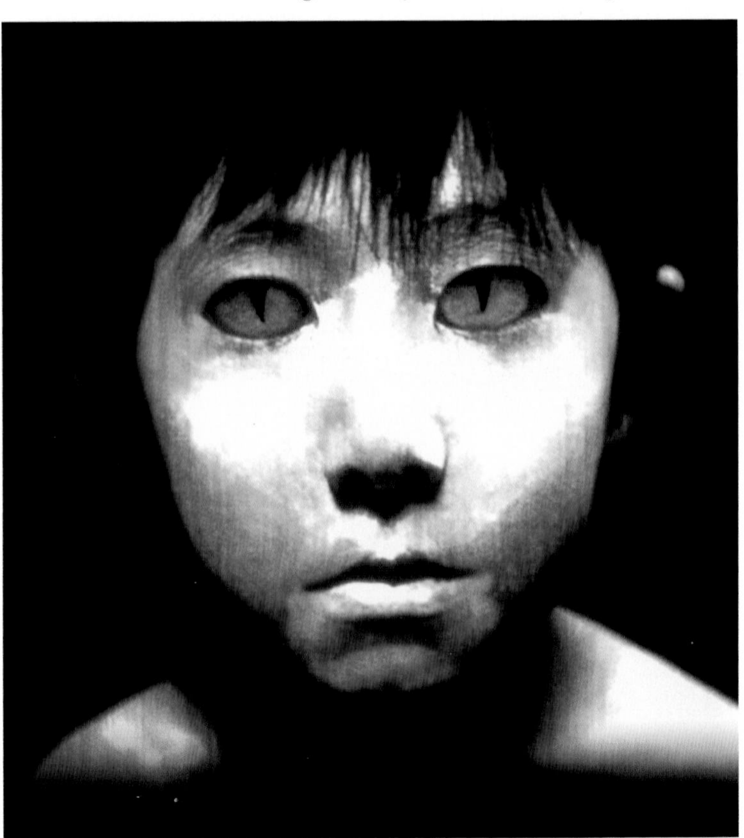

This *Ju-On* publicity still is spooky and effective. *Oz Company Ltd*

The Host

RELEASE March 7, 2007 (U.S. limited)
DIRECTED BY Joon-ho Bong
WRITTEN BY Joon-ho Bong, Chul-hyun Baek and Jun-won Ha
STARRING Kang-ho Song, Hie-bong Byeon, Hae-il Park Du-na Bae, Ah-sung Ko
RATING R, for creature violence, language

The Host hails from South Korea and was, at its release, the highest-grossing film in that country. This film is refreshing for its take on the classic monster-movie concept that deviates from the common stereotype of the Asian Godzilla-esque creature.

The day starts out like any other day for the Park family, as they work in their little shop situated in a plaza surrounding the Han River. Suddenly a crowd develops at the shore amongst cries that there is "something" under the Wonhyo Bridge. Before the amazed eyes of spectators, a creature emerges and races ashore, taking gawkers by surprise and cutting a path of death through the crowd. The creature then eats family member Hyun-seo (Ah-sung Ko).

The family, quarantined by officials for coming in contact with the creature, receives a cell phone call from Hyun-seo. He was not really killed, but rather transported to the sewers where the creature is keeping him. The family must find a way to escape the quarantine and rescue Hyun-seo before the creature feeds him to her offspring.

The Host is a great film that saw a lot of success, due both to being an excellent example of a creative and original monster movie and for the political commentary surrounding the presence of the United States military in South Korea. The monster, you see, was created when military personnel broke protocol and dumped 100 bottles of formaldehyde into the river, resulting in a mutant that would one day grow to terrorize the city. This event (the dumping of formaldehyde, not the monster invasion) actually did occur years earlier and resulted in some animosity toward the United States military presence by South Korean citizens.

The Host **has won several awards, including acting and special effects.**
Chungeorahm Film/Magnolia Pictures

"YOU ARE DIMWITS, RIGHT TO THE END. I'LL SEE YOU IN HELL."
- *SUICIDAL JUMPER*

The Horror Movie Freak can see the cultural basis and motivations for horror that originates in other lands, as well as a first-rate monster movie, by viewing *The Host*. Asian horror is not all dark images and ghostly apparitions, but also realistic happenings based on current events.

Norman Bates (Anthony Perkins)...so shy...so nervous...so *Psycho*. *Paramount Pictures/Shamley Productions*

Beginner's Shelf

There are those among us of a more sensitive nature. Sure, they may share some general characteristics of a Horror Freak, but alas, they are not the same. The sight of zombies feasting on human flesh makes them queasy. The thought of a machete slicing into a panty-clad lovely in the woods is too ghastly for words. The reality that a burned madman might slice them to ribbons while they peacefully slumber is enough to cause insomnia for weeks on end.

You know the type. They hide their eyes when the music swells in a Judith Light movie of the week, they can't sleep with the closet door open a crack, they insist on investigating every stray sound outside their window, they hesitate to leave the tent at night during a camping trip, and worse—they won't watch horror movies! This is the horror novice.

Known by many names, such as wimp, wuss, coward, and fraidy-cat, the horror novice can be a particularly painful thorn in the side of a randy Horror Freak. Got a date night, DVDs at home, or movie party planned with a novice? Get ready for Meg Ryan and a romantic comedy because horror is out of the question. Trust me, I have been there and feel your pain, but there is hope.

Horror novices CAN be broken of their anti-horror dementia and blossom into a full-fledged Horror Freak themselves, but it is a tricky proposition. Choosing the right films in the formative furlough of a future Freak requires careful planning and flawless execution. Go too far and too fast, like convincing a novice to witness a body ripped in half with entrails tracking the floor in George Romero's ***Day of the Dead***, and a lifetime of dreadful romantic comedy is the unavoidable result. The purpose of The Beginner's Shelf is to avoid this fate worse than death itself coming after you.

This chapter consists of those films that are good horror and appropriate representations of the various sub-genres, while avoiding the heavy gore, heart-stopping scares, and nightmare-inducing themes that advanced Horror Freaks crave. These films are typically separated from the rest of the collection on their own shelf so as to be easily identified when a horror novice emergency crops up. They are also enjoyable for the Horror Freak, while easing the novice into the proper level of appreciation slowly and carefully.

There are appropriate films to make up the Beginner's Shelf within just about every sub-genre of horror, both new and old. Maybe you have a horror novice in your life today that is secretly begging to be cured of this awful affliction. Perhaps the horror novice is actually you! In either case, the following selections are certain to ease the transition and put that pesky novice on the right track once and for all.

Save the world from the tragedy of romantic comedies and cure a horror novice today!

The Creeper (Jonathan Breck) puts the choke on Darry (Justin Long) in *Jeepers Creepers*. *Zoetrope/United Artists/The Kobal Collection/Gene Page*

Psycho

RELEASE June 16, 1960 (U.S. premier)
DIRECTED BY Alfred Hitchcock
WRITTEN BY Joseph Stefano (screenplay) and Robert Bloch (novel)
STARRING Anthony Perkins, Vera Miles, John Gavin, Martin Balsam, Janet Leigh
RATING R, presumably for the psychological and sexual themes, brief nudity

The 50th anniversary of *Psycho*, a horror movie classic to beat all classics, is 2010. Directed by the legendary Alfred Hitchcock, *Psycho* adheres to the director's long-held belief that "there is more fear in the anticipation of the act than in the act itself." With no distinguishable gore or direct violence, this film inspires fright by constantly alluding to horrific events that are just about to happen.

Marion Crane (Janet Leigh) is on the run, hoping to use the money she just embezzled from her company to start a new life with her secret lover. As night sets in, she finds the isolated Bates Motel, and decides it is as good a place as any to hole up and wait for her Romeo's arrival. Too bad she didn't keep driving.

Norman Bates (Anthony Perkins), the purveyor of this fine establishment, seems to take a liking to the lovely Ms. Crane…much to the chagrin of Norman's "loving mother," who continuously admonishes and berates him from her bedroom-turned-hospital room. Norman's mother will not tolerate another woman vying for his attention, and decides to take matters into her own hands. Or does she?

Psycho has been around for so long that most people, Horror Movie Freaks and novices alike, are familiar with the plotline and specifics of this film. That doesn't matter. This is a film that can be viewed over and over without getting tiresome. Hitchcock provides a template from which filmmakers around the world would take structure of for their own cinematic creations, horror and otherwise, decades later and still today. Hitchcock's masterful use of story, filming techniques, suspense, and horror combine to create an enduring classic that will likely last forever.

Hitchcock also introduced a horrifying new concept to the movie-watching public: the monster who is not obviously a monster. Norman Bates appears normal in every regard, except of course when his knife skills emerge while you're trying to take a shower. The horror subgenre of the psychotic was born with *Psycho*, and horror hasn't been the same since.

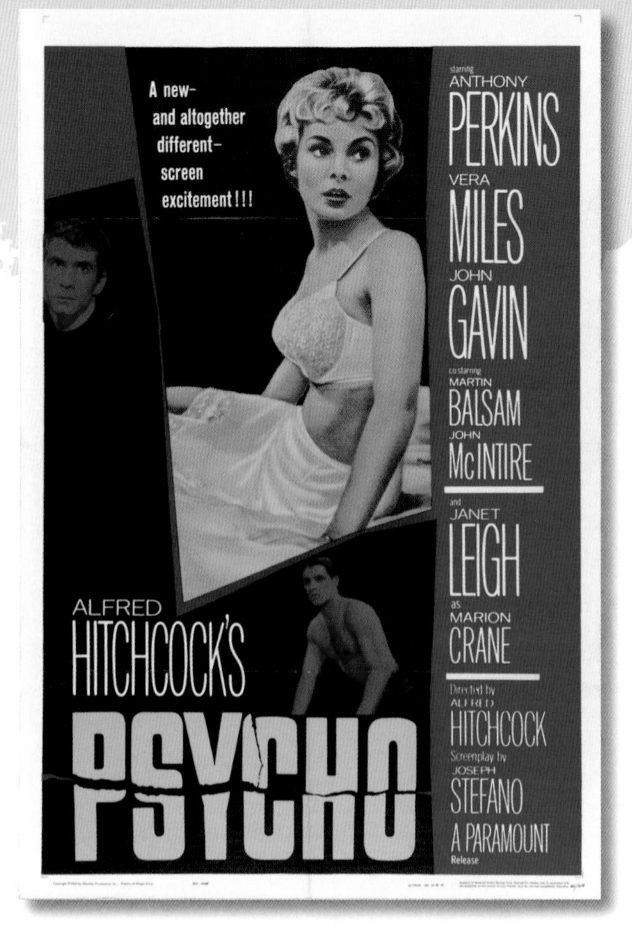

In the opening scene, Marion Crane is wearing a white bra because Hitchcock wanted to show her as being "angelic." After she steals money, the following scene shows her in a black bra to denote she's done something wrong and evil.
Paramount Pictures

Norman Bates (Anthony Perkins) at the legendary Bates Motel. Norman is ranked as the second-greatest villain on the American Film Institute's 2003 list of 100 Heroes & Villains. Hannibal Lector from ***The Silence of the Lambs*** is No. 1 (Hannibal and ***Lambs*** are on P. 132-133). *Paramount Pictures*

Marion Crane (Janet Leigh) meets her final fate in one of the most famous movie scenes ever. Horror novices will be relieved to know that any blood shown is actually Bosco chocolate syrup. That's not so scary...right? *Paramount Pictures/The Kobal Collection/William Creamer*

"I THINK I MUST HAVE ONE OF THOSE FACES YOU CAN'T HELP BELIEVING."

- *NORMAN BATES*

The Amityville Horror

RELEASE July 27, 1979 (U.S.)
DIRECTED BY Stuart Rosenberg
WRITTEN BY Sandor Stern (screenplay) and Jay Anson (novel)
STARRING James Brolin, Margot Kidder, Rod Steiger, Don Stroud, Murray Hamilton
RATING R, for terror, violence, brief nudity

The Amityville Horror is an ideal starter film for horror novices from the Ghost Stories category of films. With no discernable gore, the film relies exclusively on the creep-out factor of the storyline, and, of course, on a house that has its own ideas as to where one should reside.

"I'M COMING APART! OH, MOTHER OF GOD, I'M COMING APART!
- *GEORGE LUTZ*

George and Kathy Lutz (James Brolin and Margot Kidder) are thrilled at the amazing deal they got on their new house. It is just perfect for them in every way…except when the house proclaims that they should "Get out!" The Lutz's, of course, do not heed this warning.

After a while, George begins to behave strangely, becoming irritable and moody, even violent. Can Kathy escape the dual threat of an unfriendly house and an increasingly violent husband without coming face to face with the sharp blade of an axe?

The Amityville Horror is based on a novel that claims to be a portrayal of actual events. It is true that there were in fact folks who claimed their house was haunted and inspired violence and murder, but the validity of their story is debatable. No matter, the story is perfect fodder for a horror movie and that's what we Horror Movie Freaks care about. The psychological nature of this ghost story, combined with the 1970s styles and lack of extreme gore or effects, makes the watching experience within tolerable for the horror novice, while the classic nature of this film and performances by Kidder and Brolin up the ante sufficiently.

Amy (Natasha Ryan) senses something is wrong with the house before her parents do. Children always know... *American International Pictures*

The Lost Boys

RELEASE July 31, 1987 (U.S.)
DIRECTED BY Joel Schumacher
WRITTEN BY Janice Fischer and James Jeremias (story/screenplay) and Jeffrey Boam (screenplay)
STARRING Jason Patric, Corey Haim, Dianne Wiest, Barnard Hughes, Ed Herrmann, Kiefer Sutherland, Jamie Gertz, Corey Feldman
RATING R, for some vampire gore and violence

The Lost Boys made vampires hip and cool, casting a montage of the sexiest young stars of the time and injecting just enough humor to win over audiences and start a vampire phenomenon.

After a messy divorce, Lucy (Dianne Wiest) is forced to pack up her two sons and move in with her father. Gramps (Barnard Hughes) lives in the beach town of Santa Carla, Calif., and is a bit of an eccentric as well as a pack rat. Michael (Jason Patric), the oldest son, has more trouble than the others adjusting to his new surroundings, as his teen years come to an end and adulthood beckons.

One night Michael spies a young lovely while roaming about the beachfront amusement park and moves in to make her acquaintance. Unfortunately, the girl, named Star (Jamie Gertz), is enmeshed with a gang of roughnecks who patrol the boardwalk and generally cause trouble. In a face-off for dominance, Michael confronts the leader of this gang, David (Keifer Sutherland), and agrees to a series of death-defying dares. At the end of the evening, Michael takes a deep drink of the wine David offers him. That is his undoing.

It seems that this "wine" is actually vampire blood that starts Michael down the road to transformation and having a violent craving for human blood. It is up to his younger brother (Corey Haim) and two locals called "The Frog Brothers" to rescue Michael and the family from an eternity as creatures of the night.

Lost Boys Billy Wirth, Keifer Sutherland, Brooke McCarter, and Alex Winter. The title of the film is a reference to the companions of Peter Pan, who remained forever young - much like vampires. *Warner Bros/The Kobal Collection*

"NOW YOU KNOW WHAT WE ARE, NOW YOU KNOW WHAT YOU ARE. YOU'LL NEVER GROW OLD, MICHAEL, AND YOU'LL NEVER DIE. BUT YOU MUST FEED! - DAVID

The Lost Boys was popular in its late 1980s timeframe. Teen heartthrobs Patric, Sutherland, and Gertz, joined by "The Two Coreys," Haim and Feldman, set the stage for a frivolous "pop tart" teen movie, but there is a wrinkle. The vampire legend existing in a sleepy beach town actually works. The story and concept are intriguing and the roles well played, teen heartthrob status aside. The result of *The Lost Boys*' release was a renewed fascination with vampires and a generation of teens that thought that life as a blood-drinking immortal might not be so bad after all. Killing aside, I'm sure.

The Lost Boys holds up well against more modern vampire movies, and is a great way for horror novices to accustom themselves to our favorite genre. "Oh, THAT's horror?" they may ask. "I like that!" "Yes," you may reply, but you know in your heart that they ain't seen nothin' yet.

Ginger Snaps

RELEASE October 23, 2001 (U.S. DVD premier)
DIRECTED BY John Fawcett
WRITTEN BY John Fawcett, Karen Walton
STARRING Emily Perkins, Katharine Isabelle, Kris Lemche, Mimi Rogers, Jesse Moss
NOT RATED Has some violence/gore, language

Ginger Snaps puts werewolves squarely back where they belong—in the realm of the creature feature. Werewolves are monsters, and no amount of holy war action adventure positioning is going to change that. *Ginger Snaps* not only accepts the inherent monster elements of the werewolf, but revels in them.

Ginger (Katharine Isabelle) and her younger sister Brigitte (Emily Perkins) have trouble fitting in. Perhaps it could be because of their obsession with death and physical dismemberment, but I'm not sure. Their school photo project depicting each of them in various stages of violent death solidifies their reputation as "those weird girls."

"I GET THIS ACHE...AND I, I THOUGHT IT WAS FOR SEX, BUT IT'S TO TEAR EVERYTHING TO F***ING PIECES. - *GINGER*

One day Ginger, while walking through the woods and experiencing her first physical signs of "womanhood," is attacked by an unseen beast hungry for blood.

It is later suspected that the attacking creature is, in fact, a werewolf. Ginger's behavior over the coming days seems to reinforce this position. I'm guessing she "snaps."

Brigitte attempts to control the growing impulses of her changing sister while seeking help from the local drug dealer/werewolf expert. Can they find a cure in time?

Ginger (Katharine Isabelle) is about to show Trina (Danielle Hampton) why you shouldn't mess with a girl who has strong urges to do nasty things.
Lions Gate/TMN/Telefilm Canada/The Kobal Collection/Sophie Giraud

Ginger Snaps is an original film that has an interesting take on werewolf legends. The gore exists, but is not over the top, making this film a reasonable entry to the werewolf variety of horror film for the newbie. The story, acting, and atmosphere, however, create a compelling horror entry that will not leave the seasoned Horror Freak out in the cold.

The film sets the tone right from the beginning for the creature feature that it is, making it clear in the first few minutes that there is danger lurking in the darkness, and these strange girls will somehow wind up smack dab in the middle of it.

Jeepers Creepers

RELEASE August 31, 2001 (U.S.)
WRITTEN AND DIRECTED BY Victor Salva
STARRING Justin Long, Gina Philips, Jonathan Breck, Patricia Belcher and Eileen Brennan
RATING R, for violence/gore, language, brief nudity

Jeepers Creepers has a scary monster and an interesting plot, held together by excellent use of suspense and lurking feelings of impending doom. This film may adhere a bit to the Supernatural Thrillers horror category, with shades of Evil from Hell. Primarily, though, this is a monster movie.

It starts with two bickering siblings, Trish (Gina Philips) and Darry Jenner (Justin Long), on a road trip heading home from college. Along the way, they are passed and nearly run off the road by an ominous-looking truck with some mysterious mean guy behind the wheel. Just about the time they recover from the heart attack of their near-disastrous confrontation with this "demon on wheels," they pass the same guy, now at his house on the side of the highway. He is dumping something that looks suspiciously like human bodies into a hole in his yard, and oh no, he sees them again and takes off in pursuit, this time successfully running their car into a ditch.

"SHE DID LOSE HER HEAD THAT NIGHT, TRISH, AND YOU WANNA KNOW WHAT HE DID FOR HER? HE SEWED IT BACK ON.

- DARRY

The Jenner kids will not be deterred, however, and venture back to the house to determine the nature of the body-looking objects. Darry climbs down the hole and is shocked at what he discovers. So shocked, in fact, that he and his sister spend the remainder of the film trying to piece together the grisly mystery…and avoid becoming a shape dropped into a hole by the monstrous mean guy themselves.

Jeepers Creepers has a nice pace and edge-of-your-seat moments. The characters are good and the story doesn't skimp. For the beginner to horror, it is ideal because the really shocking horror elements of gore and panic are introduced, but not excessively explored.

Frightening a horror novice, without causing them to run for the hills, is the goal of all the films included in The Beginner's Shelf, and *Jeepers Creepers* accomplishes this goal with aplomb.

Jonathan Breck has a dual role in the film: as The Creeper, above, and as the bald cop.
Zoetrope/United Artists//The Kobal Collection/Gene Page

A hungry horde of flesh eaters tries to get at Shaun and his friends in ***Shaun of the Dead.*** *Big Talk/WT 2/The Kobal Collection*

Shaun of the Dead

RELEASE September 24, 2004 (U.S. limited)
DIRECTED BY Edgar Wright
WRITTEN BY Edgar Wright and Simon Pegg
STARRING Simon Pegg, Kate Ashfield, Nick Frost, Lucy Davis, Dylan Moran
RATING R, for zombie violence/gore and language

Shaun of the Dead is a comedy…but also a zombie movie. That's what makes this film so perfect for the horror novice. Zombie films have a tendency to be particularly disturbing and gory. They are about undead freaks feasting on the flesh of the living, after all, and there are not many ways to depict that activity without bringing up someone's lunch. *Shaun of the Dead* honors the requirements of a zombie movie, but wraps them in the bright-colored paper of a romantic comedy. Talk about tricky.

Shaun (Simon Pegg) is a hum-drum guy living a hum-drum life. He hangs out at the same bar every day, recites the same sales pitch about electronic gadgets at his job every day, and plays the same video games with the same loser friends he has had since grade school… every day. The bright spot in Shaun's life is his vivacious girlfriend Liz (Kate Ashfield), but she just dumped him.

"JUST LOOK AT THE FACE: IT'S VACANT, WITH A HINT OF SADNESS. LIKE A DRUNK WHO'S LOST A BET.

- DIANNE, DESCRIBING THE ZOMBIES

The morning after the drunken binge Shaun has to ease the pain of Liz's exit from his life, he begins to notice something strange. Women are wandering aimlessly in his back yard, trying to bite him when he asks them to move along. Strangers are lumbering down the street and smacking on his living room window. The television is out! No doubt about it—a zombie outbreak has occurred.

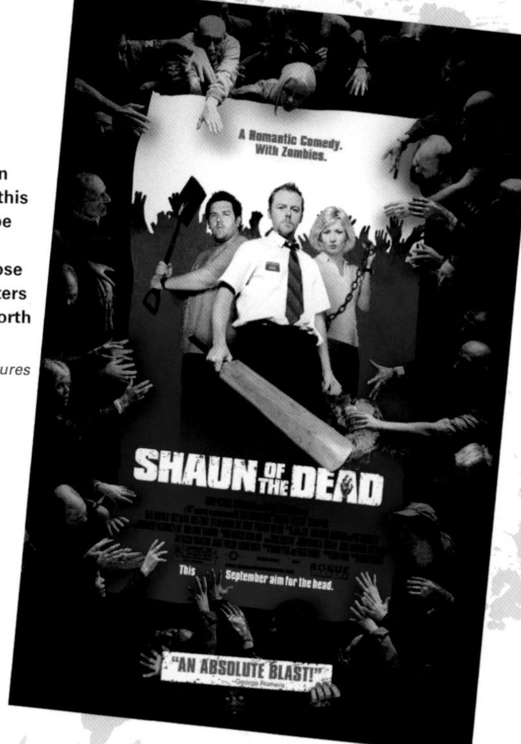

If the horror novice in your life can handle this zombie movie, maybe you can get them to eventually watch those films where flesh eaters *really* rip it up. It's worth a shot, anyway.

Studio Canal/Focus Features

Shaun has come to a turning point: either he snaps out of his lackluster existence and provides leadership and salvation to his fearful friends through this unfortunate turn of events, or he becomes zombie food. Shaun chooses the former.

Shaun of the Dead accomplishes a feat that few zombie comedies can: it respects the nature and subject matter of zombie films, while remaining hilarious and accessible to non-zombie fans. Good zombie gore and effective comedy often occur on their own, but bringing them together in a way that will satisfy both fans of zombies and of romantic comedies is indeed an amazing triumph.

Introduce your horror novice to zombie movies with *Shaun of the Dead*, and a move up to the more horrific and gory of the zombie sub-genre is sure to follow. How will things progress after that? There are no guarantees, but at least you got to watch a few zombie movies.

What entices the iconic title creature from *The Creature from the Black Lagoon* to come to land? Spotting a lovely young lady, of course. Oh, and the desire to massacre some explorers poking around where they shouldn't be. *Universal Pictures/The Kobal Collection*

The Classics

The category of "classic" is so broad it can be difficult to define. For our purposes, a horror film is considered a classic if it's more than 30 years old, made a lasting impression on the genre at large, and is still a good watch today in spite of being dated and technologically archaic.

As an additional point of separation between "modern" horror and those considered old enough to possibly be classics, consider ***Black Christmas*** (1974). This was arguably the first "slasher" film and the concept of a lurking and murderous psychotic has been used liberally in modern horror. This was followed by John Carpenter's ***Halloween*** (1978), which introduced many of the "rules of horror," and these rules were further strengthened and developed by ***Friday the 13th*** (1980). Therefore, as a general rule, B.B.C. (before ***Black Christmas***) is a logical cut-off point to distinguish the timeline where classics reside, while A.B.C. (after ***Black Christmas***) shall be considered the realm of modern horror.

Yes, I know…there will be a million examples of exceptions to this rule, and that's alright. This is, however, the most logical general divider and we're going to stick with it.

Even with such a dividing line, the universe of classic horror is vast and could easily fill an entire encyclopedia set. To provide a sampling of the classics, three groups are represented here: Universal horror, Hammer horror, and other classics. These groups will certainly provide a primer to the early days of the best movie genre, even if we barely scratch the surface.

Universal Horror

Universal horror is the name given to a series of monster movies created by Universal Studios, beginning with the ***Hunchback of Notre Dame*** in 1923. Universal brought many of the most enduring horror monsters to the silver screen and into the consciousness of the movie-going public, including ***Frankenstein, The Mummy, The Wolf Man, The Invisible Man,*** and ***The Creature from the Black Lagoon.*** Universal also employed some of the most iconic horror actors to bring these creatures to life, most notably Bela Lugosi, Boris Karloff, Lon Chaney, and Lon Chaney, Jr.

The monstrous visions brought to life by Universal Studios remain the primary visages for many Horror Freaks. Who can imagine the Frankenstein monster without that flat head, high forehead, and bolts on the side of the neck? How about Count Dracula complete with black cape and impeccable Victorian garb? These interpretations of the great monsters from literature and other sources are Universal images, brought to life by iconic performers, and are an important element of horror's roots.

Universal horror set the tone for the monster movie, and brought the public's worst nightmares to life on the silver screen. The 1930s are considered by many to be the "Golden Age" of Universal horror and spawned many of the great characters who continue to invade the nightmares of Freaks everywhere.

By understanding the humble beginnings of the world's best movie genre, the casual horror fan can set the foundation for development and elevation to full-fledged Freak. Universal horror is the place to start.

Horror legend Boris Karloff looking grim as *The Mummy.* *Universal Pictures*

Dracula

RELEASE February 14, 1931 (U.S.)
DIRECTED BY Tod Browning
WRITTEN BY Bram Stoker (novel), Hamilton Deane and John L. Balderston (play), Garrett Fort (play/script)
STARRING Bela Lugosi, Helen Chandler, David Manners, Dwight Frye, Edward Van Sloan
NOT RATED Violence is mostly implied and happens offscreen

The tale of Count Dracula has been told over and over throughout the decades. Beginning with a novel by Bram Stoker published in 1897, the legend of the Dracula vampire continues to inspire fear and Halloween costumes around the world.

The story surrounds John Harker (David Manners) and his trials with the vampire from Transylvania, Count Dracula (Bela Lugosi). Early in the film, the solicitor Renfeld (Dwight Frye) travels abroad to visit the Count, and quickly comes under his control and assists him in traveling via train to the populated centers of England.

Once Dracula arrives, he becomes smitten with the fiancé of John Harker, Mina (Helen Chandler), and casts a spell of influence on her via bites to her neck and a taste of his own blood.

Dr. Van Helsing (Edward Van Sloan) discovers the strange behavior of Renfeld, surmises that he is under the influence of a vampire, and joins the fray to investigate.

The signs present themselves to Van Helsing and Harker, notably the fact Dracula does not cast a reflection, that Dracula, too, is a vampire and that he is creating others of his kind who are now roaming the London nights in search of blood.

Renfeld (Dwight Frye) doesn't seem to like what he sees. *Universal Pictures*

It is up to Harker and Van Helsing to save Mina from the clutches of the Count and rescue England from this new-found curse.

Although this story has been told countless times with many different variations in horror movies over the years, one typical vision of Count Dracula and indeed vampires in general remains in the minds of most people, and that is the visage of Lugosi in this classic.

Lugosi IS Count Dracula, and was the first to portray the vampire wearing the long cape, slicked back black hair, and regal dress that is the mainstay of recreations and children's costumes today. Even Lugosi's voice and accent are mimicked by those wishing to instill vampiric fear and delight in others. Try saying "good evening" as a vampire and see what comes out. Chances are it is Lugosi's Count Dracula.

Universal's *Dracula* is mandatory viewing for any Horror Movie Freak, young or old. Although the film is dated and without a soundtrack in its original form, the historical significance of this film and the portrayal of Count Dracula by Lugosi is of immeasurable importance.

Dracula (Bela Lugosi) being characteristically dramatic. *Universal Pictures*

"I NEVER DRINK WINE."
- COUNT DRACULA

Frankenstein

RELEASE November 21, 1931 (U.S.)
DIRECTED BY James Whale
WRITTEN BY Mary Wollstonecraft Shelley (novel), Peggy Webling (play), John L. Balderston (adaptation), Francis Edward Faragoh, and Garrett Fort
STARRING Boris Karloff, Colin Clive, Mae Clarke, John Boles, Edward Van Sloan
NOT RATED Has mild monster violence

The Frankenstein monster, and the situations leading to his being brought to life and ultimate demise, are well known to most humans on earth. Movies, books, cartoons, and comics have all taken a stab at portraying the creature brought to life by the mad scientist Dr. Frankenstein via a bolt of lightning on a cold stormy night.

Universal Studios, again at the leading edge of fright, is responsible for bringing the most lasting and predominant image of this Mary Shelley literary monster to the silver screen. Also in the process, another iconic horror movie performer was born: Boris Karloff. Few can imagine the monster given life by a mad scientist without also picturing the flat head, obvious scars where the brain was presumably inserted inside the skull, bolts on the neck, and arms that extend well beyond the reach of mere mortal men. Karloff played this monster, and Universal Studios gave him distribution.

The story of *Frankenstein* is a sad tale, beginning with a man who takes scientific curiosity to the extreme of attempting to play God by creating life. Body parts are collected and connected and a brain is chosen to give the new creature thought and intellect. On a stormy night, the shell of a man is raised high in the air and subjected to extreme voltages of electricity and voila! "It's, it's…ALIVE!"

The Monster (Boris Karloff) joins little Maria (Marilyn Harris) in throwing flowers in the water. But what will happen once the flowers are gone? *Universal Pictures*

"...NOW *I* KNOW WHAT IT FEELS LIKE TO BE *GOD!*"
- HENRY FRANKENSTEIN

Unfortunately for the newborn creature, he's not very popular with the townsfolk. First off, there's something wrong with the brain and the creature has the mind of an infant. This doesn't match well with his giant and powerful body and results in injury and death to those who come within the creature's grasp. He is not evil, merely incapable of coming to the same conclusions of right and wrong that polite society adheres to. The monster must go, and the townspeople organize to rid the world of this abomination of nature and God.

The tragic tale of *Frankenstein* is indeed a classic, and although variations of the theme will continue to crop up, Universal's version is the standard. Horror Movie Freaks should not be content to merely accept this as fact and move on but instead experience this creature for themselves in all his Universal glory. With the foundation of the basics firmly in place, a vast library and knowledge of horror can be built to remain strong and tall.

The Mummy

RELEASE December 22, 1932 (U.S.)
DIRECTED BY Karl Freund
WRITTEN BY Nina Wilcox Putnam, Richard Schayer, John L. Balderston
STARRING Boris Karloff, Zita Johann, David Manners, Arthur Byron, Edward Van Sloan
NOT RATED Has mild mummy frights

Tutankhamun's tomb was opened and explored in 1922, revealing clear artifacts and evidence of an age wrought with mummies, jewels, and drama. As monster movies are a window into the angst of the day, it is understandable that a horror movie dramatizing the dangers of the unknown should emerge and thus, *The Mummy* was born.

The Mummy was created during the golden age of Universal horror and capitalized on the public's new-found obsession with horror and adoration of star Boris Karloff after the blockbuster hit *Frankenstein.* As with all of the early Universal horror, the "newness" of the talking motion picture allowed for a completely blank slate and filming techniques, lighting, and editing experimentation was part of the equation. Putting director Karl Freund at the helm added the additional dimension of German-influenced dark cinema with terror and dread playing heavily.

The great Boris Karloff set the standard for mummies.
Universal Pictures

The story of *The Mummy* is well known. An archeological expedition uncovers an important find: a fully intact mummy. What is not anticipated is that the mummy will come to life, find a woman he believes is the reincarnation of his former love, and attempt to mummify her and take her as his bride. *The Mummy* has been re-imagined in multiple film genres, horror to comedy to action/adventure, but this movie started it all. Horror Freaks have their favorite mummy interpretations, but in the eyes of many, the first is indeed the best and undeniably sets the standard for all future manifestations.

> ANCK-ES-EN-AMON, MY LOVE HAS LASTED LONGER THAN THE TEMPLES OF OUR GODS. NO MAN EVER SUFFERED AS I DID FOR YOU.
> *- IM-HO-TEP, ALIAS ARDATH BEY*

The Mummy may have become the villain in a series of Brandon Frasier action films later in life, but the origins of this enduring character along with the classic performance of the immortal Karloff have their roots in pure horror, and pure genius.

The Invisible Man

RELEASE November 13, 1933 (U.S.)
DIRECTED BY James Whale
WRITTEN BY H.G. Wells (novel) and R.C. Sherriff (screenplay)
STARRING Claude Rains, Gloria Stuart, William Harrigan, Henry Travers, Una O'Connor
NOT RATED Has mild violence

The Invisible Man is Universal's adaptation of an H.G. Wells novel of the same name published in 1897. Claude Rains plays the invisible man, a scientist who experiments with techniques to cause objects and animals to cease reflecting light and thereby become invisible to the human eye. When he tries the technique on himself, he quickly learns there are many things a man can accomplish when he cannot be seen by others, few of them moral. As the sense of invincibility grows and delusions of grandeur mount, the Invisible Man becomes more insane and makes plans to cause terror across the world as an exercise of his own power.

"AN INVISIBLE MAN CAN RULE THE WORLD. NO ONE WILL SEE HIM COME, NO ONE WILL SEE HIM GO." - *THE INVISIBLE MAN*

The Invisible Man is directed by James Whale, who also brought Karloff's *Frankenstein* to movie-watching audiences. This film is both a monster movie and a treatment of the adage that "absolute power corrupts absolutely." When the fear of consequences for your actions is removed by the addition of power or advantage, to what extent will a man capitalize on this fact to use and exploit those around him? The psychological demise of man and the horror that can result if all societal dictated behavioral constraints are lifted is a powerful theme more closely related to the emergence of movie monsters than may be immediately apparent. Most monsters represent some cultural fear in one way or another, and making the monster recognizable as a man is a particularly direct approach in exploring this concept.

Flora Cranley (Gloria Stuart) has no idea the Invisible Man (Claude Rains) is actually her sweetheart. *Universal/The Kobal Collection*

All heady discussion of the significance of the horror movie monster aside, *The Invisible Man* is just a fun horror movie. The effects are incredible for the time as objects seemingly move on their own, facial bandages are removed to reveal nothing underneath, and food and drink are visible being chewed and swallowed, seemingly, in mid air.

Rains does an excellent job portraying the scared and desperate scientist in the beginning of the film, slowly transforming into a violent and power-hungry madman bent on bringing chaos and death. *The Invisible Man* is certainly deserving of classic status and is a favorite of Horror Freaks and movie fans alike.

The Creature from the Black Lagoon

RELEASE March 5, 1954 (U.S.)
DIRECTED BY Jack Arnold
WRITTEN BY Harry Essex and Arthur A. Ross (screenplay) and Maurice Zimm (story)
STARRING Richard Carlson, Julia Adams, Richard Denning, Antonio Moreno, Nestor Paiva
NOT RATED The body count is high, but the violence is mild

Creature **is considered a trend-setter for other monster movies.**
Universal Pictures

Creature features swept the country in the 1950s, becoming a window into the angst of the day played out by monsters and science fiction aliens and spacemen.

The Creature from the Black Lagoon, one of the last monster movies created by Universal at the tail end of its complete dominance of the horror genre, brought horror back into the limelight in a sea of science fiction releases that were popular at the time.

An expedition ventures into the Amazon in search of fossil evidence to help explain an inhuman claw/hand that's discovered. Little does everyone know that fossil evidence is setting the bar a little low…the pre-historic creature itself is still lurking in the water's depths and doesn't much appreciate being studied.

The Creature from the Black Lagoon is a monster movie in the grand Universal style, mixing love and heartbreak into the equation. Once the creature sees the lovely Kay Lawrence (Julia Adams), he gets ideas beyond the general massacre of the human explorers—but doesn't disregard that tactic completely. The body count is high in this classic, especially for a Universal horror film from this period.

The Creature is highly recognizable to most people, horror fans or otherwise, yet there are a great number of reported Horror Freaks who have never witnessed the monster's airless swims and fights through the water or the fish-like gills that actually move on their own while out of the water…and that is a shame. This is an excellent film with one of the best "monster suits" ever created, groundbreaking underwater filming, and a musical score that adds to the experience in perfect fashion.

The Creature from the Black Lagoon is required viewing for the Horror Movie Freak who desires to rise above the casual fan and experience the classics that set the stage for the scary monsters of today.

"THERE ARE MANY STRANGE LEGENDS IN THE AMAZON. EVEN I, LUCAS, HAVE HEARD THE LEGEND OF A MAN-FISH." - *LUCAS*

Hammer Horror

Beginning with the 1955 surprise hit *The Quatermass Experiment*, Hammer studios embarked on a new and horrifying film-making direction.

I say "horrifying" in a good way, of course, as Hammer Studios began a series of horror films that resurrected many of the monsters of Universal Studios and gave them new life, and box office appeal. In the process, Hammer Studios was raised from bankruptcy and liquidation brought on by the unsuccessful foray into non-horror films to begin a new dawn in movie monsters.

Hammer Studios brought some twists to the classic monsters: new looks, new performers, and Technicolor! The revitalization of classic horror monsters did not come about without some bumps along the way in the form of copyright issues with Universal, but as these issues were settled, Hammer brought back Frankenstein, Dracula, and The Mummy, introducing a new take on the classic monsters and some new stars to lead the way. Peter Cushing and Christopher Lee became the new icons to join the ranks of Bela Lugosi and Boris Karloff, and director Terence Fisher succeeded Universal's James Whale and Karl Freund.

Although Universal will always be king of the movie monster, because of the living color and the leaning toward then-unheard of cinematic gore, Hammer Horror films are actually preferred by some to their Universal elders.

Eventually the fickle tastes of the horror movie-going public changed and the bloody monster fell out of favor leading Hammer to move to sex rather than blood to draw audiences. This was only marginally successful, however, and to the Horror Freak, Hammer Studios will always be remembered for gothic horror, compelling stars, ghastly gore, and a colorful take on the movie monsters we love to fear.

The Quatermass Xperiment

RELEASE June 1956 (U.S.)

DIRECTED BY Val Guest

WRITTEN BY Val Guest and Richard Landau (screenplay), Nigel Kneale (television play)

STARRING Brian Donlevy, Richard Wordsworth, Jack Warner, Margia Dean, Thora Hird

NOT RATED Has some mild horror

The Quatermass Experiment began as a serial run in the U.K. in 1953. The success of these serials prompted Hammer productions to create an adaptation for the big screen. Released in 1955 in Europe and the United States in 1956 (as *The Creeping Unknown*), this film achieved a high level of success and began the series of films that made Hammer an international force in revitalizing the waning horror movie landscape.

The Quatermass Xperiment dramatizes the return to earth of the first manned spacecraft. Some of the astronauts who set out on the voyage are inexplicably missing, and the surviving astronaut, Victor Carroon (Richard Wordsworth), is behaving "strangely."

"NOBODY EVER WINS A COLD WAR."

- INSP. LOMAX

It becomes evident that there was an alien visitation aboard the craft and that Victor is now the host of alien spores that threaten to take over the world.

Although this film is generally considered science fiction, the fight against global destruction via alien spores perked up the horror interest in audiences and prompted Hammer to continue on that path.

The Quatermass Xperiment met with mixed reviews upon initial release in the United States, but over time has been elevated to classic status with a lasting impact.

For the Horror Freak, especially those with a fondness for the Hammer brand of horror, this film is a must see.

Besides, if you get into a discussion with a fellow Freak and Hammer horror comes up, not having seen the *Quatermass Xperiment* is an instant credibility wrecker. I suggest you avoid the embarrassment.

An unsuspecting little girl (Jane Asher) in *The Quatermass Xperiment* tries to befriend Victor Carroon (Richard Wordsworth), who is starting to transform into something hideous. *Hammer Film Productions/The Kobal Collection*

The Curse of Frankenstein

RELEASE June 25, 1957 (U.S.)
DIRECTED BY Terence Fisher
WRITTEN BY Jimmy Sangster (screenplay), Mary Shelley (novel)
STARRING Peter Cushing, Hazel Court, Robert Urquhart, Christopher Lee, Melvyn Hayes
NOT RATED Contains some violence/gore

Hammer Studios first direct horror offering, *The Curse of Frankenstein*, took the public by storm. Technicolor, gothic themes, elaborate sets, and a level of violence and gore previously unheard of brought the horror movie monster back to top billing status. Because of copyright issues with Universal Studios at the time, *The Curse of Frankenstein* varies substantially from the classic Boris Karloff version and offers a new retelling of the Mary Shelly novel.

Curse begins with Victor Frankenstein (Peter Cushing) in a jail cell awaiting the fulfillment of a death sentence. As he tells his story to a priest, he reveals details of his sordid past creating life from dead bodies. The foundation of the story is the same one we all know: he collected parts from various sources to create the body, and the brain that was to make the creature a genius was somehow damaged, resulting in a creature that is a violent monster.

Christopher Lee as the troubled Frankenstein monster. *Hammer Film Productions*

The Curse of Frankenstein is ground breaking on several fronts. First, this film introduces the world to Terence Fisher as a horror director. Fisher's sense of style and using color to full advantage, particularly when it came to real looking blood, was a scandal to critics and a revelation to fans. Cushing as Frankenstein brings a new dimension to the movie as his British style and matter-of-fact manner make the film more about the deranged doctor than about the monster itself—a fresh approach to a classic monster movie. *Curse* also brings Christopher Lee to the attention of horror fans, and the world. His impassioned performance as the creature and violent portrayal of the classic monster shocked the world and made him a star.

The Curse of Frankenstein marks an important milestone in the development of horror through the years as it both revitalized a genre and began the reign of Hammer as one of the most influential studios in horror movie history. That, combined with bringing together Fisher, Cushing, and Lee, who changed the nature of monster movies, secures *The Curse of Frankenstein* as a member of any Horror Freak's A-list of classics.

"I'VE HARMED NOBODY, JUST ROBBED A FEW GRAVES!"
- BARON FRANKENSTEIN

Horror of Dracula

RELEASE May 8, 1958 (U.S.)
DIRECTED BY Terence Fisher
WRITTEN BY Jimmy Sangster (screenplay), Bram Stoker (novel)
STARRING Peter Cushing, Christopher Lee, Michael Gough, Melissa Stribling, Carol Marsh
NOT RATED Has a few scenes of violence/gore

After the success of *The Curse of Frankenstein*, Hammer wowed horror fans again with the release of *Dracula*. Released as *Horror of Dracula* in the United States, this film repeats the winning combination of Terence Fisher in the director's chair, Peter Cushing as the straight man, and Christopher Lee as the monster.

Although the primary storyline from the Bram Stoker novel is followed, there are a few distinct variations in the Hammer version. For starters, Harker is actually in league with Van Helsing (Cushing) from the start, determined to bring about the demise of the evil Count Dracula. And evil he is.

"SLEEP WELL, MR. HARKER."
- COUNT DRACULA

Many of the niceties of the blood-sucking Count are discarded in *Horror of Dracula*, the vampire existing for the singular purpose of extracting blood in the most gory and vicious ways possible. Liberties are taken in the ending verses the original story as well, culminating in one of the most dramatic vampire death scenes ever caught on film. Beautiful indeed.

Cushing as the determined vampire hunter is brilliant, working that cultured British gentleman shtick for all it's worth. Anyone who can give the impression that he can avoid being the victim of a vampire through seemingly insurmountable odds, slay that vampire thereby saving an entire society from the living hell of becoming a night walker, and still get home in time for tea…is doing something right.

That one's got to hurt for Dracula (Christopher Lee).
Hammer Film Productions/Warner Bros/Seven Arts

Lee shines as the evil drinker of blood, and went on to play Dracula more times than any other actor in history. The subtle evil lurking under the surface, culminating in such outrageous displays of gory bloodlust, secures Lee as the most exuberant Count and a staple of the monster movie genre.

Fisher is in his glory with *Horror of Dracula*. The pacing, the gore, and the amazingly gothic visuals and sets give the impression of having a much bigger budget than was actually available in making Hammer films. Taking nothing and turning it into a classic is a Fisher trademark and certainly evident in this film.

Vampires are an important core to horror movies, past and present. Just as it is important for the Horror Freak to be familiar with the humble on-screen beginnings of this immortal figure, it is also necessary to watch and appreciate Hammer's first entry to re-imagining the Count and keeping him alive for generations.

The Mummy

RELEASE December 16, 1959 (U.S.)
DIRECTED BY Terence Fisher
WRITTEN BY Jimmy Sangster
STARRING Peter Cushing, Christopher Lee, Yvonne Furneaux, Eddie Byrne, Felix Aylmer
NOT RATED Various mummy mischief

Hammer's *The Mummy* is the third horror entry utilizing Universal Studios' characters and together with Dracula and Frankenstein set the foundation for Hammer horror of the era. Based on Universal's *The Mummy's Hand* from 1940, with additional story elements from that film's sequel, *The Mummy's Tomb* (1942), rather than the original 1932 *Mummy*, Hammer's version brings depth, humanity, and living color to the oft-told story.

"SEEMS I'VE SPENT THE BETTER PART OF MY LIFE AMONGST THE DEAD."
- *JOHN BANNING*

British archeologists search for the lost tomb of Princess Ananka (Yvonne Furneaux) in spite of dire warnings that the tomb should not be disturbed. When are dire warnings ever heeded in horror movies anyway? If they were, we'd have a pretty boring flick. Anyway, the tomb is discovered along with the ancient Scroll of Life. Someone of course reads aloud from this scroll, and true to word, it brings the Princess' guardian, Kharis (Christopher Lee), to life.

It isn't until three years later that another fellow, a worshiper of Kharis, transports the mummy to England to exact his revenge on those who desecrated the tomb of his beloved Anaka. The Mummy, of course, spies a woman whom he believes to be the reincarnation of Anaka—the archeologist's wife—and you know the rest.

Other taglines for this movie included "Torn from the tomb to terrify the world!" and "It's evil look brings MADNESS! Its evil spell ENSLAVES! It's evil touch KILLS KILLS KILLS!" *Hammer Film Productions/Universal Pictures*

The trio responsible for making Hammer horror recognizable and lasting is part of the equation in this movie as well: director Terence Fisher and performers Peter Cushing and Christopher Lee. The masterful direction of Fisher allows for a fast-paced storyline rich with incredible visuals, flashbacks and plot twists to keep Horror Freaks on the edge of their seat throughout the film. Cushing gives his customary complex performance, moving from detached and collected English gentleman to the panicked and impassioned intensity necessary in the end to make the character human and believable. Lee as the monster is, in fact, monstrous. He also has the ability to give a quality of vulnerability to the monsters he plays in Hammer films that inspire not just terror but also a bit of sympathy. He's not really bad, he's just made that way.

The mummy theme in horror has been done over and over, but this inspired progression from the original Universal vision is a mandatory experience for Horror Freaks. Don't forget to call your mummy…

Christopher Lee as the monstrous Kharis, the mummy. Due to on-set injuries, including throwing his back out and dislocating his shoulder, Lee's mummy walk wasn't all acting.

Hammer Film Productions/The Kobal Collection

Dracula Has Risen from the Grave

RELEASE February 6, 1969 (U.S.)
DIRECTED BY Freddie Francis
WRITTEN BY John Elder
STARRING Christopher Lee, Rupert Davies, Veronica Carlson, Barbara Ewing, Barry Andrews
RATING G (hard to believe, but it's true)

More than 10 years after the rebirth of Count Dracula in the Hammer film *Horror of Dracula*, the vampire rises again in this spectacular and lush tale of violence and revenge…with, of course, vampires.

Dracula Has Risen from the Grave is actually a sequel to the Hammer vampire epic *Dracula: Prince of Darkness* and picks up at the demise of Dracula from that film. It seems that the castle where Dracula (Christopher Lee) slumbers and awaits to rise again has been redecorated with religious symbols and exorcisms. When Dracula does awake, he is not amused.

He goes on a violent and bloody rampage, determined to make those who would deface his sacred castle pay dearly. Now mobile with a horse-drawn hearse and powerful black horses, Dracula travels about inflicting death and taking vampire slaves along the way.

An accident prevented Terence Fisher from directing this film and at the helm instead is Freddie Francis, an accomplished cinematographer who worked on many Hammer films. The direct line between the director's vision and the artist's style creates one of the most beautiful and extravagant films in the Hammer horror library.

The atmosphere is dark and foreboding, the sets realistic and convincing and the camera angles and methods work to create a visual experience that is irresistible.

"Obviously," indeed. This movie was the first to get a rating from the Motion Picture Association of America, and was Hammer's most profitable film.
Hammer Film Productions/ Warner Bros/Seven Arts

Peter Cushing is also absent from *Dracula Has Risen from the Grave*, leaving only Lee from the Hammer trio of terror. Lee does not disappoint. More vicious, more ferocious, yet with more hypnotic power over women, he takes Dracula to new and horrifying heights.

For the Horror Freak, *Dracula Has Risen from the Grave* is a necessary and important film for several reasons beyond the sheer enjoyment of this dark tale of the bloodthirsty Count. This is one of the last horror films Hammer produced that achieved significant commercial success, and it is also one of the highest budgeted and highest-grossing films in the Hammer catalogue.

> "THE TRUTH? WHAT DO YOU WANT WITH THAT? IF YOU WANT TO BE A SUCCESS IN LIFE, FORGET THE TRUTH." - *MAX*

There are those brave souls who even say out loud that *Dracula Has Risen from the Grave* is the very best of Hammer's Dracula series. If you debate with other horror aficionados on this point, be sure that you are talking from a point of view of direct viewing rather than heresy. Otherwise, you are bound to get eaten alive.

Other Classics

A horror movie does not need to be a Universal or Hammer one to be a classic, to be sure. We Horror Freaks know that all you have to do is turn on the Saturday morning movie of the week to find classics galore, and the movies we came across the most often as kids sitting on the living room floor have become dead favorites well into adulthood.

But there is more to classic horror than fond childhood remembrances of *The Wasp Woman* and *Children Shouldn't Play with Dead Things*. The early horror films shaped the taste of generations of Horror Freaks…and some of those Freaks became horror filmmakers with a style unavoidably colored by Saturday morning mayhem.

Aside from being childhood favorites, many of the old and classic films surpass today's features in many ways.

The classics come from a simpler time, before computer-generated images and a film rating system that allows a level of gore that makes cable television reality shows about plastic surgery gone wrong look fake. Without sophisticated technology and big effects budgets to lean on, the classics have to rely on simpler tactics to terrify the audience, namely story, suspense, and amazing performances.

Special effects and cinematic tricks certainly add to the movie-going experience, but often those tactics are used as a crutch to make up for the fact that the film just can't get a jump out of people without them. Is the story a bit boring? Make someone's head explode! Is it hard to care whether the milquetoast lead character lives or dies? Chop them up into a million pieces more realistically than an E.R. show and nobody will care how they got there. Without the movie-making "slight of hand" afforded by technology, however, horror movie makers actually had to rely on being clever. What a concept!

Classic horror is scary because it is engrossing. The story and themes are so intriguing that all distractions fall away and we are there, staring into the eyes of that "perfect" little child who happens to be inhabited by an alien full of malaise.

The unexpected, the shocking, and the excruciating moments leading up to an unknown horror, betrayed only by swelling music, envelope the Horror Freak and take them on a fearsome ride through a nightmare that seems to never end.

In *Village of the Damned*, children with strange glowing eyes make people do things against their will.
Metro-Goldwyn-Mayer

Classic horror is all about the basics, and while today's Horror Movie Freak loves to shriek and squirm to CGI blood as much as the next guy, the soulful roots of psychological terror deserves a respectful place in the repertoire. In fact, it is highly recommended that all Freaks make time for at least one classic per month. That way, not only do you remain well rounded, but you always have at least one classic reference to pull out of nowhere in a conversation with friends, leaving them to wonder how often you are allowed out of the house and whether you actually have a life outside of horror movies.

It works to the Horror Movie Freak's advantage to always keep them guessing.

The unnerving Graf Orlok (Max Schreck) from *Nosferatu*. It's reported that director F.W. Murnau thought Schreck's lack of real-life handsomeness required that only pointy ears and false teeth would be needed for the vampire makeup.

Prana-Film/The Kobal Collection

"IS THIS YOUR WIFE? WHAT A LOVELY THROAT." - GRAF ORLOK

Nosferatu

RELEASE June 3, 1929 (U.S.)
DIRECTED BY F.W. Murnau
WRITTEN BY Henrik Galeen
STARRING Max Schreck, Gustav V. Wangenheim, Greta Schroeder, Alexander Granach
NOT RATED Contains nothing too objectionable

Produced before the invention of the "talkie" and without appropriate copyright permissions, *Nosferatu* is the vampire movie that you almost never saw. It is also possibly the first appearance of the evil Count Dracula on the movie screen.

It follows the plot and story of Bram Stoker's novel closely, so by this time, most Horror Movie Freaks know how it goes. What might throw you are the name changes, made in an attempt to avoid a copyright infringement lawsuit. Avoiding the suit wasn't quite as successful, though, but more on that later.

Hutter (Harker from Stoker's novel) travels a great distance to Transylvania to assist Orlok (Count Dracula) in a land deal. Hutter (Gustav V. Wangenheim) escapes with his life, but Orlok (Max Schreck) succeeds in getting transported via ship to the populated centers of England. Vampiric mayhem ensues.

Nosferatu is a tremendous horror film, made even more so by the facts that it is silent and created in 1929 before any discernable movie effects existed. Most of the versions you find today will have musical accompaniment, but originally a musician played this live in the theater. There are occasional panels of written dialog, but for the most part the action plays out without conversation, and it is still clear what is transpiring.

The performance of Schreck as Orlok is astounding and a very different interpretation of Count Dracula than we're accustomed to. Not at all the charmer, Orlok is a hideous creature that actually looks as if he is a walking evil corpse. All the more amazing, then, that he has the ability to bring people under his control and lure women into his web, even though he has no resemblance to attractiveness.

The movie was banned in Sweden due to excessive horror, but the ban was finally lifted in 1972. *Jofa-Atelier Berlin-Johannisthal/Film Arts Guild*

There actually are some groundbreaking special effects in this film, including stop-motion photography to make objects appear to move on their own, double exposures to create the illusion that Orlok vanishes, and physical tricks to allow him to rise to an upright position while keeping his body stationary.

Nosferatu was almost lost forever as a copyright suit ended in an order that all copies of this film be destroyed. Fortunately for Horror Freaks, some pirate copies survived and, as the film entered the public domain, became available far and wide as an homage to the evil Count Dracula and the first vampire to enter the awareness and nightmares of a public starving for fright.

Cat People

RELEASE December 25, 1942 (U.S.)
DIRECTED BY Jacques Tourneur
WRITTEN BY DeWitt Bodeen
STARRING Simone Simon, Kent Smith, Tom Conway, Jane Randolph, Jack Holt
NOT RATED Most of the terror is implied

Cat People is a classic psychological horror film from the active RKO studios. In 1993, it was preserved in the United States National Film Registry by the Library of Congress as being "culturally, historically, or aesthetically significant." Beyond that, the film is suspenseful, scary, and claims invention of the oft-used horror technique, the "bus."

The beautiful and mysterious Irena Dubrovna (Simone Simon) believes she's cursed to turn into a killer cat.
RKO/The Kobal Collection

Fashion designer Irena (Simone Simon) has a fascination with panthers, and some skill at drawing them. Irena meets Oliver (Kent Smith) at the zoo, and later over tea discovers that he, too, enjoys panthers, demonstrated by his interest in her statue of a panther being impaled by a spear. She tells Oliver a tale of an ancient legend of a band of Satanists that invaded the village where she grew up, turning all the inhabitants into devil worshipers. When King John visited the village and discovered what had happened, he ordered all of the villagers killed. A few of the most dastardly, however, escaped execution. Irena believes she is a descendent of these evil villagers. Worse yet, Irena is also certain that she will transform into a panther should her emotions be aroused.

Inexplicably, Oliver marries Irena in spite of her delusions of cat-dom. Fearing the passions associated with consummating her marriage, however, Irena denies Oliver any "marital activities." There is also evidence of dark lurking as people are attacked and killed by what appears to be a giant cat.

"OH, IT'S ALRIGHT. IT'S JUST THAT CATS DON'T SEEM TO LIKE ME." - *IRENA DUBROVNA*

Cat People had a small budget compared to other RKO productions, so has to rely on creativity and cleverness to induce the desired states of fear and dread. Most of the terror is not depicted but rather implied, ultimately having much more impact than a gallon of gore laid out for all to see.

Illustrating the cleverness is the use of a horror technique the "bus." In one particular scene between Irena and Oliver's confidante Alice, the audience is led to expect that Irena will turn into a panther at any minute and rip Alice to shreds. At the climax of the scene, Alice's horrified face consumes the screen when suddenly a loud hissing noise erupts that sounds just like a panther…but it is only the air brakes on a bus that has stopped to pick Alice up. The claim is that all instances of tension building to a climax that turns out to be nothing at all, yet gets the jump scare of an actual event, is a variation of the bus technique—at least that's what the producers of *Cat People* claim.

The Horror Freak will benefit from watching *Cat People* and seeing the results of clever filmmaking in the lack of budget dollars. The concepts of good and evil are complex compared to other films of the times, making sure that the lines between the two are blurred and subject to interpretation. This film is considered one of the best of all time by some well-known critics, and is a required element to a Horror Freak's library.

Cat People **was in theaters for so long that some critics who had originally bashed it were able to see it again and rewrite their reviews in a more positive light.** *RKO Radio Pictures*

The Fly

RELEASE July 16, 1958 (U.S. Premier)
DIRECTED BY Kurt Neumann
WRITTEN BY George Langelaan, James Clavell
STARRING Al Hedison, Patricia Owens, Vincent Price, Herbert Marshall
NOT RATED A few scenes may be disturbing for younger viewers

The Fly begins with Helene Delambre (Patricia Owens) admitting to murdering her husband by crushing him under a heavy safe. After initial reluctance to admitting why, she tells her story.

Helene's husband Andre (Al Hedison) invented a device he called a "disintegrator-reintegrator" that could teleport objects from one cabinet to another.

After several unsuccessful attempts to teleport a living creature (including reducing the family cat to a simple "meow"), he finally is able to teleport a guinea pig with no discernable negative effects. The next step is to transport himself.

Unbeknownst to Andre, a housefly enters the cabinet with him, and the teleportation jumbles the two together creating a man with a fly's head and claw. His wife is, understandably, horrified. Over time, Andre realizes his mind is being taken over by the fly and he deplores his wife to put him out of his misery…so she does.

"YOU'VE COMMITTED MURDER JUST AS MUCH AS HELENE DID. YOU KILLED A FLY WITH A HUMAN HEAD. SHE KILLED A HUMAN WITH A FLY HEAD."
- FRANÇOIS DELAMBRE

The Fly is a surprisingly excellent film that successfully mixes horror in with the science fiction so popular at the time. It also unexpectedly saw a lot of box office success in spite of a meager budget and short shooting time.

***The Fly*'s climactic "help me" scene is one of the best in B movies.**
20th Century Fox/The Kobal Collection

The subject of a successful 1986 remake, this film keys into the growing concern surrounding scientific experimentation and, possibly, man's attempt to move into the realm of God by exercising control over life and matter.

This film also features the legendary Vincent Price, the master of horror who, beginning in 1939 with *The Tower of London*, came to define the horror film for many—including a new generation as the creepy voice in the Michael Jackson video *Thriller*.

For the Horror Movie Freak, *The Fly* is good to be familiar with, not only because of the popular remake that followed decades later, but also as an example of the kinds of special effects and cinematic trickery used during this age.

Additionally, the "twist ending" was well received and has become quite famous. Besides, if you squeak out "Help me…help me…!" you will be able to tell those horror fans "in the know" by which can name the reference and which merely gaze at you with a puzzled expression. Refer those who don't get it to the Beginner's Shelf and hope for the best.

Village of the Damned

RELEASE December 7, 1960 (U.S.)
DIRECTED BY Wolf Rilla
WRITTEN BY Stirling Silliphant and George Barclay (screenplay) and John Wyndham (novel *The Midwich Cuckoos)*
STARRING George Sanders, Barbara Shelley, Martin Stephens, Michael Gwynn
NOT RATED The creepy kids may give parents the heebie jeebies

June Cowell, Martin Stephens and other evil children descend upon a village to, uh, do evil things. The blond wigs the children wear had a built-in dome to give the impression they had a cranium that was larger than normal. *MGM/The Kobal Collection*

A classic story of evil children who take over a village and threaten the world, *Village of the Damned* is considered by some rating systems to be one of the 100 scariest movies of all time.

One day all the inhabitants of a British village suddenly fall unconscious, including the animals. For a time, this affliction is not limited to locals as anybody who enters the perimeter of the village also falls unconscious; even a pilot who flies his plane too low passes out and crashes.

The military is called and the area is quarantined; then suddenly, the villagers wake up and feel perfectly normal. Life goes on.

About two months later, all of the women in the village of childbearing age discover they are pregnant. All of them give birth on the same day, and all of the children are pale with blond hair and blue eyes.

These children age rapidly and within three years are the size of 12-year-olds. They speak with the demeanor of cultured adults and display no emotion. Plus they can read minds and make people do terrible things. Is this the end of the world?

This film is just great, and the glowing eyes of the children as they exercise their mental powers are beyond unnerving. In fact, the children generally are creepy, and horror movies with children as the villains can be particularly hard to take. *The Village of the Damned* has received a lot of attention from release through a sequel, 1964's *Children of the Damned*, and even a remake in 1995.

> "PEOPLE, ESPECIALLY CHILDREN, AREN'T MEASURED BY THEIR IQ. WHAT'S IMPORTANT ABOUT THEM IS WHETHER THEY'RE GOOD OR BAD, AND THESE CHILDREN ARE BAD." - *ALAN BERNARD*

The horrific nature of the children and their glowing eyes even prompted a second version for U.K. audiences where the effect was deleted so as to not emotionally scar the public.

Every Horror Freak will have different tastes and particular types of films that strike the fear bone more thoroughly than others, and *Village of the Damned* is certainly one that helps the horror fan blossom into the true Freak they are.

The Abominable Dr. Phibes

RELEASE May 18, 1971 (U.S.)
DIRECTED BY Robert Fuest
WRITTEN BY James Whiton, William Goldstein
STARRING Vincent Price, Joseph Cotton, Virginia North, Terry-Thomas, Sean Bury
RATING PG-13, for some horror violence/gore

A highly stylized and intriguing horror film, *The Abominable Dr. Phibes* stars the legendary Vincent Price in the later part of his career. After viewing the creative devices used for torture and murder, you will see shades of another film that became famous by using complex devices for death.

Dr. Phibes (Price), terribly disfigured and thought to be dead, is grieving the loss of his wife from the same accident that left him a monster. As he ruminates on the loss, he decides there are nine doctors and medical personnel responsible for her death. With the help of his lovely and mute assistant Vulvania (Virginia North), Dr. Phibes exacts his revenge in creative and grisly ways on those who took his wife from him.

This is a highly enjoyable film, and an important one for Horror Movie Freaks to have under their belts. It shows the world that Price "still had it," as he camps it up and leads the audience through black comedy, vicious fits, and beautifully crafted revenge based on the Ten Plagues of Egypt from the *Old Testament*.

One mystery that is often discussed concerning *The Abominable Dr. Phibes* is the lack of additional performance credits of North. North is a Bond girl in the one James Bond 007 film starring George Lazenby, *On Her Majesty's Secret Service* (1969). After her impressive performance in *Dr. Phibes*, she married a wealthy industrialist and completely dropped out of movies, and longing for more from the beautiful Vulvania is a common lament for many Horror Freaks.

A classic photo of Dr. Phibes (Vincent Price) with the lovely Vulvania (Virginia North).
American International Pictures

The contraptions used by Dr. Phibes in exacting his revenge on several of his prey before causing death are ingenious and torturous. The popular *Saw* series of horror films is known for, among other things, the use of devices to teach losers to appreciate their lives. Watch *The Abominable Dr. Phibes* and decide for yourself what impact this film had on the creators of *Saw*.

"LOVE MEANS NEVER HAVING TO SAY YOU'RE UGLY." - *DR. PHIBES*

Influential, extravagant, dark, and campy describe this film, and it is a treat that no Horror Freak should miss.

The Wicker Man

RELEASE June 1974 (U.S.)
DIRECTED BY Robin Hardy
WRITTEN BY Anthony Shaffer
STARRING Edward Woodward, Christopher Lee, Diane Cilento, Britt Ekland, Ingrid Pitt
RATING R, for some violence and gore, sexuality, nudity

Mixing horror, paganism, and sex into an intricate tale of suspense, betrayal, and murder, *The Wicker Man* is a true cult classic.

Sergeant Howie (Edward Woodward) is on the trail of a missing woman and receives an anonymous note leading him to an isolated island off the coast of Scotland.

Howie is mortified at what he finds on the island as the pagan rituals and free sex run directly contrary to his staunch Christian values. Beyond that, the inhabitants of the island are extremely secretive about the true goings on in their home and all claim to know nothing of the missing girl.

As Howie's investigation continues, he realizes that there is a human sacrifice brewing, and he fears that the missing girl is not only alive and on the island, but may actually be the victim in the ritual being planned.

After playing Dracula more times than any other actor, as well as the Frankenstein monster and the Mummy, Christopher Lee has said he considers his role in this film to be one of his greatest ever. *British Lion Film Corporation/The Kobal Collection*

DO SIT DOWN, SERGEANT. SHOCKS ARE SO MUCH BETTER ABSORBED WITH THE KNEES BENT.
- LORD SUMMERISLE

The Wicker Man is considered by many fans and critics to be a classic of the horror genre and has been described as an example of existentialist horror, focusing on the potential nonexistence of God. This film stars Christopher Lee as the magistrate of the island, marking a significant change in direction for the man who played Dracula more than any other actor.

The film, however, was not stellar at the box office initially. It gained critical acclaim, but not a high level of commercial success, possibly because of the "art-house film" components.

The themes are deep and the soundtrack itself is responsible for a large amount of the emotional impact and even story development. This film is not "mindless entertainment" and was possibly a bit too complex for audiences initially.

Over time, *The Wicker Man* has come to be appreciated much more fully, and is an excellent film for Horror Movie Freaks to be familiar with. Even if art films are not your preference, sitting through this one just might change your mind. Just make sure and try it before you make your final decision.

Christine Brown has a good job,
a great boyfriend, and a bright future.
But in three days,
she's going to hell.
DRAG ME TO HELL
COMING SOON
WWW.DRAGMETOHELL.NET
GHOST HOUSE
THIS FILM IS NOT YET RATED

There are all kinds of evil. There is the evil of that guy in the BMW who will not let you get in front of him and out of the turn-only lane during rush hour. There is the bully in school who pulls girls' pigtails then pounds away, and the "convenience" store clerk who will not hang up her cell phone and ring up your Cheetos so that you can get on down the road. But, you say, that's not REAL evil.

How about the murderous monster wearing a burlap sack over his head and wielding a machete, seeking panty-clad coeds to slash and hack? The walking undead zombie craving that delectable treat, BRAAIIINNNSS!? Maybe an enormous sea creature with a singular intention to not only make a meal of you but to cause as much fear and suffering as possible along the way? We're getting closer, but to get to pure evil, you must go to the source: hell.

The concepts of heaven vs. hell, light vs. darkness, angels vs. demons and God vs. Satan run deep in modern culture, whether you are religious or not. Pure goodness is light, heaven, and of God…and pure evil is darkness, hell, and of the Devil. That's some heavy stuff, ripe for use in horror movies depicting Evil from Hell.

Evil from Hell is one of the most powerful villains in horror because there is no escaping it. We're not talking about some mean guy or run-of-the-mill walking undead here, but actually the source and beginning of evil itself. To make matters worse, for those who spent time in Sunday school learning about the eternal conflict between heaven and hell, many of the outcomes have already been written. The biblical prophecies are what they are, and no amount of rooting for the demise of the anti-Christ will change that.

Not all Evil from Hell horror movies deal with biblical prophecies, of course, but they do deal with the ultimate evil that shall not be denied. Be they demons, devils, or bringers of the apocalypse, these frightful fanatics have the full faith and credit of the guy downstairs on their side, and we Horror Freaks are in for it. The more you believe in conventional religious teachings, the more frightening these movies become because in that context, these things could really happen!

Horror movies depicting Evil from Hell are among the most popular and can tend to cross over into the realm of mass audience appeal. Why? Most members of society are familiar with the dark themes and religious overtones already, making the prospect of having those nightmares brought to life on screen strangely compelling. For the Horror Movie Freak, however, it is par for the course. Whatever you find the scariest will eventually end up the main attraction in a horror movie, and frightening visions of hell's fury are no exception.

Horrific things start happening to young Regan (Linda Blair) after she becomes possessed by a demon in *The Exorcist*. Warner Bros. Pictures

Rosemary's Baby

RELEASE June 12, 1968 (U.S.)
DIRECTED BY Roman Polanski
WRITTEN BY Roman Polanski (screenplay) and Ira Levin (novel)
STARRING Mia Farrow, John Cassavetes, Ruth Gordon, Sidney Blackmer, Maurice Evans
RATING R, for violence, sexuality, adult situations

The excellent *Rosemary's Baby* gained critical acclaim, as well as box office success. This film, and others like it, also marked the end of popularity for Hammer Horror films as audience tastes changed.

The story begins with Rosemary and Guy Woodhouse (Mia Farrow and John Cassavetes) as they move into a beautiful new apartment. The building and space are fantastic—who cares that the building has a reputation of having harbored a coven of witches long ago?

Guy is an unsuccessful actor, but his luck starts to change after he befriends an older couple in the building, and Rosemary's does as well when she finds out she is pregnant. The older neighbors, however, become extremely overbearing and start to take control of Rosemary's prenatal care and interfere in her life generally. What is their interest in this baby, and why does the doctor they recommended insist she continue taking drugs that make her sick?

> "HE CHOSE YOU, HONEY! FROM ALL THE WOMEN IN THE WORLD TO BE THE MOTHER OF HIS ONLY LIVING SON!"
> - *MINNIE CASTEVET*

Rosemary (Mia Farrow) becomes convinced her neighbors have special plans for her unborn child. *Paramount/The Kobal Collection*

Rosemary's Baby gained a lot of attention upon release, even winning Gordon a Best Supporting Actress Oscar for her performance as the nosy elderly neighbor. This film is purely psychological without much notable gore, yet draws you in as the situations become darker and more ominous.

This is a true classic that should be on the shelf of honor for any Horror Freak. The dramatizations of the coming of demons and the devil to earth are numerous, but *Rosemary's Baby* is one of the better efforts.

Drag Me to Hell

RELEASE May 29, 2009
DIRECTED BY Sam Raimi
WRITTEN BY Sam Raimi and Ivan Raimi
STARRING Alison Lohman, Justin Long, Lorna Raver, Dileep Rao, David Paymer
RATING PG-13, for horror violence, disturbing images, mild profanity

Elderly gypsy Sylvia Ganush (Lorna Raver) teaches Christine Brown (Alison Lohman) a hard lesson about denying a mortgage extension.
Mandate/Universal/The Kobal Collection

Drag Me to Hell is the first return to horror for the legendary Sam Raimi after a long run as the CGI master of the *Spider-Man* trilogy of films. We're glad to have him back.

Christine Brown (Alison Lohman) is a young country girl trying to make a name for herself by earning the coveted assistant manager's position at the local bank where she works. Also vying for the position, however, is a young man who is aggressive and conniving, so Christine has to show that she, too, can make the "tough decisions"

Her chance comes when an old gypsy woman (Lorna Raver) looks for a third extension on her mortgage. Christine denies her the additional extension and as a result, the old woman lays a curse on her that will result in her soul being dragged into hell after three days. Christine must find a way to counteract the curse and avoid the taunting of the evil demon before her three days are up.

Drag Me to Hell has an excellent story and is well acted. Many of the horror elements prevalent in Raimi's early work, *The Evil Dead* trilogy, also exist in this film. The difference is in the execution.

Back in the old days, Raimi didn't have much budget, nor did he have access to expensive and highly technical effects' techniques. Not so today. The influence of the highly artistic *Spider-Man* movies is evident in this horror film and most of the effects are the result of beautifully done computer-generated imagery, rather than the oatmeal and corn syrup that oozed from the wounds of zombies in *The Evil Dead.*

What didn't change is Raimi's desire to completely gross out the audience. The old woman at various times vomits bugs, embalming fluid, and other brightly colored concoctions into Christine's mouth at regular intervals throughout the film, and the gypsy's dead body has a tendency to bite at her face while coated with sticky phlegm. It's really gross.

> "I BEAT YOU, YOU OLD BITCH!"
> – CHRISTINE BROWN

Horror Freaks should check out this film for a few reasons. For one, this is good horror with a solid story and great theme. For another, the gross-out visuals are unmatched in other horror movies today and will certainly inspire a yell or two. Finally, this film represents an interesting look at how a director's vision may stay the same, while the execution of that vision changes due to enhanced technology. From that perspective, *Drag Me to Hell* becomes a must see.

"TEXAS CHAINSAW MASSACRE MEETS DAWN OF THE DEAD.
A MEGA-SPLATTERY ZOMBIE-STREWN SLASHER FLICK!"
— Scott Weinberg, Cinematical

Foreign Horror

What a funny concept, foreign horror. Foreign to whom, you might ask? As this book is from the point of view of a Horror Movie Freak from the good ol' U S of A, foreign horror is any movie that originates outside the country, and there are a lot of good ones.

The best thing about foreign horror is the cultural and societal differences and how they affect what is scary, how situations are presented, and the local myths regarding monsters, ghosts, killers, and other fear inspirers.

Often foreign horror carries extremely original themes and highly disturbing imagery, because although they may be "old hat" in their land of origin, they are certainly unique to those in another country.

Familiarity with the formulas and concepts of horror movies can desensitize even the Horror Freak over time, and the completely differ[illegible] a movie conceived on the opposite side of the glob[illegible] prescription to cure what ails you and finally find t[illegible] of dread.

Dive into the murky waters of foreign horror, f[illegible] be warned—this ride is not for the timid. If ther[illegible] sociated with foreign horror, it is that sometimes t[illegible] imagery are, in fact, too unique and we just might[illegible]

With an open mind and a craving for fear, h[illegible] cated Horror Freak can overcome the trepidation [illegible] ritory and submerse in a frightful fantasyland full[illegible] and gasps in bodily horror centers you didn't eve[illegible] That, my fellow Freaks, is what we all crave.

A note on Asian horror: dark and distur[illegible] the Asian countries is prolific and extremely pop[illegible] quite a few tremendous films from this region. Be[illegible] volume, Asian horror has its own section; see P. 4[illegible]

Now, onward Horror Movie Freaks, into the u[illegible]

A creepy masked child watches and waits in the Spanish movie *The Orphanage*. Warner Bros Pictures Espana

Black Sabbath

RELEASE May 6, 1964 (U.S.)
WRITTEN AND DIRECTED BY Mario Bava
STARRING Michèle Mercier, Lydia Alfonsi, Boris Karloff, Mark Damon, Jacqueline Pierreux
NOT RATED May have mild frights for some

Italian horror film *Black Sabbath* is written and directed by the influential Mario Bava. The Italian title is *I tre volti della paura* and the film features horror icon Boris Karloff, who has a role in one of the three vignettes and provides narration between the segments.

The three stories, "The Telephone," "The Wurdalak," and "The Drop of Water," tell different tales of ghosts, paranormal happenings, and murder, and the film as a whole is a good representation of Bava's style and the mark he made on modern horror.

The director's use of light and dark within the context of black and white films is considered unique, as well as his imaginative use of color in later films.

His background as an artist and later as a cinematographer certainly shows itself, as each film Bava created has a definite artist's sensibility in terms of visuals and atmosphere.

Bava was influential beyond his prominence in what has been described as the golden age of Italian horror. He has been credited as the first to direct (actually co-direct with Paolo Heusch) an Italian science-fiction film and the first director of a "Giallo" film, an Italian crime mystery based on cheap novels with trademark yellow covers.

Bava also influenced the alien-invasion horror film, *Alien* (1979), as well as 1980s' slasher films and many elements characteristic of Asian horror.

Although a scene from the story "The Wurdalak" depicted on the poster has shades of the Headless Horseman, it's about vampires, including one who feeds on the blood of his loved ones, played by Boris Karloff. And yes, the title of this movie is where heavy metal band Black Sabbath got its name. *Alta Vista Film Production/American International Pictures*

"YOU HAVE NO REASON TO BE AFRAID." - ***MARY***

Freaks interested in foreign horror or any of the sub-genres utilizing dark imagery can gain much by watching *Black Sabbath* and a host of other Bava films. Undoubtedly the influences of horror favorites will be noticed with an astounded, "Ah-ha! That's where that comes from!"

Haute Tension

RELEASE June 10, 2005 (U.S.)
DIRECTED BY Alexandre Aja
WRITTEN BY Alexandre Aja and Grégory Levasseur
STARRING Cécile De France, Maïwenn, Philippe Nahon, Franck Khalfoun, Andrei Finti
RATING R (edited version), for graphic violence, sexual content, profanity

Haute Tension, known as *High Tension* in the United States and *Switchblade Romance* in the U.K., is a French film that found a good deal of success in other markets.

The film begins with two women, Marie (Cécile De France) and Alex (Maïwenn), visiting Alex's parents in the French countryside. One night a ferocious serial killer arrives and delivers some incredible Technicolor gore on the poor unsuspecting family. Marie escapes the onslaught by hiding from the deranged killer, and searches for a way to rescue her beloved Alex…but there is something not quite right. The question becomes, who is friend and who is foe?

"YOU CAN'T ESCAPE FROM ME, BITCH!"
- *LE TUEUR*

This film is particularly gory and over the top in terms of violence and blood. Release in the U.S., for example, required some significant cuts to avoid the dreaded NC-17 rating. The uncut version became available later on DVD. The special effects were created by Giannetto De Rossi, well known for realistic carnage and a favorite of Italian director Lucio Fulci. The effects are so graphic and bloody that most mainstream film critics refuse to acknowledge that any positive aspects may exist at all.

Marie (Cécile De France) is on the trail of the killer who kidnapped her friend.
Alexandre Films/Europa Corps/The Kobal Collection

High Tension also receives quite a bit of attention for the shocking plot twists, and is admonished for the fact that some of them require a significant leap of faith, to say the least.

For Horror Movie Freaks, *High Tension* can be appealing for a number of reasons. First, the level of gore exceeded the tolerance of the U.S. MPAA, illustrating what may be acceptable in foreign lands verses here at home. In that regard, it is also an excellent example of the extreme work of De Rossi. Second, there is a significant difference between the median rating of this film between horror movie fans and mainstream critics and even the dreaded "horror intelligentsia." Fans generally like the film, but the critics pan it. This could possibly illustrate the disconnect between the general movie-viewing public and Horror Freaks.

Finally, *High Tension* is indeed a tense trip down gory lane and is also not afraid to break taboos in terms of sexuality and character development.

My impression is that Freaks crave the gore and are willing to accept more serious leaps of logic to appreciate a film than other folks. See this good, scary film and you be the judge.

Wolf Creek

RELEASE December 25, 2005 (U.S.)
WRITTEN AND DIRECTED BY Greg Mclean
STARRING John Jarratt, Cassandra Magrath, Kestie Morassi, Nathan Phillips, Gordon Poole
RATING R, for gruesome violence, profanity

Australian film *Wolf Creek* claims to be based on true events. The validity of this statement is highly questionable, but the film was banned from release for a time due to fears that it might influence an ongoing murder trial.

Three friends on holiday decide to visit the site of the Wolf Creek meteor crater. Shortly after their arrival, they encounter car trouble and are stranded out in the Australian outback. "Lucky" for them, a charming bushman comes to their rescue and tows their ailing vehicle to his remote home/camp. It quickly becomes clear that the helpful stranger is anything but benevolent, as the teens are drugged, tortured, and killed one by one.

The location for Wolf Creek really exists, sort of. It is actually "Wolfe" Creek and is indeed the site of the second-largest known meteor crater where fragments of the meteor have been found. The basis of "true events" is also slightly possible, as there were a couple of known murder cases in Australia where some similar torture and killing methods were reportedly used. This film is, however, a complete work of fiction. Still, this didn't stop the film's ban in the Northern Territory of Australia while the trial of Bradley John Murdoch was going on. Murdoch was accused of allegedly abducting a British tourist and assaulting his girlfriend in 2001. There are also references to the infamous "backpacker murderer" Ivan Milat in some of the killing techniques, and the mining company sign shown in the film reads "Navitalim," which is Ivan Milat reversed and spelled backward.

Mick Taylor (John Jarratt) is the murderous bushman some unwitting backpackers fall prey to. *True Crime/Best FX/The Kobal Collection*

BEN MITCHELL: WHAT DO YOU DO NOW?
MICK TAYLOR: I COULD TELL YOU. BUT THEN I'D HAVE TO KILL YOU.

Wolf Creek is a good film for Horror Movie Freaks to be familiar with as possibly being a precursor to ones sometimes referred to as "torture porn" because of having human torture as a primary theme. Beyond the violence and torture, however, *Wolf Creek* is suspenseful and scary, effectively making the gentle savior into the violent killer before our eyes. Many of the scenes are indeed over the top in terms of the pain inflicted and the gore, but do not go as far as some later torture-themed films do, but the movie pushes the envelope of "acceptable society" without a doubt.

Hell's Ground

RELEASE April 7, 2007 (Philly Film Festival, U.S.)
DIRECTED BY Omar Ali Khan
WRITTEN BY Omar Ali Khan and Pete Tombs
STARRING Kunwar Ali Roshan, Rooshanie Ejaz, Rubya Chaudhry, Haider Raza
NOT RATED Contains strong gore/violence of zombie flesh eating, profanity

Hell's Ground is promoted as "the first Pakistani gore flick." We can't verify this is true, but it certainly makes a serious attempt.

The story surrounds the experiences and mishaps of five friends who drive across Pakistan to see the country's most famous rock band. They all climb into a very Scooby-Doo-like van and head out, stopping along the way at a small shop selling spice cake and tea. There they encounter a creepy old couple who warn them of dire consequences if they do not turn back immediately—they are headed for the dreaded "Hell's Ground." Of course, they ignore the warning and continue on anyway…to their doom.

Hell's Ground is an interesting movie for Horror Freaks for a variety of reasons. On the film's face, it is a straight-ahead slasher film that borrows liberally from several popular American films, namely George Romero's *Dead* series and *The Texas Chainsaw Massacre*. What sets this apart from standard slasher fare is the perspective.

How do people in the Middle East view horror movies, and what scares them? The general themes may be intact in this film, as are the "rule of horror" that state that sin equals death—but what is sin?

In *Hell's Ground*, the kids are continually asked why they are driving around instead of going to school and praying, for example. A bit of a different take on what a "good kid" is supposed to be doing with his time.

Part slasher fest, part zombie flick, *Hell's Ground* is a gorehound's paradise.
Bubonic Films/Mondo Macabro

There are also many elements of pagan religion and healers worked into the mix, further evidence that the cultural norms of everyday life depicted during the opening credits are not being adhered to. So, then…of course the kids will meet an untimely demise.

Beyond the cultural insights, this film is a gore-lover's paradise, and if you waver between preferring slasher films or zombie invasion, you are in for a particular treat. The Pakistani carnivorous dwarf zombie will be of special interest to be sure.

"YOU ARE ON THE ROAD TO HELL MY CHILDREN."
- *DEEWANA*

The Orphanage

"A TALE OF LOVE. A STORY OF HORROR."
- *One of the movie's taglines*

RELEASE December 28, 2007 (limited U.S.)
DIRECTED BY J.A. Bayona
WRITTEN BY Sergio G. Sánchez
STARRING Belén Rueda, Fernando Cayo, Roger Príncep, Mabel Rivera, Montserrat Carulla
RATING R, for some disturbing content

The Orphanage, a compelling creation from Spain, is of the ghost story variety and blurs the line between actual haunting and a psychotic episode.

Laura (Belén Rueda) decides to move with her husband and young child back to the orphanage where she grew up and open it for business again. What she doesn't realize is that the spirits of children, who disappeared from the orphanage years earlier, reappear in an attempt to bring Laura back into the fold.

The Orphanage is lush and well made, with cinematography and music designed to envelop the viewer in the dark atmospheric beauty of the abandoned place, and set the tone for powerful ghosts to arise and make contact. Produced by Guillermo del Toro of *Pans Labyrinth* fame and directed by J.A. Bayona, who has experience in music videos and short films, *The Orphanage* is as much a haunting drama as a ghost story.

Horror Movie Freaks will appreciate the fact there is more attention to the emotions of the lead players than to the ghosts themselves, if ghosts actually exist at all. Are we watching the spirits of the past looking for resolution of unaddressed conflict, or the slow unraveling of a woman overcome with tragedy and guilt? Interestingly, many new generation horror fans become bored with too much character development and lingering storyline and opt instead for the immediate gratification of fast-moving slashers and gallons of gore. *The Orphanage* has none of this and instead relies on the unnerving build-up of unanswered questions and visions that may or may not be real.

As a creepy and atmospheric ghost story, as well as an example of a completely different point of view when it comes to creating horror, *The Orphanage* is required viewing by Freaks and can even help turn non-horror fans in the right direction.

Laura (Belen Rueda) dines with dolls as she slowly goes insane. *Warner Bros Pictures Espana*

[REC]

RELEASE July 14, 2009 (U.S. DVD premier)
DIRECTED BY Jaume Balagueró and Paco Plaza
WRITTEN BY Jaume Balagueró, Paco Plaza, and Luis Berdejo
STARRING Manuela Velasco, Ferran Terraza, Jorge-Yamam Serrano, Pablo Rosso, David Vert
RATING R, for bloody violence, profanity

[REC] follows the terror of a news reporter as her documentary on a day in the life of a firefighter turns into a fight for survival against viral infection and "not-a-zombie" zombies.

Angela Vidal (Manuela Velasco) and her cameraman Pablo (Pablo Rosso) are on assignment, spending the night at a local fire station to get an up close and personal account of the heroes who risk their lives every day to save the public from burning buildings. After several scenes within the firehouse and even a few rides down the fire pole, the entire experience looks as if it's going to be just another boring feature without any real meat—and then the call comes in.

There is an emergency transpiring at a downtown apartment house, and Angela is allowed to tag along to document it. As firefighters and police officers venture into the building to determine what the ruckus is about, they see an old lady covered in blood, and seemingly psychotic and deathly violent. Shortly after the first devastating encounter with the woman, everyone who is inside the building discovers they are now trapped by SWAT teams with no way out; meanwhile, each person succumbs to a growing sickness and the resulting "zombieism" one by one.

[REC], the title refers to the "record" button on most video cameras, took the critical world by storm when it first released in a series of film festivals in Europe before it opened to an accepting public in Spain in 2007. The entire film is from the perspective of the news camera, so the production is shaky and raw, but not to the extent that it causes dizziness or nausea as some other films presented this way do. The depiction of a sickness, the violent "zombies" that result, and the desperation and claustrophobia of being trapped inside the building give a realistic account of what might transpire should such an event actually occur.

A day of heroics soon turns into a terrifying fight to survive the horror going on inside an apartment house, as people don't want to end up like this poor little girl.
Filmax/The Kobal Collection

"THERE'S SOMETHING MORE TO THIS PLACE. OUR CELLS DON'T WORK. NEITHER DOES THE *TV* OR RADIO. WE'RE ISOLATED." - *CESAR*

[REC] is one of the better foreign films to come out in modern times and inspired a remake for U.S. audiences just one year after its initial release. The Horror Freak should be aware of the original and realize that subtitles do not mean a film lacks power or scare-factor.

Mary Shaw (Judith Roberts) seeks revenge on the townspeople who murdered her in ***Dead Silence***. *Universal/The Kobal Collection*

Ghost Stories

Things that go bump in the night, a fleeting glimpse of a hazy figure passing by a doorway, strange sounds that cannot be explained…all evidence that there is a ghostly presence in our midst. Ghost stories are as old as the campfire and told by tour guides and slumber party guests with frightening results worldwide.

The dictionary describes a ghost as "the disembodied spirit or soul of a deceased person," but Horror Movie Freaks are more concerned with those we can see, hear, or feel.

Horror movies convey tales of ghosts of many types and temperaments from the poltergeist capable of moving physical objects in the room to houses saturated with the presence of angry spirits ordering residents to "Get out!"

A common component for most ghost stories is atmosphere, and that is the allure for many Freaks. Spooky and uncomfortable rule the day in these tales of tormented terror, as every childhood fear of an unexplained household sound is given the possible explanation of an unsavory spirit looming overhead. Settings are dark, ideally with a bit of unnaturally thick fog hovering outside, and just enough moonlight to cast a beacon on the darting ectoplasm down the hall.

Ghosts don't just quip "how ya doin'," but instead wail and moan with the suffering of an eternity trapped in purgatory.

Ghost stories are particularly good at creating a heightened state of alertness and apprehension long after the film is over. Otherwise-benign sounds suddenly require immediate investigation as the Horror Movie Freak creeps up the stairs with a thumping heart and a scream on the lips.

Movement is seen out of the corner of our eye, even though we know our parents are out to dinner and will not return for hours. Does it feel like somebody is watching you? It is probably a distant descendant trying to warn you of an unspeakable evil, or maybe there was a tragic injustice perpetrated right in this very house and the spirits of the maligned have chosen this night to seek their revenge…on you!

Ghost stories are scary, emotional rides that can stay with you for hours, days, or a lifetime. Based on a true story? Even better to lend credibility to the tale and convince us all that rumors of the haunting of that weird house on our street are not only founded, but cause to pass on the other side of the street where it's safe.

From left: Alan Napier, Ray Milland, Gail Russell, and Ruth Hussey have a seance to try and get some answers as to why an old seaside house in *The Uninvited* is

The Uninvited

RELEASE February 10, 1944 (U.S. premier)
DIRECTED BY Lewis Allen
WRITTEN BY Dorothy Macardle (the novel *Uneasy Freehold*), Dodie Smith, and Frank Partos
STARRING Ray Milland, Ruth Hussey, Donald Crisp, Cornelia Otis Skinner, Dorothy Stickney
NOT RATED Has creepy moments, but no real scares

The Uninvited is one of the first films in history where ghosts are portrayed as actual supernatural phenomenon instead of the fodder for comedy or the result of an attempt to mislead.

The movie opens with narration that sets the tone: "They call them the haunted shores, these stretches of Devonshire and Cornwall and Ireland, which rear up against the westward ocean. Mists gather here, and sea fog, and eerie stories. That's not because there are more ghosts here than in other places, mind you. It's just that people who live hereabouts are strangely aware of them."

A young couple discovers a beautiful oceanfront house while on vacation and insists on buying it, not realizing that the house is haunted by an angry ghost seeking revenge.

This film is a classic and old ghost story that is not necessarily scary but is certainly creepy.

"...THEY CAN'T UNDERSTAND WHY WE DIDN'T KNOW WHAT IT MEANT WHEN OUR DOG WOULDN'T GO UP THOSE STAIRS. ANIMALS SEE THE BLASTED THINGS THAT APPEAR."

- RODERICK FITZGERALD

Charles Lang was nominated for an Academy Award in 1945 for Best Cinematography.
Paramount Pictures

The cinematography was nominated for an Academy Award and the soundtrack features music that was later remade by some of the most famous musicians and vocalists of the time.

The Uninvited is not of specific appeal to Horror Freaks for the scare factor, but rather as a history lesson of the beginnings of the on-screen ghost story and the beautifully eerie quality that lush black and white film work can create. Those who appreciate the ghost story flavor of horror movies will certainly benefit from watching this film and seeing first hand how the stylized 1940s interpreted the concept of a haunting of a house by a woman bent on revenge.

The Legend of Hell House

RELEASE June 15, 1973 (U.S.)
DIRECTED BY John Hough
WRITTEN BY Richard Matheson (novel *Hell House*/screenplay)
STARRING Pamela Franklin, Roddy McDowall, Clive Revill, Gayle Hunnicutt, Roland Culver
RATING PG, for mild horror, brief nudity/sexuality

The Legend of Hell House is about as classic a haunted house story as there ever was. The concept of an evil house cursed by an evil man has been done before and since, but seldom as well as in this movie.

The eccentric millionaire Mr. Deutsch (Roland Culver) is determined to debunk claims of hauntings and ghosts, and enlists a group of reported "intuitives" to explore and rebuke the haunting of the one house he has yet to disprove...Hell House.

"WHAT'S TO TELL? THE HOUSE TRIED TO KILL ME. IT ALMOST SUCCEEDED."

- BENJAMIN FRANKLIN FISCHER

This has been tried before, but all members of the previous psychic team died violent deaths inside the house save one, Benjamin Franklin Fischer (Roddy McDowall). Fischer joins this group to serve as a guide and share his previous experiences. The house, however, has other ideas and proceeds to terrorize and torment them as they seek answers and try to survive.

This is a classic in every sense. Not only is it a 1970s ghost story that has survived the test of time, but even the themes are consistent with an imagining of a haunted house ghost story. The big old Gothic house, grand furnishings, red velvet draperies—even a church inside with crosses destined to crush someone—are all present and accounted for in this epic tale.

Florence Tanner (Pamela Franklin) is part of a team investigating the mysterious Hell House. *Academy Pictures/The Kobal Collection*

The performances, all strong and compelling, lead the characters to the appropriate discussions in the drawing room, dinner in the grand dining room, ghost hunting in the study, and a series of possessions and objects moving on their own that just scream "ghost story." Heck, there's even an attack by a black cat.

Look up ghost story, or particularly haunted house, in the dictionary and *The Legend of Hell House* is sure to be the first listing. Horror Movie Freaks will love the classic themes and visuals and be surprised by the strength of the story and how fear can be stirred with little to no special effects at all. Things go bump in the night? Get out of Hell House.

The Changeling

RELEASE March 28, 1980 (U.S.)
DIRECTED BY Peter Medak
WRITTEN BY Russell Hunter (story), William Gray and Diana Maddox
STARRING George C. Scott, Trish Van Devere, Melvyn Douglas, Jean Marsh, John Colicos
RATING R, for mild violence, imagery, profanity

The Changeling is a scary ghost story starring Academy Award winner George C. Scott, best known for his role in *Patton*. As unlikely as this casting sounds, the result is an excellent ghost story with staying power.

John Russell (Scott) loses his wife and young daughter in an auto accident and moves to Seattle to begin piecing his life back together. Unfortunately for John, he is not alone in the creepy house he rents; the ghost of a child who was murdered in the house is making its appearance known.

The filmmakers create the perfect setting for a traditional ghost story with *The Changeling* and this creepy tale is just the thing to cause your heart to pound at the instant an unexplained sound is heard while in the house at night. The visions of a drowning child and the later apparitions are spooky, but the special effects are minimal. This film succeeds on cleverness and presentation, rather than relying on dramatic gore effects.

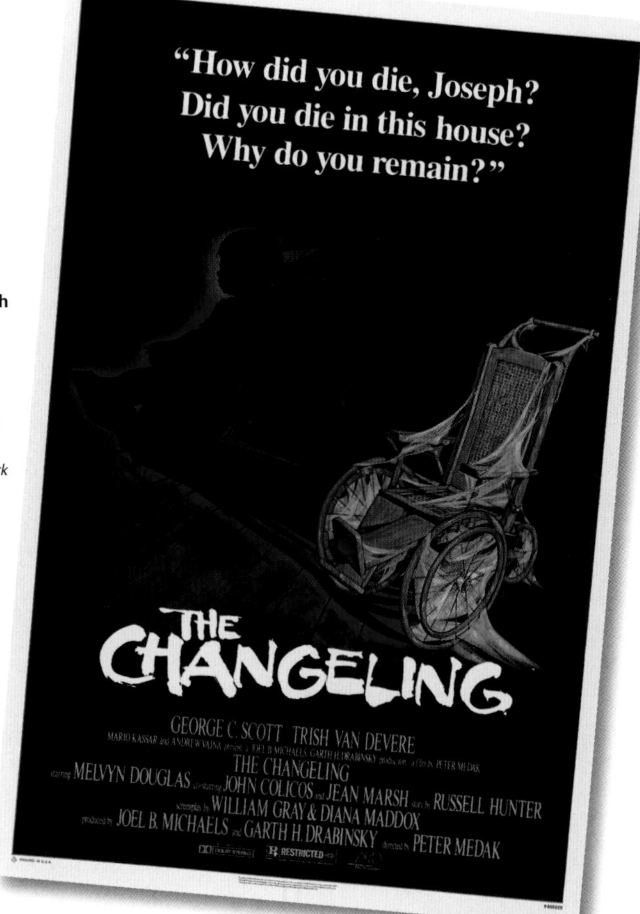

This movie is based on events which supposedly took place at a house in Denver, Colorado, in the 1960s. *Chessman Park Productions*

"THAT HOUSE IS NOT FIT TO LIVE IN. NO ONE'S BEEN ABLE TO LIVE IN IT. IT DOESN'T WANT PEOPLE." - *MINNIE HUXLEY*

The performance of Scott as the grieving widower living in a haunted house is right on and works to carry this film beyond a run-of-the-mill ghost story to being a classic of the genre that is sure to cause pleasant discomfort.

The contrast between recent and older ghost stories is an interesting treat for Horror Movie Freaks as one approach or the other is certain to have an impact. This ghost story is not necessarily subtle, but the effects and events are a bit understated compared to the CGI-infested horror of late, so torment of the characters involved takes center stage. Scary story, great performances, and ghostly settings rule the day, as well as the fears of ghost story aficionados.

Dead Silence

RELEASE March 16, 2007 (U.S.)
DIRECTED BY James Wan
WRITTEN BY James Wan (story), Leigh Whannell (screenplay/story)
STARRING Ryan Kwanten, Laura Regan, Judith Roberts, Donnie Wahlberg
RATING R, for violence and gory killings

During the climax of this movie, in the storage area with all the dolls, you can see the doll Billy from the *Saw* movies sitting on the floor. *Universal Pictures*

Ghostly legends and trademark plot twists gather to give that bump in the night a real punch in *Dead Silence*, the first offering by James Wan and Leigh Whannell after the runaway success of their *Saw* franchise.

Jamie (Ryan Kwanten) and Lisa (Laura Regan) are in love, but when a mysterious package appears on their doorstep containing a ventriloquist's dummy, their lives take a turn for the worst. Jamie returns home with Chinese takeout to discover that the doll has ripped his wife's tongue out of her mouth, killing her.

Jamie tracks the origin of the doll to his hometown, and travels there to find the truth about the doll and its apparent ability to bring death to those around it. What he finds is the tale of Mary Shaw (Judith Roberts), a woman who was killed by the townsfolk after being suspected of killing young children, and her deadly promise to return and take revenge on those who took her life.

Dead Silence is all about the atmosphere, and it plays perfectly for a ghost story. The darkness, the rain, and even the eerie pure silence that precedes an appearance by Mary Shaw all result in a creepy tale and genuine scares. The dolls themselves are disturbing also, and the knowledge that Mary preferred their company to that of human beings makes them all the more so.

Dead Silence has scary ghost activity, gory killings, lots of mystery, and a twist ending that pulls everything together, even taking some clues from the film's opening credits. Ghost stories can be difficult to get right and sometimes do not appeal to Horror Movie Freaks craving a bit more action.

This film not only gets it right, but has enough other things going on to grab your attention and hold it until the curtain goes up.

"EVER SINCE SHE WAS BURIED, RAVEN'S FAIR HAS BEEN PLAGUED BY DEATH. FAMILIES MURDERED. THEY WERE FOUND WITHOUT THEIR TONGUES." - *HENRY WALKER*

Poltergeist

RELEASE June 4, 1982 (U.S.)
DIRECTED BY Tobe Hooper
WRITTEN BY Steven Spielberg
STARRING Craig T. Nelson, JoBeth Williams, Heather O'Rourke, Zelda Rubinstein
RATING PG, for some frightening scenes

What listing of horror movie ghost stories could EVER be complete without a mention of *Poltergeist* – one of the most oft-quoted and enduring tales of pesky spirits. Still, due to its early '80s release, this one may have flown under the radar for the new generation of Horror Movie Freaks.

The Freelings are a typical American family living in a typical American subdivision, chasing the typical American dream. One day something strange, and kind of fun, happens in the Freeling kitchen. Any item put in one spot is suddenly transported to another, including chairs, toys, and even people. What a rush!

The strangeness escalates, though, when young Carol Anne (Heather O'Rourke) begins peering into the white snow of a television and proclaims "They're here!" What follows is a nightmarish ordeal for the Freelings and a severely troubled spirit who wants the life force of little Carol Anne for his very own.

Poltergeist really took the world by storm, horror fans and mainstream filmgoers alike. Directed by Tobe Hooper of *The Texas Chainsaw Massacre* fame, what could have been a pop-culture bit of ghostly drivel was instead a very scary high budget and iconic masterpiece.

Horror Movie Freaks will certainly have *Poltergeist* on their "must see" list, not necessarily for the conversation surrounding the film's intricacies but really just because it is absolutely "must see." Speaking of intricacies, though, the ending scene with the house is one of the coolest effects of the time, but I can't say how they did it without giving away the effect—and there may be one or two out there who have not yet had the pleasure.

Say the line, "They're here!" to any horror fan and they will immediately know you're talking about *Poltergeist*. This line was voted as the No. 69 movie quote, out of 100, by the American Film Institute. *Metro-Goldwyn-Mayer/SLM Production Group*

Horror Movie Freaks who have been around for a while have certainly watched this one, and maybe have forgotten all about it over time, and newer and aspiring Horror Freaks may have missed it altogether. In either case, this one is necessary to watch at least once and is absolutely worth a re-watch. The scenes of the whacky cherub-esque psychic Tangina (Zelda Rubinstein) are worth the price of rental alone, and an angry ghostly presence striking right in the middle of Middle America hits exactly the nerve that horror is meant to hit. This is also the film that made a generation afraid of clowns.

> "MOMMY, WHERE ARE YOU? I CAN'T FIND YOU. I CAN'T. I'M AFRAID OF THE LIGHT, MOMMY. I'M AFRAID OF THE LIGHT." —CAROLE ANNE

Watch the original *Poltergeist* for a great look at how good a ghost story can be, and for crying out loud, "Don't go into the light!"

This scene from *Poltergeist* is a classic example of why many people think clowns are creepy.
Metro-Goldwyn-Mayer/SLM Production Group

Tangina (the late Zelda Rubinstein) does everything in her psychic power to cleanse the Freeling household of a host of ghosts in *Poltergeist*.
Metro-Goldwyn-Mayer/SLM Production Group

Steven (Kevin Patrick Walls) finds himself horribly in the wrong place at the wrong time in ***Scream***. *Miramax/The Kobal Collection*

Homicidal Slashers

What Horror Movie Freak doesn't love a slasher?

The slasher films are those horror movies that feature big, bad, machete-wielding meanies.

Not to be confused with the psychopath, who can maintain a facade of normalcy in certain circumstances (when they are not viciously filleting someone), a slasher makes no bones about his intention to impale and dismember as many nubile coeds as possible. I think of the distinction as the guy you wouldn't stand next to at a bus stop.

Whether the villains in them use knives, axes, hay hooks, their bare hands, or whatever happens to be lying around to inflict their bloody mayhem, slashers are a beloved treasure to Horror Freaks and among the most popular horror movies.

Slashers often retain popularity decades after their initial coronation and many of the early ones remain on the classic horror lists of hordes of fans and aficionados.

The most successful characters have gone on to star in many sequels over multiple decades creating franchises that are popular and profitable time and time again.

Although not a hard and fast rule, slasher villains are typically exacting bloody revenge for some real or perceived wrong committed against them.

The concept of sins and consequences runs thick through the slasher film, whether the victims of the Karma-motivated carnage are directly involved in the original egregious act or not.

To the slasher villain, friends, family, and even distant descendants are fair game and often pay the ultimate price for the behavior of those they happen to be connected with in some way. In the most satisfying of slasher films, there are even moments of rooting for the maniac and tingling joy as an annoying character finally meets their bloody demise.

The supporting characters are an important ingredient to a sumptuous stew of slasher mayhem, and at their best fall into one of three general types: The hero, the jerk, and the throw-away.

The hero can typically be spotted immediately; this is the character who lives through the end. The hero is often wounded themselves, having survived a tragedy such as losing a family member, being physically attacked in the past, or being recently jilted by a romantic interest. The hero must survive through repeated frenzied and ferocious attacks by the slasher, and in the process overcome their own demons.

The jerk, on the other hand, is the character that Horror Freaks cannot wait to see impaled on the fence post by the homicidal maniac. This character is sometimes the cause of the hero's earlier troubles, but perhaps is just a dishonorable type who has left a trail of pain

The good deed of Sally (Marilyn Burns) and her friends picking up a hitchhiker (Edwin Neal) leads to terror in *The Texas Chainsaw Massacre*. *Vortex-Henkel-Hooper/Bryanstona*

in their wake or is just an obnoxious and demanding scumbag and unendingly annoying. In any case, it is sheer bliss to see the jerk meet his fate at the hands of our slasher—the gorier and more dramatic the kill, the better.

The rest of the main characters are the throw-aways. These are like the "red shirts" from *Star Trek's* glory days; you don't know much about them, you don't care much about them, and you know from their first appearance on the screen that they are going to die a heinous death.

The throw-aways are important to keep things moving along and provide a vehicle for the incredible talents of the special-effects team. How boring would it be if the jerk died dramatically and the entire remainder of the movie showed the hero narrowly escaping death, only to survive at the end? There needs to be blood, guts, decapitations, and disembowelment along the way, and the throw-aways are happy to oblige.

The homicidal slasher is a mainstay of the horror genre and an important component of a Horror Freak's joy. Oh, and don't worry if the slasher dies at the end of the film. The sequel will undoubtedly concoct some ridiculous scenario revealing they didn't actually die at all that requires a complete suspension of disbelief…just how we like it.

Horror villain Leatherface (Gunnar Hansen) with his trademark weapon...the reason the movie is called *The Texas Chainsaw Massacre*.

Vortex-Henkel-Hooper/Bryanston

The Texas Chainsaw Massacre

RELEASE October 1, 1974 (U.S.)
DIRECTED BY Tobe Hooper
WRITTEN BY Tobe Hooper and Kim Henkel
STARRING Marilyn Burns, Allen Danziger, Paul A. Partain, William Vail, Teri Mcminn
RATING R, for violence and terror

The Texas Chainsaw Massacre is classic 1970s horror that influenced an entire genre of film and introduced the world to an iconic villain.

A brother and sister, along with three friends, are traveling out to a family homestead after hearing reports that their grandfather's grave has been defiled.

Along the way, they meet a gas station attendant who tells them of a nearby fishing hole, and the group decides to take a look. Instead, they find an old house and a crazy cannibalistic family, including the chainsaw-wielding Leatherface.

The Texas Chainsaw Massacre takes some elements from Wisconsin serial killer Ed Gein, but claims of being "based on a true story" are unfounded. No matter. *Chainsaw* is a gritty and frightening film that has had an impact on horror movies generally, and slasher films specifically.

The slasher mainstays of the killer hiding their face, being a big and hulking presence, and killing victims with chainsaws, drills, knives, and blunt weapons lying around, are sometimes credited to this film as being the pioneer.

Beyond any influence the film may have had on the genre, Leatherface is among the most recognized horror movie villains of all time, gaining his name from his habit of peeling the faces off of his victims and wearing them himself to hide his own disfigured profile.

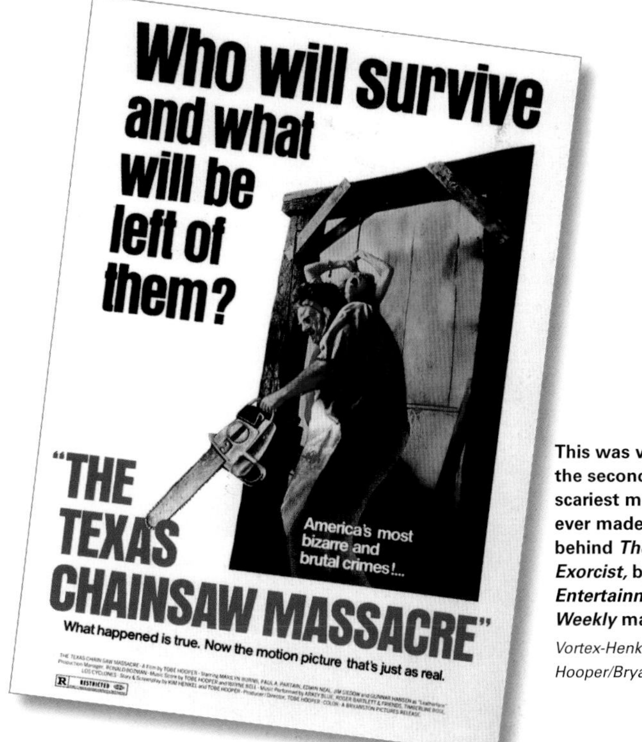

This was voted the second scariest movie ever made, behind *The Exorcist*, by *Entertainment Weekly* magazine.

Vortex-Henkel-Hooper/Bryanston

Leatherface has been redone and re-imagined many times (the 2003 remake is on P. 109), and what commercial haunted house would be complete without some guy chasing screaming visitors out of the exit with a chainsaw?

> FRANKLIN: I GOT AN UNCLE WHO WORKS IN A SLAUGHTER HOUSE.
> HITCHHIKER: I USED TO WORK THERE. MY BROTHER DID, TOO. MY GRANDFATHER, TOO. MY FAMILY'S ALWAYS BEEN IN MEAT!

Tobe Hooper has had an interesting career creating horror, with some films hitting the mark and others falling flat on their face. In spite of it all, Hooper is considered a master of horror for his creation of *The Texas Chainsaw Massacre*, and this film is a certified cult classic that must be seen to be believed.

The Hills Have Eyes

RELEASE July 22, 1977 (U.S.)
WRITTEN AND DIRECTED BY Wes Craven
STARRING Susan Lanier, Robert Houston, Martin Speer, Dee Wallace, Russ Grieve
RATING R, for gruesome violence and terror

"WE'RE GONNA BE FRENCH FRIES! HUMAN FRENCH FRIES!" - BRENDA CARTER

The Hills Have Eyes takes a typical American family and thrusts it into an isolated setting among violent monsters determined to deal destruction.

The Carter family is on vacation, traveling across the country. Dad decides to take a shortcut that leads through an isolated patch of desert with no services in sight, and the car breaks down. Dad sets off to find help, only to be attacked by some monstrous creatures. The hills are full of deformed and evil beings who torture, torment, and murder the family, seemingly for the sheer joy of it.

The Hills Have Eyes is a suspenseful and frightening film that puts a family in possession of utter helplessness. That's part of the scare factor. It is one thing if a slasher maniac is chasing you and you can run to the police station looking for help, but what if there is nobody around for miles to hear you scream?

The interaction of the family through the film provides some depth beyond the slasher carnage, as old battles come to the surface and must be handled as a means of survival. Also, when the chips are down and death is around every turn, there are a couple of directions an individual can take—the courageous and forgiving or the scared and meek—and each of these is played out to the joy and frustration of Horror Movie Freaks.

Brenda (Susan Lanier) struggles against the murderous grip of mutant freak Jupiter (James Whitworth).
Blood Relations/The Kobal Collection

The Hills is the creation of Wes Craven, a director well known for his slasher-themed horror films and for creating successful franchises. *Hills* has spawned sequels and remakes with varying degrees of success. Craven is also known for pushing the boundaries of violence and gore in his films, and this movie is no exception. Reportedly garnering the dreaded X rating from the MPAA initially, the film had particularly graphic sequences cut out to reach the acceptable rating of R. Still, the gore and violence are extremely disturbing in this film and will not fail to get a reaction from even the most jaded horror fans.

The Hills Have Eyes is a cult classic that is necessary viewing for Horror Freaks. The dark mind of Craven shines brightly in this film, and it is sure to inspire nightmares and a bit of thought before taking that short cut through the desert.

My Bloody Valentine

RELEASE February 11, 1981
DIRECTED BY George Mihalka
WRITTEN BY Stephen Miller and John Beaird
STARRING Paul Kelman, Lori Hallier, Neil Affleck, Keith Knight, Alf Humphreys
RATING R, for gore and violence, some profanity

JESSIE "T.J." HANNIGER: WE'LL HAVE A PARTY IN THE MINE!
HOWARD LANDERS: YEAH. BEWARE OF HARRY WARDEN! OOOOOOOHHHHH!

My Bloody Valentine came at the tale end of a string of successful slasher horror films and sought to continue the then-popular tradition of naming the film after a known holiday.

Twenty years ago in the mining town of Valentine Bluffs, some miners were trapped in a shaft after the foreman left early to attend a Valentine's Day dance. One man, Harry Warden, survived the accident by eating the corpses of his fallen friends, and later landed in a mental institution. Warden escaped and killed the offending foreman by cutting out his heart, and proclaimed that if the town ever had a Valentine's Day celebration again, he would exact bloody revenge.

Today, a group of youngsters decides that the time has come to disregard the old legend and get down to partying on February 14. Murderous mayhem ensues.

My Bloody Valentine is rich with controversy and history beyond the fact that it is a slasher film from the "golden age" of slashers. Censorship accusations flew when it was reported that eight to nine minutes of the film were cut to achieve an R rating rather than the first-offered X (now known as NC-17). The presumed lost footage was not released until 2009, and even then there are only 3-1/2 minutes of additional stuff. Does more graphic footage still remain? The world may never know.

Never mind the censorship drama, though, as *My Blood Valentine* is one of the most underrated slasher films of the period with a great villain and credible concept. The killer dresses like an eerie miner and commits his atrocities in bloody and creative ways. The heroes are sufficiently stupid in their actions and the different expected players among the hapless future-victims are accounted for in grand slasher style.

Instead of using his ax to extract minerals from the earth, this killer miner is using it to extract blood from his human victims.
Paramount/The Kobal Collection

The fact that a 2009 remake was created in 3-D (see P. 208) makes watching the original even more mandatory. Know the original, watch the remake, and pass your judgment on how they did from the point of view of a well-informed Horror Freak.

A Nightmare on Elm Street

RELEASE November 9, 1984 (U.S. limited)
WRITTEN AND DIRECTED BY Wes Craven
STARRING Robert Englund, Heather Langenkamp, John Saxon, Ronee Blakley, Johnny Depp
RATING R, for violence, terror, profanity, brief sexuality

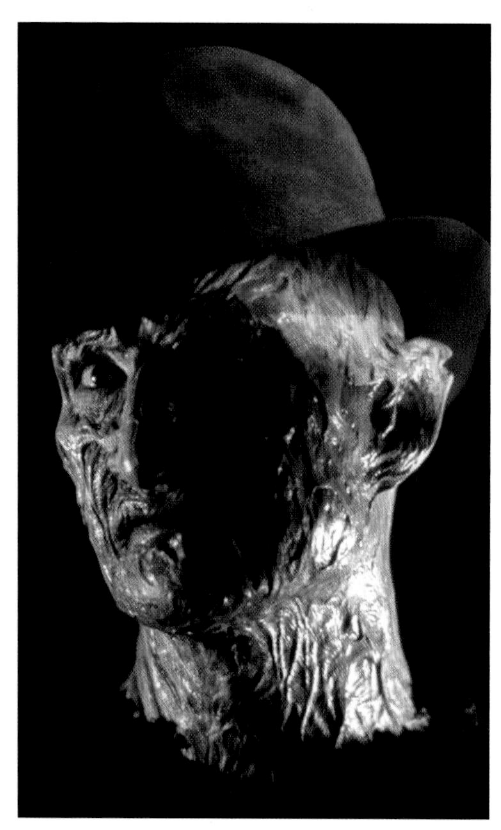

Freddy Krueger (Robert Englund) is one of the most recognized horror villains in the world. Wes Craven originally designed the character to be a "silent" type in the same vein as Michael Myers and Jason Voorhees, but over the course of the movie's sequels, Freddy developed cheeky black humor he gleefully spews.
New Line Cinema

"I'M GONNA SPLIT YOU IN TWO."
- *FRED KRUEGER*

In *A Nightmare on Elm Street*, the killer has a decided advantage: he can get you in your dreams where there is no chance of escape.

Nancy Thompson (Heather Langenkamp) is a typical and wholesome American girl. She keeps her horny boyfriend at bay with appropriate virginal vigor and barely skips a beat when her slutty friend is going crazy with her outlaw boyfriend in the guest room of her house. Nancy, though, is having nightmares that are truly terrifying and extremely vivid.

Nancy discovers that most of her friends are also having nightmares; well, not just nightmares, but the SAME nightmare about the same burned tormenter with a green and red sweater and knives for fingers. His name is Freddy Krueger (Robert Englund). Over time the dreams get worse, and there's more…when someone dies in their dream, they also die in real life.

It is up to Nancy to find the secret of Freddy and defeat him before he picks off the whole town one by one.

A Nightmare on Elm Street is a true horror classic that absolutely transcends the typical slasher offerings of both the past and present. The completely original concept of a killer in our dreams is so scary that it's hard to imagine, and Freddy Krueger has become an international icon. Freddy's sarcastic wit, maniacal glee as he kills, and his joyful torturing and terrorizing have become synonymous with horror, and made a star out of Englund. The terror themes are highly unique in *Nightmare* also, as the boundaries of real life do not exist in dreamland. Incongruous happenings and horrible settings are all possible when the limitations of the flesh are eliminated, and this film takes full advantage of that newfound freedom.

A Nightmare on Elm Street also breaks ground regarding the actions and attitudes of the heroine Nancy. She follows the "rules" of surviving a horror movie by avoiding sex, drugs, and behaving stupidly, but she also has spunk. The stereotypes of the victimized female screaming in terror and hiding in the closet do not apply to Nancy as she sets out to trap Freddy and attack him with all of the vigor of a killer herself. Her active role and anti-victim posture broke the mold of the horror heroine and proves that a Nancy Thompson scorned is a deadly force to be reckoned with.

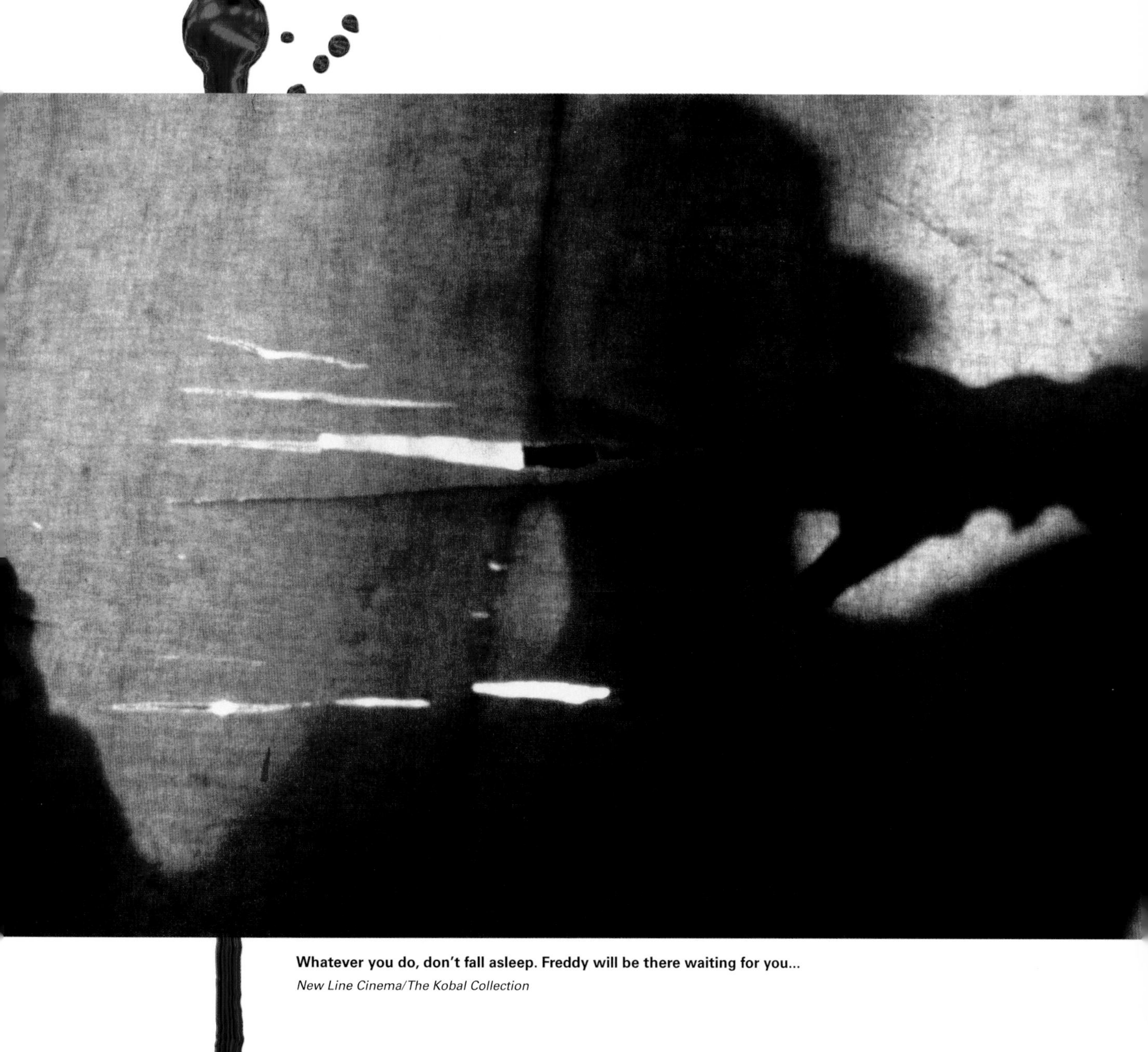

Whatever you do, don't fall asleep. Freddy will be there waiting for you...
New Line Cinema/The Kobal Collection

Scream

RELEASE December 20, 1996 (U.S.)

DIRECTED BY Wes Craven

WRITTEN BY Kevin Williamson

STARRING Neve Campbell, David Arquette, Courteney Cox, Skeet Ulrich, Rose McGowan, Drew Barrymore

RATING R, for graphic violence, gore, profanity

Wes Craven is here again, this time as director of *Scream*, the film that helped bring horror back to the big screen in the late 1990s.

Sidney Prescott (Neve Campbell) is a high school girl in despair. Her mother was murdered and it was her testimony against the killer that put him behind bars. There is a certain shock television journalist, however, who believes Sydney was mistaken in her reports and she doesn't mind telling the world about the suspected mistake.

To make matters worse, there is a killer on the loose, and one by one Sidney's friends wind up dead in bloody and creative ways.

Horror in the 1990s was slim at best. A-list actors wouldn't touch it and those films that were released generally did not do well. Horror was banished to low-budget zombie films that never got distribution in the theaters and instead were only available on the dusty shelves of mom and pop video stores. The classics of the 1980s and repeated sequels featuring known horror characters were all that seemed worthy, so Horror Movie Freaks just watched those films…over and over.

"NOW SID, DON'T YOU BLAME THE MOVIES. MOVIES DON'T CREATE PSYCHOS, MOVIES MAKE PSYCHOS MORE CREATIVE!" - *BILLY*

All that changed with the release of *Scream*. With a $14 million budget, *Scream* surpassed most horror films of the day in terms of resources. The casting included the popular actress Courtney Cox from the television hit *Friends* and Neve Campbell who also had success on television with the series *Party of Five*. Drew Barrymore was chosen for a blood-drenched cameo and the star power of the film grew even more powerful. The primary theme is sheer genius: make a horror film that details the "rules of horror" defined in the 1970s and '80s classics and accept them as truth—and then break those rules to build suspense and plot twists.

The scene in which Casey (Drew Barrymore) is being chased outside with the killer directly behind her, wielding a weapon directly above her head in the darkness, closely resembles the famous scene from the original *The Texas Chain Saw Massacre*.
Dimension Films/Fox Network

The result was a huge hit, with the film grossing over $100 million. Horror could be a box office draw after all! With renewed hope for a profitable horror film, and the taboo of name actors starring in such films broken, the stage was set for a resurgence of horror that continues to this day.

So, Horror Freaks, the next time someone complains that *Scream* is "too formula," inform them that first of all, the formula is a key component of the movie concept, and second, if it weren't for *Scream*, we would still be watching tired horror sequels and Lifetime, the channel for women. Do the math.

Behind the Mask: The Rise of Leslie Vernon

RELEASE March 16, 2007 (U.S. limited)
DIRECTED BY Scott Glosserman
WRITTEN BY Scott Glosserman and David J. Stieve
STARRING Nathan Baesel, Angela Goethals, Robert Englund, Scott Wilson, Zelda Rubinstein
RATING R, for horror violence, language, some sexual content

"IT IS GOING TO GET WET IN HERE TONIGHT. LACE YOUR BOOTS UP KIDDIES." - *LESLIE VERNON*

Behind the Mask is a low-budget independent that actually finds the right mix between horror and comedy to be effective as each.

Film student Taylor Gentry (Angela Goethals) is creating a documentary. Her subject is Leslie Vernon (Nathan Baesel), a self-professed serial killer in training, who has agreed to grant Taylor permission to follow him around and document the day-to-day life of a serial killer preparing for his coronation.

The documentary begins normally enough, with Vernon making grand statements about his background and prowess as a killer, yet there is always something underneath his facade that implies he is really just a goofy guy with delusions of grandeur. Imagine Taylor's surprise, then, when she becomes the intended victim of the elaborate massacre she thinks she is only there to film.

The excellent *Behind the Mask* is somehow able to present a horror/comedy in a way that does not ruin the horror or taint the comedy. How you ask? They do not intermingle, that's the secret. The beginning portions of the film are purely documentary and the silliness of Vernon's statements and reported background are so outlandish that it is both funny, and a little sad. Later, however, the film becomes pure slasher with every bit as much horror, suspense, and yell-out-loud moments as any established and proven horror movie classic.

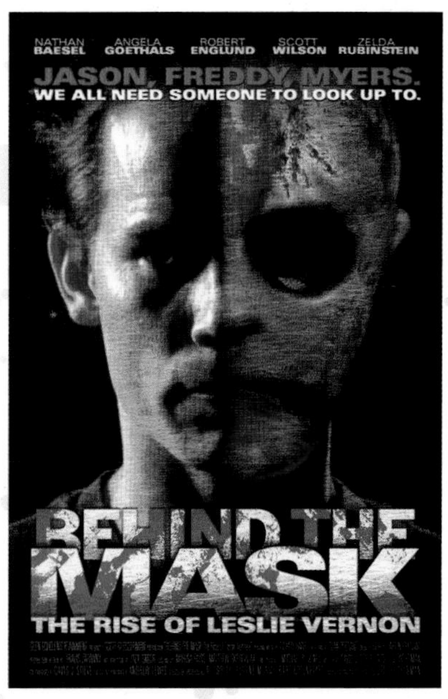

***Behind the Mask* makes various references to other horror movies, including actor Kane Hodder (Jason Voorhees), seen walking into 1428 Elm Street, the address Nancy lived at in the original *A Nightmare on Elm Street*.** *Glenn Echo Entertainment/Anchor Bay Entertainment*

Behind the Mask: The Rise of Leslie Vernon is the perfect film for Horror Movie Freaks to be familiar with, both because of its quality and because the film's indie status has kept it from the eyes of the general movie-going public. When you can bring up a horror film as one of your favorites and your friends simply stare at you confused, you know you've made it past the point of casual horror fan and into the realm of true Freak. Congratulations.

British soldiers on a training mission in *Dog Soldiers* soon discover there's something terrible lurking in the woods coming to get them.
Kismet Entertainment Group/The Kobal Collection

Monsters

Monsters are the beginning, the shin-
ng start of horror movies entering the pub-
ic's consciousness and encapsulating hu-
nan fears in one grotesque physical form.
Whether from this dimension or another,
created by humans or naturally occurring,
monsters have what it takes to bring societal
ngst to life so that they can hide under the
bed and get us in our sleep.

The evolution of monsters over the decades is a window into the collective consciousness of the day.

Conservative fears of the liberation of
women in the 1950s, for example, resulted
n a 50-foot woman terrorizing a town in her
violent rage.

Improvements in intercontinental travel
not only put visits to far away lands within
reach, but also uncover treacherous creatures never seen before.

Scientific advances in genetics open the door to new life ready to
remove humankind from the planet. And the government…it seems
that everything it does gives birth to some unique and uncontrol-
lable monster determined to bring about Armageddon.

Some monsters have a personal tragedy to correspond with thei
murderous appetites. Werewolves, when in their human form, ofter
live in torment from the atrocities they commit while under the in
fluence of the full moon.

Other monsters are merely trying to survive and don't under
stand why their prey is so darned violent. Still others are just looking
for love. Besides, it is boring hiding under the bed all the time waiting for children to fall asleep—and how frustrating for the monste
to emerge only to find out that his sumptuous morsel has the "covers of protection" up over his head, leaving him hungry.

Horror movie monsters are, really, how horror began and continue to be a mainstay in the Freak's collection. No matter where they
come from or what they are after, one thing is certain: surviving a
monster attack requires wits, determination, and making sure you
check under the bed before turning out the lights.

A violent storm ushers in a massive cloud of mist and malevolent creatures in *The Mist*. This one's got a firm hold on Norm (Chris Owen).

An American Werewolf in London

RELEASE August 21, 1981 (U.S.)
WRITTEN AND DIRECTED BY John Landis
STARRING David Naughton, Jenny Agutter, Griffin Dunne, John Woodvine
RATING R, for violence/gore, nudity/sexuality, language

An American Werewolf in London is a true classic that has stood the test of time. In a world where werewolf-related monster films often succumb to the action/adventure temptation, this one remains true to the legendary elements of the classic werewolf mythos.

Americans David (David Naughton) and Jack (Griffin Dunne) are backpacking through the Yorkshire moors in England and it is starting to get late. Luckily, the full moon illuminates their path through the countryside, but any benefits are quickly overshadowed when a mysterious animal attacks them. The beast kills Jack, while David survives and is transported to a London hospital.

The ghost of Jack appears to David in the form of a mutilated and slashed corpse and warns him that their attacker is in fact a werewolf. He advises David to kill himself before the next full moon, as he is a werewolf now, too.

Makeup and industry technological contributions became recognized by the Academy Awards in 1981 because of this film. Makeup artist Rick Baker, who created the werewolf effects for this movie, was the first to receive an Oscar in the new category. *The Guber-Peters Company/Universal Pictures*

> "THE WOLF'S BLOODLINE MUST BE SEVERED; THE LAST REMAINING WEREWOLF MUST BE DESTROYED. IT'S YOU, DAVID."
> – *JACK*

David ignores this dire warning, but four weeks later experiences excruciating pain upon the full moon and transforms into a werewolf himself, terrorizing the fair citizens of London with his murderous rage.

As the cult status of this film grew, so did Landis' reputation as a master of horror. Landis also directed *Animal House* and *The Blues Brothers*, so clearly this is a man with a warped sense of reality.

Regardless of Landis' resume, *An American Werewolf in London* is a definite classic that stands its ground, in terms of story and effects, against any monster movie today. Most Horror Freaks have seen this one numerous times, but if you haven't, then do so immediately. If you have, watch it again…you know you want to.

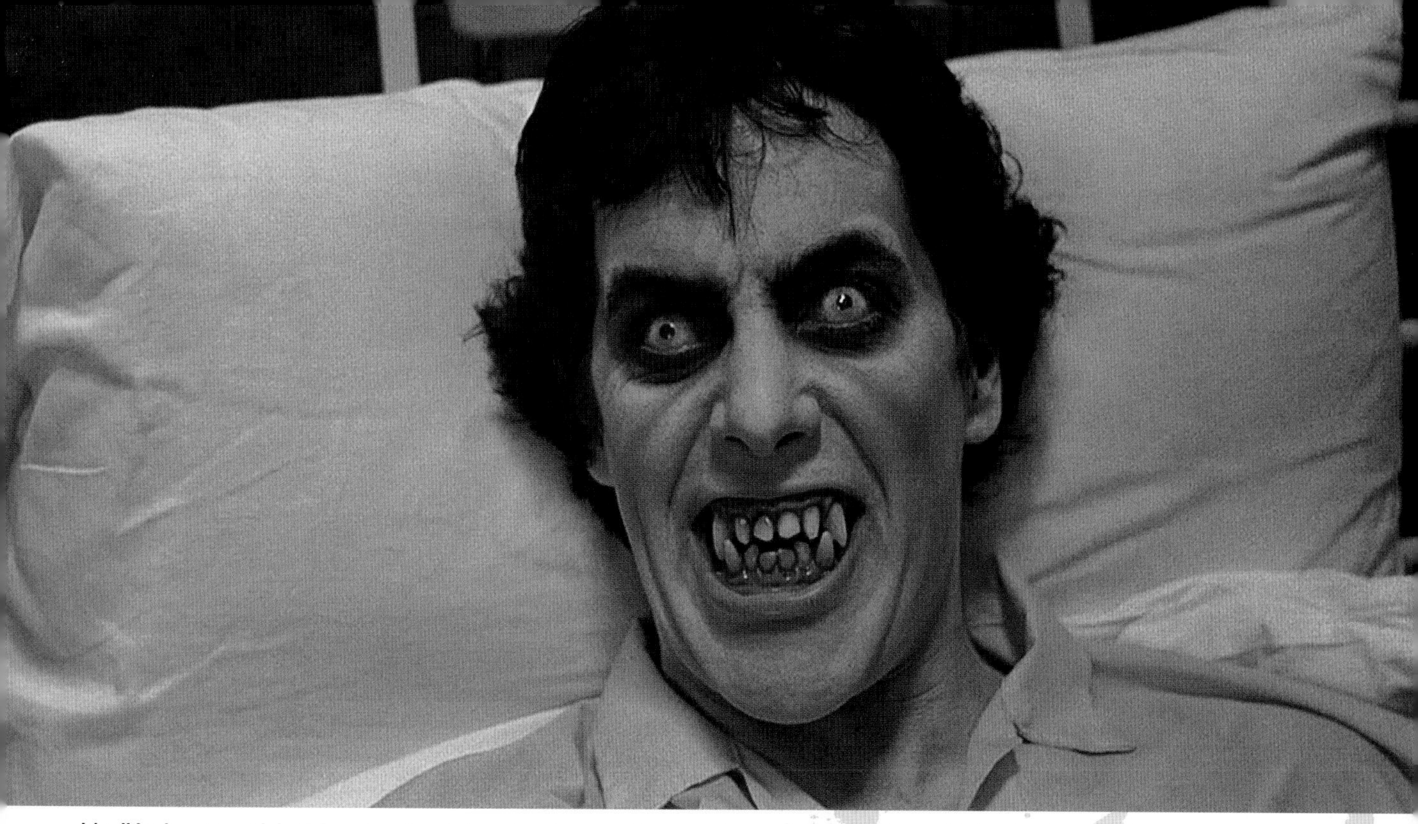

It's all in the eyes and dental work as David starts transforming into a beast in *An American Werewolf in London*. Actor David Naughton reported that this was a painful scene because glass contact lenses were used. *The Guber-Peters Company/Universal Pictures*

Killed by a mysterious creature, Jack (Griffin Dunne) appears to his friend David in mutilated ghostly form to warn him of what will happen the next time there's a full moon.

The Guber-Peters Company/Universal Pictures

The Howling

RELEASE April 10, 1981 (U.S.)
DIRECTED BY Joe Dante
WRITTEN BY Gary Brandner (novel), and John Sayles and Terence H. Winkless (screenplay)
STARRING Dee Wallace, Patrick Macnee, Dennis Dugan, Christopher Stone, Belinda Balaski
RATING R, for violence, terror, nudity/sexuality, some language

> "A SECRET SOCIETY EXISTS, AND IS LIVING AMONG ALL OF US. THEY ARE NEITHER PEOPLE NOR ANIMALS, BUT SOMETHING IN-BETWEEN." - *KAREN*

The Howling is a classic werewolf film starring the ravishing scream queen Dee Wallace. That is reason enough to watch and enjoy it, but the fact it's one of the preeminent werewolf films in existence is icing on the cake.

Karen White (Wallace), victimized by a rapist, has a miscarriage and nervous breakdown. In an attempt to leave the drama of city life and hopefully her problems behind, she and her husband Bill (Christopher Stone) move to "The Colony," an isolated resort in the California countryside. Immediately, however, Karen begins hearing howling coming from the woods that unnerves her considerably.

There are many wolf puns throughout this movie, including a copy of Allen Ginsberg's book *Howl* placed near a phone during one scene. *AVCO Embassy Pictures*

Bill tries to behave in an understanding way, but pushed further away by a belief that his wife is getting increasingly crazier, he has an affair with a local woman. On his way home from the tryst, he is attacked and bitten by a large black wolf. Bill immediately begins to change, as it was a werewolf that bites him; in fact, the entire population of The Colony consists of werewolves hungry for human blood.

The Howling, based on a novel of the same name, depicts werewolves as living together in a community while in their human form, fully accepting and comfortable with it. This concept adds a cult-like quality to the classic monster concept. The performance of Wallace as the victim/heroine is indicative of her roles in horror movies, playing a wife and mother type thrown into horrific circumstances and forced to rise above them.

The Howling won the Saturn Award in 1981 for Best Horror Film and is a necessary component of the Horror Freak's collection of classics. *The Howling* is the werewolf movie against which most others are compared.

Dog Soldiers

RELEASE November 5, 2002 (U.S. DVD premier)
WRITTEN AND DIRECTED BY Neil Marshall
STARRING Sean Pertwee, Kevin McKidd, Emma Cleasby, Liam Cunningham, Thomas Lockyer
RATING R, for violence, gore, language

A unique and creative take on the classic werewolf legend, *Dog Soldiers* is one of the best werewolf monster movies to never see theatrical release in the United States.

It starts with a lovely young couple in love, camping in the woods. Unfortunately for them, they are not alone and some unseen creature rips their tent and bodies to shreds.

A platoon of soldiers later embarks on a training exercise in those same woods, only to find their Special Forces Unit training partners massacred by some kind of vicious creatures. After being attacked by these creatures themselves, the soldiers seek shelter in a country house and slowly discover the nature of their attacker: werewolves. The soldiers scramble to keep themselves out of harm's way until sunset, with hungry werewolves lurking in every corner.

Dog Soldiers is one of the best werewolf films there is for a number of reasons. The story is strong, with good dialogue and compelling twists. The combination of costumes and animatronics in creating the werewolves themselves is excellent, resulting in scary and believable creatures. The acting is first rate with an impressive cast of accomplished performers, and writer/director Neil Marshall is responsible for some of the most terrifying and well-received horror films of the decade. There is even some notable wit and references to horror classics with character names like Sgt. Harry G. Wells (Sean Pertwee) and Cpl Bruce Campbell (Thomas Lockyer). Still, *Dog Soldiers* never saw U.S. theatrical release and was relegated to straight-to-DVD status.

Dog Soldiers is the werewolf film to watch for Horror Movie Freaks who want to experience quality fright that many casual fans have never heard of. Good monsters, great gore, solid performances, and a tight storyline come together for a monster treat that will likely end up on the shelf with your favorite horror films.

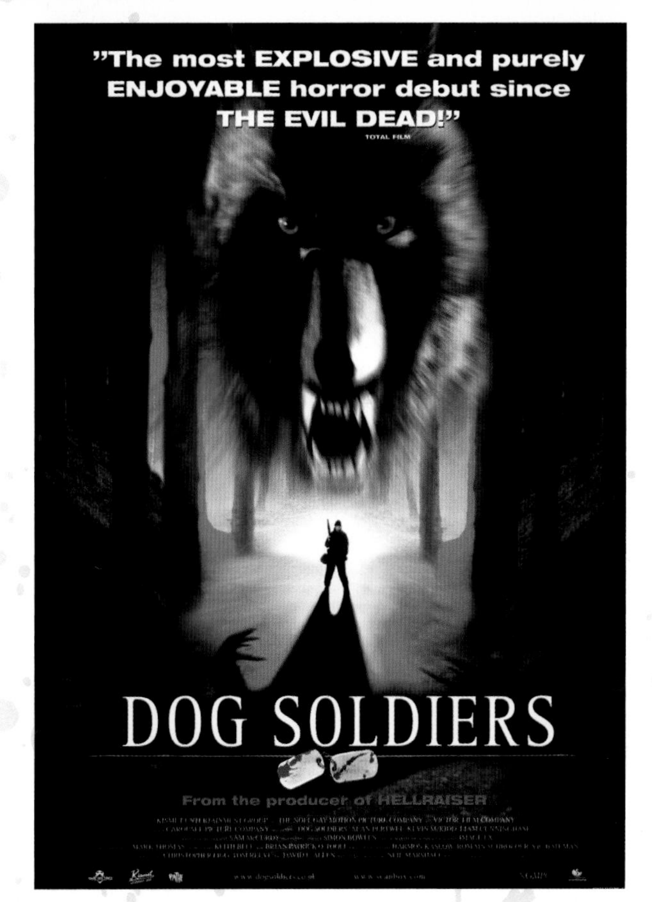

One of the soldiers in this movie is called Bruce Campbell, a reference to *The Evil Dead*, which Campbell stars in as hero Ash. *Kismet Entertainment Group*

"WE ARE NOW UP AGAINST LIVE, HOSTILE TARGETS. SO, IF LITTLE RED RIDING HOOD SHOULD SHOW UP WITH A BAZOOKA AND A BAD ATTITUDE, I EXPECT YOU TO CHIN THE BITCH."
- SERGEANT HARRY WELLS

The Descent

RELEASE: August 4, 2006 (U.S.)

WRITTEN AND DIRECTED BY Neil Marshall
STARRING Shauna MacDonald, Natalie Mendoza, Alex Reid, Saskia Mulder, MyAnna Buring
RATING R, for violence, gore, language

The Descent is a monster movie that derives only part of its appeal from the attack of monsters. The human elements of desperate times and desperate measures combine with an excruciating sense of claustrophobia to create one of the best horror films of the last decade.

A group of longtime female friends gets together every year for an outdoor adventure of some sort. This year spelunking is on the agenda (or "exploring caves" for you and me) and the women set down into a dark hole for a weekend of excitement.

Unfortunately for all concerned, the organizer of the expedition, Juno (Natalie Mendoza), switches destinations without the others' knowledge and leads them into an uncharted cave instead of the well-mapped one they are expecting. To make matters worse, there is a cave-in that leaves the women trapped with no way out. OK, to make matters REALLY worse, there are also creatures lurking in the caves that are hungry for some well-toned female adventurer meat. It gets even worse than that when the women turn on each other in their desperate attempts to survive.

The Descent exceeds expectations on every level. The story, cinematography, and acting are absolutely perfect. The tone is set for terror and intolerable unease before the monsters ever even show, due to the close quarters of the caves and the fact that there are horrifying rockslides and injuries already in progress. By the time the monsters do show up, it is almost a relief because at least where there are monsters, there is also some room to walk around.

Sarah (Shauna MacDonald) frantically pulls herself up from the caves and into the light of day. *Celador/Pathe/The Kobal Collection*

The Descent is among Horror Freaks' favorites for a good number of reasons and even if it doesn't claim a coveted spot in the collection, it is certainly worth watching. Caves, monsters, murderous catfights, and developing psychosis in one well-made horror film? Count me in.

"HEY, THERE'S SOMETHING DOWN HERE..."
- *HOLLY*

Sarah looks none too pleased to be stuck in what appears to be a pond of blood in *The Descent*.
Celador/Pathe/The Kobal Collection

Feast

RELEASE September 22, 2006 (U.S. limited)
DIRECTED BY John Gulager
DIRECTED BY Marcus Dunstan, Patrick Melton
STARRING Balthazar Getty, Henry Rollins, Krista Allen, Navi Rawat, Judah Friedlander, Josh Zuckerman
RATING R, for creature violence/gore, language, some sexuality

---

Feast, the winning result of a *Project Greenlight* film contest, is a monster movie with no discernable plot but lots of bloody gore and terrifying creatures.

The patrons in a run-down bar in the middle of nowhere have their peaceful, eventual inebriation disturbed by a young man, who bursts in and claims monsters are on the way and he is the one to "save their ass." Immediately thereafter, a monster grabs him through a window and bites his head off. His designation flashes on the screen: "Hero." So much for the hero living until the end of the movie.

The bar patrons, now convinced of a real threat, board up the windows and work through the night to fend off the vicious monsters and try to survive until morning. Most are not successful.

Project Greenlight was a documentary series focused on amateur filmmaking that aired on HBO for a couple of seasons and Bravo after that. The third-season contest for the best film featured the prize of full production, and *Feast* is the result.

Feast may not have any real plot, but it does have other things going for it. Each of the characters, when introduced, freezes in frame while a note flashes stating their "horror name," role in the film, and chance for survival. This direct take on basic horror formulas, which leaves audiences making the same determinations in their minds, is sheer wit. The thought process behind *Feast* seems to be that plot and back story can sometimes be irrelevant in the face of a good monster, and exciting fights for survival of those engaged with a monster, and in that regard this film is brilliant. Cut right to the good parts is what *Feast* seems to be saying, and for the Horror Freak with a soft spot for monsters that can have sex and create additional villains in an instant, sheer bliss awaits.

Tuffy (Krista Allen) takes no guffy from the monsters out to get her and the other bar patrons. *Dimension Films/The Kobal Collection*

"I THINK WERE GONNA BE *OK*, GUYS. YEAH, I THINK WERE GONNA BE ALRIGHT. YOU KNOW, THIS IS JUST SOME LEAKY BARREL, RADIATION, TOXIC DUMP WASTE, ENVIRO-CRAP, FREAK-BEAST ACCIDENT THAT CRAWLED OUT OF THE SEWER, MAN. THAT'S ALL THIS IS."
- BEER GUY

The Mist

RELEASE November 21, 2007 (U.S.)
DIRECTED BY Frank Darabont
WRITTEN BY Frank Darabont (screenplay) and Stephen King (novella)
STARRING Thomas Jane, M[illegible]arden, Laurie Holden, Andre Br[illegible]ones
RATING R, for violence/g[illegible] language

*"DON'T GO OUT THERE! THERE'S SOMETHING IN THE MIST!" - **DAN MILLER***

The Mist is based on a somewhat obscure Stephen King short story and brings together monsters from a presumed other dimension with monsters from the human race.

The town of Bridgton, Maine, suffers a dramatic thunderstorm that knocks out the power and ruins several buildings when large trees succumb to the wind and rain. In the aftermath, a thick mist seems to be emanating from the site of a military installation and overcomes the town. The unearthly monsters that live in this mist prevent a number of the townsfolk from venturing outside of a small grocery store where they congregated for supplies.

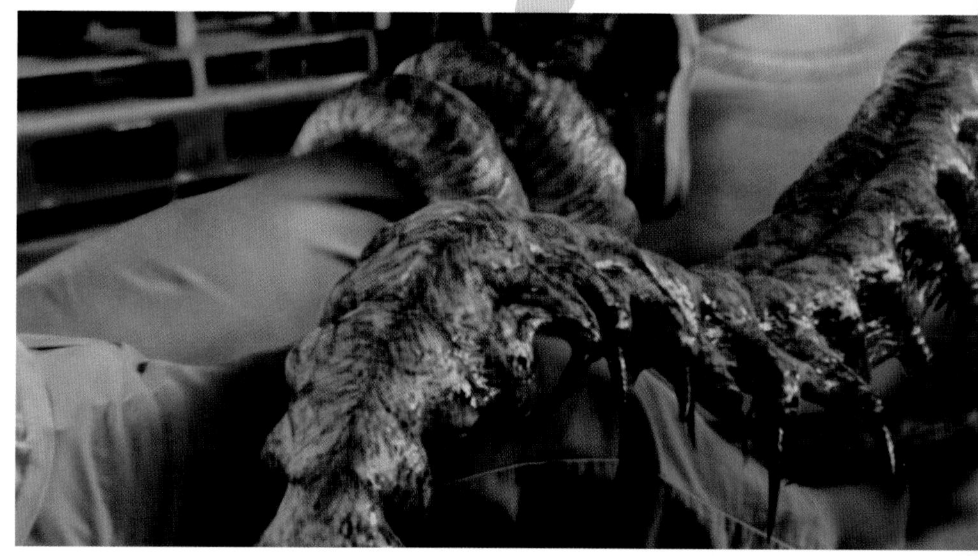

Spines in the tentacles of the mist creatures ensure you don't escape.
Darkwoods Productions/Metro-Goldwyn-Mayer

While trapped inside the store, the townsfolk begin to break under the strain, forming alliances and following the sermons of a crazy woman (Marcia Gay Harden) claiming that the monsters are sent from God to punish sinners. The followers of the newly appointed holy woman begin to turn on the others, calling for sacrifice to the demons and exorcism of the evil souls of those outside the clan.

The Mist is brilliant in its treatment of the very worst in human nature when under unimaginably difficult strain. Although this is certainly a monster movie with scary monsters artfully done, the real monsters are the humans who turn on each other in vicious and unconscionable ways.

Horror Movie Freaks will appreciate the struggle for survival against some extremely aggressive and deadly creatures and also the sheer black terror of seeing friend turn against friend, and a mob mentality develop into a force more destructive than any monster could aspire to. The ending, which varies from the ending of King's short story, is so incredibly dark that you should prepare for a period of silence after viewing, as you may not be able to utter a word for a while at its devastating conclusion.

The Midnight Meat Train

RELEASE August 1, 2008 (U.S. limited)
DIRECTED BY Ryuhei Kitamura
WRITTEN BY Jeff Buhler (screenplay) and Clive Barker (short story "The Midnight Meat Train")
STARRING Bradley Cooper, Leslie Bibb, Brooke Shields, Vinnie Jones, Roger Bart
RATING R, for bloody gruesome violence, grisly images involving nudity, sexual content, language

The meat must be properly prepared. *Lakeshore Entertainment/Lions Gate Films*

"WELCOME."
- MAHOGANY

The meat hammer of Mahogany (Vinnie Jones) is caked with goo. *Lakeshore Entertainment/Lions Gate Films*

Midnight Meat Train is a twisted tale of a photographer determined to capture "real life" with his lens, but who ends up with much more than he bargained for. Too much reality can be deadly.

Leon (Bradley Cooper) is an artistic photographer desperate for the big break that will land his work on the walls of a high-class art exhibition. When a famous artist manager looks at his work, she is not impressed, and tells Leon that if he wants to capture "real life," he needs to be willing to put himself into that life with the shutter firing.

Leon's search for dangerous and real situations to photograph brings him face to face with Mahogany (Vinnie Jones), a mountain of a man who lurks in the New York subways at night. Leon suspects Mahogany is somehow involved in a series of subway disappearances and proceeds to follow him day and night, becoming obsessed with the man and the secret he surely keeps.

Midnight Meat Train is based on a short story by Clive Barker, known for his dark and off-the-wall horror creations. The film had a limited release in August 2008 with lackluster box office draw, and proceeded to work the horror film festival circuit before being released on DVD in February 2009. The release date was continuously delayed, presumably to build buzz around the film and secure successful DVD sales, but the film instead ended up falling from consciousness for all but the most adamant horror fans that followed festival hype.

This is a shame, since *Midnight Meat Train* is an original story about obsession, murder, and monsters. Although it is too early to know for sure, this one is likely to still elevate to true cult status over time, so Horror Movie Freaks who want to get a jump on classics to come should know this film in all its gory glory.

Splinter

RELEASE October 31, 2008 (U.S. limited)
DIRECTED BY John Gulager
WRITTEN BY Marcus Dunstan, Patrick Melton
STARRING Shea Whigham, Paulo Costanzo, Jill Wagner, Rachel Kerbs
RATING R, for violence, gore, language

"IT'S *OK*, WE'RE CUTTING YOUR ARM OFF."
- *POLLY WATT*

Splinter can be called an alien invasion film, as the monsters are the result of infection from an extraterrestrial "splinter." The humans infected, however, are absolutely monsters that will chase you down via their acrobatic dance.

Splinter begins with a recent prison escapee and his drugged-out girlfriend seeking shelter after a dramatic getaway. They carjack a young couple headed to a camping trip and race along toward freedom. Suddenly a small animal leaps out in front of the car and is crushed, and the inmate stops to investigate. What is discovered is gross, indeed: a small animal both crushed by the car and impaled by hundreds of small spikes resembling large splinters. When he looks at the mass, it seems to move, and a few of the splinters embed themselves in his hand. The crew is also now without transportation, since the splinters have flattened the car's tires.

The now-stranded foursome finds a gas station and encounters the attendant, infected by splinters himself and moving in a highly unnatural way. He kills the druggie girlfriend and the three remaining folks hide in the station from the growing number of once-human monsters accumulating outside.

Splinter had a limited theatrical release after winning a series of awards at the 2008 Screamfest film festival. Horror Freaks will enjoy the creative monsters, especially how those infected bodies that have been ripped apart can re-connect with other discarded body parts to create a larger and more deadly monster. The fact that dismembered, yet infected, body parts can move and attack on their own is a nice touch.

Just because a body part is dismembered doesn't mean it still can't attack. *Indion Entertainment Group/ Magnet Releasing*

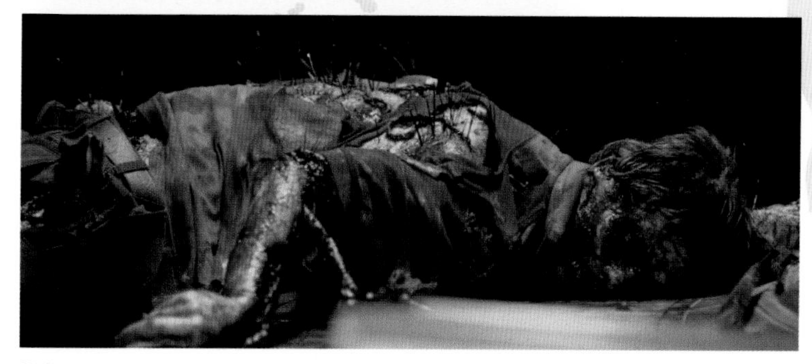

Holy cow, that guy looks splintery. *Indion Entertainment Group/Magnet Releasing*

The directing is strong and John Gulager moves the story along at the perfect pace. The music and special effects work together to create a creepy and intriguing monster movie that will surprise you. Sure, the heroes make stupid decisions throughout the film, but that is part of the fun of the monster movie—watching stupid people meet their well-deserved demise.

Psychotics

"He was such a good neighbor." How many times has this line been repeated on the nightly news by those who live next door to the bloodthirsty serial killer who's just been apprehended? The house is always tidy, the lawn always mowed, and the recycle bin always full—who knew there were dismembered bodies buried in the basement? This is the work of the psychotic.

Unlike the homicidal slasher, who single-mindedly hunts nubile young lovelies with a weapon suitable for impaling, the psychotic gives the appearance of benevolence in the bright light of day. You could stand next to the psychotic at a bus stop, even lend him the fare and share a seat, all the while in blissful ignorance of the evil derangement lurking beneath the surface. That is what makes the psychotic so frightening.

As we go about our daily lives, there are certain things we take for granted. The expectation that the clerk in the florist shop will not calmly extract a hatchet from underneath the register and proceed to chop us to bits is one of them. With the psychotic, though, all bets are off and all beliefs that we know the difference between safety and peril are discounted. Have you ever wondered about the slightly sinister look in the cable guy's eye when he came to install your HD decoder? Wonder no more…he's gonna get you.

Common situations and circumstances becoming instantly horrific are one thing, but the psychotic takes this concept to extremes. Nothing is as it seems and horror is right next door. Don't take a shower, don't go to sleep, and don't drive down the street in your car because that red scarf your grandma gave you for your birthday happens to look exactly like the one that the psychotic's childhood tormenter wore while locking him under the bathroom vanity. You will pay.

Horror movies depicting the psychotic can be particularly disturbing, which is why they figure prominently in the Horror Freak's library. Everything often starts out just fine in these films, but slowly becomes not fine. Little glimmers of dysfunction—maybe a reaction that seems slightly irrational—offer clues that "Mr. Nice Guy" is not quite so nice after all. Invariably we can see from the comfort of our living rooms that something horrific is brewing, but alas, those on the screen ignore their instincts and agree to that drive in the country anyway.

Movies about psychotics are staples of the horror genre and beyond, often crossing that line to mainstream acceptance, classified as "thrillers." Fans of these films may not know it, but they are Horror Movie Freaks through and through. It's time they fess up and admit it.

Having Annie Wilkes (Kathy Bates) be your number-one fan can lead to much *Misery*.
Castle Rock Entertainment/Columbia Pictures

The Hitcher

RELEASE February 21, 1986 (U.S.)

DIRECTED BY Robert Harmon

WRITTEN BY Eric Red

STARRING Rutger Hauer, C. Thomas Howell, Jennifer Jason Leigh, Jeffrey DeMunn

RATING R, for violence, grisly images, language

The Hitcher has been remade recently, but the creep factor and highly uncomfortable suspense of the original make it the one to watch.

Jim Halsey (C. Thomas Howell) is driving from Chicago to San Diego and decides to pick up a hitchhiker to help pass the time. The man, John Ryder (Rutger Hauer), seems calm enough until they pass a stranded car on the side of the road. Ryder informs Jim that the reason the car is stranded is because he killed the occupants, and he plans to do the same to him. Jim kicks him out of the moving car and speeds away, assuming for a moment that he is safe.

Unfortunately, Ryder has other ideas, and proceeds to follow and torment Jim, even framing him for the murders that he himself committed. What follows is a tense cat and mouse as Jim must evade the law and stop Ryder, all without becoming a victim himself.

The psychotic looks like any normal person, even someone you would consider picking up on the side of the road if they simply stick their thumb out. *The Hitcher* plays to this theme and makes the worst-case consequences of doing someone a favor come to life. This film is tense and extremely creepy, often inspiring yells and squirming in your seat as one deadly problem arises after another.

The cunning John Ryder (Rutger Hauer) is a murderous hitchhiker out to have a good time. C. Thomas Howell, who plays Jim Halsey, the young man who makes the grave mistake of picking Ryder up, has said he was actually afraid of Hauer on and off the set because of the actor's intensity in playing the role.

Silver Screen/HBO/TriStar/The Kobal Collection

"YOU WANNA KNOW WHAT HAPPENS TO AN EYEBALL WHEN IT GETS PUNCTURED? DO YOU GOT ANY IDEA HOW MUCH BLOOD JETS OUT OF A GUY'S NECK WHEN HIS THROAT'S BEEN SLIT?" – *JOHN RYDER*

Hauer as the killer is a key to the film's success. The way he plays his role and the believability of his normalcy switching over to murderous psychosis brings a sense of reality to *The Hitcher* that is critical. This is likely why the remake did not achieve the same levels of fright. The audience must believe in the seeming harmlessness of the psychotic as well as the violence for the impact to be felt. *The Hitcher* achieves this and is a likely candidate for the A-list collection of any Horror Movie Freak.

Misery

RELEASE November 30, 1990 (U.S.)
DIRECTED BY Rob Reiner
WRITTEN BY Stephen King (novel *Misery*), William Goldman (screenplay)
STARRING James Caan, Kathy Bates, Richard Farnsworth, Frances Sternhagen, Lauren Bacall
RATING R, for violence and profanity

For her performance in *Misery*, actress Kathy Bates won an Academy Award for Best Actress, and one viewing proves she deserves every ounce of tin in that statue.

Annie (Bates) is a dorky country woman who "rescues" her favorite author Paul Sheldon (James Caan) after he has a terrible accident in a snow storm. Sheldon writes trashy novels about a woman named "Misery" and Annie is his "number 1 fan." After the rescue, Annie holds Sheldon hostage and her psychosis becomes progressively more pronounced.

Misery captures the essence of the psychotic category brilliantly. Annie is sweetness and light in the beginning of the film…well, maybe a bit strange, but still, sweetness and light. Even the townsfolk have no idea what danger lurks under that calm-looking exterior. As the film progresses, little flashes of psychosis begin to show in Annie, coming to a head when she becomes abusive and violent.

This film is an on-screen interpretation of a novel by Stephen King of the same name, and King's work shows up in the Horror Freak's library quite often. This one in particular, though, was taken seriously, with a large budget and intricate attention to detail. Bates' performance steals the show and is beyond outstanding, and is the finest and most terrifying of her career. As many Horror Freaks know, *Misery* is a psychotic film that can be watched over and over, not losing impact at all from one viewing to the next. And that hobbling scene! I think I'm going to yell out loud every time I see it, and you undoubtedly will, too.

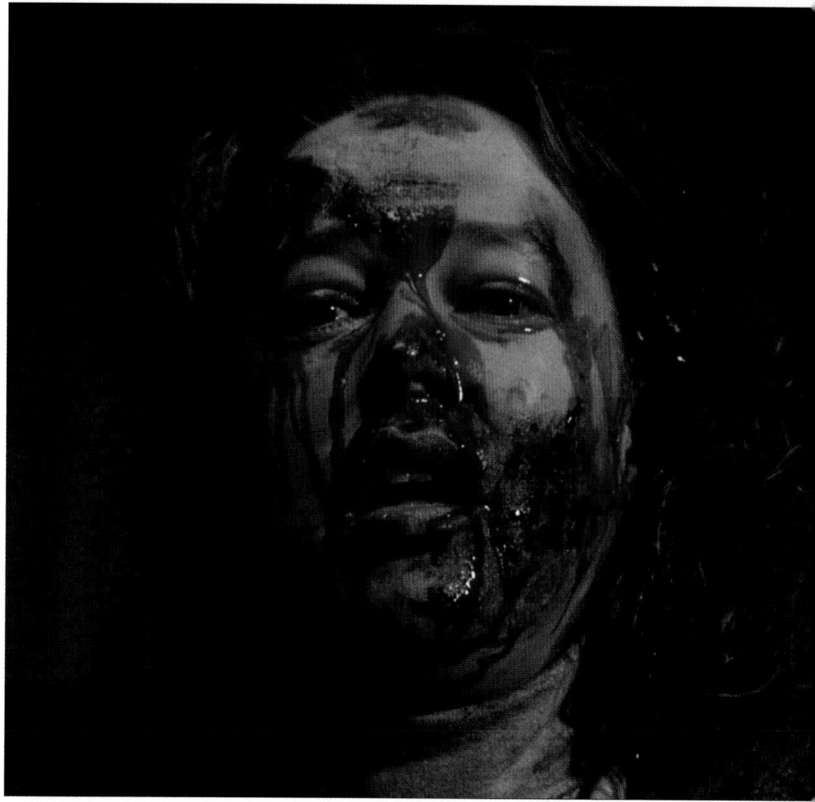

Bloodied and battered, Annie (Kathy Bates) is still creepy. *Castle Rock Entertainment/ Columbia Pictures*

"I AM YOUR NUMBER ONE FAN. THERE IS NOTHING TO WORRY ABOUT. YOU ARE GOING TO BE JUST FINE. I AM YOUR NUMBER ONE FAN." – *ANNIE WILKES*

Misery is now almost two decades old, yet still stands up against any film in the category. Classic horror from an unexpected source—that is what the psychotic subgenre of horror is all about. *Misery* delivers.

The piercing eyes of brilliant serial killer Hannibal Lecter (Anthony Hopkins) from *The Silence of the Lambs*. Although he's onscreen for less than 20 minutes, Hopkins won a Best Actor Oscar for his chilling portrayal of a villain who has left an indelible mark on movies. *Orion Pictures Corp.*

"BELIEVE ME, YOU DON'T WANT HANNIBAL LECTER INSIDE YOUR HEAD."

- JACK CRAWFORD

The Silence of the Lambs

RELEASE February 14, 1991 (U.S.)
DIRECTED BY Jonathan Demme
WRITTEN BY Thomas Harris (novel *The Silence of the Lambs*), Ted Tally (screenplay)
STARRING Jodie Foster, Anthony Hopkins, Ted Levine, Scott Glenn, Anthony Heald
RATING R, for gore/violence, profanity, sexual situations, brief nudity

---

In *The Silence of the Lambs*, Hannibal the Cannibal (Anthony Hopkins) is a horror movie villain who is charming, intelligent, and hungry.

Clarice Starling (Jodie Foster) is an FBI recruit working toward graduation. One day she gets a call to meet with the big boss, Jack Crawford (Scott Glenn), and receives a special assignment to visit with the notorious serial killer Hannibal Lecter to see if he has any information that can help in another investigation, the search for Buffalo Bill (Ted Levine).

Buffalo Bill is a serial killer who preys on plus-size women, and his most recent abductee is the daughter of a United States senator, making the search for Bill rise to the top of the to-do list. Starling gets closer to learning the identity of the killer through her interactions with Lector, but in exchange, he insists on getting inside her head: a dangerous activity with someone as capable of driving you insane as Hannibal.

Jodie Foster won a Best Actress Oscar for her role as Clarice Starling. The American Film Institution named Starling the sixth greatest film hero, out of 50, making her the highest ranked female on the list. *Orion Pictures Corp.*

The Silence of the Lambs was a huge box office success and is known to most movie fans, Horror Freaks or not. This film is pure psychotic and illustrates an important point about this particular horror category: the classification of such films is difficult and murky, as many films falling under the psychotic horror designation can also be considered crime dramas or simply "thrillers." The determining factor, from my perspective, is the gore. If the primary theme involves a serial killer and the focus is the psychological aspects of hunting this killer or the suspense as he prepares to attack—but no gore—then one of the other classifications is appropriate. Gore, however, moves a film into the horror realm to start with, and finding the appropriate category for that film then becomes semantics.

This film is a requirement for Horror Movie Freaks under all circumstances. Great film, great gore, great villain, and heroine Clarice Starling has the perfect mix of toughness and inner turmoil. Add this film to your collection immediately.

Seven

RELEASE September 22, 1995 (U.S.)
DIRECTED BY David Fincher
WRITTEN BY Andrew Kevin Walker
STARRING Brad Pitt, Morgan Freeman, Gwyneth Paltrow, R. Lee Ermey, Kevin Spacey
RATING R, for grisly killings, gore, strong language

Seven, marketed also as *Se7en*, is a crime drama that moves into the realm of horror due to the explicit gore and shocking and disturbing content.

Detectives Mills (Brad Pitt) and Somerset (Morgan Freeman) are investigating a series of murders based on the seven deadly sins: lust, gluttony, greed, sloth, wrath, envy, and pride. The resulting cat-and-mouse game between the killer and detectives puts everyone in danger.

Seven is an amazing film that mixes horror's terrifying content and gore with the star power of big-named performers and a big budget. The result is a film that successfully crossed over into mainstream cinema and achieved a great deal of box office success.

"WANTING PEOPLE TO LISTEN, YOU CAN'T JUST TAP THEM ON THE SHOULDER ANYMORE. YOU HAVE TO HIT THEM WITH A SLEDGEHAMMER, AND THEN YOU'LL NOTICE YOU'VE GOT THEIR STRICT ATTENTION." - *JOHN DOE*

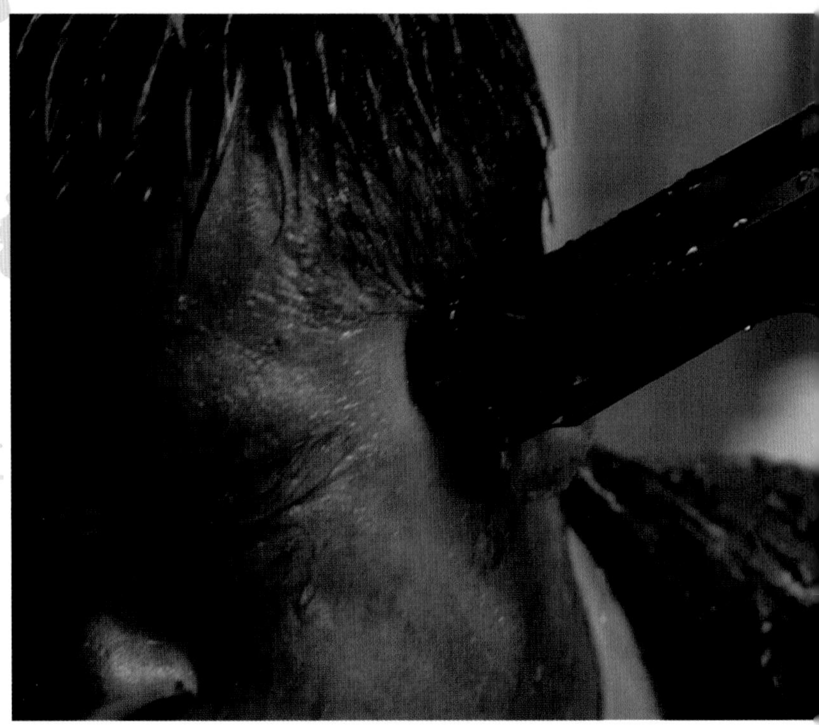

Detective David Mills (Brad Pitt) finds himself on the wrong side of a gun.
New Line Cinema

The killer in this film is a psychotic who decides he is going to teach the world a lesson regarding the error of its sinning ways, and his methods for doing so are dramatic and graphic.

The murder scenes come straight from the most horrifying haunted house and must be seen to be believed.

The interactions between the detectives and the killer are intriguing as each of the lawmen gets more involved in the mentality of it all and increasingly entangled in the killer's evil plans.

The story line is strong and the suspense is thick. This is a film that can be enjoyable for the most seasoned horror fan, as well as those who have not yet seen the light.

Horror does not need to be low budget to work, even though it sometimes seems as if this is the case. The budget in *Seven,* though, is used wisely to collect solid performances and set an atmospheric tone sure to shock and disgust.

Frailty

RELEASE April 12, 2002 (U.S.)
DIRECTED BY Bill Paxton
WRITTEN BY Brent Hanley
STARRING Bill Paxton, Matthew McConaughey, Powers Boothe, Matt O'Leary, Jeremy Sumpter
RATING R, for violence and some language

Frailty shows us how a vision from God can turn a gentle and loving man into a heartless killer who sees demons in those who turn up on "the list."

The story begins with a widowed father (Bill Paxton) raising his two sons, Fenton (Matt O'Leary) and Adam (Jeremy Sumpter). One night he wakes the boys in the middle of the night for a family meeting. He informs them he has received a message from God instructing him to seek out and destroy demons posing as normal people.

The next morning it is business as usual, and young Fenton determines that the entire exchange was just a dream, until his father mentions the vision again. He later arrives home with an ax and pair of gloves, tools he says God sends him to fulfill his duty to destroy demons. Then arrives "the list," a collection of names of those who appear to be human but are actually demons in disguise; the father will be able to see their true identities and the atrocities they commit by laying his hand upon them. Dad then goes on a killing spree leaving poor Fenton terrified and searching for a way out.

Frailty is an excellent example of the psychotic category, but with a twist. There is always doubt as to whether the father is murderously insane or if he is actually receiving messages from God.

The presentation of the story, told via flashbacks to an FBI agent by a now-adult Fenton (Matthew McConaughey), truly casts a spell on the viewer and a conflict as to what it is we're watching. The true nature of the killings and their motivation may never be known, but we can all take discomfort in knowing that psychotics like the Meiks could be living right next door.

Directors James Cameron and Sam Raimi, and author Stephen King reportedly all gave high praise to this movie. *David Kirschner Productions/ American Entertainment*

"WE DON'T KILL PEOPLE, WE DESTROY DEMONS."
- DAD

The Only Thing More Terrifying
Than The Last 12 Minutes Of This Film
Are The First 92.
SUSPIRIA
Once You've Seen It
You Will Never Again Feel Safe In The Dark

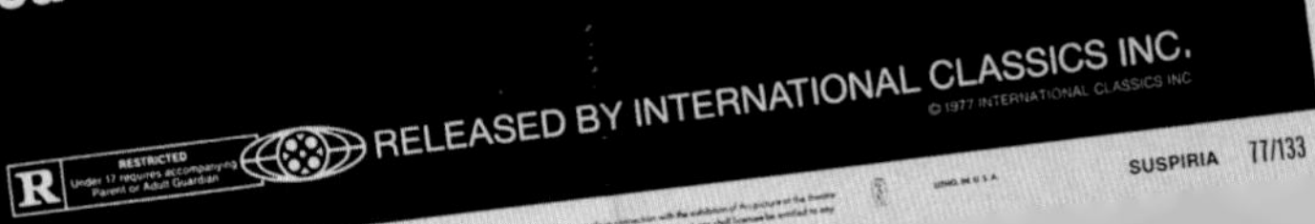
R RESTRICTED
Under 17 requires accompanying Parent or Adult Guardian
RELEASED BY INTERNATIONAL CLASSICS INC.
© 1977 INTERNATIONAL CLASSICS INC.
SUSPIRIA 77/133
© 1977 INTERNATIONAL CLASSICS INC.

Supernatural Thrillers

Horror movies with supernatural themes and villains are similar to "evil from hell" with one major difference: supernatural horror does not rely on conventional religious thought and belief to get the point across.

Evil spirits possessing the living, telekinetic abilities, and even death itself can come after you with a vengeance in a horror movie based on the supernatural, but once religion comes into the picture, the category changes.

The supernatural thriller can also have much in common with the ghost stories category, as often the grand meanie is some kind of disgruntled spirit determined to bring despair to as many hapless bystanders as possible. The primary distinction here is atmosphere and focus. Is the story dark and creepy with the primary focus on the apparition, the legend behind the spirit, or the havoc the specter wreaks on the lives of the living? If so, then it is likely a ghost story. If the atmosphere is more urgent and suspenseful with a focus on the psychosis or murderous result of the spirit's influence, then you might have a supernatural thriller on your hands. These are not hard and fast rules but rather general guidelines, and there are certainly films in either category that can disrupt the apple cart pretty quickly. The "rules" of horror movie classification are, in fact, merely suggestions.

Supernatural thrillers are a favorite among Horror Movie Freaks because they take a giant leap beyond the capabilities of a mere mortal psycho killer. Objects move by themselves, ancient legends play out in the physical world, and forgotten curses seek their targets and materialize their destruction. In some films of this type, latent powers rise to the surface allowing human villains to psychically attack others, see the future, or read minds.

Magic powers and supernatural abilities intrigue the Freak most of all, creating a scenario where the horror movie hero is at a distinct disadvantage. You can't hide from someone who can read your mind. With the cards stacked against survival for the hero, the ultimate battle to overcome the odds and live to fight another day becomes increasingly less likely, making those rare instances of triumph sweet indeed.

Then again, the supernatural is just another weapon in the Horror Freak's arsenal of angst that is sure to take us

Carrie

RELEASE November 3, 1976 (U.S.)
DIRECTED BY Brian De Palma
WRITTEN BY Lawrence D. Cohen and Stephen King (novel)
STARRING Sissy Spacek, Piper Laurie, Amy Irving, William Katt, Betty Buckley, John Travolta
RATING R, for bloody violence, disturbing images, language, nudity

Carrie, a film adaptation of a frightening Stephen King novel, contains some scenes that are among the most recognized in horror movie history.

Carrie White (Sissy Spacek) is a young high school girl with no friends and questionable bathing habits. The popular girls in school tease her mercilessly and her mother (Piper Laurie) is a religious zealot whack-job who locks her in the closet and forces her to pray. Carrie also has a secret.

While locked in the closet, she slowly develops her mental abilities that seem to give her the power to move physical objects with her mind. What happens, then, when some mean kids play a prank on Carrie that leaves her standing on a stage at the senior prom covered in pig's blood and a laughing stock? Violent bloody death, that's what.

Academy Award Best Actress winner Spacek absolutely rips it to shreds playing Carrie. The movie is a bit dated considering its initial release in 1976, but the scenes where Carrie interacts with her abusive mother are burned into the memories of horror fans forever. And the prom scene! The suspense and sense of coming dread are strong when the prank is being laid out against Carrie, and the eventual reaction is just devastating.

On prom night, Carrie (Sissy Spacek) goes from shy, mousy girl to someone her classmates really regret messing with. Spacek was apparently all for real blood being used, but a concoction of Karo Syrup and red food coloring was used instead.
Redbank Films/United Artists

"IT WAS BAD, MAMA. THEY LAUGHED AT ME."
- CARRIE WHITE

Carrie is an absolute classic film that blends psychological horror, graphic destruction, and supernatural fright with an excellent cast of performers and an amazing story. The vision of Carrie White and the look in her eyes as her wrath erupts is worth the price of admission by itself, and this film is certain to become one that is watched over and over again.

Piper Laurie, who plays Carrie's mother, Margaret, thought her character was so over the top that the movie was a comedy. But this scene shows it actually wasn't fun and games between mother and daughter. *Redbank Films/United Artists*

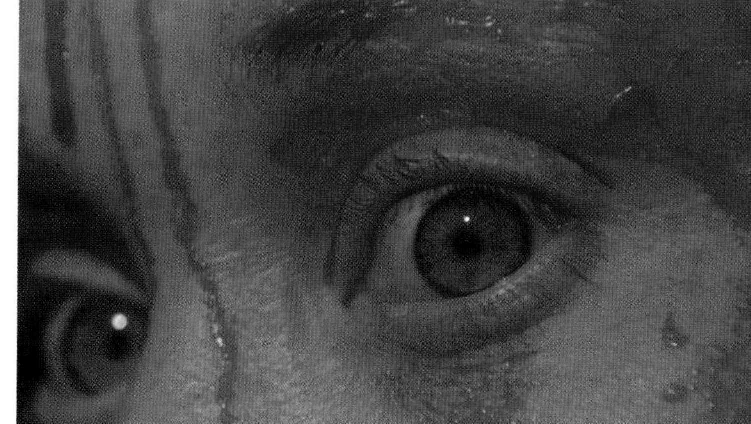

When Carrie gets this intense look in her eyes, blood and carnage follow. *Redbank Films/United Artists*

Suspiria

RELEASE: August 12, 1977 (U.S.)
DIRECTED BY Dario Argento
WRITTEN BY Dario Argento, Daria Nicolodi
STARRING Jessica Harper, Stefania Casini, Flavio Bucci, Miguel Bosé, Barbara Magnolfi
RATING R, for violence and gore

Suspiria is pure '70s with bright colors, stylized presentations, and a portrayal of violence against women that had the feminist movement up in arms.

The setting is an exclusive ballet academy in Germany and Suzy (Jessica Harper) is arriving for her first day of classes. On the night of her arrival, it is raining heavily and a woman fleeing the school almost knocks Suzy down at the front door. Unfortunately for Suzy, the woman does not leave the door open and whoever is inside will not allow her entry. Freezing and drenched to the bone, Suzy climbs back into her taxi and finds a hotel for the night. The fate of the fleeing woman is not so pleasant, however, as she is later killed in one of the most shocking and frightening horror death scenes ever.

"SUZY, DO YOU KNOW ANYTHING ABOUT... WITCHES?" - *SARAH*

When Suzy is finally admitted to the school, she may wish things had turned out otherwise. The school and teachers have a secret involving witchcraft, murder, and even a zombie!

A lot more than arabesques and tutus are going on at the prestigious ballet academy in *Suspiria*. *Seda Spettacoli/The Kobal Collection*

Suspiria is considered by many to be one of the best works of Italian director Dario Argento. It is certainly one of the most well known.

Argento has fallen under significant fire from feminist groups for his images of beautiful women being brutally murdered in graphic ways. The charge is that he has a hatred for women generally and plays out that hatred in his films. Argento's response is basically that someone is going to die in a horror film anyway, so it might as well be a beautiful woman so there is something nice to look at while we wait. It's hard to argue with that logic.

Suspiria is one of the classics that Horror Freaks discuss and analyze. That fact, combined with the beauty of this film and its trademark colors, camera angles, close ups of eyes, and violent gore, make it a necessary film for anyone who aspires to rise above the casual fan. There are other Argento works that are more disturbing, but *Suspiria* is the minimum starting point in exploring this director's work.

The Shining

RELEASE May 23, 1980 (U.S.)
DIRECTED BY Stanley Kubrick
WRITTEN BY Stanley Kubrick, Diane Johnson, Stephen King (novel)
STARRING Jack Nicholson, Shelley Duvall, Danny Lloyd, Scatman Crothers, Barry Nelson
RATING R, for graphic violence, disturbing images, brief nudity, language

The Shining is, quite possibly, the scariest film of all time. Jack Nicholson makes this film soar as he delivers some of the most remembered lines ever shouted in a horror film.

The story surrounds the Torrance family as they settle into a mountain resort for the winter. The resort becomes inaccessible due to snow and ice during the coldest months and the Torrances will be caretakers. The last caretaker of this particular resort went insane and killed his entire family, but this time things will be different.

Not different so much, though, as Jack Torrance (Nicholson) begins seeing visions and develops growing aggression toward his family, eventually becoming a raving lunatic who seeks to chop his wife and child into little bits.

The Shining is a masterpiece of fright and supernatural happenings. The slow decay of Jack's mind over time is frightening to watch and turns the concept of "father as protector" completely upside down. The performance of little Danny Torrance (Danny Lloyd) is stellar as well, as he chants the very familiar "Redrum! Redrum!" over and over while talking to his finger as if it were a little friend.

Unlike some of the classic horror films, *The Shining* has stood the test of time and any elements that seem potentially dated due to styles and language are quickly forgotten as the tale unfolds. This one is just as scary as ever, and is considered by many to be one of the scariest horror movies of all time.

Exploring the mountain resort on his Big Wheel, Danny (Danny Lloyd) encounters twin sisters who shouldn't be there. *Warner Bros. Pictures*

Horror Movie Freaks will likely be familiar with the high quotability of this film as well, including the already mentioned "Redrum!" as well as "Here's Johnny!" and "All work and no play make Jack a very dull boy." Each of these phrases, along with many others, can conjure visions of *The Shining* instantly in those who hear them, and bring up the fear that goes along with it. Great film.

"Here's Johnny!" This image of Jack Nicholson from *The Shining* is one of the most iconic and recognized images in movies, and his Jack Torrance is one of the most iconic villains.

Warner Bros. Pictures

"WENDY? DARLING? LIGHT OF MY LIFE. I'M NOT GONNA HURT YA. YOU DIDN'T LET ME FINISH MY SENTENCE. I SAID, I'M NOT GONNA HURT YA. I'M JUST GOING TO BASH YOUR BRAINS IN." - JACK TORRANCE

The Blair Witch Project

RELEASE July 16, 1999 (U.S. limited)
WRITTEN AND DIRECTED BY Daniel Myrick, Eduardo Sanchez
STARRING Heather Donahue, Joshua Leonard, Michael Williams
RATING R, for language

Reportedly created for a mere $30,000, *The Blair Witch Project* is an independent horror film that unexpectedly took the world by storm. Well, kind of unexpectedly…

Heather Donahue is a film school student determined to get an A on her documentary project, and enlists the help of friends Josh and Mike to make that happen. The plan is to travel to Burkitsville, Maryland, and interview people about a local legend known as The Blair Witch.

After spending time around town and talking with several locals, they head off to the second part of the adventure: hiking through the woods in search of the abandoned home of the legendary Blair Witch. Unfortunately, they get horribly lost and cannot find their way out of the woods; to make matters worse, there is something evil seemingly stalking them.

The setup for *The Blair Witch Project* is that some videotapes are found during a renovation project that chronicle the horror of the young filmmakers, previously reported missing. This concept was used heavily in a marketing program that resulted in blockbuster status for the film and just a few angry fans. Advertisements and viral Internet marketing campaigns were created that implied this was a true story, that videotapes were actually found that told the tale of the doomed trio, and that these tapes were edited into a movie shown in theaters. Those who believed the hype felt decidedly duped watching the film.

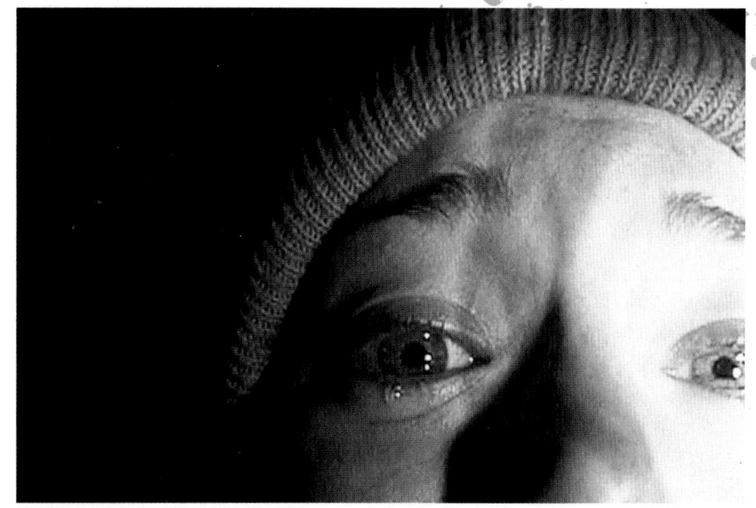

It's been reported that nearly all the events in the film were unknown to the three actors beforehand and often on-camera surprises to them all. So this shot of Heather Donahue reacting to something she hears in the woods may actually involve real tears. *Artisan Pics/The Kobal Collection*

Regardless of how it was marketed, *The Blair Witch Project* is truly excellent and scary without the use of gore or effects of any kind. There are no visible ghosts, no discernible kill scenes, and no direct threat of violence—just some creepy sounds in the woods and a depiction of the three as hunger, exhaustion, panic, and dementia overtake them.

> "YOU GONNA WRITE US A HAPPY ENDING, HEATHER?"
> - JOSH LEONARD

The camera techniques have been the subject of much discussion and regular duplication. The entire film comes from the point of view of a hand-held student's camera and is therefore shaky and real. This causes dizziness for some; to others it adds realism that would not be possible with typical studio filming techniques. This method has been used repeatedly since the movie's release and will likely continue for some time.

Horror Freaks enjoy *Blair Witch* for a variety of reasons, including as a confirmation that a low-budget independent film can actually become a widely released hit if the concept is unique enough and if the film is done well. Of course, it doesn't hurt if the marketing scheme is brilliant.

Ingenious Campaign

Like *The Blair Witch Project* before it, another low-budget horror movie, *Paranormal Activity*, also used a mountain of creative marketing to pull folks from their homes and into theaters—namely putting the power of the movie's distribution directly into the hands of moviegoers.

Before *Paranormal Activity* got wide release in October 2009, it had limited midnight-only sold-out shows. This created a fan frenzy and at Paramount's Web site for the movie, people could click a box and "demand" it come to their cities, with the studio promising to give it nationwide release when a million people voted. It was a publicity stunt, but it worked—and the ultra-low budget *Paranormal Activity*, with its simple reality-based filming techniques, got enough things right to become a smash hit.

The movie, written and directed by Oren Peli, centers around young couple Katie (Katie Featherstone) and Micah (Michah Sloat), who move into a house in suburbia. There seems to be someone (or something) else there, too, though, in the form of a malicious spirit. Micah thinks the whole thing is funny and plays with a Ouija board to try and contact the presence, but that only pisses him off. The tension mounts slowly to an explosive ending that will knock you out of your seat.

This movie is filmed completely from the point of view of a camcorder. As strange sounds escalate to moving objects and possible possession, *Paranormal Activity* builds slowly and carefully, dragging Horror Movie Freaks along hook, line, and sinker. The low budget adds to the realism of the film, giving the convincing impression that we are actually watching a young couple being slowly tormented by an unseen specter.

Paranormal Activity shows, yet again, that high-dollar effects and intricate plot lines are far from necessary when creating an effective and compelling fright flick. Everyone has heard a bump in the night and imagined the worst. This film shows us just how bad it can be.

MISSING

On October 21, 1994, Heather Donahue, Joshua Leonard and Michael Williams hiked into Maryland's Black Hills Forest to shoot a documentary film on a local legend, "The Blair Witch." They were never heard from again.

One year later, their footage was found, documenting the students' five-day journey through the Black Hills Forest, and capturing the terrifying events that led up to their disappearance.

THE BLAIR WITCH PROJECT

Makers of *The Blair Witch Project* were the first to take full advantage of viral marketing and generated massive buzz for the movie before it even opened. As part of the campaign, the three actors who star in the movie were reported as missing and presumed dead. It worked like a charm in getting moviegoers to believe the film was real. *Haxan Films/Artisan Pics*

Final Destination

RELEASE March 16, 2000 (U.S. premier)
DIRECTED BY James Wong
WRITTEN BY James Wong and Glen Morgan (screenplay) and Jeffrey Reddick (screenplay/story)
STARRING Devon Sawa, Ali Larter, Kerr Smith, Kristen Cloke, Daniel Roebuck
RATING R, for violence, gore, terror, language

Slashers, ghosts, demons, monsters, and psychos may all come to get you, but what happens when the deadly attacker is death itself?

Alex (Devon Sawa) is going on a high school graduation trip to Paris when he has a vision of destruction. In this vision, something goes wrong with the plane shortly after takeoff and after some deadly occurrences in the cabin takes the lives of several of his classmates, the entire plane explodes into a bright ball of fire.

The vision is so vivid and realistic that Alex attempts to get everyone off the plane, certain of its eminent destruction. Most think he's crazy and airport security removes him, along with a few of his friends and classmates, from the aircraft for questioning. Shortly thereafter, the plane takes off and then explodes. It seems that death does not enjoy being cheated by one boy's visions and each of the survivors dies a horrible death in freak accidents, in the order that they died in Alex's vision. Alex and his friends must find a way to cheat death again and survive against an attacker with the cards stacked in its favor.

We know this is horror, but is that look on her face natural? *New Line Cinema*

Final Destination is notable because of the originality of the concept. According to the story writer, Jeffrey Reddick, in fact, it took considerable time before a studio would consider producing the film because it felt nobody would buy a killer that has no form. No guy with a black hood and sickle, no ghostly image, no obvious attacker at all appears in this film, just random occurrences that result in the violent demise of those death targets.

Final Destination is also one of the goriest films around, with each kill happening in a graphic and extremely creative way. It is actually fun to see the random events converge on the clueless teens and their dramatically drastic results. Of course, once the survivors realize what's going on, yet continue to put themselves in harm's way, their actions become sheer stupidity, and at that point they deserve exactly what they get, and that is satisfying, too. Every Horror Movie Freak gets *that* part.

"IN DEATH THERE ARE NO ACCIDENTS, NO COINCIDENCES, NO MISHAPS, AND NO ESCAPES."
- *BLUDWORTH*

Iris (Megan Franich) is part of the ravenously thirsty gang of vampires that descends upon an Alaskan town in *30 Days of Night*.

Ghost House/Columbia/Dark Horse

Vampires

Vampires are, in fact, monsters and could be included in the Monsters category without error, but the mystique surrounding this particular creature demands a dedicated chapter. Beginning with Bram Stoker's novel *Dracula*, the vampire has become a romantic figure inspiring not only fright, but also passion and intrigue.

Even though we know eating the entire dozen of "Hot Donuts Now" Krispy Kremes or drinking a third martini will leave us regretful in the morning, we indulge anyway. The promise of momentary pleasure exceeds the gravity of the consequences. The hypnotic power of the vampire affects people the same way; we know that fraternizing with one will undoubtedly result in our untimely death or an eternity of wandering bloodlust, yet we can't help ourselves.

There is no shortage of folklore and legend surrounding vampires, beginning in early literature and further developing through horror movies, trashy novels, and comic books. In fact, an informal survey of people on the street will almost certainly reveal that a vampire's inability to tolerate the Christian cross, holy water, and garlic are common knowledge. Vampires must sleep during the day, ideally in a coffin stored underground, as sunlight is deadly. Vampires have no reflection in a mirror and can sometimes turn into bats. A wooden stake through the heart is a sure fire way to kill a vampire. These "facts" and other tidbits about the particulars of vampire lore are such a part of the general cultural consciousness that it is hard to believe they do not actually exist. Vampires don't actually exist, right?

The humble beginnings of vampires as evil creatures with an irresistible attractive power have given way to an even greater obsession with these creatures of darkness over time. There are those who actually want to "be" vampires, and some who actually claim that they are indeed eternal beings who lurk in the darkness and depend on human blood to survive. Vampire dating services and secret socials exist across the country and undoubtedly around the world.

Movies about vampires have also undergone a metamorphosis in recent years. No longer is the vampire relegated to the personal movie library of the neighborhood Horror Movie Freak but has expanded to pop culture and romance. Pre-pubescent girls fawn over new vampire stars of the silver screen searching for love with mortal girls while trying to survive high school in ***Twilight***. Television series such as HBO's ***True Blood*** chronicle the quest for an acceptance of forbidden love between vampires and mortals while this new minority strives for equal rights and an end to discrimination. Vampires are not evil, just misunderstood and the victims of close-minded bigotry.

As a card carrying Horror Movie Freak, I prefer the vampire as the villain, not as the next boy-toy to grace the cover of *Tiger Beat*. These deadly dark monsters, however sultry and alluring, are still hungry and looking for food…and we are it. Vampire movies, and those about the brave and valiant souls who hunt them, are a key component of the Freak arsenal and will continue to be so…for all eternity? That part's hard to say.

A biker vampire and rhinoplasty candidate in *From Dusk Till Dawn*.

Los Hooligans/A Band Apart/Dimension Films

Near Dark

RELEASE October 2, 1987 (U.S.)
DIRECTED BY Kathryn Bigelow
WRITTEN BY Kathryn Bigelow, Eric Red
STARRING Adrian Pasdar, Jenny Wright, Lance Henriksen, Bill Paxton, Jenette Goldstein
RATING R, for violence/gore, language

Near Dark creates an interesting twist on the vampire concept by intermixing some traditional horror themes with a new set of vampire rules, then pulling in elements of a western.

Caleb Colton (Adrian Pasdar) is a lonely cowboy abducted by a vampire "family" and bitten by the lovely Mae (Jenny Wright). To be accepted by this group, he must prove himself by feeding on a mortal, which he resists. Meanwhile, Caleb's human family is on the hunt for the vampires and determined to rescue Caleb.

Near Dark was released during a resurgence of "serious" vampire films in the late 1980s, a time when a good number of vampire horror/comedies dotted the landscape. The mixing of horror and western film genres, with elements of biker culture, worked well for the critics and the reviews were generally good. Unfortunately, the movie-going public did not agree and the box office receipts were disappointing.

Horror Movie Freaks should not take this negatively, however, as *Near Dark* is a good and gory film with some of the scariest moments to come out of horror in some time. The variations from traditional vampire legend, crucifixes and garlic being deadly for example, give a new twist to the vampire persona and add to the uniqueness of the film also having a decidedly western tone.

The actors, some well-known horror vets, include Lance Henriksen and Bill Paxton, and their performances are fantastic. The vampires in this film, especially Paxton's Severen, are violent and evil creatures, just as vampires are supposed to be. There are certainly demons with a heart of gold to be found, but fortunately they are not the only creatures of the night in this film.

Between scenes, Bill Paxton, shown on the poster above as his character, Severen, and Lance Henriksen, who plays group leader, Jesse, would go for car rides in their vampire costumes. The two were once reportedly stopped by a policeman, who was so unnerved questioning "Jesse" about his speeding that he became visibly flustered and sent them on their way instead of writing a ticket. *F-M Entertainment/De Laurentiis Entertainment Group/Anchor Bay*

Near Dark is a good addition to a vampire movie collection, not only because it stayed true to the evil nature of vampires and has great gore and scares, but because it adds something new to the body of knowledge surrounding the vampire legend, and new information is good information.

"HOWDY. I'M GONNA SEPARATE YOUR HEAD FROM YOUR SHOULDERS. HOPE YOU DON'T MIND NONE." - *SEVEREN*

The family that sucks blood together stays together in *Near Dark*. Posing for their portrait are Jesse (Lance Henriksen), Diamondback (Jenette Goldstein), and Severen (Bill Paxton). All three actors also appear in *Aliens*.
F-M Entertainment/De Laurentiis Entertainment Group/Anchor Bay

Bram Stoker's Dracula

RELEASE November 13, 1992 (U.S.)
DIRECTED BY Francis Ford Coppola
WRITTEN BY Bram Stoker (novel *Dracula*) and James V. Hart (screenplay)
STARRING Gary Oldman, Winona Ryder, Anthony Hopkins, Keanu Reeves, Richard E. Grant
RATING R, for violence, sexuality

Bram Stoker's Dracula is a lush interpretation of the classic vampire story with a huge budget and significant impact on the vampire-loving public.

The story is the one that Horror Movie Freaks have come to expect of the infamous Count Dracula, but with some additional points of information as well.

"THE BLOOD IS THE LIFE... AND IT SHALL BE MINE."
- *DRACULA*

The beginnings of Dracula (Gary Oldman) as a master of darkness is revealed, for example, prior to the escapades of Jonathan Harker (Keanu Reeves) and his travel to the castle.

The role of Van Helsing (Anthony Hopkins) is also a bit expanded as not only is he a simple scholar with uncanny knowledge of vampires, but an actual vampire killer with a bloody and violent edge.

Bram Stoker's Dracula is an excellent continuation and retelling of the classic vampire story, now from the point of view of well-known director Francis Ford Coppola. Every time a Horror Freak imagines that the same story cannot be told in a new and compelling way, this movie surprises them.

The sets are amazing, the performances fantastic, and this version of the classic story is so full of nuances and additional information, you feel you really know the nature of vampires just a bit better.

Newly minted vampire Lucy (Sadie Frost) looks pretty thirsty. *Zoetrope/Columbia Tri-Star/ The Kobal Collection*

Interview with the Vampire

RELEASE November 11, 1994 (U.S.)
DIRECTED BY Neil Jordan
WRITTEN BY Anne Rice
STARRING Tom Cruise, Brad Pitt, Kirsten Dunst, Christian Slater, Virginia McCollam
RATING R, for vampire violence/gore, sexuality

Interview with the Vampire is based on the Anne Rice novels and chronicles the adventures and heartbreak of those who live forever on the blood of mortals.

The film begins with the vampire Louis (Brad Pitt) speaking with Daniel Malloy (Christian Slater), a newspaper reporter. Louis has been alive for centuries with a heavy heart—being a vampire is not the existence he would have chosen for himself. Now he needs to get his heartbreak off of his chest and make the presence of vampires known to the mortal world.

Louis tells a tale of being abducted by the vampire Lestat (Tom Cruise), being made a vampire, and the years that followed in isolation and sadness, punctuated by satisfying kills of mortals along the way.

The Vampire Chronicles, a series of books by Rice, took the world by storm as romantic visions of asexual vampires were cast in dramatic detail—from the point of view of the vampires themselves, rather than the victims and hunters. The novels are wonderful, and this film adaptation captures much of the essence of the first installment.

Because of the popularity of the novels, this film garnered a huge budget and big-name stars, something that inspired much apprehension among both fans of the novels and horror movie fans. Ultimately, the stars do not detract from the power of the story too much, with the possible exception of Cruise, who is much more believable as a whacked-out celebrity than an eternal being who feasts on human blood.

After living for centuries feasting on human blood, the heavy heart of Louis (Brad Pitt) makes him open up to a newspaper reporter about his life and the existence of other vampires in the mortal world.

Zoetrope/Columbia Tri-Star/The Kobal Collection

"YOU ARE A VAMPIRE WHO NEVER KNEW WHAT LIFE WAS UNTIL IT RAN OUT IN A BIG GUSH OVER YOUR LIPS." - *LESTAT*

Interview with the Vampire is significant in other ways relevant to the Horror Movie Freak, however, as *The Vampire Chronicles* were one of the early commercial successful vampire tales to depict the creatures as romantic leads rather than monsters. What followed were a series of television programs and even movies, where vampires are treated like sexy yet misunderstood minorities rather than bloodthirsty killers. This film does not go as far as some of the pop culture teen movies of late in regard to casting vampires in a purely romantic light, like *Twilight*, but it certainly forms the foundation for this trend. Watch this film as one of the first to hint at the "human" side of a vampire, and one of the last that did so without simultaneous merchandising plans to plaster the vampires' images on the walls of 13-year-old girl's bedrooms as boy-toy celebrities.

From Dusk Till Dawn

RELEASE January 19, 1996 (U.S.)
DIRECTED BY Robert Rodriguez
WRITTEN BY Robert Kurtzman (story) and Quentin Tarantino (screenplay)
STARRING Harvey Keitel, George Clooney, Quentin Tarantino, Juliette Lewis, Salma Hayek
RATING R, for strong vampire violence and gore, language, nudity

Not all vampire films have to be completely serious, and *From Dusk Till Dawn* works this fact for all it's worth.

Seth (George Clooney) and Richie (Quentin Tarantino) Gecko are violent criminals fleeing from the FBI and police. When they come upon a vacationing family at a small motel, they kidnap them and force them to smuggle their fugitive selves across the Mexican border in their RV. Once in Mexico, the group proceeds to a rendezvous point, the Titty Twister bar, where the Gecko brothers expect to meet a contact who will assist them in their escape from the law.

Forced to enter the bar by the Gecko brothers, the family sits down and watches the provocative stripper (Salma Hayek) on stage perform her extended solo, but when blood drips to the ground from a wound, the stripper attacks and is revealed as a vampire. In fact, the entire staff of the bar and all of the strippers are vampires and proceed to feast on the bar patrons and threaten the group, who must now work together to survive.

From Dusk Till Dawn started with mixed feelings from Horror Movie Freaks, primarily because the concept of a scary vampire film was muddied by the casting of television star Clooney, who was on *ER* at the time. The film won many over, however, through an interesting plotline, exciting vampire-killing action, and an impressive level of gore not often associated with pop-star actors. Clooney does well also, proving to the critics that he can battle the evil undead with the best of them.

A night with vampires turns everyone into a badass, including Kate (Juliette Lewis), who takes aim at a bloodsucker. *Los Hooligans/A Band Apart/Dimension Films*

"FIGHT NOW, CRY LATER." - SETH

The primary detractors of this film are the dreaded horror intelligentsia that believes their film-school visions of vampire movies are the only credible interpretations. This film does not adhere to the dark and gothic vampire standard that has proven itself over the decades, yet it holds its own as a gory action-oriented vampire kill-fest that is fun and satisfying.

If a Horror Freak does not enjoy or appreciate *From Dusk Till Dawn*, that doesn't automatically peg them as a member of the horror intelligentsia, but may signify that further study may be in order, as well as perhaps a bit of honest soul searching, just in case.

30 Days of Night

RELEASE October 19, 2007 (U.S.)
DIRECTED BY David Slade
WRITTEN BY Steve Niles (screenplay/comic book), Stuart Beattie and Brian Nelson (screenplay) and Ben Templesmith (comic book)
STARRING Josh Hartnett, Melissa George, Danny Huston, Ben Foster, Mark Boone Junior
RATING R, for strong horror violence, language

30 Days of Night depicts a vampire's wet dream and a mortal's worst nightmare. How rampant can vampires run in a place where the sun doesn't shine for 30 days straight?

The town of Barrow, Alaska, is preparing for the annual "30 Days of Night," a time when the sun does not shine for a full 30 days due to the location of the town and the rotation of the earth. Most residents leave for nearby cities during this time but some stay and live through the darkness.

This particular season will not be like those past, as a gang of vampires converges on the town and feasts upon the residents while they fight for survival until daylight comes.

30 Days of Night is based on a popular comic book mini-series of the same name and went through some significant turbulence on the path of being made into a feature film. When it finally came out, it did well at the box office, partly due to a huge amount of promotion and advertising. Although the reviews of this film are mixed, I believe that is partly a result of resistance to the considerable hype surrounding the film's creation and release and the underground uproar by the comic book series' fans, who were not going to be satisfied with the outcome under any circumstances.

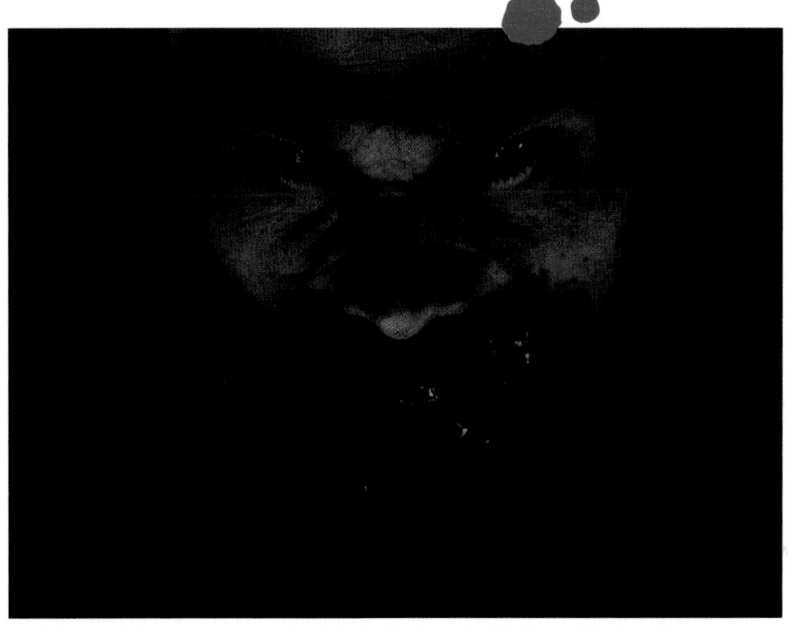

Fresh from drinking someone's blood, Arvin (Andrew Stehlin) looks like he still wants a whole bunch more. *Ghost House/Columbia/Dark Horse*

SHERIFF EBEN OLESON: HELL OF A DAY.
THE STRANGER: JUST YOU WAIT.

The fact is, *30 Days of Night* is a solid vampire film with a fantastic concept. The special effects are outstanding and the vampires themselves are intriguing and actually believable as undeads who seeks out isolated bits of population to feast upon and then make the massacre look like some other type of disaster to cover their tracks and allow the world to continue to relegate their existence to that of myth.

Vampires are supposed to be evil and scary creatures that feast on human blood with no regard for the life of mortals. In *30 Days of Night*, that is exactly what you get. Blood, gore, evil, and treachery abound in this film, making it a real treat.

Underworld

RELEASE September 19, 2003 (U.S. limited)
DIRECTED BY Len Wiseman
WRITTEN BY Len Wiseman, Kevin Grevioux, Danny McBride
STARRING Kate Beckinsale, Scott Speedman, Michael Sheen, Shane Brolly, Bill Nighy
RATING R, for violence/gore, some language

Underworld is a stunning and slick depiction of the legendary war between vampires and werewolves. Not a horror movie you say? You are correct; fantasy/thriller at best. Still, the additions to vampire lore are displayed with awesome effects and style…and talk about thriller, Kate Beckinsale is so hot in this film she will make you burst into flames.

Selene (Beckinsale) is a vampire warrior, entrusted to lurk through the night in search of the mortal enemies of her race, the Lycans (werewolves to you and me). When Selene falls in love with a member of her intended victims, however, she must choose between a race mired in lies and deceit and her one true amore. What do you think she does?

An ancient legend of rivalry between the Vampires and the Lycans is played out in Underworld, complete with flashbacks of unrequited love and the deadly war that begins as a result. A good bit of social structure for the vampire nation is also explained, making the story extremely compelling. The effects in Underworld are incredibly slick and beautiful, both CGI and via makeup. The result is an excellent action/adventure/thriller that furthers the depth and depiction of everyone's favorite bloodsuckers.

There are other reasons why this "not really a horror movie" horror movie is included among so many vampire greats. First, although not specifically horror, one would be hard pressed to find a Horror Movie Freak who has not seen this film at least once. Whether you decide this one actually does cross over to horror enough to count, or decide to debate those fools who think so, not being familiar with this film will leave you out in the cold among the non-Freaks. If you want to ensure that you are not seen by all as merely a horror fan but rather than a bona-fide Freak, be unfamiliar with *Underworld* and unable to engage in heated discussion until the wee hours of the morning.

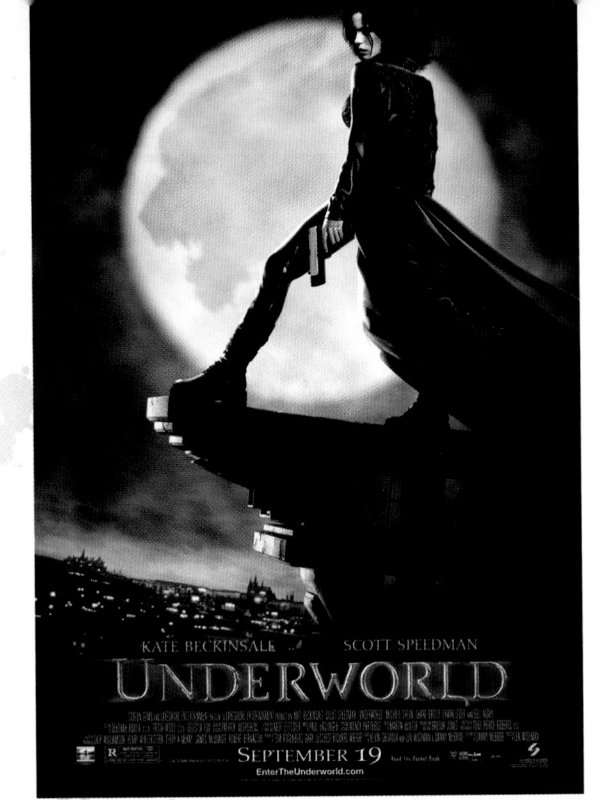

The leather-clad Selene is vampire warrior who deals death to enemies of her clan. *Subterranean/Screen Gems*

Besides, Kate Beckinsale is truly stunning in this film, So here it is, included among the vampire entries. Enjoy, know it's not really horror, and move onto the next movie.

"I AM A DEATH DEALER, SWORN TO DESTROY THOSE KNOWN AS THE LYCANS. OUR WAR HAS WAGED FOR CENTURIES, UNSEEN BY HUMAN EYES. BUT ALL THAT IS ABOUT TO CHANGE." -SELENE

Lycan Lucian (Michael Sheen) about to rip into the flesh of lycan-vampire hybrid Michael (Scott Speedman).
Subterranean/Screen Gems/The Kobal Collection/Egon Endrenyi

Let the Right One In

RELEASE October 24, 2008 (U.S. limited)
DIRECTED BY Tomas Alfredson
WRITTEN BY John Ajvide Lindqvist
STARRING Kåre Hedebrant, Lina Leandersson, Per Ragnar, Henrik Dahl, Karin Bergquist
RATING R, for some bloody violence, disturbing images, brief nudity, language

Let the Right One In, a Swedish horror film based on a novel of the same name, is about coming of age, young love, and vampires.

Oskar (Kåre Hedebrant), a young boy who lives a bleak colorless existence, is constantly bullied. Things start to look up when young Eli (Lina Leandersson) moves in next door. She's a girl Oskar's age who helps ease the loneliness of his life. But Eli has a secret…

The lovely Eli has been 12 years old for a very long time…she is a vampire. Living with her human protector Hakan (Per Ragnar), she survives on blood and develops a relationship with Oskar, amid intermittent bouts of violence that demonstrate just how dangerous she is.

Let the Right One In handles many social themes and is a deep movie on one level, but also a beautiful movie with appropriate gore and terror intermixed. The coming of age of Oskar as he learns to take charge of his life, along with the quest for independence of a young girl with the soul of a killer, work together to deliver not only a great vampire movie, but a great movie in general.

The film falls squarely into the category of vampires as romantic figures rather than pure evil, but also captures the evil and menace of the creatures as well—a bit of a hybrid. Because of the limited U.S. release and minimal promotion, it is largely unknown to the movie-going public, making it a nice strategic addition to the library of Horror Movie Freaks who want to be on the bleeding edge of the best horror around.

A number of tricks were used to create the right sound effects in the movie for some of the gorier scenes, including biting into sausages to replicate biting into skin and flesh, and drinking yogurt to sound like drinking blood. *EFT/Magnet Releasing*

Eli (Lina Leandersson) is a child wise beyond her years, and also harboring a secret in *Let the Right One In*. *EFT/Magnet Releasing*

If you're going to burst into flames, a hospital is a good place to do it.

EFT/Magnet Releasing

Bloody hands on the door make mom sad.

EFT/Magnet Releasing

OSKAR: ARE YOU REALLY TWELVE?
ELI: YES. IT'S JUST I'VE BEEN TWELVE FOR A VERY LONG TIME.

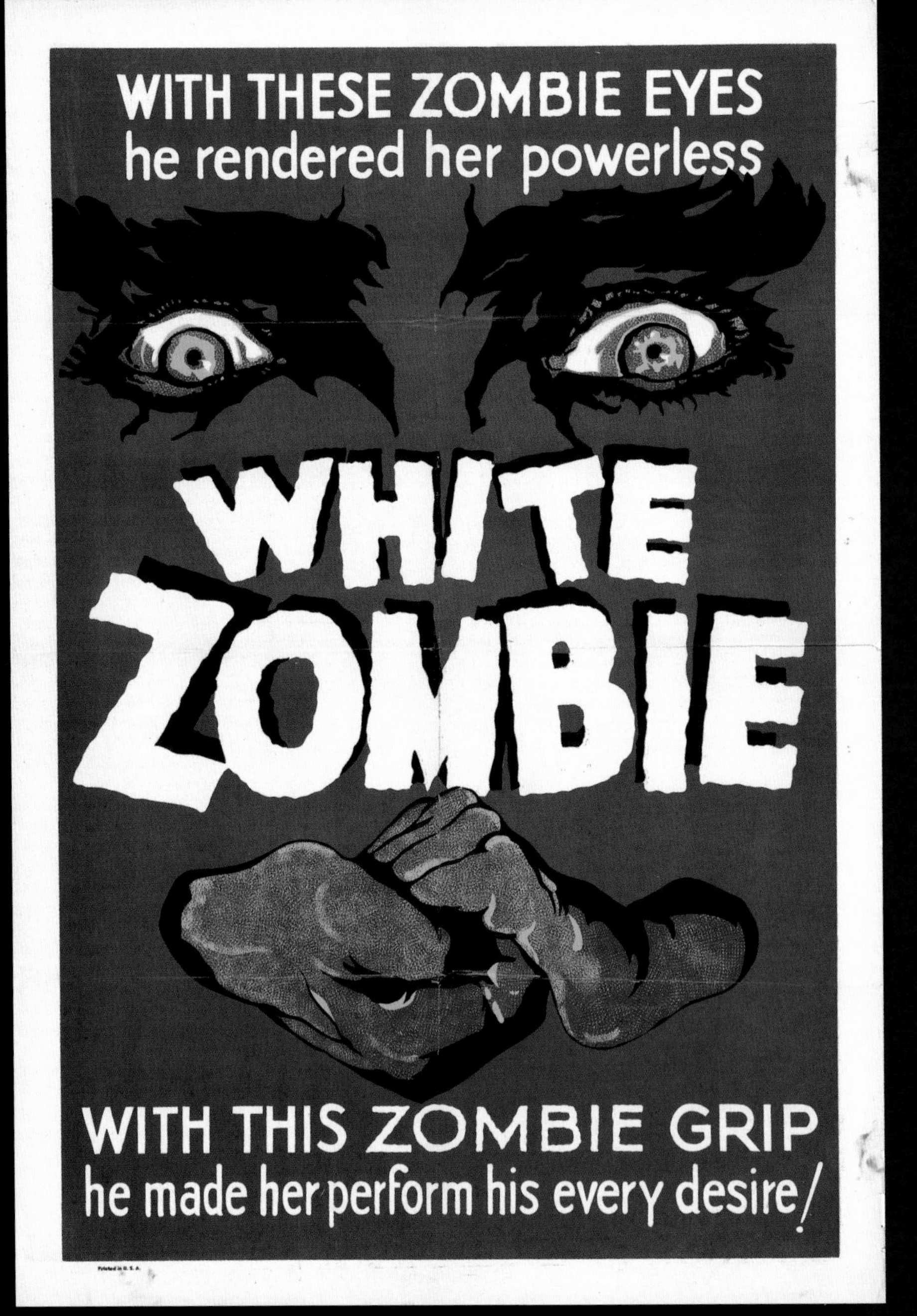

A desperate man in love with a woman betrothed to someone else turns to a witch doctor for help in *White Zombie*. *Edward Halperin Productions/United Artists*

Zombie Invasion

The nature of the zombie in horror movies has changed significantly over the decades.

Early zombies were the result of voodoo curses and magical control over one person by another. These early zombies are mindless slaves of their masters, typically with wide white eyes and no soul. Voodoo zombies are not known for their own bodies being decayed and rotted, or for feasting on the flesh of the living. That came later.

The "modern zombie" has several distinguishing characteristics from the voodoo one. There is no pulse, no breathing, no body warmth, and no thoughts, other than a blind instinct to consume human flesh. In fact, biological death is a requirement if a zombie is to, in fact, be a zombie. Death occurs first, and then the dead corpse rises to walk again. This point has been the source of quite a bit of confusion as films surface featuring ferocious folks infected by viruses or hypnotized by alien transmissions run about on killing sprees. Although these creatures may exhibit zombie-like attributes and may even be flesh-feasters themselves, if it didn't die, it ain't a zombie. Admittedly, a bit of an exception is found with those zombies created through demonic possession, even though there may not have been a defined moment of physical death followed by distinct reanimation. This can be explained when you acknowledge that demonic zombies did, indeed, die prior to bursting forth in zombiedom; it just happened so quickly as to appear as a transition straight from normalcy to undead freak.

Beyond the original voodoo ones, several categories appear in zombie films in the modern era:

Classic undead: These zombies display stereotypical characteristics including dying before reanimating, instinctively craving human flesh, and lumbering slowly, as rotting muscles are not particularly agile. Classic undead are incapable of speech and independent thought and operate on instinct alone, occasionally being drawn to areas that were familiar to them during life. Destruction of the brain or separating the brain from the spinal cord is the only way to kill the classic undead.

"BRAAIINNNSS" zombies: Sharing many characteristics of the classic undead, these zombies exhibit death prior to reanimation, crave human flesh, and have slow lumbering movement. These zombies, however, are more selective in their dietary requirements and prefer the human brain over all other cuts of meat. Rudimentary speech is also possible for these zombies, and they usually utter a single word that defines their desires "BRAAIINNNNSS!"

Demonic zombies: These zombies can be difficult to define, as some instances of simple demonic possession result in a zombie-like appearance, but not zombie behavior. Demonic zombies have a rotted physical demeanor and limited intellectual ability. Murdering their victims and dragging their souls to hell is their primary

Fresh from being turned into a flesh eater, Stephen (David Emge) is no doubt looking for some brains to munch on in *Dawn of the Dead*. *United Film/The Kobal Collection*

objective, and they may or may not consume the flesh of their victims in the process. A demonic zombie cannot recover from their undead state, as they die at the instant of possession and zombie manifestation. If the victim of such a possession can recover, it is not a demonic zombie but merely a possessed individual.

Runners: These undead monsters share most characteristics with the classic undead, with one important difference—they can sprint after their human meals. Running zombies are a fairly recent phenomenon that has sparked much debate between zombie purists and progressives. One thing is certain about runners though—they are gonna get you.

"Not-a-zombie" zombies: These "zombies" are not zombies at all, though they may display zombie-like behavior. The defining element of a "not-a-zombie" zombie is that the victim did not die prior to becoming a feasting freak. Viral infections that bring on murderous madness without killing the infected is an example of this creature, and those infected have the possibility of recovery should an anti-virus be found.

The following horror movies have the best a Zombie Invasion has to offer…and remember, when it comes to preparing for the eventual overtaking of humanity by zombies, perfect paranoia is perfect preparedness.

"YOUR DRIVER BELIEVED HE SAW DEAD MEN...WALKING." - DR. BRUNER

White Zombie

RELEASE 1932
DIRECTED BY Victor Halperin
WRITTEN BY Garnett Weston
STARRING Bela Lugosi, Madge Bellamy, Robert Frazer, John Harron
NOT RATED Has some mild zombie violence

Bela Lugosi is one of the most influential actors on the budding horror genre. His stylized interpretation of horrific characters set the tone for a variety of movie types, including the first zombie movie.

White Zombie is possibly the first commercial zombie movie ever made, although not with zombies as they have come to be known. This film is an example of voodoo zombies, the undead who are bound to obedience to their masters as mindless slaves.

White Zombie begins with a young couple traveling across the Haitian countryside in a carriage. Their trip is interrupted by a funeral being conducted in the middle of the road. It seems that the Haitians are concerned about bodies being stolen from their graves, so they bury their dead along busy roads in an attempt to deter would-be body thieves. During this stop, the couple crosses paths with an eerie gentlemen and his band of henchmen. The henchmen, they learn, are not men at all, but zombies. Mindless undead made to work as slaves in the fields.

Upon arrival at their destination, the home of Charles Beaumont (Robert Frazer), the young couple prepare for their upcoming marriage ceremony. Unfortunately for all involved, Charles has his eye on the young bride-to-be himself, and engages "Murder" Legendre (Lugosi) to assist him in winning over the woman of his dreams. The question is, what state will she be in when she is delivered to her new "suitor?"

White Zombie is an important film for Horror Freaks, especially those with a taste for zombie mayhem. The antics of the walking dead, lumbering along seeking living human flesh to satisfy their hunger, are even more appealing when the history of the zombie movie can be seen encapsulated in the first film. The shock and delight of seeing entrails dragging behind a victim newly ripped in half by a zombie horde, when framed by the tame beginnings of our favorite meat eaters and accentuated by a classic performance by the one and only Lugosi, has the power to elevate the casual horror fan to true Horror Freak status.

"Murder" Legendre (the great Bela Lugosi) uses his undead henchmen to help with his nefarious schemes in *White Zombie*. *Edward Halperin Productions/United Artists*

This shot of the blue-faced zombies reaching for human victims is a classic in ***Dawn of the Dead***. *Laurel Group/United Film Distribution Company*

"SOMETHING MY GRANDDAD USED TO TELL US. YOU KNOW MACUMBA? VOODOO. MY GRANDDAD WAS A PRIEST IN TRINIDAD. HE USED TO TELL US, 'WHEN THERE'S NO MORE ROOM IN HELL, THE DEAD WILL WALK THE EARTH.' " - *PETER*

Dawn of the Dead

RELEASE May 24, 1979 (U.S.)
WRITTEN AND DIRECTED BY George A. Romero
STARRING David Emge, Ken Foree, Scott H. Reiniger, Gaylen Ross, David Crawford
RATING R, for graphic violence/gore, language

Dawn of the Dead continues the story of a sudden zombie outbreak that leaves the world wondering what the hell happened.

It picks up where George A. Romero's *Night of the Living Dead* leaves off: The dead are rising to walk again and feasting on living flesh. The beginning scene takes place inside a television studio, where it is easy to see the confusion and chaos overtaking the world. When a zombie gets loose inside the studio, a few people take off in a helicopter to seek a safe haven.

They land on a shopping mall and attempt to make their stand there. Between the feasting freaks and the roughneck survivors attacking, however, survival doesn't look likely.

After Romero defined the new zombie age with *Night of the Living Dead*, the world was hungry for more. That "more" came with *Dawn of the Dead*. The parameters for the modern zombie movie were reinforced and further developed as the undead feasters lumbered along with only living flesh in their consciousness.

The drama surrounding those who attempt to survive in this new world is an interesting commentary on human nature and the effects that unimaginable tragedy might have on one's psyche. This film also confirms a couple of valuable lessons that any potential survivor must commit to practice if they are going to have a chance in the coming zombie invasion: Always shoot for the head, and don't get over-confident. The consequences for failing in either of these areas, Horror Freaks, are dire indeed.

Director George A. Romero has said that the zombie walk of David Emge, who plays Stephen, is his favorite out of all the *Dead* movies and Emge's performance is worthy of Lon Chaney. *Laurel Group/United Film Distribution Company*

Zombi 2

RELEASE July 18, 1980 (U.S.)
DIRECTED BY Lucio Fulci
WRITTEN BY Elisa Briganti
STARRING Tisa Farrow, Ian McCulloch, Richard Johnson, Al Cliver, Auretta Gay
RATING R, for violence and graphic flesh-feasting gore, nudity

Zombi 2 (also known as *Zombie*) is an example of the classic post-Romero zombie film, with the walking dead lumbering along slowly seeking human flesh to feed their insatiable hunger.

Anne Bowles (Tisa Farrow) is searching for her father on the island of Matool, after she is told his boat drifted into New York Harbor carrying a horrific creature that rips the throat out of a harbor patrolman with its teeth.

When Anne finds the island, she discovers the inhabitants are all inflicted with a strange disease that causes them to rise from the dead in search of living flesh.

The title *Zombi 2* implies this film is a sequel to *Zombi*, the Italian title of George Romero's *Dawn of the Dead*. In reality, this film has nothing to do with *Zombi*, except of course for the zombies. *Zombi 2* is one of the best-known works of Lucio Fulci, the Italian horror master who brought a score of creepy and complex movies to light.

Zombi 2 takes zombie gore to new levels, with a decayed look and bloody feasting that is unmatched in zombie lore even today. Fulci also seems to have a "thing" about the human eye and there is a certain scene in this film where you can see first hand what this "thing" means. No matter how many time you see this particular scene, it's still gonna get you. If you've already seen the film, you know what I'm talking about.

Fulci has been referred to as the "godfather of gore" and *Zombi 2* is one of the films to earn him this title. Zombie movie lovers will absolutely adore this, as all of the desired disgusting and horrifying elements are present and accounted for. For those Horror Movie Freaks not accustomed to really good and gory zombie films, well…maybe you should start with the Beginner's Shelf and work your way up. We don't want to cause an episode now, do we?

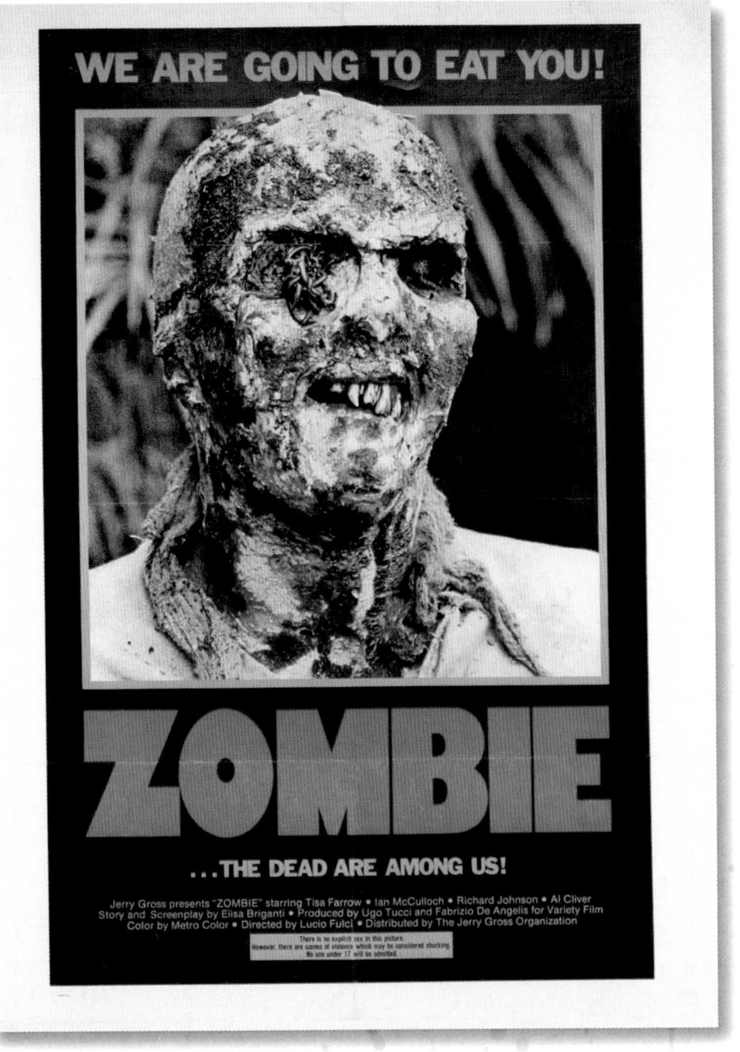

As shown in trailers before the film was released, airline "barf bags" were handed out to theater moviegoers due to the unusually high amount of violence and gore for a horror film of that time. *Variety Film Production/The Jerry Gross Organization*

The Evil Dead

RELEASE October 15, 1981 (U.S. premier)
WRITTEN AND DIRECTED BY Sam Raimi
STARRING Bruce Campbell, Ellen Sandweiss, Hal Delrich, Betsy Baker, Sarah York
NOT RATED Contains violence, graphic gore

An *Evil Dead* publicity still with Bruce Campbell as hapless hero Ash.
Renaissance Pictures/New Line Cinema

Long before Sam Raimi achieved fame for the *Spider-Man* trilogy, he was a young filmmaker with an eye for the terrifying. *The Evil Dead* is the first on-film manifestation of this eye, and his twisted mind.

The Evil Dead begins with five friends on their way to an isolated cabin in Tennessee for spring break. Exploring the basement of their cabin results in some good finds, including a tape player with a strange audio diary from the prior inhabitant. When the tape is played, however, it awakens a demonic force in the woods with the power to turn people into zombies.

The Evil Dead is an example of a movie in the "demonic zombies" category. This movie is one of the most popular cult classics in horror and leaves some lasting impressions. One of these is star Bruce Campbell as Ash Williams. Through two sequels to *The Evil Dead*, cameos in other Raimi films, and some other films of his own, Campbell has become an icon himself. Most horror movie fans know his name and the lines for his autograph at horror conventions winds down the hall and out the door. Speaking of horror movie conventions, the "women of *The Evil Dead*" sometimes appear themselves and also cause quite an uproar, as well as long autograph lines.

Raimi went on to write and direct many other movies including the popular mega-budget hit *Spider-Man*. His return to horror movies with the 2009 release of *Drag Me to Hell* (P. 82 and 89) was highly anticipated and a huge commercial success.

The Evil Dead also has the distinction of being a "banned" film, earned when the United Kingdom proclaimed it a "video nasty" and prohibited its distribution. It was released in that country later, though, after edits.

The Evil Dead is the cult classic to beat all cult classics, being the one off-the-wall film every Horror Movie Freak has either seen or will see soon. One distinction not yet bestowed upon *The Evil Dead*, "most creative use of a pencil," will surely be awarded whenever this honor is created. Watch the movie to see what I mean.

> "LOOK AT HER EYES. LOOK AT HER EYES! FOR GOD'S SAKE, WHAT HAPPENED TO HER EYES?"
> - SHELLY

Return of the Living Dead

RELEASE August 16, 1985 (U.S.)
DIRECTED BY Dan O'Bannon
WRITTEN BY Dan O'Bannon (screenplay), Rudy Ricci and Russell Streiner (story), and John Russo (book)
STARRING Clu Gulager, Thom Mathews, James Karen, Don Calfa, Beverly Randolph, Linnea Quigley
RATING R, for gore/violence, nudity, language

Return of the Living Dead is an example of the "BRAAIINNSS!" style of zombies, named so after the primary vocabulary of the film's undead flesh feasters.

Uncle Frank (James Karen) shows his nephew Freddy (Thom Mathews) around the medical supply shop on his first day of work. Frank confides in Freddy that he knows for certain George Romero's *Night of the Living Dead* is based on a true story because he himself is in possession of some secret military canisters, which contain dormant reanimated corpses.

Uncle Frank proceeds to show his nephew the containers. One of them develops a crack and leaks the dangerous chemical "Trioxin 245" into the atmosphere, which causes a corpse in the freezer to reanimate. When the duo burns this now-moving zombie in the crematorium, the ashes soar into the sky and are brought down upon a graveyard by a rainstorm. You can guess the rest.

Ernie (Don Calfa) and Spider (Miguel Nunez) lean in close – but not *too* close – to hear a secret from the half of a zombie woman. *Orion/The Kobal Collection*

"SEND...MORE...PARAMEDICS."

– A ZOMBIE

Return of the Living Dead breaks most of the rules of zombie movies, especially the part about a shot to the head taking them down, yet adds to the zombie knowledge base by creating a new type that would later be duplicated in films down the road. Romero brought zombies out of the voodoo realm and into normal life, and the creators of *Return of the Living Dead* give them speech and a finicky appetite. Finicky, you ask? Well, not just any human flesh will do for these zombies. They crave BRAAAIIINNSSS!

28 Days Later

RELEASE June 27, 2003 (U.S.)
DIRECTED BY Danny Boyle
WRITTEN BY Alex Garland
STARRING Cillian Murphy, Naomie Harris, Brendan Gleeson, Megan Burns, Christopher Eccleston
RATING R, for violence/gore, language, nudity

British film *28 Days Later* features the "not-a-zombie" style of zombies in an apocalyptic tale of infection, quarantine, and potential end of days.

Bicycle courier Jim (Cillian Murphy) awakens in a hospital 28 days after a serious accident left him in a coma. He pushes his call button but nobody answers, and finally he pulls the needles and tubes out of his body and ventures out to investigate.

The hospital is empty, littered with debris and bedpans. When Jim goes outside, he finds that there are no people anywhere and the streets are filled with crashed cars, broken glass, and bloody smears. In the 28 days that Jim was in a coma, he discovers, a virus has overtaken London (possibly the world) and reduces the citizens to mindless and vicious killers; not-a-zombie zombies, to be exact.

28 Days Later is one of the best horror films released in its time period, and the cause for distinction between zombie movies and "not-a-zombie" zombie movies. The "infected," you see, behave in a similar way to traditional running zombies and a bite from them brings on the infection, and a transformation into a hungry creature. The creatures are not easily killed without a gunshot to the head and seem to operate on an instinctive level, seeking only to bite and dismember the living.

A running zombie, right? A zombie, no. These creatures do not die and reanimate, but rather simply become infected by a virus. This is the distinction. It is theoretically possible that the infected in *28 Days Later* can be cured of the virus and return to normal, something not possible with a zombie since the zombie is already dead. If you're dead, there's no recovery, virus or not.

Shadowy figures descend upon a group of people temporarily trapped in a tunnel in *28 Days Later*. *DNA/Figment/Fox/The Kobal Collection/Peter Mountain*

"OH, GREAT. VALIUM. NOT ONLY WILL WE BE ABLE TO GO TO SLEEP, IF WE GET ATTACKED IN THE MIDDLE OF THE NIGHT, WE WON'T EVEN CARE." - *JIM*

The category of "not-a-zombie" zombies was created possibly by The Zombie Master Everett Roberts, one of the panel members for this book, as he's the first I'd heard mention the term, to combat the common belief that *28 Days Later* and films like it are zombie movies, which technically they are not. The creatures do, however, behave enough like traditional zombies to be included in zombie film discussion, with appropriate qualifiers of course. Hence a new category of zombies is born, and Horror Movie Freaks are in the know. Use your knowledge wisely, young Freaks, and take every opportunity to spread this knowledge so that it can do some good by educating the average horror viewing public.

MOTEL HELL

It takes all kinds of critters
to make Farmer Vincent Fritters

You might
just die...
laughing!

"MOTEL HELL" starring RORY CALHOUN PAUL LINKE NANCY PARSONS NINA AXELROD
and WOLFMAN JACK produced by STEVEN-CHARLES JAFFE and ROBERT JAFFE
executive producer HERB JAFFE written by ROBERT JAFFE and STEVEN-CHARLES JAFFE
directed by KEVIN CONNOR music by LANCE RUBIN

R RESTRICTED UNDER 17 REQUIRES ACCOMPANYING PARENT OR ADULT GUARDIAN

ENTER THE SECRET GARDEN IN DOLBY STEREO IN SELECTED THEATRES

United Artists
A Transamerica Company

800105

"MOTEL HELL"

Weary travelers who check in at *Motel Hell* - don't check out. *Camp Hill/United Artists*

Honorable Mention

The horror genre includes a collection of terror that is considered "must see" to appreciate what it has to offer.

These are the films that come up in conversation with other Horror Freaks, as well as the novice, and can generally be discussed openly in mixed company.

"Oh, you like horror. What's your favorite horror movie?" Nary has a Freak avoided hearing this question, perhaps several times every year.

To avoid complete excommunication from your social group or termination of employment, we typically answer with a film that we really like and that will likely also be recognized by the questioner. Well, at least that is how a "horror movie fan" might answer.

The true Horror Movie Freak may have different ideas. Somewhere off the beaten path lie the movies that bring a definite distinction between the casual fan and the aficionado.

Be they campy cult classics, banned horror, notable remakes, or from a list of early cheese by your favorite scream queen, the honorable mention horror will certainly set you apart from the huddled masses eagerly awaiting the next Hollywood studio release.

Campy Fun

Why so serious all the time? Horror movies should be scary, sure...but sometimes they just need to be fun. Goofy lines, memorable characters, and outlandish kills can elevate a horror movie from supermarket bargain-bin status to true cult classic. To be fair, just because a film is in the bargain bin doesn't automatically mean it's NOT a cult classic, and those you can't buy at Safeway for $.99 shouldn't take that fact as a testament to quality. But still.

It takes a certain kind of Horror Movie Freak to cotton to the campiest and cheesiest of the movie universe, and even then not every cheese-fest will qualify. There is a big difference, after all, between corny, cheesy hilarity and just plain stupid. The trouble is, it's impossible to get any two Horror Freaks to agree on which film qualifies as which. Some films, however, have risen above their inherent badness to gain significant followings among Freaks. Midnight showings, box sets, and independent fan sites spring up seemingly out of nowhere touting the thrill of a 20-year-old film that nobody has ever heard of...that's how you know.

Dive into the Cheese-o-Matic, and bring your boots. After all, nobody likes to go "camping" without taking an occasional day hike. Ouch.

In the cult classic *Army of Darkness,* Ash (Bruce Campbell) once again finds himself fighting the forces of the undead, but this time in 1300 AD.
Dino De Laurentiis Co./Universal Pictures

Motel Hell

RELEASE October 18, 1980 (U.S.)
DIRECTED BY Kevin Connor
WRITTEN BY Robert Jaffe and Steven-Charles Jaffe
STARRING Rory Calhoun, Paul Linke, Nancy Parsons, Nina Axelrod, Wolfman Jack
RATING R, for graphic human harvesting, profanity, some nudity

Holy moly, *Motel Hell*! How does it get its smoked meats so tasty and tender?

The story surrounds a farmer and his sister who run a farm and motel. The name is "Motel Hello," but the neon "o" repeatedly flickers on and off. It's appropriate.

The duo is known for the tastiest and tenderest smoked meats for a hundred miles. What is the secret? Well, let's just say that there is also a VERY high missing persons' rate in these parts.

If you haven't seen *Motel Hell*, be forewarned: this is extremely campy and ultra unserious. The farmers are completely over the top for such a horrifying concept. This is the kind of film that will bring older Horror Movie Freaks back to the days when, once cartoons were over on TV, the horror movie of the week would start playing. I think this one was on a high rotation.

There are some good scenes that will stick with you for quite a while, especially the ones associated with the "garden." Using human meat alone is not enough to make your meat the very best, however; it has to be "tenderized" in a way that will truly leave your visitors wanting more.

Ida (Nancy Parsons) decides Terry (Nina Axelrod) is ripe for harvesting from the garden.
Camp Hill/United Artists/The Kobal Collection

"THERE'S TOO MANY PEOPLE IN THE WORLD AND NOT ENOUGH FOOD. NOW THIS TAKES CARE OF BOTH PROBLEMS AT THE SAME TIME."
- *VINCENT SMITH*

Motel Hell is crazy and it might be hard to call it a cult classic, so let's just call it cult. You will be hard pressed, however, to find many Horror Movie Freaks who have not seen this one. It is just one of those films everyone seems to be familiar with somehow. The best way to describe *Motel Hell* is "guilty pleasure"—every Horror Freak has one, and there is a likelihood this is it. By the way, ask expert panelist for this book, The Zombie Master, about his guilty pleasure *Zombie Lake*. That one makes *Motel Hell* look like Citizen Kane.

Sleepaway Camp

RELEASE November 18, 1983 (U.S. limited)
WRITTEN AND DIRECTED BY Robert Hiltzik
STARRING Felissa Rose, Jonathan Tierston, Karen Fields, Christopher Collet, Mike Kellin
RATING R, for violence/gore, profanity, brief nudity

OK Horror Movie Freaks, here we go. *Sleepaway Camp*. This one is campy cheese, though not as much as the sequels that followed. What will get you about this one is the surprise ending.

Little Angela (Felissa Rose) has had a rough life. One day she is happily playing with her brother and father at a lovely outing at the lake, and the next, a wayward boat slams into her family members, killing them both. She is forced to go live with her extremely bizarre aunt and cousin Ricky (Jonathan Tierston), and then gets sent to summer camp.

People are not nice to Angela at summer camp, especially the mean girl Judy (Karen Fields). The fact that Angela doesn't utter a word doesn't help matters. Then, one by one, everyone who is mean to Angela ends up dead in very creative and disgusting ways. Who's doing it?

Sleepaway Camp is the cult classic to beat all cult classics. There are Web sites, articles, commentary—and Felissa Rose has become quite a celebrity based primarily on this film. What is it about *Sleepaway Camp* that keeps it top of mind for Horror Movie Freaks after all these years? Is it the dolphin shorts that the male camp counselor wears? Is it the cook that has a "thing" for young girls? Perhaps it is because so many people who are bad in some way meet such satisfying fates.

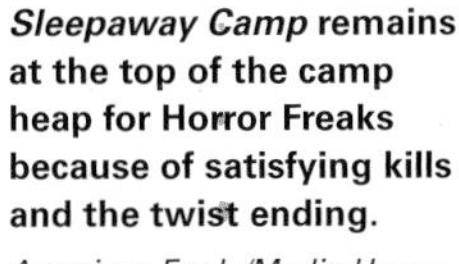

***Sleepaway Camp* remains at the top of the camp heap for Horror Freaks because of satisfying kills and the twist ending.**
American Eagle/Media Home Entertainment

"IF SHE WERE ANY QUIETER, SHE'D BE DEAD!"
– *MEG, REFERRING TO ANGELA*

All of those things exist, but they are not the main reasons. The surprise twist at the end is the clincher. If you haven't seen *Sleepaway Camp* already, don't let anyone tell you the end, and don't go looking for the answer, as you will surely find it. Treat yourself to the shock value. If you have seen it, please do not give it away to those who haven't. Just have them over for movie night and show this film. Make sure there are LOTS of adult beverages available (if you're of age, of course…) and settle in for a quite shocking and disturbing ride.

The sequels are fun and also campy and have some extremely creative kills as well. Go ahead and watch those if you like (they star Bruce Springsteen's sister instead of Felissa) but see the original first. Oh, and there is a pretty recent sequel as well that has cameos from many from the first film, including Ms. Rose. Pay homage to *Sleepaway Camp*. Any self-respecting Horror Movie Freak would.

Night of the Comet

RELEASE November 16, 1984 (U.S.)
WRITTEN AND DIRECTED BY Thom Eberhardt
STARRING Robert Beltran, Catherine Mary Stewart, Kelli Maroney, Sharon Farrell
RATING PG-13, for some graphic images, violence, some sensuality, language

As far as cheesy horror movies go, *Night of the Comet* is the Mac and Cheesiest. Big '80s hair, cheerleader zombie killers, and sinister piles of red dust are what's in store.

Regina (Catherine Mary Stewart) and Samantha (Kelli Maroney) are sisters who hate each other with all the love that only sisters can muster. They also hate their dorky stepmother Doris and find a way to be as far away from the house as possible when she has her big party to celebrate the passing of a rogue comet. The earth passed through the tail of this comet once before, about 65 million years ago. Just about the time the dinosaurs became extinct. What a strange coincidence…

Well, the comet passes and every living thing exposed to the air is reduced to piles of dust. Those who got only minimal exposure are zombies. There is almost nobody left at all, except of course for Regina and Sam. They do what anyone would do in such a circumstance—seek out a radio station, kill zombies with their impressive firearms skills, and go shopping. But will they be saved?

There really isn't any "horror" to speak of in *Night of the Comet*, but there are zombies. This is cheese-o-matic that is fun to watch. The vision of two girls with huge hair-dos, one of whom is still in her cheerleader outfit, taking target practice on zombie heads with guns their military father taught them to use is almost too much to take.

Teenage Mutant Horror Comet Zombies **was the original working title for this movie.**
Film Development Fund/The Kobal Collection

The plot thickens beyond the shopping, but it all is one great spoof of the government, comet scares, traditional sexual norms of the 1980s, and just about anything else these filmmakers can get their hands on. Great weekend film and a cult classic in its own right, that's *Night of the Comet.*

"YOU MAY AS WELL FACE THE FACTS, SAMANTHA. THE WHOLE BURDEN OF CIVILIZATION HAS FALLEN UPON US." - *REGINA BELMONT*

Puppet Master

RELEASE Oct. 12, 1989 (U.S. video premier)
DIRECTED BY David Schmoeller
WRITTEN BY Charles Band, Kenneth J. Hall, Joseph G. Collodi
STARRING Paul Le Mat, William Hickey, Irene Miracle, Jimmie F. Skaggs, Robin Frates
RATING R, for violence/gore caused by little puppets, profanity, brief nudity/sexuality

Puppet Master is considered campy, but I must admit—it scared the heck out of me!

The story begins with an old puppet maker working on his crafts; the finishing touch is an ancient Egyptian spell he learned that brings his puppets to life. These puppets are his only friends it seems and he keeps them all around him in his workshop.

"I'M TIRED OF EXPERIMENTING WITH SILLY PUPPETS."
- NEIL GALLAGHER

This movie will make you believe little puppets aren't as harmless as they may look.
Full Moon Productions/The Kobal Collection

One day the Nazis come looking for him, presumably to learn his secret of animating the wooden figures. The puppet master puts all of them into a big crate and hides it in the wall of his workshop—and then puts a bullet in his head. The Nazis will not have this power.

Years later, an heir of the puppet master gains the workshop, now part of a hotel, and hires a group of psychics to find his secrets. The puppets, unfortunately for all involved, are not about to cooperate.

Most people think this movie is cheesy, as I found out when going through the process with the expert panel to choose which movies we would include. One of the reasons is that the killer puppets are little, like a foot tall. What's so scary about that? Well, personally, they creeped me out completely, and *I* thought it was scary. One female doll even chokes up some kind of leech thing that kills people and it's completely gross.

On the cheese front, though, nobody just kicks over the dolls and runs away, and, like I said, they are only about one foot tall. There is also one that happens to have a working drill for a hat, so cheese it is—I just didn't realize it when I watched this film for the first five times. I will leave this up to Horror Movie Freaks to judge if this is cheese or horror.

The People Under the Stairs

RELEASE November 1, 1991 (U.S.)
WRITTEN AND DIRECTED BY Wes Craven
STARRING Brandon Adams, Everett McGill, Wendy Robie, A.J. Langer, Ving Rhames
RATING R, for terror and violence

The Stairmaster (Yan Birch) has been living in the cellar too long.
Universal/The Kobal Collection

The People Under the Stairs has the right mix of camp, weirdness, and suspense to actually be a worthy addition to any Horror Freak's library.

Fool (Brandon Adams) is a child from the projects, being tutored by his brother on being a thief. Fool's kind heart makes him a pretty shaky scofflaw, but he gives it his best shot.

When Fool's family finds they will be evicted from their shabby apartment, he sets out with some other miscreants to rob the house of the brother and sister who own their apartment building and see if they can steal enough to find a better place to live. What they find, however, is a whacked-out couple with dozens of secrets hiding in the basement.

This film is notable for a lot of reasons. First, it actually has some suspenseful and scary moments in spite of its camp. The basement is full of scary moments, in fact. The landlords are completely and totally over the top—like black leather and whips over the top. The level of their dementia is absurd and makes for some very entertaining moments. The little boy "Roach" is pretty great, too.

ALICE: CAN'T GET OUT. NO ONE EVER HAS.
FOOL: WELL, I'M GONNA GET OUT. I'M A WHOLE OTHER THING.

The level of social commentary in this film is high, but the execution of it is interesting. There is a spotlight on racial inequity in the inner city here that would be tiresome if it weren't so hilarious; it is portrayed through many stereotypes and expletives. Today, everyone is much too "sensitive" to use such methods, no matter how important you might feel the message to be.

This isn't a complete "message film" though; it is a campy and cheesy horror movie that is so outrageous that it's hilarious, and the fact that everyone seems to be acting as if this isn't a comedy makes it all the better. Horror Movie Freaks are familiar with Wes Craven at this point, the writer and director of this film, but this is different than most he's created. Not horrifying, not really funny on purpose, but just right.

Super Sequels

The sequel is often the unwanted step-child of the original movie that inspired it.

Sometimes, however, the sequel can stand on its own merit, occasionally even surpassing the original in terms of popularity and enjoyment. This stands true in our favorite genre as well.

The super sequels that follow are examples of those films that successfully beat the odds and actually aren't terrible.

Some succeed because they continue the story of their predecessor smoothly and believably. Others are included because conventional thought surmises that any sequel will be "bad news," yet they won over the critics delivering a quality tale. Still others may actually improve upon the theme presented in the original film.

I am not going to tell you which one is an example of which success factor, mainly because you won't agree with me anyway.

Suffice it to say that sequels aren't always bad, and sometimes become "super sequels." Knowing which ones are worth a watch and which are mindless drivel is one way that the Horror Movie Freak rises above the casual fan.

Someone is newly infected and HUNGRY in *28 Weeks Later.* *Fox Atomic, a subsidiary of 20th Century-Fox Film Corporation*

Billy, a tricycle-riding, tuxedo-clad puppet, is a frightening face from the *Saw* movies. Here he is on his way to deliver a message to a victim in *Saw II.*

Twisted Pictures/The Kobal Collection

Aliens

RELEASE July 18, 1986 (U.S.)
DIRECTED BY James Cameron
WRITTEN BY James Cameron, David Giler, Walter Hill, Dan O'Bannon, Ronald Shusett
STARRING Sigourney Weaver, Carrie Henn, Michael Biehn, Lance Henriksen, Paul Reiser
RATING R, for violence, profanity

Aliens is the follow up to the horror masterpiece *Alien* and commits a cardinal sin that leads many horror sequels straight to the bargain bin: bringing in the military. Fortunately this time, though, it works out well.

Ellen Ripley (Sigourney Weaver), the sole survivor of the encounter with the alien in *Alien*, is discovered and awakened after drifting in space for 57 years in hypersleep. After a grueling interrogation and fending off accusations of irresponsibility for damage to her prior cargo ship, she is approached to consult a military operation. It seems that, much to Ripley's dismay, the planet, which bore the alien from her prior encounter, has been colonized and suddenly the people there are not responding to radio communication.

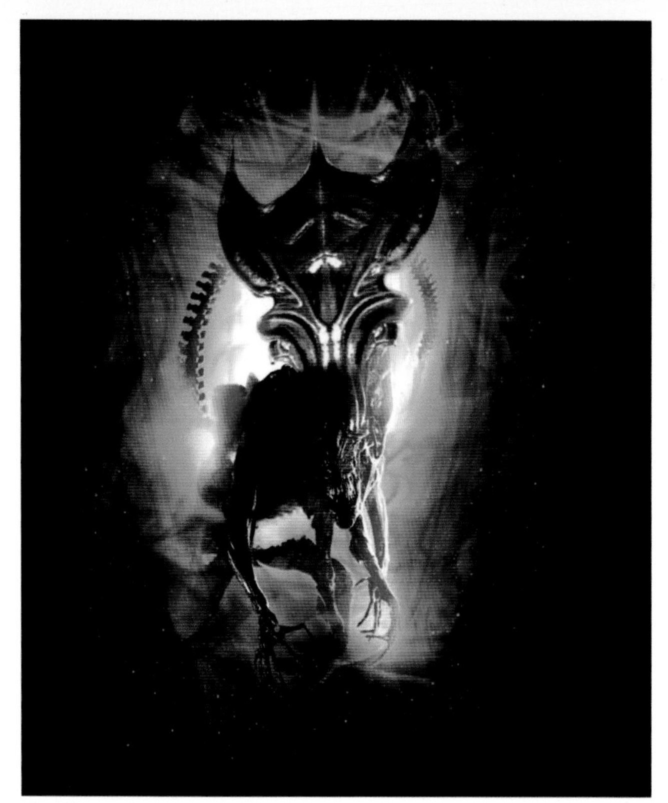

An *Aliens* publicity poster created for use in theaters and venues in the U.S. To bring the alien queen to life in the movie, it took 14 to 16 operators. *20th Century Fox*

The military platoon, along with Ripley, embarks on the journey back to the planet, but this time they encounter not one, but an entire pack of the alien beasts, as well as covert activity by representatives of "the company" that threatens to kill them all, as well as destroy earth.

There is debate among Horror Movie Freaks surrounding *Aliens*. One camp applauds this sequel as a fantastic extension of the original story that continues many of the human themes that make the first film so compelling and allows Ripley to continue developing into an alien-fighting machine. The other camp, however, resents the injection of action/adventure into the equation of horror feeling that the slasher-esque nature of the alien is lost when it becomes one big group of space creatures fighting a team of well-armed military personnel.

Although each side has good points, there are additional considerations that elevate *Aliens* beyond just a good sequel and actually make this film a horror classic in its own right. One is the development of Ripley as a bona fide horror movie heroine—not just a gun-toting bad ass, but a thoughtful, vulnerable woman who rises to the occasion when faced by unspeakable terror. Another is the concept of man as horror villain. The direct villains are, of course, the aliens, but horror movies that also address the evil lurking in a man's heart when faced with the unimaginable have a depth beyond just showing how well the killer kills. It is the human aspect that really makes *Aliens* shine, and that kind of horror can be rare indeed.

Great and vicious monsters, colorful heroes, memorable and quotable lines, and the evil of human greed come together to create a film that Horror Freaks will enjoy both as a sequel, and as a stand alone.

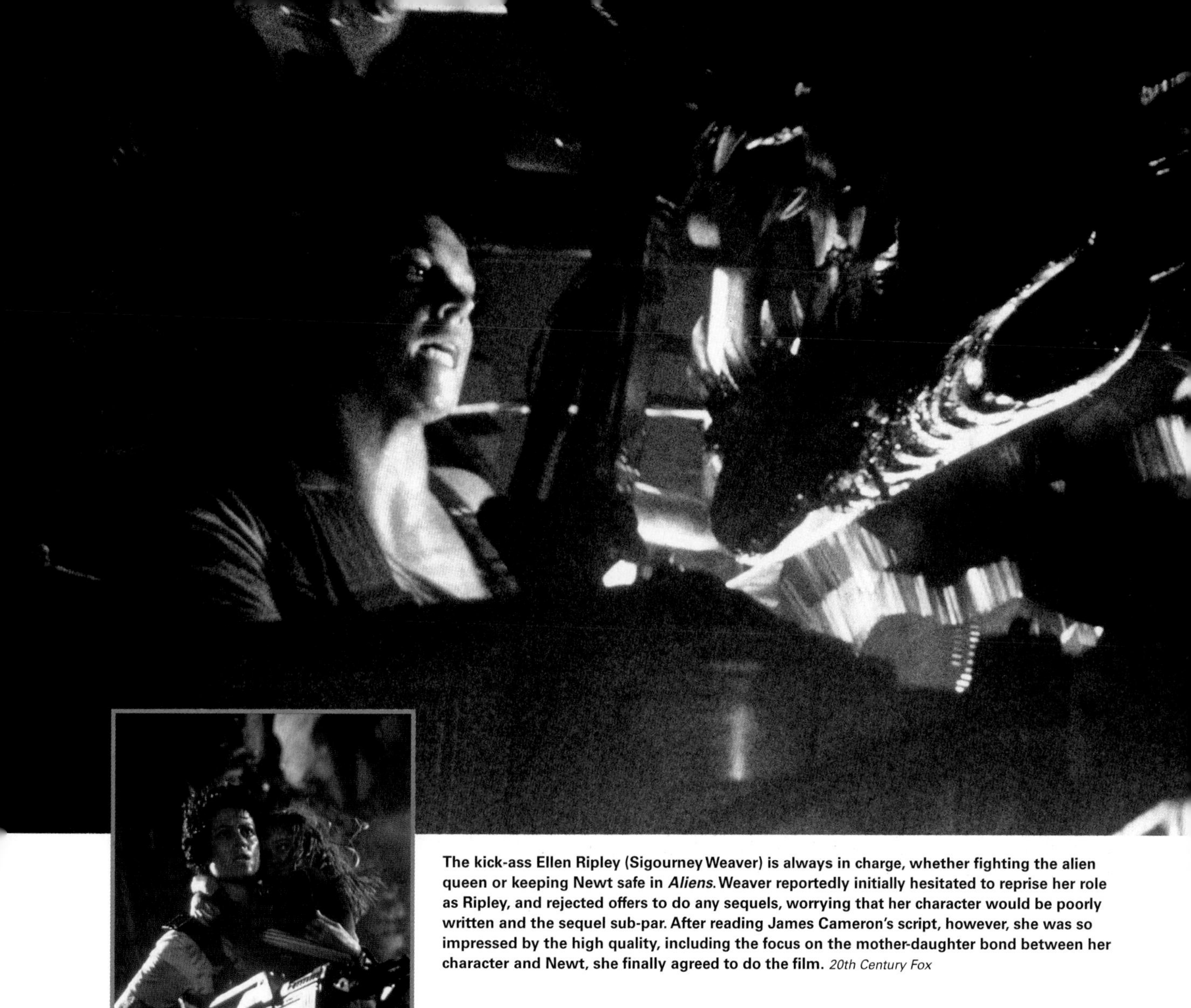

The kick-ass Ellen Ripley (Sigourney Weaver) is always in charge, whether fighting the alien queen or keeping Newt safe in *Aliens.* Weaver reportedly initially hesitated to reprise her role as Ripley, and rejected offers to do any sequels, worrying that her character would be poorly written and the sequel sub-par. After reading James Cameron's script, however, she was so impressed by the high quality, including the focus on the mother-daughter bond between her character and Newt, she finally agreed to do the film. *20th Century Fox*

NEWT: MY MOMMY ALWAYS SAID THERE WERE NO MONSTERS - NO REAL ONES - BUT THERE ARE.
RIPLEY: YES, THERE ARE, AREN'T THERE?

Sheila (Embeth Davidtz) finds herself in the scaly, evil clutches of a Deadite from *Army of Darkness*. *Dino De Laurentiis/Universal Pictures*

ARTHUR: ARE ALL MEN FROM THE FUTURE LOUD-MOUTHED BRAGGARTS?
ASH: NOPE. JUST ME, BABY...JUST ME.

Army of Darkness

RELEASE February 19, 1993 (U.S.)
DIRECTED BY Sam Raimi
WRITTEN BY Sam Raimi and Ivan Raimi
STARRING Bruce Campbell, Embeth Davidtz, Marcus Gilbert, Ian Abercrombie
RATING R, for violence and terror, although it's done with a heavy dose of humor

---

Army of Darkness, sometimes known as *Evil Dead 3*, is a sequel to the original *The Evil Dead* in regard to characters, not content.

Army of Darkness begins with a flashback to *Evil Dead 2* and a treatment of the *Necronomicon*, or book of the dead. This gives a bit of explanation as to why Ash (Bruce Campbell) has been transported into the middle ages and now must find the book and use an incantation within it to get back home.

Unfortunately for Ash, he inadvertently unleashes the Deadites and must lead the humans to conquer the evil threat.

Army of Darkness is pure camp and one of the funniest movies ever. It is a little strange to see Ash Williams in his medieval surroundings, but add in his goofy heroic posturing and a ton of Deadites roaming around, and this film works as a new action hero emerges.

There is no horror here really, but because of the witches, zombies, and other monsters, along with the fact that this is a sequel to films classified as horror, *Army of Darkness* falls in our patch.

There was a good deal of box office success for this film, but it is really the Horror Movie Freaks who keep the cult status alive. In fact, you would be hard pressed to find anyone at a horror convention who can't quote at least half of this movie from memory.

Campbell has not had enormous success outside of his role as Ash, but from the perspective of Horror Freaks, that's OK. We like him just as he is—the goofy and sometimes dumb-as-a-post victim, hero, and sometimes super-hero.

Now, whether Campbell himself would agree is another story…

Ash (Bruce Campbell) impresses the crowd with his "boom stick."
Dino De Laurentiis/ Universal Pictures

Scream 2

RELEASE December 10, 1997 (U.S. premier)

DIRECTED BY Wes Craven

WRITTEN BY Kevin Williamson

STARRING Neve Campbell, Liev Schreiber, Jerry O'Connell, Courteney Cox, David Arquette

RATING R, for bloody violence, language

Scream is notable because of its impact on revitalizing the horror genre in a time when theatrical horror releases were a bit thin. *Scream 2* plays as a second installment in a weekly serial.

Poor Sydney Prescott (Neve Campbell). After surviving the killer in the first *Scream*, her torment has been made public in a feature film titled *Stab*, based on the book by Gale Weathers (Courtney Cox) chronicling the previous murders.

To make matters worse, Sydney's ultimate fear has been realized: Tori Spelling is playing her in the movie.

The murders are not over yet, though, as people around Sydney begin to die again. The previous characters from *Scream* who didn't die reconvene and attempt to discover the killer's identity without becoming the latest victim.

Scream 2 is straight sequel in the most literal sense of the word. Nothing new is added to the storyline to speak of; the story just continues similar to the next installment of a mini-series would.

This works just fine in this case. All of the formula elements that worked the first time around are repeated including the A-List cameo (this time Jada Pinkett after Drew Barrymore in the first *Scream*), reminders of the "rules for survival in a horror movie" and the typical "whodunit" themes.

Omar Epps and Jada Pinkett Smith make a brief cameo in *Scream 2.* The killer's comments Epps' character overhears in the bathroom stall next to him are directly inspired by the killer in 1974's *Black Christmas.*

Dimension Films/The Kobal Collection/Kimberly Wright

Let's face it, *Scream* was not "deep" and *Scream 2* should not try to be either. These films are straight-ahead slasher fare that pull off the subgenre better than most. There is also a *Scream 3*, and there are actually a few surprises in that one. This film was destined to be the second in a trilogy from the start, and all three can be watched in a row for a good night of low-thought horror.

Sometimes that's all the Horror Movie Freak wants—a bit of escape from reality, some good scares and stupidity being punished by a knife through the skull. In the case of *Scream 2*, that's gonna have to be enough.

"OH PLEASE! BY DEFINITION ALONE, SEQUELS ARE INFERIOR FILMS!" - *RANDY*

Saw 2

RELEASE October 28, 2005 (U.S.)
DIRECTED BY Darren Lynn Bousman
WRITTEN BY Darren Lynn Bousman and Leigh Whannell
STARRING Tobin Bell, Shawnee Smith, Donnie Wahlberg, Erik Knudsen, Franky G
RATING R, for grisly violence/gore, terror, profanity

To say Jigsaw traps this potential victim is quite the understatement.
Twisted Pictures/The Kobal Collection

The original *Saw* introduced Horror Movie Freaks to the Jigsaw killer (Tobin Bell) and the ingenious ways he teaches society's miscreants to appreciate their own lives. *Saw 2* gets even more into the mind of the killer, who seems to believe his murderous mayhem is actually a social good.

The lair of the Jigsaw killer is found, and along with it a set of monitors showing a group of people trapped in a house that is slowly filling with a deadly nerve gas. Detective Matthews (Donnie Wahlberg) from the first *Saw* is shocked to learn that his son is one of those trapped in the deadly house, along with Amanda (Shawnee Smith), the only known survivor from the first *Saw*. As a highly intricate chain of events unfolds, Matthews tries to find the location of the trapped victims while keeping Jigsaw from pulling the trigger and killing them all.

The first *Saw* brought an original killer and some killing methods designed to give victims the option to survive their ordeals if they only take certain actions that prove to Jigsaw and themselves that they have an appropriately strong will to live. *Saw 2* takes this concept a step further.

The detail orientation of Jigsaw and his ability to anticipate actions of his intended victims and cover all contingencies is laid out in *Saw 2*, as well as the complex way each individual's "test" hinges on the actions and testing of others in a multi-faceted scenario. In many cases, the simple act of following verbal instructions is all that is needed to survive a Jigsaw test, but it is clear from the beginning that nobody is going to just sit there and let things happen to them without trying to figure a way out.

Saw 2 is an effective sequel because it does such a good job fleshing out one of the newest and most compelling horror movie villains in Jigsaw and gives brief windows into both his motivations and the extreme attention to detail inherent in the tests inflicted on his victims. The shock value of plot twists and turns is high in this film with dramatic "ah-ha" moments and scenarios that make perfect sense when revealed, without telegraphing them for early guessing. Horror Movie Freaks will enjoy the unique nature Jigsaw and learning the scope of his "educational tests" in *Saw* and *Saw 2*. The sequels following *Saw 2* do, however, become a bit more of the same. Once the dramatic twists become commonplace, there are not a lot of other places to go, so stick with the first two and see additional sequels at your discretion.

"THOSE WHO DO NOT APPRECIATE LIFE DO NOT DESERVE LIFE."
- JOHN

28 Weeks Later

RELEASE May 11, 2007 (U.S.)
DIRECTED BY Juan Carlos Fresnadillo
WRITTEN BY Juan Carlos Fresnadillo, Rowan Joffe, E.L. Lavigne, Jesus Olmo
STARRING Robert Carlyle, Catherine McCormack, Rose Byrne, Jeremy Renner, Harold Perrineau
RATING R, for strong violence/gore, language, some sexuality/nudity

28 Weeks Later is an excellent continuation of its predecessor *28 Days Later* and one of those rare sequels that releases with high hopes and doesn't let Horror Freaks down.

The conclusion of *28 Days Later* leaves a gloomy picture of a global apocalypse, brought on by a viral infection that turns the entire population of the U.K., and possibly the world, into violent creatures reminiscent of zombies. In the beginning scenes of the sequel, however, we learn it is not all that bad. It seems that the infection was contained in Britain and eventually all of the infected starved to death. Repopulation of the area is now safe.

Led by NATO forces and the United States military, old and new residents are admitted to Britain and the country begins anew…until a rogue survivor becomes infected and starts the whole thing again. The area goes into lockdown and one family becomes trapped inside the newly festering "not-a-zombie" zombie hellhole.

"ABANDON SELECTIVE TARGETING. SHOOT EVERYTHING. TARGETS ARE NOW FREE. WE'VE LOST CONTROL."

- STONE

In *28 Weeks Later*, there is no escape from the hungry infected.
Fox Atomic, a subsidiary of 20th Century-Fox Film Corp.

After the surprise success of *28 Days Later* and the subsequent worldwide release and overwhelming acceptance and praise, a sequel was both inevitable and feared. Inevitable because a huge box office draw, especially one that leaves room for continuation of the story, just about always spawns a sequel, as money talks. Feared because part of the allure of the original film is its gritty nature and lack of big studio "polish," lending a tone of realism and despair to the whole experience. Once a franchise gets some money behind it, a slick look chock full of CGI and effects is often the result, thereby killing every element that made the original unique. Bigger budget does not automatically equal better film; in fact, the contrary is often the case when the original has to make up for budgetary lacking with ingenuity and creativity.

28 Weeks Later avoids these pitfalls and retains many of the elements that made the first one great. This film also focuses appropriately on the uninfected survivors and the terror of their ordeal more than relying exclusively on the shock factor of the scary monsters. Add to the equation a world of governments that will do anything to avoid the extinction of the entire human race, and you've got drama…and horror. Just what the Horror Movie Freak ordered.

Banned!

That's just not right! How outrageous, how politically incorrect, how disturbing and graphic! Horror movies, by nature, "push the envelope" of polite society, but some head directly over the top in an effort to shock and offend. What is the result of this courageous filmmaking? The film is banned!

There are many methods used to censor and ban horror movies deemed lacking in social value by critics, governments, organizations, moralists and rating bodies. The most common in the United States is via the Motion Picture Association of America (MPAA) rating system, which rates films based on content and themes in the context of suitability for children. While not officially "banned," a horror film garnering a rating of NC-17 has no chance of wide release and is effectively dead in the water. In other words, it's banned. Sometimes films are prevented from release by pressures of consumer groups, political action committees, social organizations, and religious concerns. There are not generally enforcement "teeth" in these methods, but the threat of a boycott or other economic attack may motivate some to honor the request and refuse screening or distributing a film.

Other methods may be more direct and can be quite common in various countries. Great Britain, for example, had specific legislation that resulted in state-ordered banning of several horror films pegged as "video nasties." Other countries have lists denoting horror movies that are unsuitable for their citizens. In the eyes of the Horror Movie Freak, a banning can often intensify the desire to watch a film, or at least make us aware of the existence of an otherwise unknown one. I don't think that's what people have in mind when they choose to ban them.

Banning does not automatically make a movie desirable. It just adds to the mystique, and there are some worth a look. As a Freak, it is important to have a cursory knowledge of at least a few, and the ones that follow will start you down the right path.

The MPAA originally slapped *Last House on the Left* with an X rating. Despite director Wes Craven editing sizeable chunks out of the movie on two different occasions, the MPAA still gave it an X. Craven finally put all of the original footage back in and got the R-rated approval from the film board from a friend of his, put it on the film, and released it. *Sean S. Cunningham Films*

Freaks

RELEASE February 20, 1932 (U.S.)
DIRECTED BY Tod Browning
WRITTEN BY Tod Robbins
STARRING: Harry Earles, Olga Baclanova, Wallace Ford, Leila Hyams, Rosco Ates
NOT RATED Has some images that may be disturbing

Once a beautiful trapeze artist, Cleopatra (Olga Baclanova) is eventually transformed into a chicken lady. *Metro-Goldwyn-Mayer*

Freaks suffered controversy from the start. Even after extensive scene cuts, it was banned in some countries and halted the career of the great director Tod Browning.

The setting for *Freaks* is a circus sideshow and the performers, each of whom has some kind of oddity, help draw crowds. Midgets, bearded ladies, and deformed folks make up this crew and one of their own is set to marry the circus trapeze artist in spite of the fact that she is "normal."

After the wedding, it becomes clear to all the performers that Cleopatra (Olga Baclanova), the trapeze artist, only married the sideshow midget Hans (Harry Earles) because he has a large inheritance. A sinister plot to murder Hans unfolds and the performers band together to protect their friend and deliver some justice of their own.

The controversy surrounding *Freaks* is motivated by the fact that Browning chose to use actual sideshow performers with various physical abnormalities in the film instead of simply achieving his desired effect with costumes and makeup. The result of this dose of realism was a disastrous initial opening that even had one audience member threaten a lawsuit claiming that the film had caused her to have a miscarriage. The film was then cut severely with several of the most dramatic and disturbing scenes lost forever. The edited version didn't fare much better and Browning, known for directing Universal's *Dracula* with Bela Lugosi, had trouble finding work after this film's release. *Freaks* was banned in Britain for years.

Today *Freaks* has a significant cult following and is readily available in its post-cut form with a run time of 64 minutes. Considering the original length of 90 minutes, only 71 percent of the film remains. Still, *Freaks* is disturbing as the oddities cast are indeed odd, some of them extremely so. Horror Movie Freaks should certainly be familiar with this film, both for its banned and cult status, as well as the fact that it is primarily responsible for the early retirement of the director who brought us one of the most enduring horror movie classics of all time, *Dracula.* Interesting how fickle the movie-going public can be and how taking a filmmaking risk seems to have equal chance of moving a director to hero…or zero.

> "WE ACCEPT YOU, ONE OF US! GOOBLE GOBBLE!" - *FREAKS*

Think about *Freaks* and the effect the film had the next time you complain about a lack of originality in horror movies. There is always a fine line and to cross it can be a horror filmmaker's one-way ticket to oblivion.

The "freaks" enjoying dinner together. Author F. Scott Fitzgerald, a member of the MGM writing department at the time this movie was in production, didn't quite feel at home with all the movie stars and powerful moguls, so he often dined with the sideshow attractions during his lunch hour. *Metro-Goldwyn-Mayer*

Last House on the Left

RELEASE August 30, 1972 (U.S.)
WRITTEN AND DIRECTED BY Wes Craven
STARRING Sandra Cassel, Lucy Grantham, David A. Hess, Fred Lincoln, Jeramie Rain
RATING R, for brutal and disturbing scenes of rape and violence, and sexuality, nudity, language

ESTELLE COLLINGWOOD: I THINK IT'S CRAZY.
MARI: WHAT'S CRAZY?
ESTELLE COLLINGWOOD: ALL THAT BLOOD AND VIOLENCE. I THOUGHT YOU WERE SUPPOSED TO BE THE LOVE GENERATION.

Considering the wide acceptance of Wes Craven as a horror movie director and writer, it is hard to believe his first feature film gained the dreaded "video nasty" designation.

Mari Collingwood (Sandra Cassel) is at the family vacation house with her parents and decides to celebrate her 17th birthday by going to a concert with her wild friend Phyllis (Lucy Grantham). Mari's parents don't like Phyllis or her low-class ways, but agree to let her go anyway.

The brutally sadistic Krug Stillo (David A. Hess).
Sean S. Cunningham Films/The Kobal Collection

Phyllis causes more trouble than she is worth when she goes on a quest for drugs and draws Mari into danger at the hands of escaped convict Krug (David A. Hess) and his band of outlaws. After Krug violently assaults and kills the girls, the crew has car trouble and happens upon, ironically, Mari's parents house. The sparks start to fly when Mari's parents realize the nature of those now staying in their house and decide to get revenge for the crimes against their daughter.

The Last House on the Left is consistent with several of Craven's other early works, which are wrought with violence and cruelty. This film, though, is more sadistic and violent than any later films when it comes to rape and torture. There was controversy surrounding the release from the beginning, due primarily to the violent rape scenes and the exploitation and victimization of women. It has been reported that the final version was actually softer than originally intended, so it is difficult to imagine the trouble the film would have had with censors had it been completed as originally conceived.

Even though the film was banned in Britain, a cult following developed and some now consider *Last House on the Left* to be an important film for the period with realistic commentary on the plight of women at the hands of abusive and violent men. The concept of familial retribution being handed out is certainly a nice touch.

A 2009 remake of *The Last House on the Left* does not have nearly the impact of the original, but Horror Movie Freaks know this is typically the case. The grit and realism of the original are its power and much of that is lost through slick Hollywood production methods. The tagline for this film is "Keep telling yourself it's only a movie, it's only a movie," and though that phrase has been used since to describe other exploitation films, it holds true for this one even now as sound advice.

I Spit On Your Grave

RELEASE November 3, 1978 (U.S.)
WRITTEN AND DIRECTED BY Meir Zarchi
STARRING Camille Keaton, Eron Tabor, Richard Pace, Anthony Nichols, Gunter Kleemann
NOT RATED Has graphic scenes of rape and violence, nudity, profanity

---

I Spit on your Grave, previously known as *Day of the Woman*, opened to negative reactions and banning in several countries around the world. Today, the film is still considered controversial.

Jennifer Hills (Camille Keaton) is a magazine writer about to embark on her first novel. To avoid distractions, she decides to stay for the summer in a lakefront cottage in the countryside. Her independence and lack of reliance on a man irks several of the local roughnecks who repeatedly harass her by speeding their boat around her house and upsetting the peace she seeks.

This taunting escalates into a brutal gang rape that ends when the men leave Jennifer for dead. But Jennifer is not dead, and once she recovers, she sets out to exact revenge on each of the perpetrators one by one.

Director/writer Meir Zarchi has said he was inspired to do the film after helping a young woman who had been raped.
Cinemagic Pictures

I Spit on Your Grave met with immediate resistance for its claimed glorification of violence against women. The sexual violence beyond the initial rape sequence heightened resistance in several countries to allow the film to be distributed, even after extensive cuts were made. In Australia, for example, the film was released only to become the subject of a lawsuit to ban it. The movie survived the suit only to be banned again later for breaking yet other laws regarding sexual violence and the depiction of such acts on screen.

This is a combination of exploitation, revenge, and feminist power to overtake male oppressors in ways more harmful than their own assaults. The kill scenes are indeed highly disturbing and violent, and whether the retribution is warranted doesn't reduce the squirming that will result seeing it all happen. The moral: don't mess with an independent woman. Horror Movie Freaks will see this film crop up periodically, sometimes heralded as a realistic depiction of violent hate and revenge and other times as simply sick and reprehensible. As always, we will make our own determination, and the banned nature of this one only strengthens the resolve to see what all the fuss is about.

"TOTAL SUBMISSION. THAT'S WHAT I LIKE IN A WOMAN - TOTAL SUBMISSION." - *STANLEY*

Silent Night, Deadly Night

RELEASE November 9, 1984 (U.S.)
DIRECTED BY Charles E. Sellier Jr.
WRITTEN BY Paul Caimi, Michael Hickey
STARRING Lilyan Chauvin, Gilmer McCormick, Toni Nero, Robert Brian Wilson
RATING R, for violence/gore caused by a deranged Santa, language, nudity/sex

For its depiction of a serial killer dressed as jolly ol' St. Nick, *Silent Night, Deadly Night* met with public outrage.

Billy Chapman (Robert Brian Wilson) has an unfortunate chain of events happen that scar him for life. It starts with a Christmas Eve visit to his grandfather, who confides that Santa rewards the good kids with presents, but severely punishes those who have not been good all year. As luck has it, on the way home from the visit, a criminal wearing a Santa suit kills his parents. The last straw is the sadistic Mother Superior in the orphanage he is later forced to live at who combats Billy's growing sexuality with further acts of degradation and violence. It stands to reason, then, that Billy is afraid of Santa and gets a bit agitated around Christmas time.

To protest the film, critics Roger Ebert and Gene Siskel read the credits out loud on their television show, *At the Movies*, saying, "shame, shame, shame" after each name. *Tri-Star Pictures*

"YOU SEE SANTA CLAUS TONIGHT YOU BETTER RUN BOY. YOU BETTER RUN FOR YA LIFE!"
- GRANDPA

On Billy's 18th birthday, he is allowed to take an outside job at a toy store. Doesn't make much sense as the Christmas season is approaching and toy stores are filled with Santa imagery during this time, but Mother Superior thinks it is for the best. Think again.

Silent Night, Deadly Night suffered from several forms of banning. In Britain, the banning was direct and to the point—essentially release was prohibited even without the classification as a video nasty. In the United States, however, the banning was driven by community outrage. The Parent-Teacher Association staged huge protests immediately upon the release of this film, fueled by the fact it was released right around Christmas time. Mainstream film critics were similarly outraged and condemned the film adamantly. In response, the studio stopped advertising the film mere days after it had begun, and pulled it from theaters shortly thereafter.

Horror Movie Freaks, however, gravitated to the film and it remains a cult classic to this day, even spawning four goofy sequels and a potential remake in the works. *Silent Night, Deadly Night* is not necessarily a good film in its own right, but the controversy surrounding it certainly adds points on the cult classic meter. Proclaim the words "Naughty!" or "Punish!" in the vicinity of most Horror Freaks and you are sure to get a reaction. If the goal is to spread holiday cheer, *Silent Night, Deadly Night* will certainly put Freaks in a festive mood ripe for giving.

Cannibal Holocaust

RELEASE June 19, 1985 (U.S.)
DIRECTED BY Ruggero Deodato
WRITTEN BY Gianfranco Clerici
STARRING Robert Kerman, Francesca Ciardi, Perry Pirkanen, Luca Giorgio Barbareschi
NOT RATED Contains extremely graphic violence and gore, graphic rape and torture, graphic sexual content, and graphic cruelty to animals

The iconic image for this film of a "cannibal" girl impaled on a stick caused director Ruggero Deodato to be summoned to court in order to prove that no actors were harmed during production. Deodato explained that the girl simply sat on a bicycle seat attached to the pole's base, while holding a small pointed balsa wood piece in her mouth. The fake blood was then added. *F.D. Cinematografica/ Grindhouse Releasing*

Cannibal Holocaust is one of the best-known exploitation films of the period, primarily because of the controversy surrounding its production, release, and subsequent banning.

The story takes a dual course: one of the search for a group of lost documentary filmmakers who disappear while exploring the Amazon Rainforest, and the other of the fate of those filmmakers revealed when their films are discovered. As we see from the footage, they encounter some unfriendly natives who are hungry for flesh, but they are not completely innocent victims themselves.

Cannibal Holocaust was released in Italy and quickly seized by the courts and the director was arrested on obscenity charges. Much of the original controversy was the result of rumors that this was actually a snuff film, where actors were killed for real during filming. There is one particular scene where a woman is impaled by a spear down her throat and neck that was the subject of intense scrutiny to determine whether it was the result of special effects or if the woman was in fact murdered for the benefit of the film. The snuff charges were proven to be false.

Another source of the seizure and subsequent banning in several countries is the explicit sexual content and violence. This film includes gang rapes and other violent sexual activity that doesn't cross the line into hardcore porn, but certainly leaves out any tender or loving feelings.

The final motivation for banning *Cannibal Holocaust* is the actual deaths of animals shown on film, and this factor remains the noted reason for several that still exist in certain countries. All in all, a coatimundi (called a muskrat in the film), turtle, spider, snake, monkey, and pig are all killed in various ways on screen. Many of the DVD versions released contain a warning about this activity and state that while the artistic methods are not condoned, the freedom of expression is respected.

There are those who commend *Cannibal Holocaust* as a gripping treatment of modern civilization that gives analysis and commentary by comparing Western society to those of the indigenous tribes in the Amazon Rainforest. Others simply enjoy the film because of all the controversy, while some are appalled by the animal cruelty. Horror Freaks should know of this film's existence, regardless of whether you choose to watch it.

"HERE WE ARE AT THE EDGE OF THE WORLD OF HUMAN HISTORY. THINGS LIKE THIS HAPPEN ALL THE TIME IN THE JUNGLE; IT'S SURVIVAL OF THE FITTEST! IN THE JUNGLE, IT'S THE DAILY VIOLENCE OF THE STRONG OVERCOMING THE WEAK!" - *ALAN YATES*

The 2009 version of *Friday the 13th* mixes in elements of the first three movies and gives them its own spin. This movie also broke two records: having the largest opening day for the film series (around $19 million) and the largest opening weekend for any horror film ($40 million).
New Line Cinema

Remake Nation
Classic Horror for a New Generation

We live in the land of horror movie remakes. This is hardly a new phenomenon, but the pace of older horror movies being remade for modern audiences continues to quicken, and there is no end in sight.

Horror Movie Freaks are apt to complain about the remake landscape, and with justifiable reason. How are we going to have new horror concepts to enjoy when a majority of new offerings are retellings of familiar stories? On the other hand, there are some good reasons to enjoy remakes that Horror Freaks should never forget: new versions of old classics bring new fans into the fold. With new fans come increased sales of theater tickets and horror movie DVDs, and with the money comes an increased supply of frightful features. Let's face it, we all want to rescue our fellow man from the tyranny of the romantic comedy…do we really care how they are saved from this fate worse than death?

Besides, there is one reason for seasoned Freaks to be open minded about remakes: some of them are really great! Remakes can bring new life to an old classic, modernize dated styles, enhance the experience through evolved effects techniques, and introduce a new generation to horror movies they may miss otherwise. There is hardly a down side.

Not all remakes are created equal, however. Different ones use different tactics, depending on the filmmaker and origin of the original. For this reason, Remake Nation has a variety of categories, each with examples that illustrate the purpose and technique employed.

Take heart Horror Movie Freaks: classic horror never dies, it is just remade!

Modernizations

The modernization mode of remakes is a re-shooting of a known film and for the most part, it does not add much to the equation other than using new actors, locations, sets, and updated effects.

In the purest form, a modernization is, essentially, a frame-for-frame mulligan—a do-over of the original film matching it scene for scene. The inherent value of such remakes is questionable and the subject of much debate as the Horror Movie Freak justifiably asks, "Why?" Perhaps the goal here is to see if the hot young starlet of the day can draw a profitable crowd.

Other modernizations take a bit of artistic license but primarily stay true to the original story and format, perhaps changing some

A bit of creepy under-the-door peering in the remake of *Black Christmas*.

Dimension Films/Metro-Goldwyn-Mayer

dialogue to be more in line with current times. Technological advances in color filming, production quality, editing, and special effects are leveraged to give the remake a new look and polish that was unattainable when the original was created. Still…

Can a classic really be improved? In the eyes of the horror-movie purist, the answer is a resounding "No!" For the new-generation Freaks, however, the answer may be different. The flash and fast pace of modern media is such that the younger folks can be easily bored with those "old films." In the age of immediacy with YouTube videos and fat broadband Internet pipes, suspenseful build up and gradual character development could seem to drag on ad nauseam before something exciting happens. When something does happen, are the visuals going to stun and horrify, or seem like some fake trick readily surpassed by Saturday morning cartoons? No Horror Freak wants to see our beloved genre succumb to the whims of immediate gratification, but how will new fans be nurtured if the prospect of exploring horror seems so laborious?

The horror modernization has the power to introduce new meat to the horror arena, and those inclined to seek out the ultimate scare are sure to venture into horror movies past. Let's get those Horror Freaks on board now, and work on their appreciation of the classics later. Otherwise, we risk losing them to romantic comedies forever. Nobody wants that.

Classics become classics for good reasons, and those reasons are seldom duplicated in the modernization remake format. Well-rounded Horror Movie Freaks, however, are capable of making their own choices based on an open-minded viewing of all available options.

Invasion of the Body Snatchers

RELEASE December 20, 1978 (U.S.)
DIRECTED BY Philip Kaufman
WRITTEN BY Jack Finney (novel *The Body Snatchers*), W.D. Richter (screenplay)
STARRING Donald Sutherland, Brooke Adams, Jeff Goldblum, Jack Bellicec, Veronica Cartwright, Leonard Nimoy
RATING PG, for mild violence, brief nudity

Few films have been remade more often than *Invasion of the Body Snatchers*. Although the 1978 version is considered the favorite by many Horror Movie Freaks, if you do not like it then there are plenty more to choose from.

The story here is the same as in the original from 1956: human beings seem as if they are being replaced by imposters. Alien pods create an exact duplicate of people and then dispose of the bodies of their victims, the duplicates characterized by their complete lack of emotion.

One interesting characteristic of the multiple remakes of this film is how directly the themes point to predominant cultural elements and angst of the time. In this 1978 version, a satire of the "Me Generation" is portrayed via a self-help guru who discounts the emotions of his clients, until he himself is discovered as a duplicate.

The attitudes of paranoia that resulted from the conclusion of the Vietnam War and the continuation of the cold war with the then USSR were also present in this film, along with the burgeoning feminist movement and female empowerment.

There is also a version from 1993 called simply *Body Snatchers*, where the horror of societal conformity takes center stage as the predominant theme of the film, and a 2007 version called *Invasion*, which points out that the pod people are peaceful and have ended all wars, potentially making them better than normal humans.

The 1978 version is the best, though, due to excellent performances by the character actors, adherence to the original movie in most respects, and the lack of overt and annoying political grandstanding.

Invasion of the Body Snatchers is the one to watch, and regardless of which version becomes the favorite, this particular remake will stand the test of time.

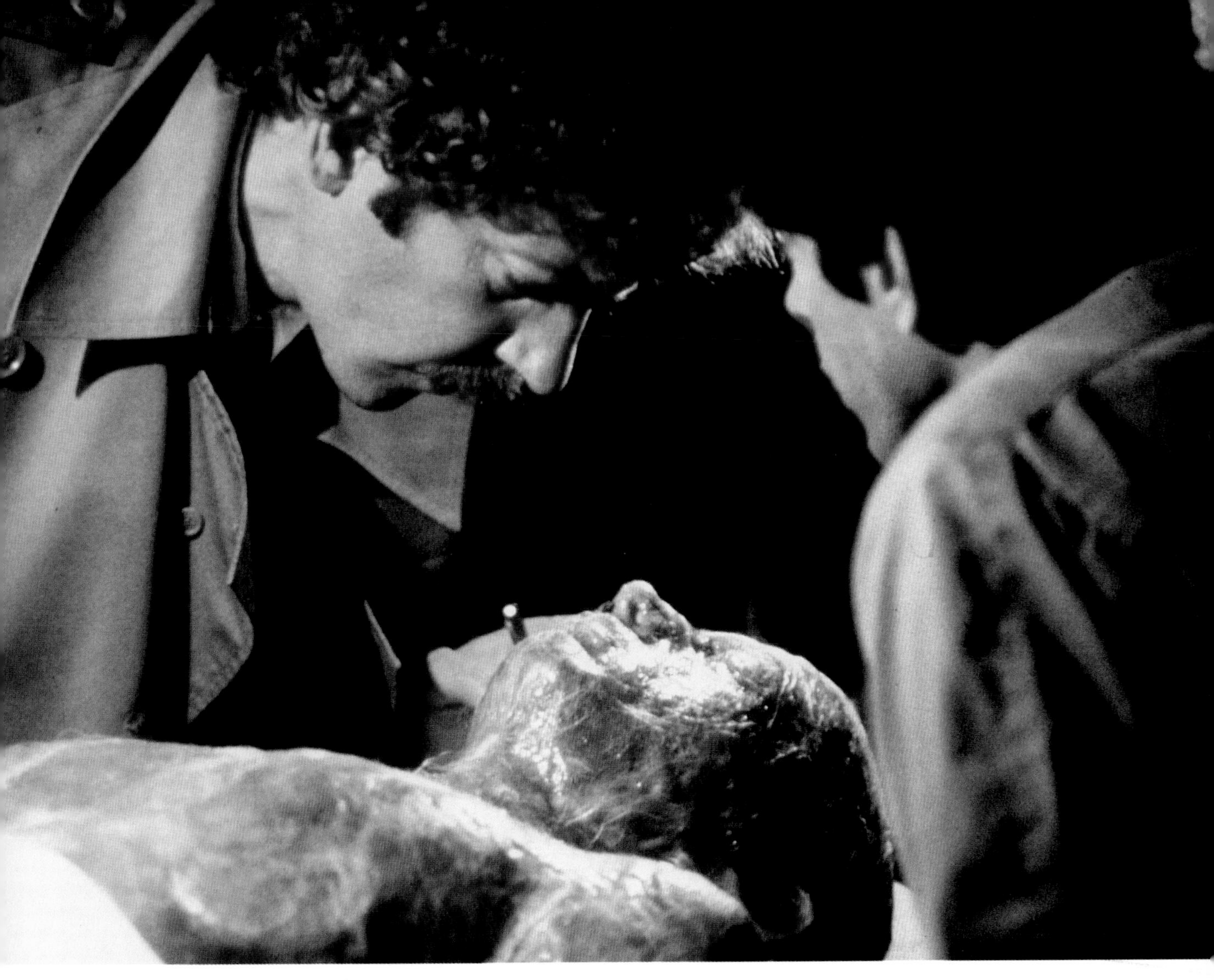

Matthew (Donald Sutherland) and Jack (Jeff Goldblum) examine a clone and try to figure out the mystery of why people are turning into duplicates devoid of emotions in the 1978 *Invasion of the Body Snatchers*. *United Artists/The Kobal Collection*

"I KEEP SEEING THESE PEOPLE, ALL RECOGNIZING EACH OTHER. SOMETHING IS PASSING BETWEEN THEM ALL, SOME SECRET. IT'S A CONSPIRACY, I KNOW IT."
- *ELIZABETH DRISCOLL*

Night of the Living Dead

RELEASE October 19, 1990 (U.S.)
DIRECTED BY Tom Savini
WRITTEN BY George A. Romero, John A. Russo
STARRING Tony Todd, Patricia Tallman, Tom Towles, McKee Anderson, William Butler
RATING R, for violence/gore, some profanity, brief nudity

George A. Romero produced and wrote this remake with famed make-up artist Tom Savini at the director's helm, and the story is primarily the same as the original.

Inexplicably the dead begin to rise from their graves to roam the earth in search of human flesh. A group of survivors defends itself in an old farmhouse, searching for both answers and a way to escape becoming zombie lunch.

In the grand scheme of remakes, this one stands tall as one that really didn't need to be made. Savini reportedly was disappointed that he didn't get to do the effects for the 1968 version and after working on other films with Romero, got the nod to apply his own sensibility to the classic story.

Most of the elements are the same with one striking exception—the character of Barbra. In the original, Barbra can barely speak and is pretty much useless in every respect; in this remake, Barbara (Patricia Tallman) is a bit more of an ass-kicker. Her name is also spelled different.

Otherwise, this is a classic example of modernization remakes with no additional value created other than updated clothing styles and better gore.

It is possible that this version will be more accessible to horror fans, and that is just fine... just make certain that all Freaks watch the original as well before settling on a favorite.

Johnnie (Bill Mosley) tries to fight off a flesheater attacking his sister Barbara (Patricia Tallman). *Columbia Pictures/The Kobal Collection*

"THIS IS SOMETHING NO ONE'S EVER HEARD ABOUT, AND NO ONE'S EVER SEEN BEFORE. THIS IS HELL ON EARTH." - *BEN*

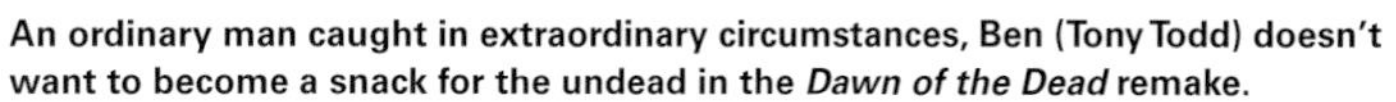
An ordinary man caught in extraordinary circumstances, Ben (Tony Todd) doesn't want to become a snack for the undead in the *Dawn of the Dead* remake.

Columbia Pictures/The Kobal Collection

The Fo

RELEASE October 14, 2
DIRECTED BY Rupert Wa
WRITTEN BY Cooper Lay
John Carpenter (1980 s
STARRING Tom Welling, Ma
Selma Blair, DeRay Davis,
RATING PG-13, for violence,
brief sexuality

The Fog is certainly an example of a modernization with no apparent purpose other than to re-release the classic story to a new audience. The town of Antonio Bay is under siege by the spirits of lepers sent to their deaths years before by townspeople who didn't find their kind "desirable." It is up to a chosen few to determine the source of the curse and put an end to it before the entire town is killed.

The original from 1980 is a classic for a few reasons including its creation by horror legend John Carpenter and the dual starring of scream queens Jamie Lee Curtis and Adrienne Barbeau. How, then, anyone thought a remake that includes none of these elements would be good is anyone's guess.

"NOW, WHAT KIND OF FOG MOVES AGAINST THE WIND?" - *STEVIE WAYNE*

Still, this remake was successful from a financial perspective even without the approval of critics or horror fans, supporting the push for old classics to be remade for new audiences. It is often difficult for Horror Movie Freaks to make fair assessments of remakes, especially if the remake in question retells a classic story that we love dearly. This is absolutely the case here. This version is not as terrible as certain reviewers and critics would have you believe, but almost. The original film required a bit of "disbelief suspension," something that we Horror Movie Freaks are somewhat accustomed to. *The Fog* remake, unfortunately, asks for even more.

This film is likely available in bargain bins across the nation, so if you come across it for about 99 cents or so, pick it up. If it's more than that, exercise caution.

Stevie Wayne (Selma Blair) and her son, Andy (Cole Heppell), brace themselves for the evil heading their way. *Sony Pictures/The Kobal Collection/Rob McEwan*

The Omen

RELEASE June 6, 2006 (U.S.)
DIRECTED BY John Moore
WRITTEN BY David Seltzer
STARRING Liev Schreiber, Julia Stiles, Seamus Davey-Fitzpatrick, Pedja Bjelac, Carlo Sabatini
RATING R, for violent content, graphic images, some language

This remake is included in modernizations for the simple reason that it is exactly the same as the original from 1976.

Robert (Liev Schreiber) and Katherine Thorn (Julia Stiles) are expecting a baby, but when the child reportedly dies at birth, he is replaced with another. This other child (Seamus Davey-Fitzpatrick) begins to exhibit signs that he is, in fact, the Antichrist, a biblical figure signaling the end of days on earth.

The Omen falls squarely into a subset of the modernization category, frame-for-frame remake. This is a modernization of a film without adding any value to the equation other than the injection of current fashions and weaving in current events to make the story appear more modern. Not only are the clothing and hairstyles more in line with modern times, but other disasters from the last 10 years are referenced as further evidence that the end is approaching.

There are those who are a bit put off by horror from decades ago, as the pacing can move a bit more slowly than modern norms and the sets and characters are a bit dated. For those horror fans, *The Omen* is a good way to experience the story without all of those annoyingly old-fashioned elements. The more established Horror Freaks may be best served to stick with the original, and even the younger-generation Freaks who appreciate a modernized view will benefit from also viewing the inspiration for the remake and judging the differences in atmosphere and storytelling for themselves.

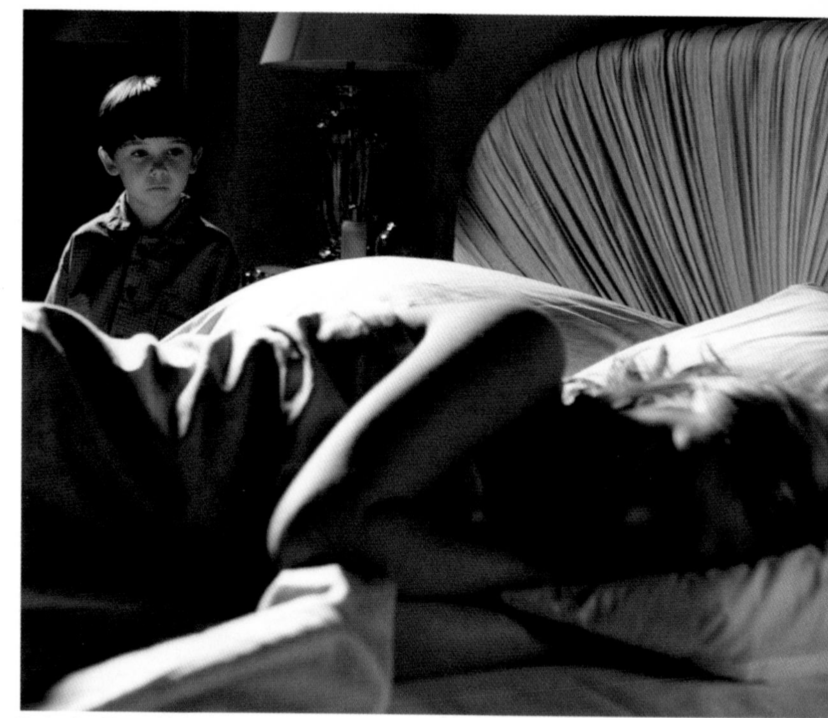

Katherine Thorn (Julia Stiles) peacefully sleeps under the watchful eye of her son Damien (Seamus Davey-Fitzpatrick), who may actually be the Antichrist.
20th Century Fox/The Kobal Collection/Vince Valitutti

"DID I SCARE YOU, MOMMY? I DIDN'T MEAN TO." - *DAMIEN*

Black Christmas

RELEASE December 25, 2006 (U.S.)
DIRECTED BY Glen Morgan
WRITTEN BY Glen Morgan, Roy Moore (1974 screenplay)
STARRING Katie Cassidy, Michelle Trachtenberg, Kristen Cloke, Lacey Chabert
RATING R, for strong horror violence/gore, sexuality, sorority girl nudity, language

Black Christmas is one remake with several notable elements, punctuated by a good deal of controversy surrounding the studio's decision to release the film on Christmas Day.

The Alpha Kappa Gamma sorority house is preparing for the holiday and the sisters are packing their things for Christmas vacation. There is a murderer lurking in the house, though, and one by one he is going to kill the young girls while also taunting them with strange phone calls and general fear-mongering. What's a sister to do?

Black Christmas is included in the modernizations category of remakes, but could also be considered a bit of a reimagining, as the background and motivations of the killer are addressed—something that doesn't happen in the 1974 original. Except for these flashes of insight, however, this film plays almost like a frame-for-frame remake.

This version is also notable because of its release timing compared to the recent rash of remakes of horror classics and the effect that this film's box office success had. Horror remakes have been around for as long as horror movies have existed, but this particular one is a remake of an established classic, often credited as being the first film of the "slasher" horror subgenre. The original *Black Christmas* is not obscure and doesn't have any particular reason to be remade other than modernizing it to see if it could be commercially successful for a second time—and it was. Not hugely successful, mind you, but certainly profitable in spite of fan response that was less than favorable.

Melissa (Michelle Trachtenberg) doesn't meet a pretty end.
Dimension Films/Metro-Goldwyn-Mayer

Many classic films from the 1970s and 1980s have since been remade, possibly as a result of the success of this one. Even if critics pan a film and hard-core fans reject it, 40 percent profitability will always rule the day. *Black Christmas* is not nearly as bad as critics say, though; a good part of the bad feelings result from the fact the classic has been "messed with" more than anything else. Once again, Freaks may want to catch this film and file it away as part of their "Freakdom," but let that not take the place of viewing the original film in all its glory.

"I'D LIKE TO BURY THE HATCHET WITH MY SISTER. RIGHT IN HER HEAD!"
- *DANA MATHIS*

Reimaginings

The remake style of "reimagining" is tricky at best. Often just the title and the general theme of the film, say, zombies, remain of its predecessor and the filmmaker takes many liberties regarding the characters, setting, and even the story.

Debate among horror aficionados is keen regarding the reimagining just as it is modernizations, but for different reasons. At its worst, a reimagining is simply a new film attempting to capitalize on the success and name recognition of another with no regard to it whatsoever. At its best, however, the reimagining can be a Horror Movie Freak treat, indeed. For the purposes of this discussion, the former will be disregarded. No self-respecting Horror Freak can get behind that tactic. The latter, however, can have considerable value.

By taking the name and general theme of an original film and re-aligning the vision via a reimagined remake, two credible goals are accomplished. First, the original film, likely a classic in its own right, is not disrespected by a filmmaker, who believes they can somehow do it better using the same script, setting, and characters as in a modernization. It was just fine the first time around, thank you very much. But second, a new and unique horror film is created that must stand on its own and win audience approval by actually being a good original horror offering. Sure, the cards are stacked in its favor due to the past popularity of the original film, but a well made reimagining can actually gain its own following independent of the predecessor.

The horror movie reimagining, then, is really not a remake at all, but rather an alternate view of the original horror concept. Both the original and the remake can stand tall, side by side, scaring the bejeezes out of horror freaks young and old. On top of that, a new generation of potential fans can find the reimagining accessible and in line with their modern technical sensibilities.

OK, so, I am presenting a utopian vision of reimaginings, and we do not live in utopia. Many filmmakers try for the reimagining that will garner critical acclaim and huge box office receipts, yet few succeed. When they do succeed, though, Horror Freaks rejoice. The Freaks' first choice is a wide array of new and unique horror movie concepts, artfully displayed to invoke hidden fears that shake the very fiber of our being. In lieu of that, a great reimagining will do in a pinch.

***Grindhouse* is an homage to the days of double-bill thrillers and cheesy exploitation movies. *Death Proof* is a rip-roaring slasher flick where the killer pursues his victims with a car instead of a knife, while *Planet Terror* gives the grim view of the world in the midst of a zombie outbreak.** *Dimension Films/A Band Apart*

The Thing

RELEASE June 25, 1982 (U.S.)
DIRECTED BY John Carpenter
WRITTEN BY John W. Campbell Jr. (the story, "Who Goes There?") and Bill Lancaster
STARRING Kurt Russell, A. Wilford Brimley, Keith David, T.K. Carter, David Clennon
RATING R, for bloody violence, grisly images, language

John Carpenter has said that of all his films, *The Thing* is his favorite.
David Foster Productions/Universal Pictures

A fantastic reimagining of an old-time science fiction film, John Carpenter's *The Thing* brings alien invasion squarely into the realm of horror.

It opens with what looks like a sled dog dodging bullets from a hovering aircraft and running along in the frozen tundra in Antarctica. The dog comes across a scientific camp and is protected from the helicopter by the inhabitants. The helicopter shooter tries to warn the scientists about the dog, but the language barrier prevents this, then the helicopter explodes.

Later, the dog is kenneled with the other sled dogs at the camp, and suddenly a commotion is heard. The "dog" they saved is not a dog at all but an alien that can create copies of other beings and bring murder and mayhem all the while.

The Thing is presented as a remake of *The Thing from Another World*, a 1951 science fiction film, but other than the fact that the supposed origin of the villain is a planet other than earth, the similarities are few. This movie is based more on John W. Campbell Jr.'s story, "Who Goes There?" The special effects in Carpenter's movie are extreme and disgusting even by today's standards—clearly ahead of their time for 1982.

The Thing is considered a classic in its own right, a rare occurrence for a remake. In true reimagining style, however, this film is less remake and more a stand-alone film that uses a few elements of a previous film to present a completely new vision.

The apocalyptic *The Thing* is a staple for the Horror Movie Freak's library and stands tall in a string of classic horror films by Carpenter. If any Freaks have not seen this, we suggest you do. If you have, what the heck…watch it again.

"I DUNNO WHAT THE HELL'S IN THERE, BUT IT'S WEIRD AND PISSED OFF, WHATEVER IT IS."
- CLARK

At least the aliens are attractive. This film is considered a benchmark in the field of special makeup effects, which were created by Rob Bottin, who was only 22 when he started the project. *David Foster Productions/Universal Pictures*

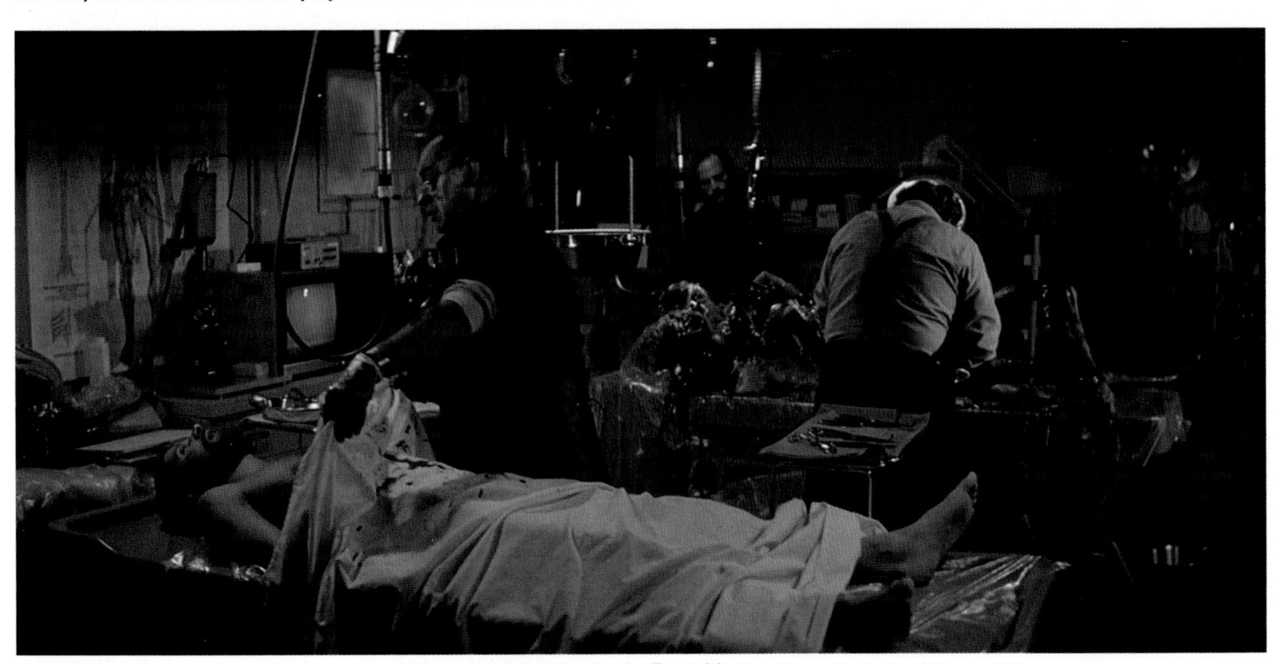

Scientists conduct an alien autopsy to try and figure out what they're dealing with. *David Foster Productions/Universal Pictures*

Kathy Kriticos (Shannon Elizabeth) remains blissfully unaware there's someone scary lurking over her shoulder.
Warner Bros/Columbia Pictures/The Kobal Collection/Alan Markfield

Thirteen Ghosts

RELEASE October 23, 2001 (U.S. premier)
DIRECTED BY Steve Beck
WRITTEN BY Robb White (story), Neal Marshall Stevens, Richard D'Ovidio
STARRING Tony Shalhoub, Embeth Davidtz, Matthew Lillard, Shannon Elizabeth
RATING R, for violence/gore, nudity, some language

The primary premise of *Thirteen Ghosts*, also known as *Thir13en Ghosts*, is the same as the William Castle film from 1960. The difference is in the execution.

The Kriticos family has inherited an old house from an uncle they never knew, and their current dire financial condition dictates that they move in and make the most of it. When they see the place, they are overwhelmed: the walls are mostly transparent and covered with cryptic writing in a language they do not recognize. There are also a bunch of ghosts in there.

The family becomes trapped inside the house and the ghosts are set free from their cages as a plot to add a thirteenth ghost to the group and thereby gain immortality for the spirit of the dead uncle unfolds and is executed.

The horrific ghosts and dramatic sets shine in this movie.
Warner Bros/ Columbia Pictures

Thirteen Ghosts is pretty good as a horror movie, but really shines as an example of dramatic sets and horrific ghosts. The ghosts here are outrageous, with each more scary than the last. The scenes where the family can see through special glasses designed to make the ghosts visible are particularly dramatic as it becomes clear that each room is not really as it appears. What looks like water coming out of the faucet, for example, is actually blood. The bathtub that looks so tantalizing has a woman's ghost inside it with flesh and body parts strewn about. It's very cool.

Thirteen Ghosts is enjoyable for the visuals primarily, but the story holds up for the most part. Well, the wheels fall off at the end, but by that time, we're so entranced by the violent ghosts that much can be forgiven. Horror Movie Freaks will appreciate the creative spirits and the cool elements of the mechanized house, even if there are no heroes really to root for. Let the ghosts get them—that's what I say.

MAGGIE: CAN I RELY ON YOU NOT TO GET ME KILLED?
DENNIS RAFKIN: I GUARANTEE NOTHING.

Dawn of the Dead

RELEASE March 10, 2004 (U.S. premier)
DIRECTED BY Zack Snyder
WRITTEN BY James Gunn, George A. Romero (1978 screenplay)
STARRING Sarah Polley, Ving Rhames, Jake Weber, Mekhi Phifer, Ty Burrell
RATING R, for zombie violence/gore, language, sexuality/nudity

Zombies create chaos in the neighborhood, and they run!
Strike Entertainment/Universal Pictures

Dawn of the Dead 2004 is considered by many to be one of the best horror remakes of modern times, as it's a film that stands on its own rather than a rehash of a classic.

Ana (Sarah Polley) comes home from a hectic day at work and hastily jumps in the shower with her husband, missing the news broadcasts of a strange epidemic causing the dead to reanimate and feast on human flesh. After a neighbor girl-turned-zombie barges into her bedroom and bites her husband, he, too, becomes a zombie and Ana barely escapes with her life.

Later she and other survivors make a stand in a shopping mall and create a vehicle that can transport them away from town and presumably to safety.

This movie has the shopping mall concept, and, of course, the zombies in common with the George A. Romero classic *Dawn of the Dead*, but here the similarities end. The characters are different, with different plans and goals and the endgame of creating a vehicle and heading out among the zombies adds a new component that is exciting and action packed. Plus, there's another thing…

Dawn of the Dead 2004 is the first time that many people saw running zombies! Not "quickly lumbering" or even "slightly jogging" zombies, but fast, sprinting, deadly, and hungry running zombies. The first time I saw a zombie sprint after a victim I almost had a heart attack. How outrageous! Zombies don't run!

What followed is a series of zombie films and "not-a-zombie" zombie films with running flesh feasters, and the debate over whether the traditional lumbering zombies or running ones are better has not let up since. Although perhaps slightly irrelevant to the casual horror fan, Horror Movie Freaks know zombies are slow and poorly coordinated which makes escape possible—the danger is in being overtaken by a mass so large that getting away without a bite is difficult. Once they start to run after you with all the zeal of an Olympic track star, all bets are off and defensive tactics must be rethought.

Dawn of the Dead 2004, then, is notable not only for taking a classic story and remaking it into a new horrific delight, but for the creation of the runner. Zombies will never be the same.

KENNETH: IS EVERYONE THERE DEAD?
STEVE: YEAH, IN THE SENSE THAT THEY ALL SORT OF, UH…FELL DOWN…AND THEN GOT UP…AND STARTED EATING EACH OTHER.

This messy girl ruined some good husband and wife time.
Strike Entertainment/Universal Pictures

A mass of zombies swarm and attack what are supposed to be the escape trucks. *Strike Entertainment/Universal Pictures*

Grindhouse

RELEASE October 14, 2005 (U.S.)
DIRECTED BY Robert Rodriguez (*Planet Terror*) and Quentin Tarantino *(Death Proof);* the fake trailers are directed by Eli Roth, Edgar Wright, Rob Zombie
WRITTEN BY Robert Rodriguez *(Planet Terror)* and Quentin Tarantino *(Death Proof);* the fake trailers are written by Rodriguez, Rob Zombie, Edgar Wright, Eli Roth, Jeff Rendell
STARRING Kurt Russell, Rosario Dawson, Rose McGowan, Freddy Rodríguez, Josh Brolin, Danny Trejo, and dozens more
RATING R, for strong graphic violence/gore, language, some sexuality, nudity

---

Grindhouse is not a reimagining of a particular film, but rather of an entire phase in horror film history of exploitation films. In that regard, it truly succeeds in bringing us back to a simpler time.

Grindhouse consists of two distinct stories designed to be presented as a double feature. The first is *Planet Terror*, a not-a-zombie zombie film, and the second is *Death Proof* about a psychotic.

In *Planet Terror*, a town is overtaken by zombie-like creatures after a toxic gas is released into the atmosphere. Campy characters use their wits and lots of firepower to make their last stand against this monstrous menace.

Death Proof is a bit more subtle as we follow Stuntman Mike (Kurt Russell) interacting with young women in bars and on the road before strapping himself into his indestructible and "death proof" hot rod and killing them in dramatic and violent auto crashes. But look out Mike, because in grand exploitation style, the women victims don't take kindly to being mistreated.

Stuntman Mike (Kurt Russell) has a friendly face - until he gets behind the wheel of his car in *Death Proof*. *Dimension Films/A Band Apart/The Weinstein Company*

Intermixed between the features are previews for other exploitation and horror films, along with vintage screen shots urging moviegoers to buy popcorn and other snacks.

Grindhouse has been split up into two different movies for DVD release, which is frankly a shame. The theater experience is one of an old grindhouse double feature complete with all the trappings of actually sitting through two movies and related marketing efforts in the 1970s and 1980s. As a recreation of that experience, this film is sheer brilliance. It did not sweep the box office, though, so there are a good number of Horror Movie Freaks who have not experienced *Grindhouse* in its entirety, and to those my heart goes out. The next best thing is to watch both *Planet Terror* and *Death Proof* in rapid succession and hope that the DVD versions you have include the trailers and other messages. Reimagine another time—good stuff.

In *Planet Terror,* Dr. William Block (Josh Brolin) needs some zombie Clearasil. *Dimension Films/A Band Apart/The Weinstein Company*

"LADIES, WE'RE GONNA HAVE SOME FUN."
- *STUNTMAN MIKE*

My Bloody Valentine 3-D

RELEASE January 16, 2009
DIRECTED BY Patrick Lussier
WRITTEN BY Todd Farmer and Zane Smith (screenplay), John Beaird (1981 screenplay), Stephen Miller (1981 story)
STARRING Jensen Ackles, Jaime King, Kerr Smith, Betsy Rue, Edi Gathegi
RATING R, for brutal violence, grisly images, some strong sexuality, nudity, language

"HAPPY F***ING VALENTINE'S DAY." - BURKE

My Bloody Valentine 3-D has attributes of a remake and some of a sequel of *My Bloody Valentine.* The creative use of new 3-D technology, however, makes the reimagining qualities move to the top of the heap.

Years ago, a mining accident left Harry Warden in a coma and several other miners dead, after Harry ate their flesh to stay alive while trapped in the bowels of the earth.

The accident would not have happened if the supervisor had not left early to attend a Valentine's Day dance, so when Harry recovers from his coma, he proceeds to massacre everyone who insists on celebrating this now deadly holiday.

Ten years later, Tom Hanniger (Jensen Ackles) inherits the mine and decides to sell it. But, as the anniversary of the Warden murders approaches and the day of love grows near, the killing resumes. Is Harry back and seeking revenge on Tom and anyone who dares mess with the mine or Valentine's Day?

My Bloody Valentine 3-D does a better job than most horror remakes at capturing the essence of 1980s horror and retelling it for new audiences, and the addition of 3-D results in a true reimagining.

In the old days of 3-D, glasses needed to be worn to enable some three-dimensional trickery and then a few specific instances capitalized on the effect. You know the ones I mean, the spear thrusting out of the screen, birds flying in your face, that sort of thing. The technology used for *My Bloody Valentine 3-D,* though, goes way beyond the limited effects of the past by making the entire film experience 3-D. No waiting for specific instances of objects thrusting in your face but rather seeing deep inside the screen at all times as if you are sitting on a stool in the middle of town while the action is going on. The effect is quite impressive.

But all the effects in the world don't make a movie good to be sure, and *My Bloody Valentine* does not disappoint in that regard, either, presenting straight ahead slasher fare that doesn't insult the Horror Movie Freaks intelligence…well, any more than others do. There are still the required moments of suspending disbelief, but not to such an extreme that it is noticeable at every second. That, in my book, is a win.

Ten years after a Valentine's Day massacre, someone hellbent on revenge goes on a rampage, leaving blood-and-guts carnage in their wake. *Lions Gate/The Kobal Collection*

Foreign Horror for U.S. Audiences

Of all the horror movie remake variations, this category has the most promise and suffers from the most saturation.

Horror movies from far away lands offer highly original concepts and intriguing themes when compared to the standard fare produced domestically.

This source of new terror is a goldmine for Horror Freaks, if you can find the films. Often the products of this foreign horror banquet are relegated to art house openings and dingy back-corner shelves of the local mom and pop video store.

Quarantine **is an American remake of the Spanish movie, *[REC]*.** *Andale Pictures*

Even if you can find them, the language barrier can be too much for some Freaks to handle, even if there are subtitles. There are other hindrances, too.

Sometimes the scare factor of horror depends on familiar settings and situations turning upside down into unexpected trips to terror land. So what happens when those familiar settings and situations, so common to citizens of the originating land, are anything but familiar to Horror Freaks in the States? The films may still be dark and foreboding, but the to-the-core terror experienced by those in one culture may be lost on those from another. These challenges are overcome by the foreign horror for U.S. audiences remake style.

This concept was proven beyond a shadow of a doubt by the U.S. release of *The Ring* in 2002. A remake of the popular J-horror film *Ringu*, *The Ring* quickly became one of the most popular and nightmare-inducing horror films of the decade, earning hundreds of millions of dollars worldwide.

While the old guard Freaks had their first horror-induced nightmares by watching the classics of the 1980s, the new generation cut their horror teeth on *The Ring*. The realization that foreign horror could impact new cultures and reach new audiences in this way was astounding…and the beginning of a downward spiral.

Soon every horror movie that experienced a modicum of success abroad, particularly Asian horror, ended up being remade for U.S. audiences. Many of these films are good and some are decidedly not good, but the sheer volume inspired by the financial success of an early few has resulted in foreign horror remakes becoming a monstrous mainstay in the domestic horror landscape.

The dreaded horror intelligentsia will tell you that every single foreign horror film remade for U.S. audiences is an abomination, so inferior to their original counterparts that they are a waste of time and celluloid. This is not completely true. A good number of these remakes are indeed inferior, simply capitalizing on the current public obsession with foreign remakes instead of striving to create a compelling and horrifying film. Others, however, are absolute gems that bring eerie foreign concepts of fright to American audiences starving for a good scare. There are a lot of them, however, so the Horror Movie Freak seeking an expanded horizon of fearfulness must choose wisely.

The Grudge

RELEASE October 22, 2004 (U.S.)
DIRECTED BY Takashi Shimizu
WRITTEN BY Takashi Shimizu (film *Ju-On: The Grudge*), Stephen Susco
STARRING Sarah Michelle Gellar, Jason Behr, William Mapother, Clea DuVall, Takako Fuji
RATING PG-13, for disturbing images, terror, violence, some sensuality

The Grudge, based on the 2000 J-horror film *Ju-On*, is particularly notable as an English-language remake because the same director created both movies.

The Grudge involves an Asian legend about spirits who harbor grudges against the living and attempt to infect them with their angst; this then spreads to others with the eventual goal of ending humanity. The story surrounds an American nurse (Sarah Michelle Gellar), who is exposed to this curse.

The original *Ju-On* is popular and spawned several sequels as the curse jumps from one group to another. *The Grudge* has inspired similar remakes as well. All of these films, Asian and English language, have some involvement by Takashi Shimizu. This is notable, as typically it is a different director who takes the helm for the remakes rather than the same person creating both.

The effect is an excellent translation of the original film for U.S. audiences. While generally well reviewed and received, *The Grudge* experienced a high level of commercial success world wide, and therein lies the film's downfall in the eyes of critics. Clearly if a film is a blockbuster smash, then it must be lacking, right? Horror Freaks generally do not agree with this assessment, but the opinion does indeed exist. The confusing nature of the film is also a point of criticism for some, but that is the nature of J-horror much of the time. The fact that the English-language translation should also be a bit confusing is par for the course.

Vengeful spirit Kayako (Takako Fuji) doesn't like when people come into her house.
Columbia Pictures/The Kobal Collection

The Grudge is counted as the scary movie that introduced them to horror by a number of younger Horror Movie Freaks, and for that fact we are thankful. It is painful to imagine the dreary life full of romantic comedies these souls may have endured had it not been for this remake.

"CROAKKKKKKKKKKKKKKKKKKKKKKKKKKKKKKKKKKKKK!" - *Kayako Saeki*

Pulse

RELEASE August 11, 2006 (U.S.)
DIRECTED BY Jim Sonzero
WRITTEN BY Wes Craven, Ray Wright, Kiyoshi Kurosawa (2001 screenplay *Kairo)*
STARRING Kristen Bell, Jonathan Tucker, Ian Somerhalder, Christina Milian, Rick Gonzalez
RATING PG-13, for terror, disturbing images, language, sensuality

It's up to Mattie (Kristen Bell) to help devise a plan to save mankind, but you can bet that malevolent spirit will try and stop her. *Distant Horizons/Neo Art/The Kobal Collection*

Pulse is a remake of the 2001 Japanese horror film *Kairo*, where the "plugged in" world of cell phones and broadband provide a conduit for malevolent spirits to push people to suicide.

Josh (Jonathan Tucker) encounters a spirit in the school library prior to meeting his girlfriend Mattie (Kristen Bell) there. The ghost sucks the will to live right out of Josh, and he wanders home and commits suicide.

A short time later, Mattie receives a package that Josh sent before killing himself that includes red tape and a message saying that the tape will help keep "them" out. Who "them" is and what's happening in the world becomes clear to Mattie as she fights to survive an attack of spirits who use the world's wireless networks to feed on the life force of the living.

Talk about social commentary. Danger in the wireless networks and broadband? Sucking the life out of people? Dissolving the will to be near people so that victims die isolated and alone? There are those who would say our current technology, even without ghosts, is already doing this to our society.

Pulse was not well received by the moviegoing public, primarily because the film critics and horror intelligentsia of the world panned it horribly for not living up to the standards of the Japanese predecessor. After watching the original with its hopeless atmosphere and dark dread, I tend to agree with this assertion, but that does not mean *Pulse* is not good. In fact, many of those who viewed *Pulse* without knowledge that it is a remake of a J-horror cult film thought it was pretty great…those who were not poisoned by false reviews by J-horror snobs with delusions of grandeur, that is.

> "DO YOU KNOW WHAT DYING TASTES LIKE? METAL."
> - ISABELL FUENTES

Pulse is an interesting example of Asian horror remade for U.S. audiences because it is not a remake of a blockbuster, but rather a cult film with a smaller following in Asia. Interesting, then, that the reviews have been so terrible but that would seem to speak not only to the nature of the horror intelligentsia but also the nature of fans of cult films—there is an emotional attachment that becomes easily offended by anyone tampering with a beloved favorite. In any case, judge this one for yourselves Horror Freaks. If it sucks, it sucks; but if it simply isn't the same as the movie that inspired it, that might just be alright.

The Eye

RELEASE January 31, 2008 (U.S. premier)
DIRECTED BY David Moreau and Xavier Palud
WRITTEN BY Sebastian Gutierrez and Jo Jo Yuet-chun Hui, Oxide Pang and Danny Pang, writers of 2002 screenplay *Jian Gui*
STARRING Jessica Alba, Alessandro Nivola, Parker Posey, Rade Serbedzija, Fernanda Romero
RATING PG-13, for violence, terror, disturbing content

The Eye is a remake of a 2002 Chinese horror film known as *Jian Gui*, and created by the prolific and popular Pang Brothers.

The story is about a woman (Jessica Alba), who, after a cornea transplant, begins to regain the sight she lost at age five. Along with the newfound vision, however, comes terrifying scenes of death and murder.

After tracking down the donor of her transplanted eyes, she realizes she shares a frightening power with her.

The Eye tells a good concept story that is interesting and intriguing and did pretty well at the box office internationally. The performances are solid and the presentation of the concepts of the supernatural, precognition, and mental illness allow for a sense of not knowing what is true and what is the result of psychosis, which adds much to the suspense and thriller aspects.

As so many Asian remakes are, this film was massacred by the critics. More than any other remake categories, Asian horror for U.S. audiences seems to glean the ire of movie critics, and the horror intelligentsia in particular.

This may be because there are not many in the general horror fan population who have actually seen the foreign counterparts of these films, so the intelligentsia types have a bit of superior knowledge to wield like a sword.

No matter. Horror Movie Freaks are a cut above the casual fan and more able to judge a film on its own merits rather than taking the word of some goofball with a semester of film school under their belt and a chip on their shoulder. *The Eye* is an example of a successful version of foreign horror for U.S. audiences that may not stand the test of time as the original might, but is a good glimpse into what scares other cultures nonetheless.

"I'M SEEING THINGS I SHOULDN'T SEE!"
- SYDNEY WELLS

If your eye gives you trouble, just rip it out like Sydney (Jessica Alba) is trying to do. No big deal.
Lionsgate

Quarantine

RELEASE October 10, 2008 (U.S.)
DIRECTED BY John Erick Dowdle
WRITTEN BY John Erick Dowdle, Drew Dowdle, and Jaume Balagueró; Luiso Berdejo and Paco Plaza (motion picture *[REC]*)
STARRING Jennifer Carpenter, Steve Harris, Jay Hernandez, Johnathon Schaech
RATING R, for bloody, violent, and disturbing content, language

Quarantine is effectively a shot-for-shot remake of the Spanish horror movie *[REC]* in the English language.

The story begins with Angela (Jennifer Carpenter), a television news reporter, capturing a day in the life of a group of firefighters in the station. She follows them through preparing their uniforms, cooking their meals, even sliding down the fire pole. It's all pretty boring and Angela longs for an actual emergency so that she can capture the guys in action. She soon gets her wish.

That's gotta smart. *Andale Pictures/Screen Gems*

The call seems to be a relatively routine domestic disturbance and the police are already on the scene when the firefighters arrive, Angela and her cameraman in tow. What they discover is a crazy and sick old woman covered in blood who viciously attacks one of the rescue personnel with a bite that rips out the flesh of his neck, killing him. Suddenly the building is sealed off by SWAT teams and Disease Control agents armed with sniper rifles, leaving Angela and the firefighters trapped inside as one after another of the inhabitants succumbs to a disease that causes radical zombie-like behavior.

Quarantine is a great film shot from the point of view of the cameraman's lens. Except for a few minor adjustments, it is exactly like *[REC]*, with the obvious exception of the language spoken. So now Horror Freaks have a choice: watch the original story with subtitles or the remake spoken in their native tongue.

There is much commentary surrounding this particular remake and there are those who proclaim the original is better because of (add reason here); that is really not the case. This remake is the same. The performers are different, of course, but they all do a credible job and don't really add or detract from the story compared to the original.

The timing of this remake is a bit odd, releasing in the United States just over a year after *[REC]*'s release in Spain. Perhaps the point was to get *Quarantine* in front of horror fans before they had a chance to see the original and make a comparison. I guess the fact that *Quarantine* was a commercial success suggests this tactic worked like a charm.

"SO, LET'S JUST PRETEND YOU'RE FIVE YEARS OLD AND ON FIRE." - *JAKE*

Tale of Two Sisters/The Uninvited

RELEASE January 30, 2009 (U.S.)
DIRECTED BY The Guard Brothers
WRITTEN BY Craig Rosenberg, Doug Miro, Carlo Bernard, Jee-Woon Kim (motion picture *Changhwa, Hongryon*)
STARRING Emily Browning, Arielle Kebbel, David Strathairn, Elizabeth Banks, Maya Massar
RATING PG-13, for violent and disturbing images, sexual content, language

The Uninvited, a remake of the 2003 Korean movie, *A Tale of Two Sisters*, is directed by Thomas and Charles Guard (the "Guard Brothers") and had a great deal of commercial success.

Anna (Emily Browning) returns home after spending some time in a mental institution and is reunited with her sister and best friend Alex (Arielle Kebbel). The girl's mother has died recently in a fire after suffering a long illness, and her mother's nurse is now their stepmother.

Before long, the cruel and manipulative nature of the new stepmother becomes clear, and to complicate matters, there seems to be a ghost lurking about and causing trouble.

A Tale of Two Sisters is considered one of the better Asian horror films by many Horror Freaks. The film is based on South Korean folklore and is complex and somewhat confusing, especially for those who are not completely familiar with the myth being portrayed. The film is dark and psychological and a great example of Asian horror with all its complexities.

"YOU KNOW ANNA, I DON'T THINK THIS IS GOING TO WORK OUT."
- RACHAEL

Anna (Emily Browning) is curious to know what's behind the curtains.
DreamWorks SKG/Paramount Pictures

This remake by the Guard Brothers is not nearly as confusing but is still a psychological thriller that combines dark family secrets, hidden agendas, and dysfunction with vengeful spirits and creepy horror. It is always good form to be familiar with an original film that inspires a remake, particularly foreign remakes for U.S. audiences, but in this case, be warned. It is possible that the confusing nature of the original may put off the casual horror fan, making the remake much more accessible.

Freaks will likely enjoy this film, whether they are familiar with the Korean film that inspired it. Our recommendation is that both be viewed and, if nothing else, noted for the differences between them and how those differences speak to cultures from opposite ends of the world.

Encapsulations

There are some horror movies that have been around for a number of years and spawned several sequels along the way. When one of these horror series features a compelling and well-known villain, a franchise is born. The villain becomes the real star of the show, with all others merely existing to give the bad guy somebody to get. Every Horror Movie Freak knows the names of the most famous of the slash-'em-up anti-heroes: Jason Voorhees, Michael Myers, and Freddy Krueger.

A curious thing happens when movie after movie is made surrounding the same villain: the horror-loving audience learns more about the background, motivations, family, and goals of the dreaded doer of despair. The details become part of the mystique of these characters, giving them a depth that becomes part of pop culture. How, then, does a filmmaker determined to create a remake of one of the classic films that introduced these characters accomplish the task in light of the volumes of knowledge revealed in subsequent sequels? Encapsulation.

The encapsulation method of horror remaking is a new phenomenon that acknowledges the secrets revealed in later installments and incorporates them into the remade film. Jason Voorhees is merely an off-the-cuff mention in the original *Friday the 13th*, for example, and doesn't begin his own killing spree until *Friday 2*. Then, in Part 3, Jason dons the famous hockey mask for the first time. A remake of the original *Friday the 13th* sans Jason and no hockey mask in sight, in light of all that has transpired, wouldn't make any sense, but encapsulation enables all common knowledge about the character to be pulled together into one gut-slicing movie.

The encapsulation is the purest form of making classic horror accessible to a new generation. There is nothing boring about encapsulations, which tend to move quickly with gory precision. No need to labor over explaining details, since everybody already knows the score walking into the theater. Simply acknowledge the facts and move onto the slaughter…nice and clean like.

The most notorious of horror villains are already the subject of encapsulation remakes, but the success of this remake style at the box office suggests these beginnings are just the tip of the iceberg. Skip the boring parts, read the cliff's notes, and get right to the killing—that's what encapsulations are about, and they are here to stay.

The new, and dirtier, Michael Myers (Tyler Mane) from Rob Zombie's 2007 encapsulation of *Halloween*. *Dimension Films*

Halloween

RELEASE August 31, 2007 (U.S.)
DIRECTED BY Rob Zombie
WRITTEN BY Rob Zombie, and John Carpenter and Debra Hill (1978 screenplay)
STARRING Malcolm McDowell, Scout Taylor-Compton, Tyler Mane, Sheri Moon Zombie, Daeg Faerch
RATING R, for brutal, bloody violence and terror throughout, sexual content, nudity, language

Michael (Tyler Mane) confronts Laurie's mother, Cynthia (Dee Wallace). *Dimension Films/Spectacle Entertainment/The Kobal Collection*

The *Halloween* remake by Rob Zombie was a tough film to make considering the almost universal love of the John Carpenter original. Using the encapsulation method was the only way to go.

Life is hard for little Michael Myers (Daeg Faerch), a disturbed boy living with a white trash mother, abusive stepfather, and slutty sister in a dump on the wrong side of the tracks. Some of the signs of Michael's troubles start early as he mutilates small animals and hides his violence from his family. Finally Michael snaps one day and goes on a killing spree.

After spending 16 years in an asylum and not speaking a word for most of that time, the adult Michael (Tyler Mane) escapes and seeks out the one person who never betrayed him: his sister Laurie (Scout Taylor-Compton). She has no knowledge of Michael or her humble beginnings, however, as she was adopted as an infant by the Strode family and lives a pretty normal life. Then "he" comes around and changes her safe little world forever.

This movie is an interesting twist on the category, as this is not necessarily an encapsulation of several films but rather an encapsulation of "facts" gained in snippets through the subsequent sequels. To start with, the background of Michael is fleshed out considerably; the original film begins with a short sequence of Michael killing his older sister and being confronted by his parents as they arrive home from a Halloween party. Michael is not directly dramatized again until he escapes the institution and goes on his murder fest back home. In the encapsulation, however, we meet Michael before his murder spree and see his trouble brewing. We also witness his time in the institution, leading up to his silence and eventual escape.

We also see many other elements that are known of Michael Myers in the remake, now with history attached. The background of the particular mask he wears is explained, along with why he wears it at all, and where he got the jumpsuit he wears. We hear of Michael's mother killing herself in one of the sequels, but in the remake we see the despair that led to that act. We even learn more about why he targets Laurie, a fact that is only implied in the original versions. We also see the beginnings of the breakdown of Laurie in this remake, something that took several original sequels to dramatize.

Overall, the *Halloween* encapsulation that brings these facts together makes the legend of Michael Myers complete. Considering the long history Horror Movie Freaks have with Michael and the *Halloween* franchise, this is how it should be.

"THE DARKEST SOULS ARE NOT THOSE WHICH CHOOSE TO EXIST WITHIN THE HELL OF THE ABYSS, BUT THOSE WHICH CHOOSE TO MOVE SILENTLY AMONG US."
- DR. SAMUEL LOOMIS

Friday the 13th

RELEASE February 13, 2009 (U.S.)
DIRECTED BY Marcus Nispel
WRITTEN BY Damian Shannon, Mark Swift, Mark Wheaton, Victor Miller
STARRING Jared Padalecki, Danielle Panabaker, Amanda Righetti, Travis Van Winkle
RATING R, for strong bloody violence, some graphic sexual content, language

Whitney (Amanda Righetti) finds herself trapped by Jason, who no doubt has nothing but the worst intentions for her. *New Line Cinema*

The remake of *Friday the 13th* is a teen-slasher movie that brings in elements from the original Parts 1, 2, and 3.

In an opening sequence, the story of Pamela Voorhees' murderous rage on the counselors of Camp Crystal Lake is revealed, ending in her decapitation. Pamela goes crazy after her only son, Jason, was allowed to swim without supervision and drowned. Jason, however, is not dead…

For years after the massacre at Camp Crystal Lake, residents of the small town nearby know it isn't safe to wander into the woods. "He" just wants to be left alone. Some teens haven't heard the warnings, though, and venture into the woods in search of a rumored grove of marijuana. Jason is not pleased.

The *Friday the 13th* remake represents a perfect example of an encapsulation. Jason Voorhees has been around since his debut in 1981's *Friday the 13th Part 2,* although, of course, his name is mentioned in the first installment from 1980.

Since that time, he appears in many sequels and takes many forms, is killed and brought back to life, and is even remade as a cyborg in *Jason X*.

The name Jason Voorhees is every bit as recognizable as O.J. Simpson or Jeffrey Dahmer. A remake, then, had to be an encapsulation, otherwise the whole thing would have just been dumb.

In this movie, we meet Jason's mother Pamela, see the shrine to her, and witness Jason wearing a sack over his head and later the famous hockey mask as he slashes through unwitting teens.

"KILL FOR MOTHER."
- *PAMELA VOORHEES*

In the original franchise, it takes three installments to get this far in the story: *Friday the 13th*, where mother is the villain; *Friday the 13th Part 2*, where we find out Jason lives through the ordeal, keeps his mother's disconnected head as a remembrance, and kills while wearing a burlap sack; and *Friday the 13th Part 3* (in 3-D!), where Jason finds an old hockey mask in a shed and completes the now-famous image.

Of course, after watching this movie, it is extremely important to view the originals, and in order. Allowing this story to unfold naturally via the original films will always be the preferred method of getting to know Jason, not to mention seeing that sex scene with Kevin Bacon that precedes an arrow through his neck from under the bed. That's a classic.

In the 2009 encapsulation of *Friday the 13th*, Jason (Derek Mears) finds what will become his trademark hockey mask, at left. Below, he wears the mask for the first time. In this version of the movie, Jason is bigger, stronger, meaner...and kind of has a turkey neck. *New Line Cinema*

A Nightmare on Elm Street

RELEASE April 30, 2010
DIRECTED BY Samuel Bayer
WRITTEN BY Wesley Strick, Eric Heisserer, Wes Craven
STARRING Jackie Earle Haley, Rooney Mara, Kyle Gallner, Katie Cassidy, Kellan Lutz, Thomas Dekker
RATING R, for the bloody carnage Freddy causes with his razor claws

A Nightmare on Elm Street is one of the longest running horror franchises, Freddy Krueger is one of the most recognized villains ever, and pretty much everyone knows he attacks his victims where they cannot escape: in their dreams. This remake necessarily encapsulates much that has been learned about this deformed killer over the years.

Years ago, a gang of enraged parents tracked down and burned the suspected child killer Freddy Krueger (Jackie Earle Haley). Now Freddy is back, invading the dreams of the children of his executioners and killing them there, which also brings death in their waking lives.

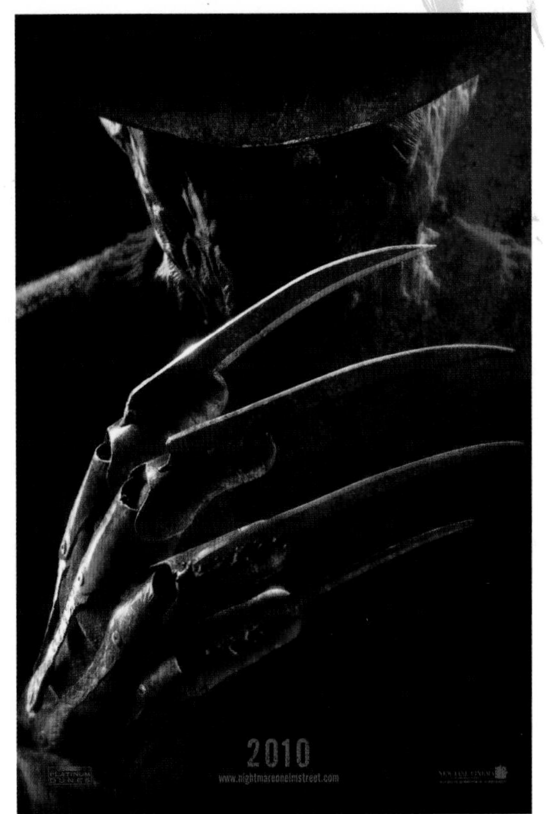

A teaser poster for the new *A Nightmare on Elm Street*.
New Line Cinema/Warner Bros.

"YOU HAVE NOTHING TO WORRY ABOUT. THIS WON'T HURT ONE LITTLE BIT." - *FREDDY KRUEGER (FROM THE TRAILER)*

Most Horror Movie Freaks, as well as casual fans, are familiar with Freddy. The original Wes Craven film from 1984 brought Freddy into theaters and living rooms all around the world, and into the nightmares of budding horror freaks of all ages.

Then there were the sequels. Several of them. Freddy gets campier, Freddy gets darker, Freddy battles the dream warriors, and Freddy even fights Jason Voorhees. Through all of these films, key details are revealed: Freddy's background, motivations, origins, and weaknesses.

Again, encapsulation is the only true answer to completing a remake of this film. The encapsulation won't necessarily be appropriate for most horror remakes, but for those with iconic characters like Freddy Krueger, there really is no other option.

The real question for Horror Freaks to answer, then, is not what type of remake is appropriate, but whether the *Nightmare on Elm Street* story can survive without actor Robert Englund as Freddy. That one remains to be seen…

nie Lee Curtis fights off vengeful spirits lurking in *The Fog*.
CO Embassy Productions

Scream Queens

It seems that every young starlet who has EVER performed in a horror movie of any sort is instantly touted as the newest "scream queen." Hogwash.

The scream queen is a diva. She is the reason why you choose to watch a certain horror movie over another or seek out an unknown title from the bottom of the heap with her name in the credits. She is the cameo performance that makes an entire film worth renting and the name that inspires inclusion in our library of beloved horror classics.

True scream queens become, uh, queens of scream for several reasons. In some cases, a certain actress has simply starred in so many horror movies that the title is undeniable, but there is more to it than that, even when volume stacks the odds in her favor. There must be something special about her. That certain Junoesque quality, if you will. Maybe she defines an era or perhaps brought to life some enduring horror films. It is hard to pinpoint what it takes for someone to become "queenly," but Horror Movie Freaks know it when they see it.

Most Freaks, unlike the casual fans, have a preference for one particular scream queen or another and can get pretty passionate about it. Just like attempting a singular list of the 100 "best" horror movies, encapsulating every scream queen preference in a short list is an exercise in futil- their particular preference is represented, ideally in some kind of throne-like top spot. I'm not even going to attempt it.

What I have done instead is gather several scream queens who most acknowledge as "undeniable" and then further pared the list by including just one from each of four different categories: the virgin, the seductress, the mom, and the bad girl. Each brings her own immeasurable quality to the horror films they present, and each is an irreplaceable entity who gives life to horror and joy to the black little hearts of Freaks everywhere.

Scream queens, we love you! Horror would not be the same without your regal presence, and I, for one, would never have watched half of the low-budget cheese I have without the promise of your shining face and piercing screams to look forward to again and again.

Dee Wallace on the theatrical release poster for *The Hills Have Eyes.*
Blood Relations Co./Vanguard

Jamie Lee Curtis

Partial horror credits: *Halloween, The Fog, Terror Train, Prom Night, Halloween II*

Jamie Lee Curtis is the scream queen at the very epicenter of the slasher-film formula and the rules for survival in a horror movie. Although interestingly Curtis' characters are not always pure as the driven snow, she has become known playing the virgin in horror movie lore. When the other kids are out having sex, doing drugs, or behaving in some other way that is sure to draw the ire of the local homicidal slasher, Curtis is sure to be found at home studying, baby-sitting, or performing some other responsible task that guarantees she will be where she is supposed to be and doing what she is supposed to be doing. That's why she lives.

There are actresses who have performed in more horror movies than Curtis, but the iconic nature of the films she has appeared in make horror queen status inevitable. Being the daughter of Janet Leigh from *Psycho* (P. 50) fame did not hurt her chances either. Good lungs for screaming clearly run in the family. A quick succession of horror movies also contributes greatly to her royal status. Curtis burst onto the scene in 1978 with *Halloween* (P. 249), starred in three horror movies that came out in 1980—*The Fog, Terror Train,* and *Prom Night*—and then reprised her role as Laurie Strode in 1981 with *Halloween II.* For that period in history, if there was a scare, Jamie Lee was there.

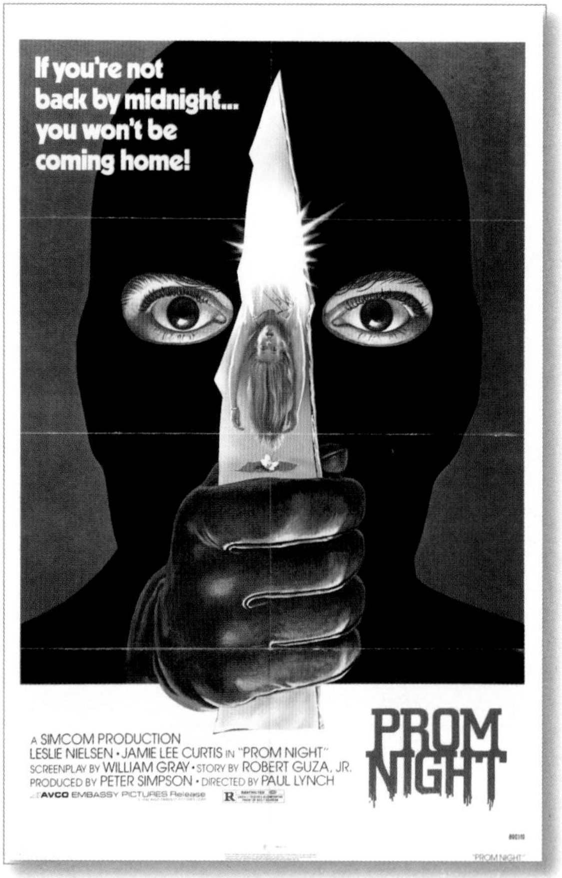

Prom Night is the third horror film Jamie Lee Curtis starred in.
AVCO Embassy Pictures

The archetype of the virginal "good girl" has been replayed over and over in horror movies and has become such a typical basis for slasher films that one is hardly recognizable without it. Curtis personifies this type of character and is the standard against which all others are judged. In fact, Curtis is so bound to this role in the eyes of Horror Freaks that even when she does not fulfill the requirements of a saintly persona, her "less than virginal" activities are not only forgiven, they remain largely unnoticed. *The Fog* is a shining example of this "selective memory," as she is only in the town of Antonio Bay to witness the onslaught of vengeful spirits because she shacks up with a guy who lives there. Every time I watch *The Fog*, I think to myself how strange it is that she isn't a complete virgin in the film…then promptly forget the seedy parts and put her back on her pedestal, where she belongs.

Curtis has had an extensive acting career outside of horror, but it is in those early horror movies where she made the most dramatic impact. The rules for survival are based on her. The "victim who lives" is the one who acts like her and her pristine presence has made an indelible mark on the horror genre that will remain for decades to come…possibly forever.

Jamie Lee Curtis in her iconic role as Laurie Strode in *Halloween*. *Halloween* director/co-writer John Carpenter considered the hiring of Curtis as the ultimate tribute to Alfred Hitchcock, who had given her mother, Janet Leigh, legendary status in *Psycho*. *Falcon International/The Kobal Collection*

Dee Wallace

Partial horror credits: *The Stepford Wives, The Hills Have Eyes, The Howling, Cujo, Critters, Alligator II, The Frighteners*

Dee Wallace, also known as Dee Wallac and Dee Wallace-Stone, has a list of horror movie credits a mile long. Somewhere along the way she also made time to take the world by storm in *ET: The Extraterrestrial* and gain a Saturn Award nomination for Best Supporting Actress. It is in horror, though, where Ms. Wallace has the most fervent fans.

Although Wallace has played a variety of characters, it is that of the mother (or dutiful wife or domestic sister) where she defines a horror movie archetype and holds the undisputed status of diva scream queen. In spite of her physical attractiveness, Ms. Wallace is consistently the comfort—the woman who will either stand by her man or take matters into her own hands when the chips are down. Never the panty-clad co-ed who ventures off into the dark woods to her doom, Wallace is more likely to be the cool mom who all the other kids wish was theirs.

Wallace made her film debut in the science fiction/horror film *The Stepford Wives* in 1975, followed by playing the mother of the victimized family from *The Hills Have Eyes* in 1977 (P. 110). Then came the role that would define Ms. Wallace's career in the eyes of Horror Movie Freaks and secure her position as scream queen: *The Howling* in 1981 (P. 120). *The Howling* is considered by many to be one of the best werewolf films ever made, and Wallace's performance is a key component in that designation. The way she transitions from risk-taking career woman to traumatized rape victim to up-ender of an entire cult of furry wolf creatures is extraordinary, and she pulls it all off while maintaining that comfortable persona reminiscent of baseball and apple pie.

Wallace is a special kind of scream queen: pure but with an edge, and always the voice of reason in a maternal way. She proves that when things get really, really bad, running home to mom is never a bad idea.

In *Critters,* Dee Wallace stays strong in the wake of furry creatures from another world eating their way through her town. This is the Pakistan poster. *New Line Cinema*

Dee Wallace's character in *The Frighteners*, Patricia Ann Bradley, says she's in the mood for a little "vivisection."
Wingnut Films/The Kobal Collection/Pierre Vinet

In *Terror at London Bridge*, a 1985 TV movie, Adrienne Barbeau's character may or may not be being attacked by Jack the Ripper.

Charles Fries Productions/The Kobal Collection

Adrienne Barbeau

Partial horror credits: *The Fog, Swamp Thing, Creepshow, Two Evil Eyes, Open House, Terror at London Bridge (aka Bridge Across Time), Unholy*

Adrienne Barbeau has the voice of a seductress. From the moment Horror Movie Freaks heard her portrayal of Stevie Wayne doing her midnight radio show from the Antonio Bay lighthouse in *The Fog*, we were hooked.

Barbeau did not start her acting career in a way that would suggest that one day she would reach diva status as the horror movie scream queen representing the seductress category. Her earliest days were on television where she was not the queen of screams, but rather the queen of bit parts showing up on such gems as *Eight is Enough*, *Fantasy Island*, and *The Love Boat*. Then she became the queen of shock television as a regular on the series *Maude*, a spin-off of the non-PC *All In The Family*. Later she did the game show circuit and goofy shows like *Battle of the Network Stars*. All that changed when she met and married director John Carpenter and starred in his 1980 movie, *The Fog*.

What could have been a simple case of nepotism ended up introducing the world to the ultimate in a seductress scream queen. Barbeau's portrayal of the midnight radio host with the seductive voice made *The Fog* "pop" and contributed greatly to the film's success.

Since that time, she has worked with the likes of Wes Craven and George A. Romero, adding her sensual sensibility to the horror genre and solidifying her place among the most influential scream queens.

Barbeau continues to make her mark on the entertainment industry, but even today her best roles are those of the tough horror victim who dominates the screen with her vixen-like presence. The best scream queens are those who can inspire a Horror Movie Freak to travel to a theater or rent a DVD based solely on the fact that she will appear. Barbeau is such a queen who forever lives in our hearts as the sexy radio host working from an isolated lighthouse in a spirit-infested coastal town.

In *Swamp Thing*, Adrienne Barbeau's character Alice has what it takes to soothe the savage beast. But who would ever wear a dress to the swamp?
Swamp Films/Embassy Pictures Corporation

Debbie Rochon

Partial horror credits: *Citizen Toxie: The Toxic Avenger IV, Mistress Frankenstein, Sandy Hook Lingerie Party Massacre, Head Cheerleader Dead Cheerleader, Hellblock 13, Terror Firmer, Rage of the Werewolf, Bikini Bloodbath Car Wash, Satan Hates You*

Debbie Rochon is possibly the hardest-working woman in horror, with 146 films to her credit since 1986, 17 films in production in 2009/2010, and four more (and counting) film projects in development as of this writing. She is also a horror movie scream queen diva.

Rochon is the consummate bad girl scream queen, who is so prolific you wonder how she could possibly star in so many films in a single year. Interestingly, many Freaks are not yet familiar with this ravishing vision of horror movie fright. This is because the films Rochon does typically fall into a specialty category of low-budget independent films that only the most passionate of Freaks regularly view. After gaining prominence as a character in the well-known Troma film, *Citizen Toxie: The Toxic Avenger IV*, Rochon went on to become every conceivable horror character, from villain to victim, serious to comedic foil. Through it all, the underlying grit of her bad girl tendencies shine through, adding a compelling element to every film she appears in.

An appreciation for Rochon is, in a way, the yardstick by which the Horror Movie Freak is distinguished from the casual fan. Although unknown to the casual fan, Rochon is simply a superstar in the eyes of those in the know. Lines out the door at horror conventions attest to this fact as dedicated Horror Freaks wait for hours for the chance to shake her hand, get her autograph, or a picture with her.

The bad girl scream queen category belongs to Rochon and her persona simultaneously encapsulates toughness, sexiness, and vulnerability while also being clear that messing with her may just result in you getting cut. Although Horror Freaks do hope for more mainstream and wide release horror films from this diva, that might kind of wreck it, too. As it stands, a mention of Debbie Rochon in the presence of horror fans is a sure fire way to separate the fans from the aficionados, and after she breaks through to the mainstream, we will be left with only the knowledge that "we knew her when." Then, of course, everyone will proclaim their love for Rochon. Until that day, this wonderful lady will be our little secret.

Debbie Rochon is one of the hardest working scream queens in the business. This is a still from *Satan Hates You*, where she plays Tina. *Glass Eye Pix*

In the goofy and fun low-budget indie *Bikini Bloodbath* (2006), Debbie Rochon plays a sassy and hormone-engulfed lesbian P.E. teacher battling the evil "Chef," who tries to add the body parts of nubile coeds to his delectable French stew. *Blood Bath Pictures*

The U.S. publicity poster for *Halloween II*. This movie picks up on the same night where *Halloween* leaves off.

Universal/Compass International Pictures

Ten Days to Halloween
Movies to Watch as the Big Day Approaches

No matter how you slice it, Isaac (John Franklin) in ***Children of the Corn*** **is one creepy kid.** *New World Pictures/Angeles Entertainment Group*

Halloween is the most wonderful time of the year for the Horror Movie Freak. Costumes, parties, horror movies—what could be better!

As the "big day" approaches, it is important that everything be perfect and the mood appropriately set. The horror movies watched as the final countdown presses on can make or break the whole experience, so put some planning into it.

After years of research, I have compiled what I believe to be the perfect mix of horror movies to watch in the ten days leading to Halloween. Three guesses which movie is recommended for the night itself, but the other nine evenings represent a collection of the best in horror, new and old, all with themes sure to set the stage in darkness and the mood of gloomy panic. They should be watched in the order presented, starting with day ten.

Press on then, oh Horror Movie Freaks, and make this Halloween the most panic-stricken ever!

Night of the Living Dead

RELEASE October 1, 1968
DIRECTED BY George A. Romero
WRITTEN BY George A. Romero, John Russo
STARRING Duane Jones, Judith O'Dea, Russell Streiner, Karl Hardman, Marilyn Eastman
NOT RATED Contains gore and violence caused by the undead, and human flesh eating

Night of the Living Dead is considered by many to be one of the greatest horror movies ever made. No other film has had more impact on an entire genre of movies than this zombie classic.

Barbra (Judith O'Dea) and her brother Johnny are visiting a cemetery, and it is not easy on poor Barbra. She is afraid of cemeteries, you see, and Johnny is taking full advantage of that fact. Who hasn't heard the line, "They're coming to get you Barbra!"

"DON'T YOU KNOW WHAT'S GOIN' ON OUT THERE? THIS IS NO SUNDAY SCHOOL PICNIC!"
—BEN

Well, karma is a bitch and "they" do, indeed, come. One lone man walking strangely approaches the duo and promptly rips Johnny's throat out with his teeth. Barbra flees to an old farmhouse and basically loses her mind.

In the meantime, the dead are rising all over the world and seeking to feast on the flesh of the living. Barbra and a group of others take shelter in the farmhouse and battle for survival against the lumbering flesh feasters.

George Romero and *Night of the Living Dead*

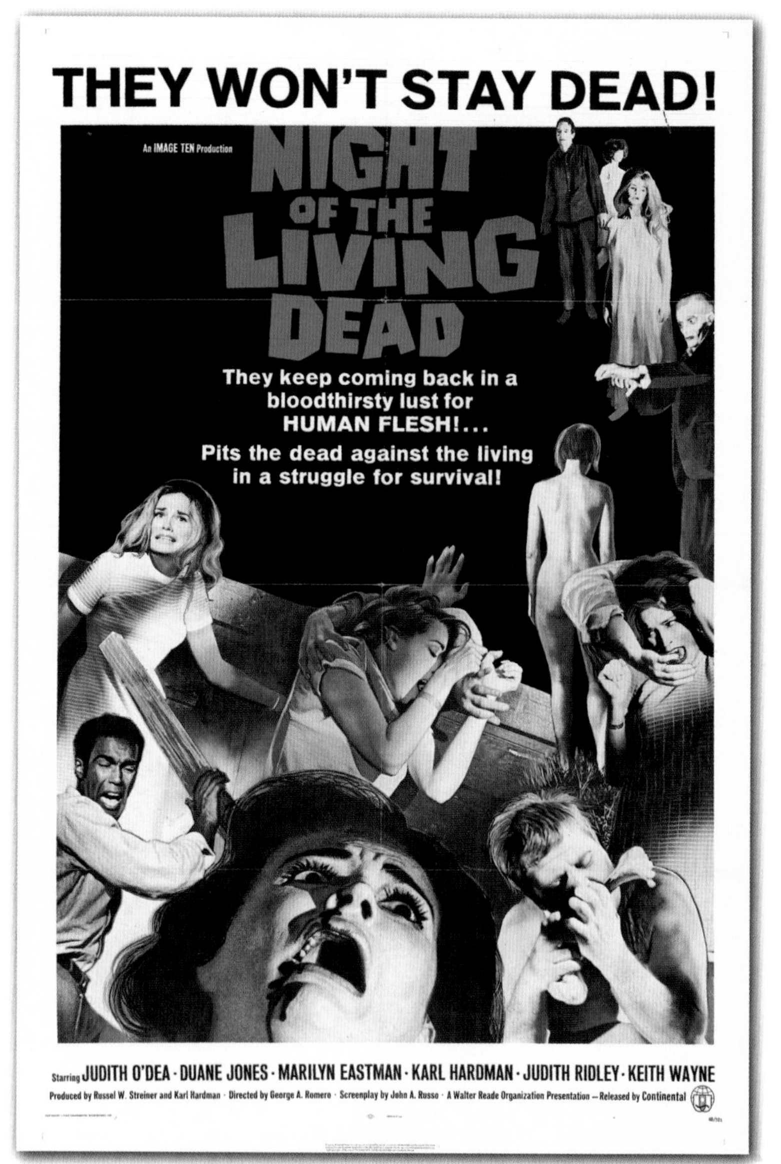

Although *Night of the Living Dead* is considered one of the best zombie movies ever made, the word "zombie" is never used in it. *Image Ten/Walter Reade Organization*

Yummy yummy human flesh. Zombies tear into some meat in *Night of the Living Dead*. *Image Ten/Walter Reade Organization*

single-handedly reshaped the horror genre as it pertains to zombies. Prior to this film's release, zombies were mindless slaves, victims of voodoo curses who merely did their master's bidding. With *Night of the Living Dead*, zombies became actual horror movie monsters and gained "rules" of their own.

Zombies are the reanimated dead and not merely disease-infected people; zombies crave living flesh to survive and the unavoidable reality that a head shot takes one down are now standard features of zombie lore.

Although the gore is somewhat tame by today's standards, this film was met with a mountain of controversy upon its release for the flesh feasting and headshots. Even without modern-quality gore, however, this film holds up to this day with terrifying images and overwhelming monsters.

Any fan of horror and certainly fans of zombies should watch *Night of the Living Dead* repeatedly, and on Halloween this is an absolute must. The beginning of the modern zombie is still the best portrayal of them, and the next time you see a man in a black suit lumbering clumsily toward you, I hope you will remember this one and aim for the head. Body shots won't do it.

Children of the Corn

RELEASE March 9, 1984
DIRECTED BY Fritz Kiersch
WRITTEN BY Stephen King (short story) and George Goldsmith
STARRING Peter Horton, Linda Hamilton, R.G. Armstrong, John Franklin, Courtney Gains
RATING R, for some violence and gore

Via murderous children and particularly creepy villains, *Children of the Corn* is a Stephen King film adaptation that achieves the desired goal of terror inspiration.

Burt (Peter Horton) and Vicky (Linda Hamilton) are driving through rural America on their way to a new beginning. Their marital problems make a new life necessary, as the old one is a complete drag. When they happen upon a small town, they are struck by the complete lack of people. The town seems completely abandoned.

The couple ventures into shop after shop, and finally a farm house, finding only corn husks made into religious symbols and then finally a small child…that's the beginning of the end.

The children in this town have killed all of the adults and follow a little creepy kid named Isaac (John Franklin) and a dark demon that lurks "between the rows" in this isolated Nebraska corn town.

VICKY: *CAN YOU TAKE US TO ISAAC?*
SARAH: *NO.*
VICKY: *WHY NOT?*
SARAH: *HE'S SCARY.*

The tagline, "And a child shall lead them," comes from Isaiah 11:6 in the *Old Testament*, which reads, "And the wolf shall dwell with the lamb, and the leopard shall lie down with the kid; and the calf and the young lion and the fatling together; and a little child shall lead them." *New World Pictures/Angeles Entertainment Group*

The services this morning were a bit corny. *New World Pictures/Angeles Entertainment Group*

The power of *Children of the Corn* is in the characters. Sure, the story is good and the concept of children rising up to kill all adults is scary to be sure, but the "church" services led by the young Isaac and the activities of master at arms Malachai (Courtney Gains) really make the film intense.

Leading up to the big day of Halloween, lots of different types of fright could suffice, but a film that illustrates the evil lurking in the eyes of those little tykes knocking on your door begging for candy is an absolute no-brainer. The sermons of the scary little Isaac will stay with you long after the movie ends, and that Malachai…what a FREAK! He is scary just to look at, even if you don't count the evil gleam in his eyes and the taste for blood he clearly has.

Children of the Corn is a classic and perfect addition to the calm before the storm of Halloween. Watch this one and beware the children…they're gonna get you.

Pumpkinhead will help you get revenge, but it comes at a terrible price. *United Artists/The Kobal Collection*

Pumpkinhead

RELEASE October 14, 1988 (U.S. limited)
DIRECTED BY Stan Winston
WRITTEN BY Stan Winston, Ed Justin (poem), Mark Patrick Carducci, Richard C. Weinman, Gary Gerani
STARRING Lance Henriksen, Jeff East, John D'Aquino, Kimberly Ross, Joel Hoffman
RATING R, some gore/violence, mild profanity

Pumpkinhead is great old-time horror with a gloomy atmosphere and hellish demon sent on a quest for revenge.

Ed Harley (Lance Henriksen) is a widowed man raising his son in a small rural town. Ed runs the local market and is met by a group of city-dwelling teens on their way to a cabin in the woods. He leaves the store to deliver some goods and tells his son to mind the shop; meanwhile, the teens decide to ride their dirt bikes and have a bit of fun. It's not very fun, though, when the youngster ventures too close to the off-road festivities and is run over.

When Ed returns and finds his pride and joy dead, he is enraged—so much so that he pays the local witch to cast a spell of revenge on those who took his son from him. This revenge has the ghastly physical form of a demonic monster, and the name Pumpkinhead.

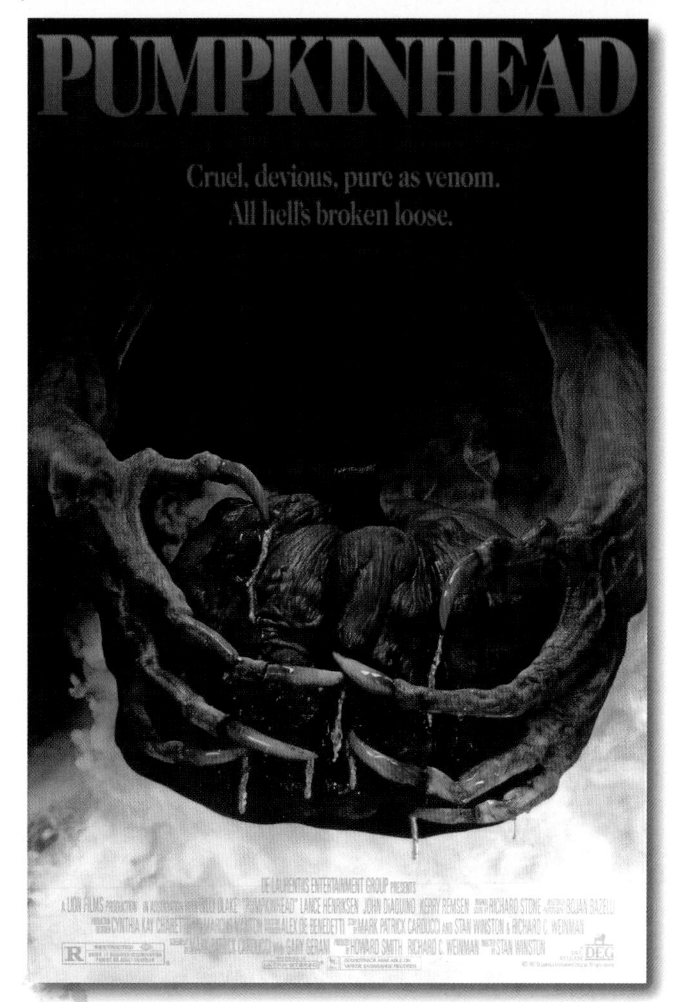

Thanks to Stan Winston, the screenwriters made Pumpkinhead and the witchy old woman much darker in the final movie than they were in the original script. *De Laurentiis Entertainment Group/United Artists*

TRACY: CAN'T YOU STOP THIS? CAN'T YOU CALL IT OFF?
ED HARLEY: NOTHIN' CAN CALL IT OFF...BUT I'M GONNA SEND IT BACK TO WHATEVER THE HELL IT COME FROM!

Pumpkinhead is a perfect movie for the days leading up to Halloween. The settings are dark and misty, the monster large and mean, and the kids are swept away in its grasp one by one. There is also a very gross and creepy witch and some magic spells involved which round out the picture nicely.

Pumpkinhead is a bit lesser known than other horror movies, probably because the critics didn't like it much when it was released. These critics must have both been of the horror intelligentsia vein or simply mainstream movie reviewers who don't "get" horror, because *Pumpkinhead* is an atmospheric tale of revenge and massacred teens. What's not to like?

Friday the 13th, Parts 1 and 2

PART 1 RELEASE May 9, 1980
DIRECTED BY Sean S. Cunningham
WRITTEN BY Victor Miller
STARRING Betsy Palmer, Adrienne King, Jeannine Taylor, Robbi Morgan, Kevin Bacon
PART 2 RELEASE May 1, 1981
DIRECTED BY Steve Miner
WRITTEN BY Ron Kurz
STARRING Amy Steel, John Furey, Adrienne King, Kirsten Baker, Warrington Gillette
RATING Both movies are rated R, for violence/gore, sexuality, nudity, profanity

These counselors sure look healthy. Must be early in *Friday the 13th*. *Paramount Pictures*

Friday the 13th is mandatory viewing in the days leading to Halloween. Don't watch only one, however, as Parts 1 and 2 must be viewed together.

The story is well known: a young boy, Jason, drowns while staying at Camp Crystal Lake because counselors aren't paying attention, and these counselors pay dearly for their mistake.

"HE NEGLECTED TO MENTION THAT DOWNTOWN THEY CALL THIS PLACE CAMP BLOOD."
- NED

Years later, the camp reopens in spite of the bloody past and the town crazy who proclaims that all who stay within the camp are "Doomed!" The curse continues, though, and one by one the new counselors meet their bloody demise, often while wandering outside wearing nothing but panties.

The story continues in *Part 2*, where the notorious killer Jason Voorhees makes his appearance and continues the massacre that started at a peaceful summer camp.

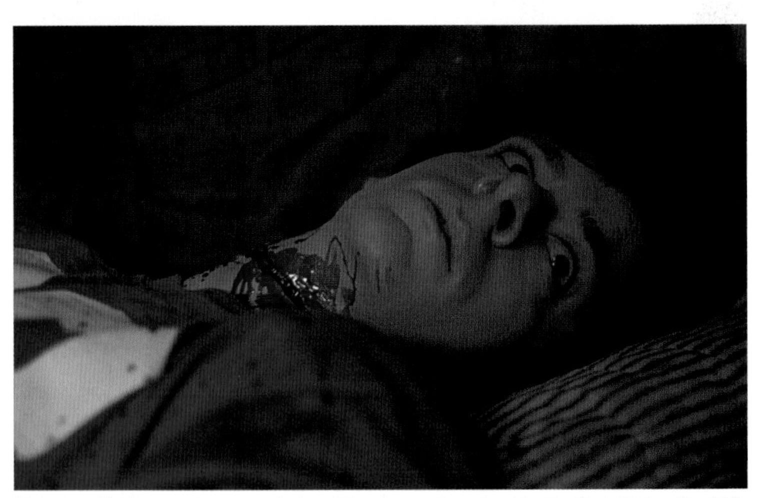

Note to self: Those who dance in headdresses end up dead in the first *Friday the 13th*. *Paramount Pictures*

The original *Friday the 13th* should be watched several times a year in actuality, but failing to revisit this horror classic on Halloween is an absolute sin. These first two movies in the franchise should always be watched together if possible, though, to get the whole story. In fact, if you're feeling particularly adventurous, *Part 3* is a good addition to this lineup as it REALLY completes the story. Going beyond these three is fun, but not as necessary to experience the full effect of Jason Voorhees, horror villain extraordinaire.

Ginny Field (Amy Steel) is a heroine with smarts in *Friday the 13th Part 2.* *Georgetown Productions/The Kobal Collection*

In *Friday the 13th Part 2,* we see a grown Jason (Warrington Gillette) before he donned his trademark hockey mask.

Georgetown Productions/The Kobal Collection

As *Darkness Falls*, a mother and son (Emma Caulfield and Lee Cormie) are unaware of the evil lurking behind them.
Columbia/Revolution Studios/The Kobal Collection/Imageworks

Darkness Falls

RELEASE January 24, 2003
DIRECTED BY Jonathan Liebesman
WRITTEN BY Joe Harris, John Fasano, James Vanderbilt
STARRING Chaney Kley, Emma Caulfield, Lee Cormie, Grant Piro, Sullivan Stapleton
RATING PG-13, for horror images, brief profanity

Darkness Falls is one version of the tale of the tooth fairy, but this one takes the story to frightening lengths if you dare to spy her slipping that quarter under your pillow.

The story begins with a young boy placing his newly lost tooth under his pillow and anxiously awaiting the tooth fairy and the big haul he's gonna get when she arrives. Soon he sees some kind of monster in his room. His mom doesn't take his cries seriously and this costs her dearly in a horrifying and shocking scene that will remind you of the worst thing that could have happened as a child. The boy hides with his flashlight under the covers and survives the night, but it's not over.

"REMEMBER, WHEN THE TOOTH FAIRY COMES, DON'T PEEK."
- YOUNG CAITLIN

Years later, the now grown boy is afraid of the dark…not just afraid but refuses to ever be in the dark for fear that the tooth fairy will come and get him as punishment for seeing her face.

Darkness Falls is a perfect film for the days leading to Halloween because it plays on the fears that almost every child has had regarding monsters under the bed and lurking in the closet. In this film, she is really there.

This creature continues grabbing folks who pass in the shadows, and plucking folks from groups and ripping them to shreds. No dark corner is safe, and after watching this, you will start to question yourself and wonder if that was really movement you saw out of the corner of your eyes.

This movie may make you think twice about leaving a tooth under the pillow.
Columbia Pictures/Revolution Studios

Black Christmas

RELEASE December 20, 1974
DIRECTED BY Bob Clark
WRITTEN BY Roy Moore
STARRING Olivia Hussey, Keir Dullea, Margot Kidder, John Saxon, Marian Waldman
RATING R, for violence, profanity, sexual language

Black Christmas is arguably the first slasher movie of that horror genre, at least as slashers have come to be known.

The scene is a sorority house gearing up for Christmas break. Many of the sisters are heading home for the holidays while others are preparing to stay around and brave the winter. A series of obscene telephone calls threatens to kill the holiday spirit, but the mass consumption of adult "spirits" relegates these disturbing calls to "mere annoyance" status.

Unbeknownst to the remaining sisters, a heavy-breathing man is lurking outside and makes his way inside the sorority house and takes up camp in the attic. He peers at them through cracks in the doors, and when he catches one alone, he turns his murderous rage upon them. As they start to disappear, the remaining women hunker down in defense of their lives.

Horror movies do not typically have a particularly creepy guy systematically and graphically killing lovely young coeds one by one prior to *Black Christmas*. Previous films often portray monsters or possibly a lone psychotic who will in fact kill, but seldom will that psycho venture out to slice and dice over and over, hiding the evidence of one kill to enable another. The methods of murder used by early movie monsters are also not often very creative and certainly don't use new and more vile methods with each new victim.

Director Bob Clark has said the murder scenes were more graphic in the original script, but he felt it would be more effective if they were toned down and made more subtle on screen.
Film Funding Ltd. of Canada/Warner Bros. Pictures

Enter *Black Christmas*, and the modern horror movie slasher. The killer in this film is true slasher with unknown motivations and a desire to cause fear and panic, but not right away. First victims need to be picked off subtly so that the remaining pool has no idea what's coming. This, of course, leads to a big massacre where bodies are found and terror ensues. This general formula is the basis for most of the famous and popular slashers we've come to know and love.

"I'M GOING TO KILL YOU."
— *THE KILLER*

Black Christmas is perfect for the Halloween countdown, both because of its holiday theme and the reality that there may be a determined killer lurking in your very home as you watch. Just don't go out wearing only panties.

It always starts with a creepy phone call, doesn't it? In *Black Christmas*, Jess Bradley (Olivia Hussey) probably wishes she hadn't even answered it. *Film Funding Ltd. of Canada/ Warner Bros. Pictures*

The trademark plastic bag in rocking chair trick from *Black Christmas*. *Film Funding Ltd. of Canada/Warner Bros. Pictures*

Andrew Bryniarski cuts a striking figure as Leatherface in *The Texas Chainsaw Massacre* remake. *New Line Cinema/The Kobal Collection*

The Texas Chainsaw Massacre

RELEASE October 17, 2003
DIRECTED BY Marcus Nispel
WRITTEN BY Kim Henkel (1974 screenplay), Tobe Hooper (1974 screenplay) and Scott Kosar
STARRING Jessica Biel, R. Lee Ermey, Andrew Bryniarski, Eric Balfour
RATING R, for strong horror violence/gore, profanity

Erin (Jessica Biel) keeps her wits about her throughout the movie, despite the chainsaw-wielding maniac Leatherface, who keeps trying to carve her like a turkey.
New Line/The Kobal Collection

The original *The Texas Chainsaw Massacre* by Tobe Hooper is one of the classic horror films of all time. This remake from 2003 tells the same tale but with some more outrageous gore.

Some teens are headed across Texas on their way to Mexico for a bit of R and R. Along the way, they pick up a strange girl hitchhiking who seems dazed and distraught. This feeling is confirmed when she shoots herself in the head. There is a great visual effect of seeing the shocked faces of the teens through the newly blown hole, by the way.

They call the local sheriff (R. Lee Ermey) to report the incident and get some assistance, but end up becoming his prisoner and being held captive by him and his cannibalistic family. The headliner of the show is the huge and violent Leatherface (Andrew Bryniarski).

The story of *The Texas Chainsaw Massacre* must be experienced on the days leading to Halloween, and purists may decide to substitute this remake for the original as the big day approaches. The remake, however, is potentially more accessible to those who might resist the gritty filming and slightly dated themes in the original. Then there is the gore. This remake takes the gory basis of the original story and makes it shine blood red, using more modern effects techniques. The result is a good bit of "yell out loud" horror and an excellent primer as Horror Freaks work through the necessary movies leading up to All Hallow's Eve.

"WELL I GUESS THAT'S WHAT BRAINS LOOK LIKE...SORT OF LIKE...LASAGNA...KIND OF...*OK,* I'LL SHUT UP NOW." - *ANDY*

Perhaps, for Horror Freaks inclined to view a double feature, both films should be included in the night's festivities. A good bit of comparative debate will surely follow an exceptional night of blood, guts, human stew, and scares.

The Ring

RELEASE October 18, 2002 (U.S.)
DIRECTED BY Gore Verbinski
WRITTEN BY Koji Suzuki (novel *Ringu*) and Ehren Kruger
STARRING Naomi Watts, Martin Henderson, David Dorfman, Brian Cox, Jane Alexander
RATING PG-13, for some disturbing images and profanity

The Ring, a remake of the J-horror classic *Ringu*, is considered the scariest movie ever by an entire generation of new fans to the genre. The aficionados seem to like it, too.

The film begins with two young women discussing urban legends, and a story about a videotape that, when watched, causes a telephone call to the viewer with an announcement of "seven days," marking the time that person has left to live before dying a violent and disfiguring death. One of the teens then confesses that she and some friends watched such a tape themselves and subsequently received the ominous phone call. Her friend, of course, doesn't believe her until she leaves the room, only to return and discover her friend is stone dead with a face that's contorted beyond recognition. One by one all of those who watched the tape meet similar fates.

Rachel Keller (Naomi Watts) is a journalist and relative of one of the dead teens and embarks on an investigation into the cause of the deaths. In the process, she herself views the tape and receives the death call. Rachel must now find the secret of the tape if she wants to survive.

What a creepy movie! From the tape itself to the visions of vengeful spirits and the path to finding the cause, *The Ring* is sure to inspire fright and nightmares. Many of the scenes will have you glued to the screen in paralyzed fear and the suspense is enough to give even the seasoned Horror Freak a possible heart attack.

This has several visual references to the films of Alfred Hitchcock, including *Rear Window* (1954), *Psycho* (1960) and *Family Plot* (1976). Coincidentally, Hitchcock himself once directed an unrelated boxing movie called *The Ring* (1927). *DreamWorks*

The Ring is a horror movie that will stay with you long after the flicker of your screen has diminished and the room is dark. As a lead-in to Halloween, this one will certainly elevate the mood to the proper level of horror and dread. The original *Ringu* is an option for this selection, but not particularly recommended. The holiday requires being completely absorbed in the terror-inducing dramatization, and subtitles just aren't gonna cut it. Not on this night.

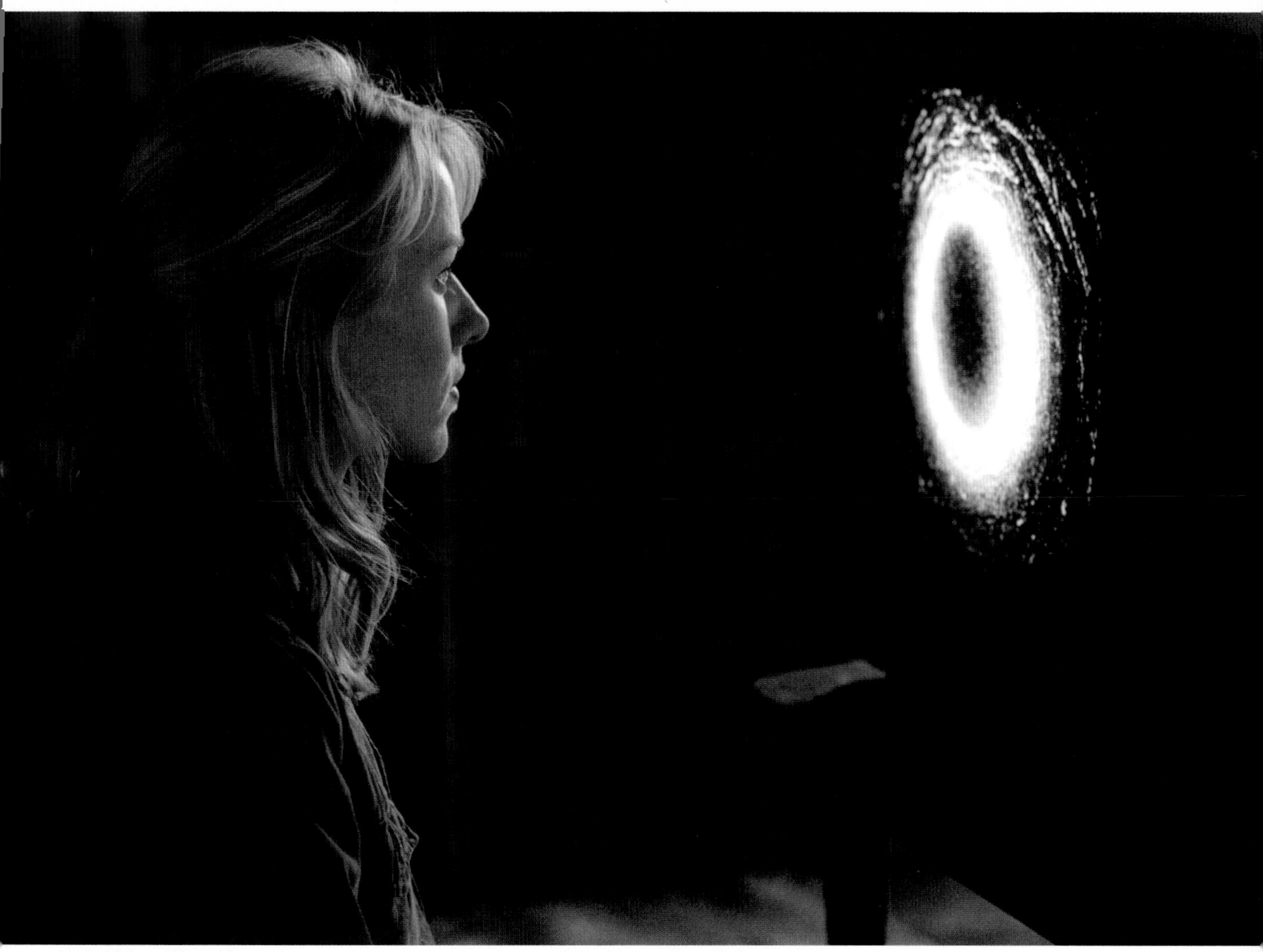

Rachel (Naomi Watts) has only seven days to solve the mystery of *The Ring* or she will die. *DreamWorks/The Kobal Collection/Merrick Morton*

"I THINK BEFORE YOU DIE,
YOU SEE THE RING..."

-RACHEL KELLER

Trick 'r Treat

RELEASE October 6, 2009 (U.S. DVD premier)
WRITTEN AND DIRECTED BY Michael Dougherty
STARRING Dylan Baker, Rochelle Aytes, Quinn Lord, Lauren Lee Smith, Moneca Delain
RATING R, for horror violence, some sexuality/nudity, profanity

---

Trick 'r Treat is a relatively new addition to the horror anthology lineup, and the series of vignettes blend together seamlessly for this spooky night of nights.

This film travels through four separate short stories, all transpiring on Halloween night and are about a woman who breaks the tradition of waiting until after Halloween to blow out the candle in her jack-o-lantern, a school principal who murders children with candy, a group of kids venturing to the site of a bus accident to pay homage to the spirits, and a group of young women attending a Halloween party in the woods.

It goes without saying, as this is a horror film, that much mischief transpires during all of these stories and victims drop like flies in the process.

Trick 'r Treat is a great movie, but is particularly enjoyable for those who love the holiday itself, as it speaks to various myths and legends associated with the pagan-inspired festival. Who knows what goes on outside the protective walls of your house on the night of ghosts and witches? *Trick 'r Treat* gives some possibilities.

A joke on the set was that no pumpkins were harmed in the making of this movie, as most were made out of foam or ceramic.

Bad Hat Harry Productions

"SAMHAIN, ALSO KNOWN AS ALL HALLOWS' EVE, ALSO KNOWN AS HALLOWEEN. PRE-DATING CHRISTIANITY, THE CELTIC HOLIDAY WAS CELEBRATED ON THE ONE NIGHT BETWEEN AUTUMN AND WINTER WHEN THE BARRIER BETWEEN THE LIVING AND THE DEAD WAS THINNEST, AND OFTEN INVOLVED RITUALS THAT INCLUDED HUMAN SACRIFICE." *-RHONDA*

Halloween 1 and 2

PART 1 RELEASE October 25, 1978
DIRECTED BY John Carpenter
WRITTEN BY John Carpenter and Debra Hill
STARRING Donald Pleasence, Jamie Lee Curtis, Nancy Loomis, P.J. Soles, Charles Cyphers
PART 2 RELEASE October 30, 1981
DIRECTED BY Rick Rosenthal
WRITTEN BY John Carpenter and Debra Hill
STARRING Jamie Lee Curtis, Donald Pleasence, Charles Cyphers, Jeffrey Kramer, Lance Guest
RATING Both movies are rated R, for violence/terror, sexuality, profanity; *Halloween II* also contains more graphic violence

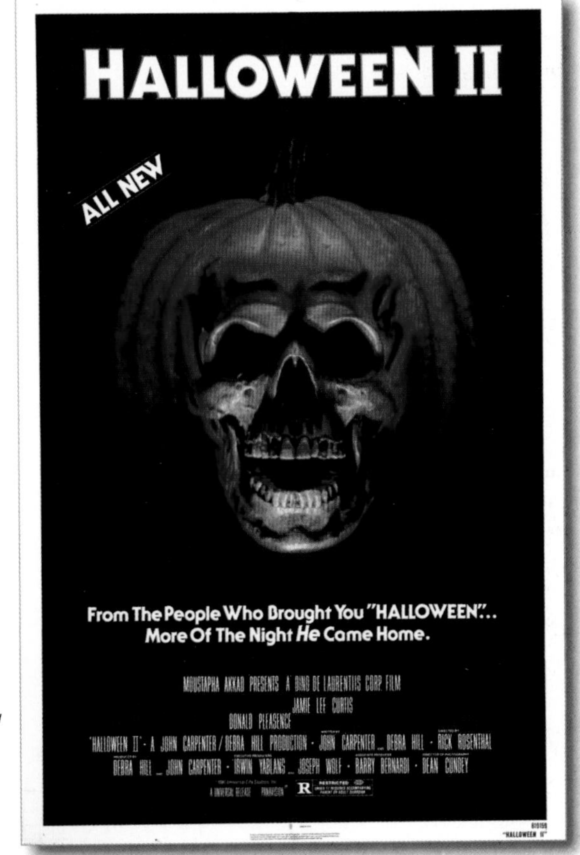

***Halloween II* is the movie debut of comedian Dana Carvey of *Saturday Night Live* and "Church Lady" fame. He's the guy receiving instructions from a blond reporter in front of the Wallace house.**
Compass International Pictures

So, finally the big day has arrived—Halloween. What to watch, what to watch? As if it weren't obvious enough, the John Carpenter classic has it all for the night of nights.

Halloween begins with a first-hand view of young Michael Myers as he suddenly snaps and murders his sister Judith with a kitchen knife. The fact that he's wearing a clown mask does not make his deed less dastardly, and his parents are shocked to find him standing in the front yard with a blank expression on his face and blood dripping from his blade.

Years later, Michael escapes from the insane asylum where he has been imprisoned and returns to the town of his childhood to seek out and kill the young and virginal Laurie Strode (Jamie Lee Curtis). With his psychiatrist (Donald Pleasence) hot on his trail, Michael slashes his way through Laurie's friends until the final showdown between the monster and the saint.

In part 2, the drama continues as Michael follows Laurie to a hospital and does his best to finish what he started. The candy stripers never know what hit them.

Even aside from the title, *Halloween* IS Halloween. The action takes place on Halloween night and Michael Myers has become over time the consummate Halloween villain. Laurie Strode, the horror heroine/victim represents the perfect fodder for a deranged killer and displays all of the appropriate qualities to make her the poster child for the "rules" of surviving a horror movie.

So much of what has become cliché in horror over the years had to begin somewhere, and *Halloween* is it. See the source of it all, back when slashers were new and the rules had yet to be written.

LAURIE: *IT WAS THE BOOGEYMAN.*
DR. SAM LOOMIS: *AS A MATTER OF FACT, IT WAS.*

Michael Myers is one of the most famous and recognized villains in horror-movie history and a pop-culture icon.
Falcon International/The Kobal Collection

Dr. Sam Loomis (Donald Pleasence) hunts down Michael Myers throughout *Halloween* and *Halloween II*. *Universal/The Kobal Collection*

Index